BLOOD ZERO SKY

BLOOD ZERO SKY

A Novel
by
j. gabriel gates

Health Communications, Inc.
Deerfield Beach, Florida

www.hcibooks.com

Library of Congress Cataloging-in-Publication Data

Gates, J. Gabriel
  Blood zero sky : a novel / by J. Gabriel Gates
    p. cm.
  ISBN-13: 978-0-7573-1610-4 (pbk.)
  ISBN-10: 0-7573-1610-7 (pbk.)
  ISBN-13: 978-0-7573-1611-1 (ebook)
  ISBN-10: 0-7573-1611-5 (ebook)
  I. Title.
  PS3607.A78854B56   2012
  813'.6—dc23

2012012124

Publisher: Health Communications, Inc.
3201 S.W. 15th Street
Deerfield Beach, FL 33442-8190

Cover illustration and design by Joshua Mikel at Sharkguts Design 2012
Interior design and formatting by Dawn Von Strolley Grove

To my grandparents:
George and Martha Goheen
and
Wendell and Peg Gates
Without you, I would not be where I am or who I am.

Thank you

You're a slave and you don't even know it.

—CHAPTER 001—

Gone now is the gun from my hand. Gone, the laughter of my friends. Gone, my father's protective glare. This is the path one walks alone.

Behind me, the N-Corp headquarters building thrusts from the earth like a giant spear, impaling the sky. It, this building, is the axis around which the whole world turns. From its doors flow all the wealth, all the abundance, and all the horror that mankind has wrought. That I have wrought.

Its glistening steps are speckled with blood.

In its mirrored doors I see myself: a skinny, pale young woman, standing alone.

Those black-clad men at the foot of the steps are coming for me. The crack of their bullets shouts my name. And no, this is not a dream.

From all around come murmurs of shock and uncertainty. Hundreds of frowning, watching faces surround me. Women in their designer-cut skirts, men in their impeccable ties, they pull back, dreading to soil their clothes with a drop of my blood. Of all the terrors in the world, they fear for their cleanliness the most.

They would rather slip past me and begin their workday immediately, so they can finish early and go home to dine on steak, sleep in silk. Already, they're desperate to forget me, this sight, this morning. Already they cannot.

All this, after all, has been for them.

There is a snap in my chest as a bullet strikes a rib, and seemingly from nowhere a kaleidoscope of painfully vivid images is unleashed upon me: my life, the Company, the revolution. I see it all. Every breath, every heartbeat, every prayer. A vision so bright I could cry.

1

But this is not the beginning.

Four hours until the Battle of Detroit.

Ethan, standing on a dusty tabletop, calls out:

"For those of you who are new, welcome. The first thing to know is this: if you're here, it's already too late to turn back. So listen well and understand what you'll be bleeding for.

"We are the Protectorate, the fourth branch of American government. Before there was a president, we were here. Before the Constitution was scratched onto paper, we walked the streets. In the year seventeen eighty-three, George Washington founded our organization in secret. We were and are a group of citizens assembled to live and die in the service of the people, to defend a liberty more basic than free speech, more fundamental than the freedoms of press or assembly or suffrage. We protect the last human right: the right of rebellion."

There are raucous shouts of assent. Energy courses through the crowd, making the air around us almost seem to vibrate.

"Never forget, my friends, how much blood has been shed in the name of freedom. Any student of history knows it is enough to wash us all away. But do not forget what the word *freedom* means: we face an enemy today who uses the very word against us. Freedom, to the Company, is the freedom to bleed the poor, to assault our minds with their greedy, warping propaganda, to hold liens against our every possession and our every minute of waking life, to watch us, track us, judge us, and execute us, without our having any recourse at all. Does this sound familiar to anyone? Am I ringing any bells?"

We yell out in agreement.

"The few of us who have been able to learn the true history of our world are filled with regret. There was a time when these atrocities could have been prevented. Once, and many times in history, the people of the world stood together in opposition to those who would make slaves of them, who would drink their blood and sweat like wine. Well, the spirit of freedom—of defiance—might slumber, but it never dies. I see it stirring again, in all of your eyes."

There are nods and whistles among the crowd. All around, the excitement builds. The atmosphere is electric.

"We are the Protectorate, guardians of freedom. We are the fourth branch of American government, the last one that remains. Today brothers, today sisters, the second American Revolution begins."

The crowd roars. They wave their white guns high. Some weep, some laugh. All seem ready to die.

I can't speak for the rest of us, the hundreds huddled with me in this dark and abandoned place, gripping simple weapons, preparing to face the most advanced and ruthless fighting system humankind has ever devised—but as for me, I'm scared as hell.

But this is not the beginning.

Morning, three months ago.

I hurry along the electric sidewalk, feeling its polished, stainless steel surface gliding along swiftly and fluidly beneath my fast-moving feet. On the opposite sidewalk, tie-men rush to work at the headquarters' South Tower complex. Everyone on my side of the walkway is heading for the greatest monolith in the Hub—the Headquarters itself. I can see it rising before me from among the other great buildings that pass by on either side.

Above each doorway, a sign: the letter "N."

I hear a slight hiss and glance up at one of the scent machines, dispensing a waft of pleasantness as it always does throughout the morning commute. The entire Hub smells of freshly baked muffins today. Sometimes it's pumpkin pie, sometimes chocolate chip cookies, sometimes jasmine or honeysuckle. Workers are an average of 5 percent more productive and 15 percent more content when presented with pleasant olfactory stimuli, according to the latest study from Cranton. So the whole city is sprayed with simulated eau de muffin.

Except I don't feel 15 percent more content today. Far from it.

Standing in line at the N-Coffee bar moments later, packed in among fifty other bleary-eyed office workers, I'm subtly aware of being a shadow of myself.

This tragic realization begs the question: Who was I before? Who is it I've become a shadow of?

The truth is, I've completely lost track.

I can still see scraps of myself. I remember in school, when all the other kids would have their lesson-goggles on, learning economics or mathematics or whatever the N-Ed program demanded for that day, I'd be staring at the sky out the classroom window, my goggles pushed back on my head, daydreaming. Invariably, I would get caught and yelled at. Teachers worked only on commission, of course, so when a student did something that threatened to diminish her test scores, that student tended to get her arm yanked out of its socket. Eventually, in keeping with the N-Corp tradition of innovation, they just replaced the windowpanes with frosted glass. Problem and solution.

I remember throwing grapes at our maids when I was about seven or eight and hiding at the bottom of the stairs to try to look up their skirts. The beginnings of a bad little girl . . .

I remember starting my career with N-Corp—it seems like decades ago now, though it has only been a few years. Even then, I was bossing around men twice my own age. Even then, people feared me.

But as I stand here now, watching the machine fill my coffee cup, I wonder, *Do any of these scattered memories actually constitute me? The real me?*

The answer is no. The equation doesn't add up. This life, these days, these memories don't equal the sum of me. There's something else I can't put my finger on. Something missing.

Above the coffee bar, an imager screen flashes a 3-D holographic ad for the new N-Roadster. Zero to sixty in nothing flat. Nice lines. Well designed. Supple interior. Very ergonomic. And just like that, my previous thoughts flutter away like a flock of birds, and I'm lost in distraction again.

Which new rug should I buy for my apartment? When should I trade my car in for the new model? Tomorrow? What about that new platinum-series toaster?

Was it this hard to think before I got the cross implant? Somehow, I don't know. It was years ago now. . . .

At the counter, the pimple-faced coffee boy recognizes me.

"Wait a minute, you're May Fields! You're the CEO's daughter, right?"

Only twenty-four years old and I'm already world famous. I hate it.

The kid grins. The other people in line turn to look at me. A few gasp.

Before I become completely incapacitated with embarrassment, I shoot the coffee boy a glance that freezes him like an icicle through the heart.

"That's right," I say. "I'm May Fields. And you're the pathetic little scab who sells me my coffee." And I pick up my cup and walk away without another word.

Cruel, maybe, but this is me. This is who I used to be. And in my defense, it's not as easy being the daughter of the most revered man in the world as everyone might think.

My high heels clatter against the polished steel as I hurry out of the N-Coffee store toward the Headquarters building. Hustling tie-men pack the walkway. It's so crowded that some people (mostly low-credit-level workers who can't afford the sidewalk fee anyway) have to walk in the street.

Suddenly, the light around me changes. The imager screens that normally paint the entire length of each surrounding skyscraper with colossal, fast-moving advertisements have shut off, leaving the buildings naked-looking, clad now only in glass and steel and not in their customary coats of fiber-optic brilliance.

The shutting off of the ads signals the end of rush hour. It means we're all late.

Instantly, chaos erupts. Car horns blare. Pedestrians elbow one another. Now that they're late for their shift, the crowd's desperation to get to work is nearly palpable. A girl next to me, the heel of her shoe snaps beneath her and she breaks down sobbing as she hobbles forward. One man screams at another to get out of his way. A large woman shouts at both of them to shut up as she wriggles her way past them.

Their stress is understandable. If you're late, a five-hundred-dollar tardiness fee is assessed to your N-Credit account, automatically. These people, they're sweating, pushing, fighting to beat the half-hour-late deadline. After that, the fee goes up to a grand.

Me, I'm late every day. But then, I can afford it.

From among the N-Roadsters and N-Troops and N-Wagons that clog the street, a bus pulls up. There, on its side, is my newest imager ad. The one from the diamond campaign. There's the girl, her little half-naked teenage body all airbrushed and perfect, with a huge, glittering diamond lodged in her cleavage. The smile and wink she gives as the bus passes seem to be directed only to me.

Given my proclivities, one might imagine I would love this campaign. Add to that the fact that it's raised diamond sales by 7 percent across the board and garnered me a crapload of accolades, and one would think I'd be positively thrilled to stare at it over my morning coffee. But no. I hate the ad. And the bus. And the cars crammed together, unmoving, honking at one another under a glaring red stoplight.

The cars are all one-seaters. N-Corp doesn't make two-seat cars anymore. This way, there's no sharing. If you want to ride in a car, you have to buy your own. Sales in the N-Auto division went up 12 percent when my father cooked up that policy.

I fall into the tussling crowd along with everyone else, feeling uncomfortably like a fish swimming in a school. A bunch of ugly, suit-and-tie-wearing cods, maybe. One guy, a fat catfish of a fellow, jostles me as he comes out of a store. I shove him back so hard he nearly topples to the sidewalk. If it weren't for a gaggle of passing school children who break his fall, he'd probably have cracked his head open. He looks at me with big, wild-looking eyes, but says nothing. Instead he rises, dusts off his suit, and hurries away from me, obviously more interested in saving himself a thousand dollars than picking a fight with a small-framed young woman in the middle of the sidewalk on a Wednesday morning.

Me, I'd rather have fought him.

On I go, through the mass of people, between the sleek glass N-Corp towers, under a sky so distant and hung with smog that it might not be blue at all.

"May! May!"

I wince. But when I turn around, I find it's only Randal, my oldest friend, jogging toward me—all jiggling belly and round, whiskery face.

"Randal," I say, giving him a little smile. "Thank God. I thought you were going to be another brownnosing tie-man asking me to get him a credit raise."

"I know better than that," he jokes. Then his expression becomes serious. "I wanted to c-catch you before you got into the office. I've gotta talk to you about something. About the presentation. It's important. Can we g-grab lunch later?"

"No can do. Gotta work on the new IC launch. It's going to be huge."

"So is this p-p-presentation, May! It's for the board—it'll be televised, for heaven's sake!"

"Keep your pants on, Randal," I say, glancing at my watch. "The presentation is going to be fine."

"B-but, May! I found something in the numbers. Something important."

I look at him. His eyes are wide, his forehead covered with sweat. He's all worked up—and it's not just the Peak they give him over at Cranton.

"Look, I'm late, I've gotta run," I tell him. "We'll talk tonight. You still up for Rocketball?"

He nods, and I hurry past him. "Alright. We'll talk after I beat you, then!" I shout over my shoulder.

In the Headquarters courtyard, I hike up the grand marble staircase toward the building's glass front entrance, moving fast among the throng of people. We all fight against one another, shoulder to shoulder, to pass through the row of doors. Above, the massive N-Corp sign with its logo—a stylized "N" next to a black cross—ushers us inside.

I'm pondering the new product launch I've been working on all month but get immediately distracted upon seeing a young clerk in a

knee-length skirt. Her hair is clean and shiny and the little calf muscles beneath her milky white, deliciously smooth skin bunch up tight
with every step. Her hips move hypnotically.

She's a lovely distraction, but my eyes were drawn to her only out
of habit. The truth is I would never dare to give this beautiful stranger
more than a surreptitious glance. I've fought too hard to develop an
ironclad policy of self-control to let it slip now, when I'm finally attain-
ing a degree of success. And anyway, when one spends long enough
denying one's self, certain kinds of hunger are prone to die.

Now, as I search for that once familiar feeling, that subtle rush of
blood, that aching twinge of desire, there's nothing. Just the coffee in
my hand, just a herd of humans grazing the fields of commerce, heading up to work, to their slow, slow slaughter.

Exposition for the dying:
In N-Hub 3, on the west coast of America Division, two hundred
teenagers were having a party. They were drinking illegal alcohol,
engaging in lewd dancing, and, according to official accounts, partici-
pating in unspecified "perverse acts." It's unclear how the tragedy happened—maybe the security squadmen followed some of the kids to the
party, or maybe one of the partygoers was secretly an HR informant—
who knows? According to the news report, the squadmen ran across a
discarded flyer with an anarchy symbol on it and the word "EMAN-
CIPATE," along with the address of a big abandoned warehouse on
the edge of the city, in an area called the industrial arc. At the time, I
believed what the newsmen said about how the party was discovered.
Now, it doesn't seem at all likely. Why would the kids be so stupid as to
put something that damning into print? It would be suicide.

However it happened, the security squad surrounded the teenagers, barred the doors, and set the structure ablaze without regard for the cries for help, the cursing, the screaming, or the last dying strains of music coming from within as the loudspeakers finally melted and the roof caved in. At least half the kids inside died in the fire.

The rest disappeared.

The following Sunday, Reverend Jimmy Shaw referenced the incident on his biweekly television program as an example of, in his words "God's punishment to those who stray from the narrow path of righteousness," and all across America Division millions of heads solemnly nodded their agreement. Hallelujah.

N-Hub 27 (formerly Buffalo, New York): a man dies in his office, a five-by-five-foot cubicle, his IC (mind-integrated computer/phone) interface still in his hand. N-Corp's regional coroner discovered that he died of sleep deprivation. He was sixty-one million dollars in debt. The interest rate on his loan was a little over 30 percent—pretty standard. He lost his apartment. He lost his car. He lost his seat in the Church since he could no longer tithe, and because of it, he lost his highly religious wife to another man. A lesser person might've jumped off a tall building or gone the standard route and allowed himself to be shipped to a work camp to pay off his debt by indenturing himself for sixty years. But not this guy. He was working day and night to earn his life back. Admirable.

Unfortunately, this proved an impossible task. Though he was in N-Corp's upper management, he was unable to earn overtime—just a straight, hourly wage. The trouble was there weren't enough hours. Who'd have thought you could actually die of sleep deprivation? Turns out, you can.

These events are common knowledge. They made it onto a couple of the lesser-known N-Info news sites, but nobody cared. Nobody.

Especially not me.

❖   ❖   ❖

Randal and I are sweaty, breathing heavily. Our voices echo against the walls of this empty, twenty-foot-wide square room, the home of my 3W3DI, a three-wall 3-D imager. It's a pretty expensive toy, but I enjoy watching sports—and with an imager like this, where the picture appears on three walls and is augmented with holographic technology, one truly feels in the center of the game. At least that's what we tell the people who spend two years' wages on one.

Right now, Randal and I are using it to play one of our favorite video games. It's basically the same as that old sport racquetball—except in Rocketball rallies are occasionally interrupted by attacking holographic pterodactyls or dragons, and the games can take place in any number of virtual environments, from the courtyard of a Mayan temple to the surface of Mars.

"May, you g-gonna serve it, or wait for it to hatch?" Randal asks, as I bounce the ball—a holographic fireball that looks kind of like a comet—off the floor a few times. Randal's spinning his plastic racket in his hand, bouncing back and forth on the balls of his feet and looking comically rotund. His headband is soggy with sweat, but the look on his chubby face is fierce.

He's never beat me at Rocketball in his life, and normally he never could—except for today, for some reason, I'm thinking of letting him win. The score on the screen says 13–14. *What the hell, why not give the guy a break? I'm feeling generous,* I think, and I serve.

It's a good point, long and hard fought—but at the end, I make a show of running into the wall and missing my shot, giving him the victory.

The room erupts into a shower of multicolored, holographic fireworks that sizzle around us like burning confetti as dramatic music plays and a banner appears on the screen declaring: RANDAL WINS!

"Dammit!" I yell, chucking my racquet against the wall. If I don't make a show of poor sportsmanship, he'd know immediately that I threw the game. If he ever actually beat me, I'd break a lot more than my racquet; I'd probably hang myself.

"Well, well, well," says Randal loudly. Though his face is ruddy and he's still wheezing, he stinks of pride. "David has slain G-g-goliath."

As he grins and dances a comical little victory jig, I immediately regret giving him the pity-win. What possessed me to do it anyway? If Dad knew I deliberately let someone beat me at anything, he'd say I've gone soft.

"Lucky you," I grumble.

"You alright? You hit that wall pretty good," he says.

"I'm fine. You should ask the wall."

I can tell he buys my sore-loser act, because his grin gets even bigger. He shakes his head at me.

"Man," he says, "I'm sure glad I'm your friend, because whenever I imagine myself on your bad side—whew!"

He laughs, and I smile in spite of myself. Randal, my oldest friend. Hard to believe we hadn't seen each other for almost eight years, then—bam—we're assigned to work together on this budget presentation. Talk about luck.

It's good to have him back—but unsettling, too, because of how much he's changed. Take his stutter, for example. He wasn't always like that. Back in high school, he was just a quiet, handsome, normal guy. But smart as hell. Then he got accepted to Cranton. Cranktown, everyone calls it. Now, they have him on one of N-Corp's proprietary neuroenhancement drugs, nicknamed Peak. Thanks to this wondrous advance in medical science, he's a genius. And he can hardly say a sentence without stuttering. And he can't sleep at night. And he's gained forty-five pounds. And he works twenty-one hours a day.

But he has a great penthouse apartment.

Despite how much he's changed (or maybe because of it) Randal is a good friend. And we've made the Rocketball a regular thing. Only who'd have thought I would ever let the lard-ass beat me?

"So, May . . ." he begins, "we really have to talk about these numbers."

I'd forced him to hold off on talking business until our Rocketball match was done. I could tell it was hard for him—Peakers are notoriously single-minded when it comes to work—but he'd managed to restrain himself. Now that we're getting into it, though, he's like a dog that just got let off his leash.

He wrangles his gym bag out of a cubby in the wall and digs his IC out of it. This is last season's IC model. The new one is sleeker and smaller, and can be strapped to your wrist like an old-fashioned wristwatch. Still, this IC will do the trick. It has all the computing power a person could want; it's fully integrated with the Company network, cross-controlled, and has a 3-D holographic display setting. Not bad—although as soon as the next gen comes out in a few months, this one will be completely obsolete.

As soon as he looks down at it, the screen changes as the device begins pulling the files Randal is thinking of showing me off the Company network.

"See, I was going over the numbers and I kept finding discrepancies with the revenue p-p-p-projections. . . . Oh, sidebar: there's something strange with the Africa Division accounting. There's a ridiculous amount of money being allocated to the Human Resources budget, which doesn't make any sense because we're just now ramping up there. Of course, recruiting new personnel is expensive, but nothing like this—not even close. You should talk to your dad. He should really ask Blackwell about it. . . ."

Blackwell. Vice President of Human Resources, overseer of N-Corp's security division—and jackass extraordinaire. But as usual, Randal has veered off topic.

"The revenue projections?" I remind him.

"Right, right. The p-projections . . ."

Randal blinks twice, and the screen of the little IC in his hand changes. He squints, and it casts a holographic projection into the air in front of us. The blinking and squinting aren't really necessary, of course, but the new ICs were only released last year, and most people are still getting used to using them.

The mandatory IC/Cross Interface program was my first major project when I started with the Company. Cross implantation had started quite a while ago, and most higher-credit-level people in the Company, like me, had their cross implants for years before it became required. It was our job to get the holdouts excited about the process.

The task seemed pretty daunting at first. I had to convince everyone in America Division to get a black implant in the shape of a cross put in under the skin of their left cheek. Oh, yes—and it's wired into your brain. It seemed so much different from selling an imager or a new car, but I soon discovered that all the sales and marketing tricks I learned in school applied perfectly. Features and benefits: the cross allows everyone to control their electronic devices with their thoughts—no more pesky touch screens or keyboards! It speeds up security procedures at airports and Company security checkpoints because your ID information is stored inside it! It makes cash and credit cards obsolete since all your account information is encoded in the cross, which can be scanned at every cashier station Companywide! And it even ensures that the marketing you receive—the imager ads, IC ads—all of them are tailored to your thoughts! You think about ice cream, we advertise ice cream to you. Talk about convenience! *Get yours today!*

But the real genius was the way we rolled the program out. For the first year, only the high-credit-level workers and their families were allowed to get a cross implant, so it became a symbol of social status, power, success. As the months went by, we released it to mid-credit-level workers, then the low-level ones. By the time crosses became mandatory, everyone was clamoring to have one. And we gave it to them—at a considerable profit.

The program was an incredible success. My father was never more proud of me.

But now, Randal is talking numbers.

" . . . But if you look at the next chart, you can see these projections are inaccurate. When you adjust for all the variables, the real growth in these sectors is slowing. And when you take into account the p-projected demographics changes—"

"Randal, cut to the chase."

He clears his throat, shifts on his feet, tugs at his beard.

"The C-Company is going to lose money this year."

I stare at him, stunned.

"That's not possible."

"B-but it is. Look at the numbers again. . . ."

We set up in the dining room of my condo and spend all night poring over the data. Finally, even without a high dose of Peak flowing through my brain, I realize that Randal is right. N-Corp, the Company that literally runs half of the world, is poised to experience a financial loss for the first time in over thirty years.

"What do we d-do?" Randal asks as we sit together at midnight amid the remnants of our takeout dinner.

I sit for a moment, drumming my fingers on the table.

"We tell the board," I say finally. "That was our assignment, right? You assess the computer's revenue projections and I present the findings."

"B-but, May, they're not going to like the report."

Randal is right. There's no telling what might happen when we announce news like this. To say that the Company is going to have a loss is the modern-day equivalent of Galileo saying the Earth isn't the center of the universe. Then there's my dad. For the last twenty-five years, he's had the nickname "Doctor Profit." He's not going to be too happy, either.

Randal looks distraught. "It's going to get ugly, May. No matter who your d-dad is, the board is going to *crucify* you up there."

I give Randal the most reassuring smile I can muster. "Maybe," I say, "but it's the truth. And like Jimmy Shaw says, the truth will set you free."

—CHAPTER 0Ø2—

"We walk a path rife with distraction! *Lust, laziness, violence; these vices might come at you from anywhere. The Devil is great with booby traps. He's a wily hunter. You'd better watch out, or you might get caught. Then, even the Company can't help you. No, then you'll be on your own. Unprofitables, anarchists, queers, cross-dressers, they've all fallen into the Devil's grip. But I'll tell you how to say clear of those traps. Hard work. Piety. Follow those Company policies and your Ten Commandments, you'd better believe it. Turn with me to the book of Deuteronomy. . . .*"

So sayeth Jimmy Shaw from his bejeweled Company pulpit. I turn off the imager screen.

Jimmy: the consummate jovial Southern gentleman, my father's old college roommate and long-time best friend. I still remember the candy treats old Uncle Jimmy used to bring me when he'd come by the house for Sunday dinner. Even after he stopped visiting, I still never missed an episode of *The Jimmy Shaw Hour in Christ*. The show's host was always warm, friendly, loving, and around at least two nights a week (on the imager, at least)—all things that my father was not. His sermons made me think of something bigger than myself. And late at night as I lay in bed alone after my evening prayers, I used to think I could really feel God there with me, just like Jimmy said he was.

I still pray twice a day, still believe in God and in Jesus—although in a much more vague way than I used to. I still hear Jimmy Shaw's homey sayings drifting through my head, especially when I'm contemplating doing something he wouldn't approve of. But lately, my taste for the show has soured, along with my taste for just about everything else in my life.

It's the evening after Randal beat me at Rocketball. I'm at home,

17

showered, styled, wearing nice clothes. Alone.

I rise from my N-Lux suede reclining couch and pace my apartment like a panther, watching the shapes my shadow makes on the wall as I pass.

From somewhere below a sound bleeds through, the washed-out blare of music and the braying of laughter from some unknown neighbor's imager. As much as they charge for this apartment, the Company still didn't go to the expense of soundproofing the floors.

As alone as I am, humanity still seeps in.

Now I stalk faster, trying to outrun the sound or distract myself from it, but there's no escape. Through the floor rise the words of a commercial. This jingle is particularly inane and pervasive:

> *You wanna get it, you gotta face it!*
> *Face it, it's your identity!*
> *N-Corp!*

Even now, with no imager in sight, the vision of the goofy guy from that commercial stumbles through my head. There he is: walking, swinging his cane, falling down, looking like—who's that film star, from black-and-white silent films? Charlie Chaplin. This guy in the commercial falls down and hits his face on a manhole cover and gets that mark of the cross on his cheek, then suddenly his black-and-white world becomes color; doors open for him, birds land on his shoulders, women come to fawn over him, and his hard-luck antics seem to be at an end. Welcome to the wonderful world of credit, Charlie! Welcome to the life of an N-Corp debtor-worker!

Welcome.

The maddening commercial plays all the time, just to make sure no one forgets that the cross implant is a wonderful thing. Naturally, all commercials played in this region are N-Corp commercials, designed to market N-Corp products, just as all imager shows are produced by N-Corp Media division. The repetition is enough to drive a person insane, but research shows it's the most effective way to get a message across—and anyway, it's all I've ever known.

As suddenly as it rose, the auditory apparition descends back into the floor. My downstairs neighbors, whoever they are, seem to have given up on the imager and gone to bed.

Thank God.

Still wandering, I cross to the window. It's twice as tall as I am and runs the whole length of my apartment. Viewed from the exterior, my entire building, all 106 stories of it, looks either like a huge mirror or a massive imager, depending on the time of day and whether the ads are on or off. Now they're off. Gazing out from here, thousands of other mirrored buildings stand in row upon endless row, as far as the eye can see. Each streetlight below has fifty twins by the time it reaches my eye. Everything is a reflection of a reflection of a reflection. The sky is in the last throes of sunset, and by now the city is mostly dark. My apartment is quiet all around me. I reach out, putting my hand to the glass, and see one more reflection: there's me—or a reverse image of me—staring back.

I lean my forehead against my forehead.

There: my short, messy dark hair; my big, dark eyes; pale, white skin; thin arms; awkward lips.

And of course, there's the black cross implanted in my left cheek, two inches by one inch. I know it's sifting through my mind and try my hardest to divert my thoughts to an acceptable subject—like work, or friends, or what I want to buy myself next—but tonight it's impossible.

Instead, a scene fills my mind of an old-fashioned bar, full of laughter and loud voices and cigarette smoke, where everyone is packed in so close they can't help but touch one another. In one corner, somebody bangs away on an old piano. Here, nobody is worried about money, about cars or clothes or plastic surgery. Nobody is afraid of being judged or demoted or fined for cursing. Nobody is worried about their credit level or about Human Resources agents watching them. They blurt out jokes, sacrilegious comments and double entendres, carelessly and endlessly. Young lovers go home together—to their own little houses, not big fancy apartments—and nobody whispers as they leave. The music follows them out the doors, into the streets, and when people pass the stumbling, laughing couples, instead of calling the security squad, they smile.

I don't know where this imaginary bar came from. Certainly, no place like it has existed in my lifetime. Most likely, I gleaned it from one of my father's stories about his epic college years. Wherever I got it, my mind wanders to this fictitious bar a lot. Maybe everybody has their own ridiculous utopia; this is mine.

And, of course, it's filled with hot, flirtatious young women. Some vices are too much a part of you to be torn away completely.

I turn back to my apartment. The air-conditioner hums. The carpet stretches away across the living room, a vast field of perfect white. There's my imager, my stereo, my desk, my table and chairs, my N-Art signed prints of holo-photos from that famous photographer—I forget his name. All of it's here, everything I could ever want. I take this inventory a lot, as a sort of mathematical exercise. I am equal to the sum of these treasures. That's the formula. By everyone's calculations, I'm doing brilliantly. Within fifteen years, I'll be a Blackie, free and clear of any Company debt.

There's my elaborate fish tank, my robot cat, my leather sofas . . . and silence.

My few friends are all working late and will have to wake up early for work. My father is in N-Hub 119, a place once called Mexico City, on business. I am alone.

Outside my door, the security squadmen pass by, laughing. They patrol every building like this. They are everywhere. I could invite them in, I suppose, give them a drink, share a little cake. If one of them was a woman, maybe ...

I walk to the fridge and take out a cupcake purchased especially for the occasion. Chocolate cake with chocolate frosting.

But why invite the squadmen in? They aren't my friends. They don't know me, and I don't like them.

Nobody knows me, whispers a voice in my mind.

And that's true, no one does. Some vices do that to a girl.

So I sit and eat my cake alone. I try not to think of Randal's dire prediction of the Company's coming loss.

I put on my N-Elita silk pajamas, wash my face, say Jimmy Shaw's prayer for health, wealth, and power, and go to bed.

So ends my twenty-fifth birthday.

The next day.

I sit at the conference table with my team, dreaming up ways to make people buy things they don't need. It's not a difficult task by any means. The way it works is simple: we only produce a few models of each product, and we promote them so much before they come out that everyone goes out and buys them instantly, no matter the cost.

The challenge, as my father confided to me on the day I was hired into the N-Corp marketing department, is that, truthfully, N-Corp products aren't that exciting. We're the only company operating in the

Western Hemisphere, and that means that there are no other companies' products on the market for us to compete with. Since there's no competition, there's no financial incentive for us to innovate. So this new IC is no better than the last one, except that it's green instead of silver, it has a slightly narrower screen, and you can strap it to your wrist. Of course, the fellows at Cranton are coming up with new stuff every day, but most of it is never developed, or if it does get developed, it's never brought to the market.

"Just enough to keep the lemmings entertained," was my father's axiom when it came to rolling out new products. "It's not the product they need, May, it's the need itself. They need to need something. It could be a sports car or a can of peanuts. It's the distraction they crave."

To make that distraction work to the fullest, my mission is to make the new product, whatever it may be, more than just a necessity; it must be an obsession. The desire for it must eclipse all else in the consumer's life.

Easy.

Ads appear on the imagers located inside your shower, on the doors of public toilet stalls, on the surface of your desk at work, inside commuter trains and elevators, in shopping plazas, inside your car, in the backs of the pews at church, in street signs, on the screen of your IC, in the living room of your apartment, in the ceiling above your bed, on the exterior of every building, of course, and in a million other places. The line between thought and suggestion is forever and irrevocably erased—that's my job.

Today, my marketing team and I sit in suede chairs around a huge ebony and mother-of-pearl inlaid conference table. A giant crucifix hangs on the far wall. I'm almost falling asleep as my team brainstorms about the launch plan for the new IC.

They'll be mandatory equipment for all Company employees by the end of the year, but those who want to buy it now can do so—at a 300 percent markup.

My job is to make everyone want it now.

"She should hold the IC next to her bra, like this," says Miller, a pasty young man in a wrinkled tie.

The screen at the center of the table lights up and displays Miller's sloppy sketch of a ferocious-looking, half-naked girl standing before a fireworks-laced night sky, holding her IC. On the top right-hand corner of the sketch, the N-Corp logo with its big, black cross appears.

"Yeah," Dagny says thoughtfully, "I like that, but we need a man in there, too. And text. Something like: 'I know what you're thinking.'"

"Not bad," Jeff says.

"That's good," Kate agrees.

"Is the guy shirtless?" Carter asks.

"Of course," Dagny scoffs.

"Does he have an IC, too? Or are they both holding on to hers? Maybe he's looking at her screen—you know, trying to see what she's uploading," Miller offers.

"Or should he have his own? Maybe they're back-to-back, both engrossed. Like the IC is so fascinating, they don't even notice each other," Carter says.

Dagny shakes her head. "One IC says luxury. It says there aren't enough ICs for everyone, so if you're lucky enough to get your hands on one, you'd better snatch it up."

"What do you think, May?" asks Miller, turning his bloodshot, sleep-deprived eyes to me.

Dagny watches me expectantly, too. Her face is round and plump, and the cross under her left eyes makes her features look strangely proportioned, as if she's just stepped out of a painting by Picasso. Or maybe I just need more coffee.

"Hmmm," I yawn. "What market is this going to be focused on again?"

"Mostly prime time imager—and we were thinking of using a variation of it as the tag during *The Jimmy Shaw Hour in Christ,*" Dagny replies.

I nod, but before I can speak, there's a din in the hallway, and we all look out the glass wall of the conference room. Four members of the security squad march down the hallway toward us. As they approach, the white letters "HR" stitched on the chest of their black military uniforms are clearly visible.

"Uh-oh," Carter says under his breath.

"Who do you think it is this time?" Jeff whispers.

"You," Miller jokes, then cackles quietly at his own joke.

"Shut up," I bark. The squadmen are coming right toward us.

The glass conference room doors slide open as they approach, and the leader steps forward. "Dagny Marot?" he asks.

For the first time since the squadmen appeared, I notice Dagny's demeanor. Her face pale, she stares down at the screen of the IC clutched in her trembling hands.

"Dagny Marot?" the squad member asks again, and when she doesn't respond, he nods to one of the other men. "Scan her cross."

The squad member lifts his IC—a slightly larger, more durable version of the one I carry. It beeps.

"Identity confirmed," the squad member says. "Dagny Marot, you are hereby repossessed by N-Corp."

Dagny is on her feet now, her chair tipping over as she backpedals toward the window.

"No," she says. "I'm working on the IC launch. I'm scheduled for a raise. And I'm saving credit. I moved into a smaller apartment. I—I—you need me! Tell them, May!"

The squadmen grab Dagny. She fights for a moment, then groans pitifully and goes limp as the squadmen put the handcuffs on her and lead her from the room. As they depart, the lead squad member's speech drones on: ". . . Per your employment contract, you will be incarcerated in a Company work camp until your debt load has been reduced to a satisfactory level. If you should fail to—"

The doors slip shut behind them. Through the glass, my team and I watch as they drag Dagny away down the hall, leaving a tense silence in their wake. A few curious heads poke out of the cubicles they pass before quickly disappearing again.

"Dammit," I murmur. One less employee means one thing: more work for the rest of us. *And Dagny was probably the strongest member of my team—although apparently HR's Profitability Department didn't think so.*

"I can't believe they got Dagny. She has to have a higher credit limit than me," Carter muses nervously.

"Pretty skirt. I wonder if they'll let her take it to the work camp," Kate says.

"Dagny was good. It's going to be rough without her," Miller says, then looks at me. "What do you think, May?"

Instantly, every set of eyes in the room snaps toward me, the CEO's daughter. I feel their stares burning into me, but I can find no words.

"One IC, like they're fighting over it," I manage to say finally, tapping the screen in the middle of the table with my finger. "And put them both in metal swimsuits or something—him in a Speedo, her in a bikini. Make the fireworks green to match the color of the IC. Do a couple of different mock-ups and send them to Shaw's people, see what they think."

The members of my team all squint down at the ICs in their hands for a moment, letting their crosses translate their thoughts into text, which will be saved for them to refer to later.

"Anything else?" I ask gruffly, and they shake their heads, all of them carefully avoiding eye contact with me. "Good. Thirty minutes for lunch. Go."

After everyone gets up and exits, I rise and linger for a moment, pacing the room. There's an uncomfortable pain in my chest, and I can't for the life of me figure out what's causing it. Certainly, it's not the fact that Dagny was repossessed. Human Resources is constantly evaluating all N-Corp employees. In the event that a person's debt load (plus interest) outstrips the profit they generate the Company, then they're designated an "unprofitable." They get relieved of their possessions and transferred to a work camp. It's a perfectly natural and reasonable solution. As my father has always pointed out, the greatest crime of all would be to let lazy and greedy people leach off Company profits and mess up the bottom line. With a repossession, the Company gets paid back the money they've loaned out, and the worker gets to atone for his or her lapse in productivity. It's a perfect trade. Problem and solution.

So why is my heart racing? Why do I feel like I'm about to throw up?

I pace for a moment longer. The feeling has almost passed when I notice something under Dagny's chair and pick it up. It's one of her shoes, a charcoal-colored N-Splash Pump, fall collection, the one with the ivory heel. Not a bad shoe—for a mid-credit-level tie-girl like Dagny. I drop it in the trash as I head out of the room. After all, she won't be needing it any time soon.

Walking briskly down the hall, I'm feeling much better, as if throwing out that shoe got rid of whatever was causing my discomfort. And why not? I have nothing to be upset about. HR will send me a replacement employee automatically within two weeks. There are people all over the world who would love to step into a glamorous, mid-credit-level job like Dagny's. And people get repossessed every day.

The real question is, what should I have for lunch, baked ziti at N-Roma or stir-fry at N-Orient Café?

I return here over and over again, to this long-ago place.

A breeze cuts the night, breathing into the white sails, filling them. The air is warm across my face. The only sounds are the slight rustle of the jib and the whisper of the hull through the water. Dad's cigar smoke smells sweet, comforting. If he's still smoking, that means I must only be—what? Nine? Ten years old?

He sits, one lax hand on the boat's oversized steering wheel, the other gripping his cell phone—this is before introduction of the ICs. His voice is deep and gravelly, but there's something comforting in its sonorous rumble.

"Jimmy, mark my words. The shareholders mean nothing. They'll follow us wherever we lead them. The merger is happening. . . . No, like I said, I'll be back in the office on Wednesday. You're going to take care of this. You're the one with the golden tongue, buddy. . . . What? You're goddamned right—or, G. D. right, I mean. And you can tell Yao I'll be back on Wednesday, not a minute sooner. I'm teaching May to sail. . . . Of course she can sail; she's my daughter! She's a goddamned conquistador!"

The dark shape of his body turns toward me for a second, then back.

"My shrink said I should spend some quality time with her. I told him, 'Bullshit, my little girl is doing fine—more than fine—she's going to be the goddamn—er, G. D. president of the Company. She's going to own us all one of these days!' But here I am anyway, and here I'll stay until Wednesday. You tell them if they don't like it they can go piss up a rope. Now stop bugging me before I run us into a damned rock. . . . Okay, buddy. Cheers."

He shuts off his phone, takes a puff of his cigar. I lean over the edge of the stern—Dad won't let me say "back," it has to be "stern"— and stare into the black water. The sky above and the foam below are tinged with pink—Dad says no matter how far we sail, we'll never quite escape the stain of city lights.

There!

I gasp. Below the foam, there's something amazing in the wake. A magical green light shines among the churning bubbles.

Of course, I'll later learn that this is just phosphorescence caused by a type of plankton or something that glows when it gets stirred up, but today, and for years to come, I'll truly, fervently believe that this is proof of magic. I'm on a path marked by magic, and if I look closely enough, I'll be able to see it all around me. Pointing down to the radiant froth, breathless, I turn to my father—but he speaks before I get a chance.

"May," he says through cigar-clenching teeth, "grab the wheel so I can take a leak."

Awed by this new responsibility, I jump up, dodging lanyards and winches, and grip the wheel with my tiny hands, just like Dad taught me. He wordlessly tosses his cigar into the drink—we never call it "the water," it has to be "the drink"—and lumbers down into the cabin. His urine starts up. I like the sound.

"Hey, May?" he says, his voice muffled.

"Hey what?" I say. He taught me to answer like that.

His voice drifts up from the cabin below: "I know you're different, but don't ever let the other kids give you crap about it, alright?"

Right now I don't really understand what he means by "different."

In a few years it'll make sense, but by then it'll be too late. For now, I think maybe he means I have special powers, like Superman or something.

"Okay," I say.

This is the only time in my life he will ever mention my "difference."

Sounds float up to me: he zips up his fly, he cracks another beer.

I steer us straight through the dark on a path marked with magical light.

I walk the shopping plaza's marbled halls. The grand, vaulted ceiling soars 120 feet above me, smooth white buttresses holding at bay a fragmented, glass-clamped night sky.

My IC beeps, and the screen shows that it's Randal calling again.

I understand his anxiety about the presentation tomorrow morning; God only knows what will happen when we tell the Company's board that they're headed for the first financial loss in a generation. But talking about it endlessly with my madly neurotic best friend won't help. When he's stressed, he rambles and stutters and pulls his own hair, and it drives me nuts.

Me, when I'm stressed out, I wander the shopping plaza.

I ignore the call.

Amid the crush of countless milling shoppers, a couple walks past me, holding hands, all perfect hair and plastic skin. Do I imagine it, or are their eyes vacant, windows into the souls of mindless dolls? (It's the pills that do it. Smiles on their faces and nothing behind their eyes. N-Pharm, at your service.) Their lips move, but they don't speak to one another. Each of them is talking to someone else on their ICs. The man mumbles about interest rates, the woman chirps about the fall line, and they pass me by.

My gut knots up as they drift into periphery, and my neck seizes with pain and tension. The hatred, the contempt I feel for these people scares me, but it isn't their vapidity that bothers me. No, it's their love. Because like all the couples I see in this place they can be together openly, and they take that blessing for granted.

They're gone, and I pass a planter where a tall palm tree grows, surrounded by a bristling pot of fake flowers. I pass a bench. I pass a makeup store with a tall, thoroughbred of a woman standing out front handing out samples of lip gloss. She gives some packets to a group of teenage girls as they pass, favoring them with a smile dripping with self-satisfied boredom. When I pass, she doesn't even hold out a packet.

In the dark hollows of my heart, a voice cackles at her: *You bitch, you don't even know: I'll be a Blackie one day.* And I hate her for not noticing me, not seeing me.

Of course, I shouldn't be surprised by her not handing me lip gloss: I'm dressed like a man.

Women wearing pants went out of fashion years ago, when N-Style first decided to go with gender-specific clothing as a matter of policy. Since then, Cranton studies showed that nonconformist dress was a workplace distraction and a drag on productivity, and the practice was strictly forbidden by the HR handbook.

Unfortunately, it's only when I'm wearing pants and a tie with my hair pulled back and stuffed under a hat like this that I truly feel like myself. It's my release, my happy place. And, yes, maybe the forbidden nature of the act adds to the thrill.

So far I haven't been caught. But even if my dirty little secret were to get back to Blackwell and his HR cronies, I have plenty of credit to pay whatever fines they might charge me, and they wouldn't dare give me a demotion—not me, the daughter of CEO Fields.

Thinking of my father, I take out my IC and try to call him again. Again, his voicemail greets me. Ever since Randal's revelation I've been trying to get a hold of Dad, to warn him, to get his advice. I've left messages at his office and at his house. I've sent them to his IC. No response. Typical. He's too busy for me. Well, fine—he can be blind-sided by my news like everyone else.

"Entry fee: fifty dollars. Your account has been debited," a synthesized voice croons as I enter N-Lumin, a candle shop.

The disembodied voice belongs to Eva, the artificially intelligent avatar who acts as my interface with the Company network and greets me from speakers hidden all over the N-Corp empire. She also lives in my IC, as my digital personal assistant. She greets me at the entrance to every Company building, and reads my mail to me, and reminds me of appointments. She's everywhere, like a computer-based stalker following every Company employee in the world around during every minute of every day. God, how I hate her.

"Welcome, Miss Fields," she says, and I roll my eyes.

No one seems to notice that I'm not May Fields at all, but perhaps her long-lost, slightly effeminate brother.

I'm only a few steps into the store when raucous laughter echoes behind me, and I turn to the entrance of the store in time to see three squadmen amble past. Silver stars hang from large chains around their necks against their black, military-style shirts. The chrome and mother-of-pearl inlaid grips of the guns on their hips glint as they pass. Their baseball caps, each black and emblazoned with a white-embroidered "HR," are cocked low over their eyes. These young men—each probably no older than eighteen years—walk slowly, joke loudly. A woman walking toward them changes her course, giving them plenty of space.

One of them sees me staring and looks back at me, his eyes filled with cold mirth. I don't want to look away, don't want to give him the satisfaction of bowing to his alpha-dog status, but I can't help it.

Their strident voices fade, blend into the cacophony of bland music and inane conversation and disappear. With a hiss, I release the breath I hadn't been aware of holding. My neck aches with tension.

All these years, and the squads still do that to me.

I pick up a red candle, sniff it. Coconut and cherry—or something like that. The smell reminds me of her, and I inhale again. *Kali.*

I close my eyes, thinking of her, of summertime and the smell of her skin when she would come in from the sun, of the taste of her lips and the salt of her sweat and the feeling of giddy, electric fear at the thought of being caught in the divine act that was supposed to be so wrong but was really so right. Sweet Kali, long gone.

I put the candle down, then pick it back up. I'll buy it, burn it tonight for her, and send a prayer her way, wherever she is. Whenever I think of her, I fear the worst.

The register is at the back of the store, and I weave my way through what must be fifty people crammed into the little shop, around table after table filled with elaborate candelabras, candles, pricks of quivering light. Before stepping up to the counter I sniff and blink my tears away.

Then I perform the checkout ritual without a second thought. Start by stepping on the black square. There's no tingling, no pain, no feeling whatsoever as the checkout computer scans the black cross on my face, extracting all my information: name, age, credit history, medical information, buying habits and preferences, criminal record, and Company account information. Eva's disembodied voice says: "*Welcome, Miss Fields,*" and I set the candle on the plastic shelf in front of me, wait for the sound of the beep, then place the candle in a plastic bag and leave. As I step out of the store, Eva's eerie, endlessly friendly voice is there, too:

"Thank you, Miss Fields. Please come again."

Even though the cross-identification program was my dad's baby, even though I know it cuts crime, saves time and money, and sets apart all N-Corp debtor-workers from the unprofitables, there's something disconcerting in never being able to escape my own name.

My IC goes off again, and this time I answer the call.

"Randal! Relax, would you? Everything is going to be fine!"

But even as the words leave my mouth, part of me knows I'm lying. Everything isn't going to be fine. It never was. It never will be.

My apartment, morning. I've already clambered out of bed, off a mattress made of a highly advanced foam-polymer-sponge compound with a synthetic goose-down pillow-top; showered surrounded by the steam from the eighteen platinum-covered titanium showerheads that assail me from all angles; lathered with N-Spa Diamond series body wash, stuff that reeks of mint and innumerable varieties of flowers; and dried off with my new N-Spa series towel, a luxurious, cashmere-cotton blend with the gold stitching.

Dry now, I apply my deodorant and style my hair (as much as I ever style it—which amounts to pulling it back into an uncomfortably tight ponytail).

Every article of clothing I own is from the N-Elita collection, hand-tailored and made of the finest fabrics. The styles are patterned after the work of the greatest clothing designers who ever lived: Giorgio Armani, Coco Chanel, Donatella Versace, people like that. The N-Textile division stopped producing new clothing designs years ago, instead cycling through collections created in years past. The move saved the Company billions in design costs. And, of course, people buy the clothes anyway. The only competition for N-Corp's clothing—in America Division, anyway—is nakedness. And nakedness is strictly forbidden by the HR handbook.

I couldn't care less about fashion anyway. The only reason I have these fancy clothes is because I'm expected to dress nicely—and because as a high-credit-level worker, I can.

As I dress, Eva goes over my schedule for the day.

"Hello, May Fields. Your day's schedule is as follows: Arrive at work—8 AM. 8 AM until 9 AM—Board meeting, attendance required. 9:15 AM until 9:44 AM—

Complete digital correspondence. 9:44 AM until noon—IC launch team meeting in conference room K15 . . . "

She goes on and on, reminding, nagging, confirming. I like to imagine her as a hot Asian woman with green eyes and a mini-skirt. It makes me want to choke her less.

Dressed now, I hurry down the hall to the elevator, nibbling at an N-Nourishe bar, trying to choke a few crumbs into my stress-clenched stomach.

The walk to work, the journey through the Headquarters lobby, the vertigo-inducing high-speed elevator ride up to the two-hundredth floor of the Headquarters building: all a blur. Before I know it, I'm standing in the boardroom. It's an imposing space, three stories high and all windows, interspersed with a few sections of polished cherry-wood paneling. Even the scent-machine odor is different here in the boardroom: mingled essences of leather and musk. Brandy. A hint of cigar smoke. It's the smell of success, intimidation. Power. The boardroom can accommodate up to one thousand people in the church-pew-style seats that border the room on three sides, and the seats are almost full. All the Company's most important tie-men and women are here. One by one, they finish their chatter and take their seats, preparing for the start of the meeting.

Amid the commotion, Randal hurries up to me, his awkward gait somewhere between a goosestep and a skip. As he approaches, I corral him and try to fix his tie and tuck in one side of his shirt while he hisses in my ear, "May, I don't know if we should go through with it. I d-d-don't—"

"Randal," I interrupt, trying to ply him with my calmness, "we were ordered to make a report to the board. That was our assignment, and that's what we're going to do. Now try to pull it together."

Even though we've already decided that I'm going to be the one doing all the talking, I'm still slightly mortified that Randal will do something to embarrass me, like start weeping in the middle of my speech. For a second, I consider walking out of the room and letting him do the presentation himself. If they're going to shoot the messenger, I'd rather it were him than me. In this Peaked-out state, no one would probably believe him anyway.

Except I can't do that. It would be disloyal to the Company. The news we have to deliver is too important.

I glance around. The board meetings are televised Company-wide, and everyone is required to watch. Imager cameras, suspended on cranes, move back and forth above us, their lenses trained on the fourth wall of the room. There, a gigantic, backlit N-Corp logo—the N and the cross—stand in relief against the granite wall. Beneath it runs the raised dais where the board members sit. If Randal doesn't get it together by the time those chairs are occupied, we're going to look like idiots.

"There's something else, May," he's saying. "Not only is the C-Company heading for a loss—there's also a discrepancy in the Africa Division accounting. Trillions of dollars are unaccounted for, May. Trillions."

"Randal, you mentioned the Africa Division stuff before. It wasn't part of our assignment, all right? Forget about it." Donning the most commanding voice I can, I grip his shoulder hard and steer him into a chair. "Sit down," I say.

He does, but his lips keep moving, silently continuing his protests. The squeal of a microphone wheels me around, and I take my seat just as Jimmy Shaw steps up to the mic and asks, in that soft, pleasant drawl of his, for everyone to please stand up.

Just the sight of old Uncle Jimmy instantly puts me at ease.

In many ways, Jimmy Shaw is an average sixty-three-year-old man:

he's of normal stature, with shoulders slightly stooped from age. His hands, large and perfectly manicured, rest atop his signature black cane with its cross-shaped handle. His hair is thick, wispy, and white, and the skin of his face is pink and supple looking, probably softer than a baby's hindquarters. He's had fairly extensive plastic surgery like everyone else in the Company, but he still looks fairly normal. Not like half of the tight-skinned monstrosities I've seen running around Headquarters.

He clears his throat and everyone bows their heads.

"Mighty Lord of Hosts, we thank you for your presence here today. We know that your will has led our great Company to its current state of unprecedented prominence, and we ask your guidance as we continue in our quest to raise the entire world on the wings of our humble industriousness. It's in your name we pray, Amen."

The lights glisten off Shaw's sapphire eyes as he steps away from the podium with a satisfied nod. In a rush of shuffling and soft clunking sounds, everyone takes their seats.

That's when I feel her watching me. She sits on the far side of the aisle, and when I look over at her, her hazel eyes hold my gaze. We stare at one another, frozen in time, as if in a contest to see who will look away first.

As the moment stretches on, I study her. She must be my age, no older. Her skin is china-doll smooth. Her hair, long and honey blond, is tied back from a flawlessly sculpted face. Her full lips bear a smile laced with an almost smug sense of self-assurance. Even the cross in her cheek can't diminish the extraordinary harmony of her features. She is exquisite.

I have no idea who she is, but God would I like to find out.

My heart beats an uneven cadence in my chest, and I'm suddenly aware that my cheeks are burning, my shirt soaking through with sweat. I snap my head back toward the stage just as the Company song starts playing, sounding strangely tinny even over the ultrapremium N-Audio speakers installed somewhere in the ceiling.

I hazard one more glance at the woman, but she's looking away now, gazing at the screen of her IC. I swallow the wave of disappointment I feel and look away from her again. There are more important things on my plate right now than flirting with girls—even ones as beautiful as her, I remind myself. Besides, she was probably just staring at me because I'm May Fields, the CEO's famous daughter.

And I'm about to be thrown to the dogs.

The music reaches its triumphant crescendo, and from an inconspicuous door beneath the logo, my father appears. The sight of him disappoints me. It's been five months since I've seen him, and I imagined I might see some change in him: he might have gained some weight, gotten a few more gray hairs. His skin might be sagging a bit; there might be bags under his eyes. But no, he looks tan, fit, eager. His face is that of a man half his age; his hair is speckled with just enough gray to lend him a distinguished air, and his white teeth stand out against the dark tan of his skin like stars against a night sky. He looks the same as ever.

With one hand, he deftly unbuttons his perfectly tailored suit coat, and with the other, he waves to the adoring crowd.

He pauses next to his chair, basking in the applause, an easy smile on his face. If he had his choice, this is probably what he'd do all day, I think with habitual bitterness: stand around grinning while the world applauded him. The sad thing is, he has enough money that he could actually pay people to do just that. For my father, unlike almost everyone else on earth, is a Blackie.

Dad sits at his throne-like chair at the center of the long conference table, with Jimmy Shaw at his left and the stoic, nearly mute CFO,

Bernice Yao, on his right. On the far end of the table sits Mr. Blackwell. The dark military uniform of the HR squads is stretched across his broad shoulders, his square jaw is clenched, his Neanderthal brow furrowed beneath a bristle of close-cropped, salt-and-pepper hair. As usual, he sits silently, his hands folded carefully in front of him, watching the proceedings unfold.

With a little flourish, Dad clacks the gavel and the applause gives way to silence.

"Welcome, N-Corp family. I'm thrilled to see you all, and to all of you out there watching us in imager land—well, I can't see you, but I hope you're thrilled to see us."

A wave of pleasant laughter runs through the crowd then quickly falls away.

"I'm proud to say we've had a great quarter," Dad continues, making eye contact with various members of the audience as he speaks. "N-Corp has continued its strategy of expansion with mind-boggling success."

The wall behind him opens, revealing a massive 3-D holo-imager screen. On it, a map of the world. America Division, South America Division, Australia Division, and Africa Division are all blue and bear the N-Corp logo. For the last twenty years, since the great crisis ended and the world's governments were forced to privatize, N-Corp has had a monopoly over these territories. EuropeBloc, RussiaBloc, ChinaBloc, and IndiaBloc are colored red and bear the logo of Briggs & Stratton—B&S for short—the only other corporation in the world. In school, most of our history classes told the story of how corrupt and inefficient the world's governments were before privatization came to the rescue and these two companies began to dominate the globe, so everyone in the room knows the information on screen by heart.

Dad continues: "Since Africa Division has been our primary focus for production growth and Company expansion this year, we're going to have a brief presentation about progress there, followed by a profit projection for the next year. Okay, take it away."

The lights throughout the room dim, and the imager grows brighter. The speakers in the ceiling cough once, then cheesy music comes in, playing over idyllic scenes of African lions and galloping gazelles, interspersed with shots of shiny new N-Corp buildings.

A voice-over:

"The Africa project is among the Company's most profitable endeavors of this decade. Due to its success, millions of Africans have been provided with safe, sanitary housing."

(Image: a plastic "beehive" unit, capable of housing twelve hundred debtor-workers on a single acre of land. Image: a family of three sitting Indian-style next to each other in a five-foot-by-five-foot, sterile-looking plastic room. They're smiling, playing cards.)

"These new employees and customers of N-Corp have been provided with a plentiful food supply, safe drinking water, and the chance to purchase hundreds of low-credit-level items. Each new worker is granted a fifty-thousand-dollar line of credit, which on average will keep him in the Company's service for fifteen to twenty years, not counting any additional credit he may accrue during his employment."

I glance down at the field of numbers on the IC clenched in my trembling hand and my mind drifts to the terrible news I'm about to drop on everyone in the room. My stomach turns and my mouth starts to fill with saliva. I glance around for a trashcan to puke in, but there isn't one handy. Typical. I close my eyes and try to breathe deeply.

"It's okay, May," Randal whispers in my ear. "They can't get mad at us. It's the t-t-t-truth."

If Randal's trying to comfort me, I must be pretty far gone.

The imager continues: *"The Africa Division Growth Project has, to* *date, netted the Company over twenty-five million new debtor-workers, worth approximately $12.5 trillion over the next ten years and 2.3 trillion lifetime man-hours of labor. Today's proposal calls for the expansion of the project beyond the pilot phase to include another nine hundred million workers, surpassing the number of debtor-workers in America Division and rivaling Briggs & Stratton's enormously successful debtor-worker program at their Trans-Asiatic production facilities. . . . "*

The presentation seems to go on forever. Pictures of happy Africans riding N-Moto scooters, playing video games and working in factories dance across the huge face of the imager, *ad nauseum.* Toward the end, an image lingers on the screen that catches my eye. There is a tall, lean African man wearing a sharp-looking suit. He holds hands with an emaciated, naked, pot-bellied child. They both smile into the camera, displaying teeth of the purest white.

That's what the Company is, I remind myself. It's civilization. The difference between prosperity and oblivion. That's what I'm working for. I have to pull it together.

I close my eyes and breathe deeply again. In, out, in, out.

The next thing I know, I'm hearing my name. There's a beep as the IC in my hand syncs with the room's audio/visual system, and suddenly Randal's numbers appear on the massive screen for everyone to see.

Applause. Half the world is watching me. I rise, half walking, half floating up the red-carpeted aisle. I carefully avoid looking at the hazel-eyed young woman sitting in the front row—the last thing I need now is an extra butterfly in my stomach.

As I near the podium, Dad grins at me then glances down at his own IC. Ms. Yao frowns, her arms folded. Jimmy Shaw gives me a wink. I step up to the microphone, clear my throat. The mic squeals. Suddenly, I panic. In my mind, I flash back to last night, walking through the shopping plaza in a tie and pants.

I love wearing a suit, love winning at Rocketball. I love to wear pants. I love women. Everyone can see through me. I am a fraud.

Pull it together, May . . .

I adjust the microphone, and it squeals again.

I begin. "In reviewing the revenue and expense projections for the next year . . ." My voice sounds too low. I am a sinner. Everyone knows. I wipe the sweat from my brow, clear my throat, try again. "In reviewing the numbers, Randal Watson and I have discovered an unfortunate trend. . . ."

The pause seems to last a decade as I build up the courage finish. "It appears that in the next fiscal year, N-Corp is projected to suffer a considerable financial loss."

I expected a long, stunned silence, a few outraged questions, laughter and disbelief, maybe then a vigorous discussion.

But the words are barely out of my mouth when all hell erupts around me.

—CHAPTER 004—

The explosion sends a tongue of flame through the double doors in the back of the auditorium, and everyone in the room screams as one. Shards of glass glitter past, like a hail of diamonds. People are panicking, slamming into one another, screaming, rolling on the floor to put out burning suit jackets and skirts. To my left, a small army of security squadmen has appeared seemingly from nowhere, wearing helmets and bearing riot shields. They've positioned themselves between the board members and the hysterical crowd. Already, my father is being hustled out of the room, followed by Jimmy Shaw and Blackwell. That's all I see before a curtain of smoke rolls in and obscures everything around me. Half blind, choking on the hot, dusty air, I stumble down the steps, away from the podium.

"Randal?" I shout. "Randal?"

He's my only friend. Other than my dad, he's the only one in the room who I have to make sure gets out of this alive. But this was his seat, I'm sure of it, and he's already gone. I look around, searching for him, but everywhere I turn it's the same: roiling, billowing smoke, churning limbs of fleeing tie-men, shrill screams, fluttering flames.

Then, suddenly, there's a hand gripping my elbow. I turn and see her, and that's when I finally panic. Hazel eyes bloodshot with smoke, strawberry-blonde hair disheveled.

"I'm Clair," the beautiful stranger shouts over the din. "Come on."

It helps that the world is burning around me, that I have no idea how to get out of the conference room, that smoke obscures all the emergency exits, but who am I kidding? Even if the Headquarters weren't crashing down around me, I would follow her anywhere.

❖ ❖ ❖

Inside the echo-filled stairwell, a red emergency light flashes in rhythm with my pounding heart. The air is better here, though still unclean. Clair and I clamor down the steps, side by side now. The descent seems endless. Once, something in the walls coughs and the whole building shutters and seems to rock on its foundation. Shouts linger all around us, some piercing, some low, all terrifying.

"We have to get out of the building," Clair shouts over the chaos. "Is there a faster way?"

There might be, but I haven't used my dad's "special exit" in years. I'm not even sure if this is the right stairwell.

"Follow me," I say, and take the lead.

Flight after flight we descend, until my legs ache and tremble beneath me. My hope at being Clair's savior is giving way to despair when finally I see a door with a sign on it. Through the smoky haze, I can barely make out: Floor 125—Rooftop Access

"Here," I cough, hardly recognizing the inhuman rasp as my own voice.

I shove through a heavy steel door, and Clair follows me into the whispering breeze of the South-Annex rooftop.

Stumbling into the afternoon light is like awaking from a nightmare. Bizarre serenity. Behind us, the rest of the building rises up, a smooth shard of blue-black mirror, fractured somewhere above. Down here, the only signs something is wrong are the tiny particles of debris that fall onto us from above, drifting as placidly as flakes of black snow.

"Thanks—" I try to finish with *for getting me out of that conference room*, but I'm wracked with a violent coughing fit before I can.

Clair doesn't even look at me. She's glancing around the rooftop, back toward the door from which we emerged. "We have to get out of here," she says.

From above comes the low rumble of another small explosion, and in my mind I'm back up in that room, remembering that lashing swirl of yellow flame, the people who were sitting in the back few rows of the auditorium, who are probably now burned to ash. How could this have happened? An accident? It seems impossible. But if it wasn't an accident, then who could have done it? Unprofitables? Anarchists? But Dad told me they were just myths, made up for newscasts, fictional boogiemen for the workers to root against. . . .

"Hey," Clair says, "Come on." There's a harshness in her tone that, judging from the sweetness of her features, I would never have thought her capable of. Her hand, still on my arm, clamps down harder as she tries to drag me across the rooftop, but I pull away.

When she turns back to me, her demeanor has gone from harsh to downright dangerous.

"Come with me," she repeats.

"No," I say. "What's going on?"

I'd never seen her before in my life, I remind myself. And she was staring at me minutes before the explosion. As soon as it happened, she found me and dragged me away, and now she's dying to get away from the scene of the crime. What if she had something to do with it? What if that was her intention all along, to cause a diversion and then kidnap me? What if—

She reaches into her coat and comes up with a gun—a strangely shaped pistol the pale color of bone.

"You're an anarchist, aren't you?" I whisper.

"Of course not. Don't be an idiot." She grabs the lapel of my jacket and is once again hauling me across the rooftop, her gun barrel jammed into my ribs. This time I'm too confused to resist. My mind races as I try to put it all together.

"Why?" I ask, my anger finally setting in. "Why did you kill those people?" I pull away from her again, halting. "Tell me the truth, or I'm not taking another step with you. You can shoot me right here!"

For a second, the rage in her eyes looks so potent I think she might shoot me after all.

Then Clair, if that's even her name (but it must be, because the cross-identification program can't be fooled, can it?), chokes back a cough and makes herself stand up straight. She's taller suddenly, stronger looking. Her carriage is regal though her face is smudged nearly black with soot. Her eyes burn into mine.

"We had nothing do with that explosion," she says. "That's the truth."

Her eyes, red around the edges and full of unspilled tears, meet mine. I try to stare into her soul. I give her no quarter. But I can see no trace of a lie inside her—and I don't think all her tears are because of the smoke.

"Who's 'we'?" I press.

Before she can answer, a sound interrupts us. From somewhere below: the lamenting warble of sirens.

We both look off into the distance, listening, and then her eyes return to mine. "I need your help, May," she says, suddenly softening. "If you don't help me, they'll kill me."

By *they*, I assume she's referring to the men behind the sirens: the HR security squads.

"If you had nothing to do with what happened, why would they do that?" I ask.

"Please," she says, and cocks her gun. Now that's persuasion. For an instant, I could almost crack a smile—if I wasn't so worried that she might actually shoot me.

But it's not the gun that makes the decision for me: it's the curiosity. I want to know this woman. I want to know what's going on.

She grabs me again—this time taking my hand. (And yes, a thrill runs through my body at her touch.) Her eyes locked on mine, she says, "Please, May."

And before I know it, I'm leading her across the rooftop. I haven't been up here in years, but it's all just as I remember it. And when we round a corner of the building, our hoped for destination comes into view on the far side of the rooftop.

"May, you're my hero," Clair says.

Ahead, my father's N-Falcon personal helicopter waits.

Mountainous glass buildings flash by us one by one, rising from the jumble of traffic-choked streets below.

Clair and I are in the chopper, running away.

Flying low under the radar grid just as Clair instructed, I slalom past the countless skyscrapers, all of them monuments to N-Corp's seemingly infinite wealth. The tilting and turning, the speed, the blurred world racing past, it makes me want to puke and laugh all at once.

"Executive Two, come in," the radio belches. I glance at it, then at Clair.

"Don't answer," she says. She's mostly recovered from all the soot she inhaled, but her eyes are still red and watery. She keeps running one hand through her hair nervously, but her gun is still pointed at me.

"Executive Two, come in, this is an emergency."

A web of thick power lines confronts us around a blind corner, and I yank us upward. The roller-coaster feeling twists in my stomach, except this no N-Fun Park. There's nothing safe about this ride.

"Executive Two—" Then, in the hollow-sounding world of radio waves, we hear the speaker address someone else in the room with him.

His words are soft, but audible: "No answer. The anarchists must've stolen the chopper."

Then, someone else comes on: "Executive Two, we know what you've done. If you think you can get away, you're mistaken." I recognize the voice immediately; it's Blackwell. I don't know much about security-squad procedures, but I know he probably has the means to shoot down a helicopter with the push of a button.

"What are we going to do?" I ask Clair.

She just shakes her head. Her face is horribly pale.

The first voice comes back on: "Executive Two, come in."

Before Clair can stop me, I snatch up the radio receiver.

"Executive Two here, over."

A moment of stunned silence, then: "Who am I speaking with?"

"Who do you think? May Fields." Maybe if I act annoyed they'll leave us alone.

"Oh. Everything alright up there, Miss Fields?"

"Yeah, why, you don't think a woman can fly a chopper?"

"No, no, sir—ma'am—it's just that we saw the explosion during your speech, and then you were missing. . . ."

"I took off down a stairwell and evacuated. Would you prefer I waited around for another bomb to go off?"

"No, ma'am, of course not. But you didn't log your flight. I need to know your current destination."

I hesitate for an instant, then say, "My apartment. I'm going to take the rest of the day off, if that's okay with you. I'm not exactly used to being blown up, and I frankly don't feel like I'd be very productive today. If anyone needs me, tell them to use my IC. Bye."

"Miss Fields," the man interrupts before I can shut off the radio. "It's just . . . is there anyone with you?"

"No," I say quickly. "Why would there be?" I glance at Clair to gauge her reaction to my lie, but she continues to stare out the windshield, pale and lost in thought.

There's a silence on the other end of the radio, then a shuffling, and a new voice greets me: "Miss Fields, this is Blackwell. We got reports you were being kidnapped at gunpoint."

Of course, the squad has cameras on the rooftop. I'm such a moron. Clair looks over at me, her eyes wide.

"Well, you were misinformed," I say. "Anything else?"

"Yes," he says slowly. "If you're going back to your place, why do our satellites have you heading in the opposite direction?"

I open my mouth a little, but nothing comes out. My mind's a blank. Surely there should be some easy answer, some logical, simple lie, but at this moment I'm completely bereft of thought.

"Fields?" Blackwell says.

Clair reaches over and snaps the radio switch to "off."

"You just got me killed," she says.

"I'm trying to help you!"

"Well, you're doing one hell of a job of it."

I grit my teeth. "You kidnapped me at gunpoint, and I'm still trying to save your life! What more do you want from me?"

She ignores me, turning back to the window, leaving me seething in frustration. I'm not supposed to be helping her. I'm *supposed* to get her killed! She's an anarchist or something, a traitor to the Company, an unprofitable and probably a heathen. She has a gun pointed at me, for God's sake! Why should I help her? But I am. And she has the nerve to complain about it.

We roar on through the flawless blue sky. Sirens bellow up from the street below, a dissonant soundtrack to our doomed escape.

"So where am I taking you?" I ask.

She shakes her head. "I'm thinking about it. They'll be tracking us with their satellites. Even if we go out of the hub and land in the forests, by the time we touch down they'll have us surrounded. As long as the sats can see us from above, we have no chance."

"Maybe we should land here, take off on foot," I suggest, peering out at the street below.

"Same problem. The squad trucks will run us down." There's an ominous undercurrent in her tone. Judging from her demeanor, the situation is hopeless.

"So what do we do?"

"I have to get a hold of Ethan," she says.

"Who's Ethan?"

She doesn't answer.

I weave us around another tall building. In a few minutes we'll be at the edge of the hub. Already, the glass-tower temples of commerce are becoming scarce, replaced by the sea of whitewashed square structures, N-Corp housing for the low-credit-level workers. Shortly, we'll pass over the countless factories of the industrial arc, then the miles upon miles of horribly polluted forests and grasslands, abandoned fields, and rotting old houses beyond.

Almost all agriculture is now done by our divisions outside America Division for efficiency reasons. The land here is too poisoned to support crops anyway.

"We don't want to get too far outside the hub city," Clair says. "Then they can just shoot us down and nobody will even know."

"They couldn't do that," I say. "It would be on the news. Besides, my father is the CEO of N-Corp. He'd be furious."

"Yeah, Blackie?" she says sardonically. "What makes you think he'd ever find out?"

Now we're reaching the industrial arc. We pass through a column of white steam rising from a power plant. The bright afternoon sun is eclipsed by it, and it feels like we've passed into a new world, a barren place peopled by ghosts where all life is choked away by cement and steel.

The sirens have passed out of earshot now, but they can't be far behind. I know that Clair is right about the satellites—they don't blink, they don't sleep, and there's no shadow in which to hide from them. I think back to the many episodes of *N-Squads LIVE* I've watched on the imager. It's a great program—the second most highly rated show behind Jimmy Shaw's—and I've seen it a million times. Each *N-Squads LIVE* episode plays out the same way: somebody breaches the Company's HR policy and then tries to escape. Many of the criminals have ingenious hiding places, fast cars, or clever disguises. Still, every show ends the same way: the squads close in like a pack of wolves surrounding their prey, and the fugitive is caught. He's dragged, usually bloody, into the back of a big, shiny black squad truck. Blaring music from the truck's stereo and raucous laughter of the squadmen form his eulogy as the truck doors slam behind him, and the criminal, the unprofitable, is gone.

Sunday Hangings is the show that tells us where they go after that. It plays on the second Sunday of every month and is the third highest-rated show in the N-Corp lineup, with top ratings in the fifteen to twenty-two age group. Normally watching these shows makes me feel good—especially *N-Squads LIVE*. It's exhilarating, with lots of action and lots of drama, and the good guys always win. It reminds me that the world is in order, the Company is in control, and I'm safe. There is no denying the moral of *N-Squads LIVE*: nobody gets away from the squads. But as illogical as it is, the thought of Clair being the one surrounded and dragged away by those laughing squadmen remakes this entertainment masterpiece into a work of horror.

I look over at her. Her face is downturned; she holds the gun in her lap delicately now, seeming to mourn over it as if it were a dead bird. Her eyes are closed in thought—or in prayer.

What's really going on here? I ask myself. *Is she kidnapping me, or am I helping her escape? And if Blackwell finds out I helped her, what's going to happen to me?*

Before I can come up with an answer, the chopper shudders. I glance down at the fuel gauge and my heart sinks: almost empty. There used to be a refueling crew on duty twenty-four hours a day, but last time I talked to my dad, I vaguely remember him mentioning cutbacks in the Headquarters aviation department. He was proud of himself for squeezing an extra half a million dollars of profit out of the operating budget—now, his cut is about to kill me. I curse at myself for not checking the fuel level before we took off—but it's too late now.

"What's going on?" Clair asks.

"We're out of fuel."

Clair doesn't even react. She just stares out the windshield, already resigned to her fate.

"Don't worry, we're going to be fine," I lie. Actually, we're probably going to crash and die, which is why my heart is fluttering faster that a hummingbird's wings.

I'm looking out the side window, desperately scanning the gray concrete landscape for a place to set down, when the chopper shudders again. Great rolling clouds, some gray, some black, some white, rise from factory smokestacks on all sides of us. Directly below are several rows of N-Corp housing units—these only a few stories high. To the right I see a red flash, and then it comes: the sound of sirens. I bank left.

"This is it," says Clair, despondent. "I failed."

The chopper shudders again as I bank. The fuel is very low, dangerously low.

"I have an idea," I say.

Ahead, a pale silver line, etched in the face of the gray concrete landscape, cuts toward the waning, smog-enfeebled sun.

"Look," gasps Clair. She points, and my eyes follow her finger to my left, back toward the city. Five black dots grow larger before my eyes. Squad choppers.

"What do we do?" she says—to herself, not to me.

"You're going to pray," I say, clenching my teeth as I fight to hold the chopper level.

"What are you going to do?" she asks.

"I'm either going to save us or kill us," I say, gripping the chopper's controls tighter. "Now seriously, start praying"

Ahead: the river.

A drop of sweat rolling down my brow; the scream and shutter of the chopper; Clair next to me, talking to God or her gun or herself; the black steel birds no doubt filled with leering squadmen growing larger and closer: all these things shred my concentration, unravel my nerve. Still, I bring us lower, throttle up our speed. The chopper's shaking worse now. The whirring blades above seem almost to groan as they slice through the air. The engine's howl is pinched and broken with coughs.

I press the button labeled "auto."

The river shimmers below, seeming to hold the only shards of light left in this desolate place.

I rise from my seat and almost pitch back into the rear cargo area, but manage to maintain my footing. I grasp the door handle. Turning back, I find Clair's questioning eyes on me.

"Jump when I jump," I scream over the dying engine.

She looks at me, shocked. "Are you kidding?"

"We're over water. The satellites will lose us when we jump, and the choppers will see this thing crash and think we're dead."

"If we jump we *will* be dead."

"Maybe not."

She blinks at me, still cradling her gun like a dead parakeet.

"We gotta go now," I yell. "If the squads are close enough to see us when we jump, they'll just pick us out of the water. They have to think we went down with the chopper."

"Why are you helping me?" she asks suddenly.

Maybe it's because I believed her when she said she had nothing to do with the bombing. Maybe it's because she's pretty. Maybe it was just an excuse to get out of the office for the day. I don't know what to say, so I ignore the question.

"Just jump, there's no time!" I shout, glancing out the window. The squad choppers are close. Any closer and they'll see us fall. Wind from the open door tugs at my ponytail, stirs wisps of loose hair to lash against my face, but I can still manage to see the river below, entombed in its cement-walled channel. Ahead, perhaps five hundred yards, it changes course. This is our only chance to jump. If we time it late, we'll wind up a couple of red punctuation marks on the pavement of the far bank.

The rush of wind is cold, biting, exhilarating. We pass through a plume of smoke, in it the scent of life and death, creation and destruction. I look back at Clair. She's half risen, but still grasps her seatback with graceful, desperately clinging hands.

"One," I say.

"You're crazy," she says, standing.

"Two."

"No wonder Ethan wanted to recruit you!"

Both our hands are on the door handle now. Our eyes lock. Her smile reflects mine.

Together, we say: "Three!"

And we throw ourselves into the wind.

"Hush, little baby, don't say a word."

Late at night, after her parents and sister have gone to bed, before my father comes and picks me up, Kali sings me lullabies: *Your Kali's gonna buy you a mocking bird . . . "*

I lie on the couch, my head laid in her lap, as she runs her fingers through my hair. I run my fingers up her leg.

"And if that mocking bird don't sing . . . "

It never fails; when she does this, tears always come to my eyes. No matter how I fight it, thoughts I never normally allow to surface crowd into my head: like, where is my mother now? Heaven? Hell? Nowhere? How could she die and leave me alone?

I sigh. The imager chatters away quietly, trying to sell us things. With one arm around her waist, I cling to Kali, already understanding instinctively—despite my youth—how fragile this moment is, how fleeting this perfection.

The smell of tuna casserole still lingers in Kali's family's cramped apartment, but if I turn my head, I can smell the skin of her smooth tanned legs instead. It's the smell of summer sun and chlorine, sweet lotion, and above all *her*, the essence of her, the essence of love and want and being fifteen.

"Kali's gonna buy you a diamond ring" she sings. *"And if that diamond ring don't shine . . . "*

There's a sound in the hall and Kali sits bolt upright, shoving my head off her lap. She edges to the other side of the couch, away from me, and looks over her shoulder at the door. A toilet flushes, a door shuts. Just one of her parents taking a pee.

"Why'd you push me?" I ask, outraged. When you're fifteen, everything stings.

"I'm sorry," she whispers, still looking over her shoulder. "I just don't want my dad to catch us. I don't think he could take it. I'm really worried about him right now."

She looks down at her lap, finished with the conversation, but I press on.

"Why?"

She sighs, hesitating. "There's something going on at his work, I think. He's been acting really weird. I'm afraid of what he would do if he found out about us."

"So you're ashamed of me?"

My arms are crossed. I look at my bare feet, propped on her parents' coffee table.

"No!" Kali says. "I mean . . . I'm sorry, May. Okay?"

I refuse to look at her.

"If that diamond ring don't shine," she sings into my ear softly, *"Kali's gonna kiss you a million times,"* and she presses her lips to mine. The smell of her, the taste of her is so delicious that my anger instantly melts and I pull her toward me. This is love, real love; nothing in the universe is more real. I defy anyone to tell me otherwise.

That song . . . Even now, her voice still rings in my ears.

The sound will stay with me, like a thorn in my heart, forever.

❖   ❖   ❖

In a smog-induced twilight filled with shifting smoke and scream-ing engines, I tumble through the wind. There, a glimpse—of a bil-lowing white cloud, of the river as it springs to meet me, of one tiny blink of sunlight on the water's darkened face—and now I'm skipping like a stone.

Slapping, my limbs glance off the river's surface over and over. I shut my eyes tight. Panic. I feel the crushing power of God all around me. And I will die. And this is the end.

My knee hits me in the face. My arms feel torn from my body.

The world is a blender set on puree.

Floating, now, all I taste is the blood on my teeth. All I hear is the liquid murmur, that amplified silence, laced with the distant lament of a whale or sonar or my own submerged screams.

Outer space, that's where I am.

Any minute now, God will whisper four small words and create the All, but for now there's only me, drifting here, bodiless.

This is better than life, somehow. Being without a body is good, carefree. I never liked life much, anyway. Too much buying hairstyling products and sitting in quiet, white-lit offices. Not enough . . . every-thing else.

Somehow, instead of whispering for the unveiling of light, God belches a raucous yell.

One eye opens. There's that same cloud I saw on the way down—saw it between my own wildly flailing legs, I think. There's a tattered-looking seagull, wings spread wide, relaxing against the sky. I wonder how he can live in this soiled, ruined place. He calls out, sounding the same as God did a minute before, but if there are any other birds around to hear him, I don't see them. This guy might be the very last.

Who would have even thought a wild animal could survive in the industrial arc, anyway?

You're drowning, my brain tells me casually, like it's an offhand comment, and I realize I haven't breathed in a long time. Most of my face is still submerged, and when I open my mouth to take a breath, I get a throat full of what tastes like fish-flavored bathwater tainted with bitter, burning chemicals. Drowning. I try to flutter my feet, to paddle with my arms, but I can't feel my limbs at all.

I finally get my head above water and take a breath. Instantly, sharp pain gouges my lungs. Every time I breathe too deeply, the agony almost causes me to black out.

I am broken.

There's no way I can swim.

Suddenly, the sound of a terrible concussion rends the world. I try to turn myself around to look, to see the source of the blast, but I can't—it's too difficult. All I can guess is that the chopper crashed. I crane my neck around, until in the distance I can see a column of black smoke solemnly ascending, mingling with the smoke of the factories then blending away.

Now I'm sinking again. I've still only managed to open one eye. Sinking. All I see is green water. Even my shallow breaths are stolen from me. I descend, and all gets darker, colder.

I'm sinking to hell, and it's actually a relief. The suspense is finally over.

—CHAPTER 0Ø5—

Dad looks down at me from the deck of his sailboat, *Green Back*, and puffs a cigar, leaning lazily against a lanyard. He might be looking down at a floating jellyfish or a lost fishing lure instead of at his daughter, drowning.

Me, I'm thrashing around, my scrawny arms beating ineffectually against the water, my little seven-year-old feet churning wildly, uselessly. I sputter, cough, weep.

"You can swim," my dad tells me matter-of-factly through cigar-clenching teeth. "All mammals are evolved from sea creatures, for God's sake."

Somehow, this doesn't comfort me. "I can't—I can't swim! Dad!"

I had more to say than that, but a swell surges over my mouth, muting me, before receding and leaving me choking, coughing, terrified.

"You can swim," my dad assures me. "You're a Fields, you can do anything."

He sips his brandy.

"Help!" I scream. "I can't—" Another swell slaps me in the mouth, choking me.

"May," he says, and looks down at me with a slow, warm smile. "You can."

Something in his tone, his face, his demeanor, relaxes me and suddenly, as if purely by will—not mine, his—I'm actually doing it. I'm treading water. I'm swimming!

For a second, I smile in spite of myself.

"See," Dad says. He smiles and ashes his cigar. That's when I get angry.

"I almost drowned! Are you happy?" I shout.

"Yes," he says. "I am."

Just then, his cell phone rings. He answers it.

"This is Fields. . . . Dammit, I'm trying to teach May how to swim here! . . . How should I know what the stock price is, I'm on a god-damned sailboat!"

"Dad!" I call. "Dad!"

He glances down at me, then back out to sea as he listens to his caller.

"Pull me up!" I yell. Even in the cold water, I can feel my face going red and hot with rage. I paddle to the edge of the boat, reach up my hands. But instead of reaching down for me, he turns away for a second.

I hear him say, "Pushed her in. She's gotta learn sometime, right? . . . Well what the hell do you know about parenting? You can't even handle a tiny goddamned acquisition without me there to hold your hand."

"DAD!" I scream.

"I'll call you back in ten," he says, and I hear the slap of his boat shoes as he crosses the deck and comes back toward me. I reach up again, groping for rescue. But instead of my father's hands reaching down for me, a rope ladder slaps down the side of the hull.

Now I'm trembling with anger, with emotion, with the remnants of terror. I grab the ladder and start pulling myself up, rung by rung.

Dad smiles at me as my head rises over the deck. He puffs on his cigar. "You want to get to the top," he tells me with a wink, "you gotta learn to climb."

❖   ❖   ❖

"You're going to be okay. We're gonna take care of you. Everything's going to be fine."

In all my life, I never believed words like those when I heard them used. Now, here, baptized in this polluted, desecrated tributary with my body broken and my mind scrambled, somehow Clair's promise inspires faith.

Above, five black helicopters bellow past. In the streets and in my heart, sirens scream, and I already know nothing will ever be the same again.

"Stay with me. Stay awake." Clair's words are furtive, desperate whispers, barely audible over the splash of the poisoned water and the howl of the sirens, hardly registering in the drift and spin of my mind.

As my head lolls back I see the bleak, gray concrete wall, cracked and sheer. A rusted metal ladder affixed to it leads up to a lip over which the pallid sun peers down at us. The corroding iron rungs paint two streaks the color of dried blood all the way down to the black, lapping waterline.

Clair still has one arm wrapped firmly around my chest. With the other hand, she tries to grip the ladder and pull us both up out of the river, but it's impossible.

"I can do it myself," I mumble.

"You sure?"

I'm not sure, but I pull away from her anyway.

"You go up first," she says. "If you start to fall, I can catch you."

The controls of my body are foreign to me; I feel like a marionette with tangled strings. Gripping one slippery rung and finding another one with my foot, I pull myself slowly, tremblingly upward. My head throbs. I can't feel my feet, and my hands are shaking. I look down at myself as I climb. My shirt is dyed with what can only be my own blood, but on this subject my brain can form no opinion—this is all too unreal, too much like a video game or a movie, too unlike my life. So I disbelieve it, and I climb on.

From below, Clair whispers, "Hurry. They're close."

And indeed, I realize, the sirens are screeching at us now from both sides of this sad river, their volume increasing as more and more electronic screams add to the chorus.

Each handhold is slick, smeared with algae and oil—or something worse—and twice I almost fall, but somehow I make it to the top and pull myself over the lip. I take a few shaky steps forward and lean against a rusted chain-link fence.

The world is spinning. I puke on a dandelion growing through a crack in the pavement.

Now Clair's face is here, her big, beautiful eyes appearing over the edge of the man-made riverbank, the lipstick smeared from her sensuous lips, her face fraught with sympathy, terror, and bewilderment, all lacquered beneath a veneer of resolve.

In an instant she's with me, my arm over her shoulder as she leads me through a break in the fence, across a deserted street, through an empty courtyard full of cracked pavement and lonely weeds, and down a series of empty, debris-strewn alleyways. All the while, she whispers to me in this eerie, singsong, almost motherly, lullaby way, her voice underscored now and then with the blood-curdling warble of sirens or the percussive chuckle of a gunship helicopter.

"We have people here. It'll be okay. We have friends waiting, in one of the empty factories. If nobody saw us jump, they'll think we were in the chopper. They'll think we're dead."

In my delirium, that prospect seems wonderful. "I wish I were dead," I mumble.

She doesn't understand what I'm getting at. "I know you might be in a lot of pain," she says, "but you'll be fine. We have people who can help. They aren't doctors, but they know medicine."

"No," I say. "I wish I were dead because—because I hate the world."

She snorts derisively. "Why would you hate the world, Blackie?"

"If you want to get to the top . . ." I begin, but nausea overtakes me and the rest of my words get lost.

I should be resisting, I remind myself. I should be fighting my kidnapper, not helping her. But I don't. I'm in no condition to fight, even if I wanted to.

Clair doesn't stop. A siren comes our way and she looks over her shoulder and drags me along faster. Toward what, I have no idea.

Starving.

The blood on my head has curdled to a dark, sharp crust, and the whole world throbs every time I move my neck.

Lying prone, staring up at layer after layer of rusted catwalks and dust-laden piping, I watch the lamplight make the shadows dance.

I must have passed out, because I don't know where Clair found the lamp.

I don't know how long she's been gone or where she went. It feels like I've been lying here forever, falling in and out of time.

When the man's voice comes, it seems to drift from among the catwalks, resonating through the hollow hearts of the pipes, echoing off some unseen ceiling with cathedral-like acoustical clarity. I try to move my head and look for whoever is talking, but the effort is too much.

The unseen speaker says: "The Company, before they were even called N-Corp, bought out hundreds of other companies. *Acquired* them. Mergers, they were called. Stop me if you know this. The Company started out, decades ago, dominating the food industry, then appliances, then restaurants. They were purchased, next, by one of the largest media conglomerates—even at that time, there were only a few companies controlling nearly all of the media. For years, each new acquisition kept its former name, so that few people realized that the same corporation that made their car and financed their house also sold them most of the food they ate. Later, they decided to put all the combined companies under one brand. They chose the name of the division with the most positive brand association, according to their marketing surveys."

"Nabisco," I murmur. "N-Corp." I strain to see the speaker, but he must be behind me.

He continues, his cadence hypnotic: "What about the government, you might ask? What about antitrust laws, if you've even heard of such things? I'll bet you never even learned about monopolies or antitrust laws in school, did you?"

I try to shake my head, but it hurts too much.

"N-Corp runs the schools, that's why. I'll tell you what happened to the government. For decades, N-Corp and other corporations had used their money and influence to buy political power. Company candidates, applauded by the Company-owned media, won almost every election. That's when there was actually a choice. More often, the electorate was given only two options when they went to the polls—both candidates controlled by the Company. Company lobbyists wrote the laws. Company consultants set the government agenda. N-Corp made billions in subsidies and interest-free loans, handed out by the government they controlled, based on laws their lobbyists had written. Of course, tax rates for corporations and the wealthy plummeted. As a result, government income dropped and government debt soared. Nations around the world teetered on the verge of bankruptcy. Media stoked fears of an impending financial disaster. Markets tumbled, and N-Corp bought up thousands of weaker corporations at pennies on the dollar."

A shadow moves against the far wall as the speaker draws near to me.

"Are you paying attention, May? Because you're going to be tested on this material, and the test is going to be a matter of life and death."

I can't tell if the man speaking is joking with me or threatening me. And before I can glimpse his face, he paces away again, his shadow receding down the length of the wall as he continues: "The American populace, many of them already unemployed because of the Company's constant job-cutting, outsourcing, efficiency-boosting measures, panicked. Drastic steps had to be taken. You know how they solved the problem of government debt?"

The sound of gunfire in the distance, coming closer. . . .

"Privatization. You know who was there to step in, the shining savior? N-Corp. They got contracts to run the schools, the universities, firefighting, and police services. Even the military. Soon, four out of every five federal dollars went straight into N-Corp coffers. Washington had become a mechanism for taking money from the people and giving it to the Company. But it was too late to turn back.

"Now that the government was too weak to enforce what few regulations remained, the company was free to pursue their agenda more aggressively. They raised prices, cut wages. Now, to afford food, appliances, transportation, housing, people had no choice but to turn to credit. Conveniently enough, N-Corp controlled the largest bank in the world. It was happy to lend hungry citizens money to buy the food and clothing they needed—at usurious rates, of course."

Shouts and sounds of battle are alarmingly close now. Panicked, I try to sit up, but a wave of dizziness sends me back down again.

My unseen lecturer presses on.

"Meanwhile, angered by the last gasps of dissent in the government, N-Corp execs began pushing Christianity, hard. By weaving some mention of Christ and the Bible into every television show and movie, and making *The Jimmy Shaw Hour in Christ* the top-rated show in prime time, they captured the moral high ground. They became the defenders of virtue, proponents of the family. They wielded the weapon of religion. If God was on their side, those who opposed them had to be evil. Anyone anti-Company was branded immoral, wicked, scheming. Unprofitable. A witch hunt started. Dissidents, labor-union leaders and intellectuals were blacklisted, smeared, demonized, and driven into obscurity. Non-Christians either converted, learned to keep quiet, or disappeared. All opposition ceased."

I've heard most of this before, in N-Academy high school—and from my father. It is the story of his triumphant ascension. But from the tone this speaker is using, it sounds more like the tale of Judas betraying Christ. I'm about to curse at whoever it is, to defend my father. But when the silhouetted figure paces between me and the lamplight, I see a wicked-looking knife in his hand.

"Now, there was no telling where the government stopped and the Company began," he continues. "There was no telling where the Church stopped and the Company began. The Church they kept, since it served their purposes, but the government they simply phased out. And the people were glad to see it go. Think of all the evil things governments did: make wars, imprison people, lie to the populace. Certainly, a publicly owned Company would never do any of those things to its own employees! With the government gone, there was nobody to oppose the will of the Company, because the people were all employees, the employees were all stockholders, and the stockholders were all going deeper and deeper into debt thanks to the generous and unprecedented credit opportunities offered by the Company. Nobody could quit—they were Company property, through and through. There was nobody to complain to. No escape. The entanglement was complete. The ensnarement was total."

Somewhere, the sound of sirens. More gunshots.

My thoughts spin around me, a vortex of confusion. I've heard this story before, but it always sounded so different. After the great economic collapse, the Company rescued the world from a corrupt and inefficient government system; that's what really happened. The way this speaker is telling it, the Company was the problem all along. And he acts like people don't have any choice but to work for the Company! The more I think about it, the angrier I get.

"If somebody doesn't like N-Corp, they can quit and go to B&S," I say.

"That's right," the voice says. "B&S was the only other company to realize the genius of the N-Corp strategy and emulate it. They were a Chinese-based electronics manufacturer, but they quickly acquired huge holdings all over the world. They took up the name of a small American engine company, Briggs & Stratton—later shortened to B&S—for its positive brand association, just as N-Corp chose to use Nabisco. They followed N-Corp's business model precisely, all the while protecting themselves fiercely against any N-Corp takeover attempt. Then, before the world governments were completely subjugated, they put into place territorial divisions to separate the last two companies, so that the giants would not become one. N-Corp was given one half of the world market, B&S the other. But the truth is, there is no difference between them. In their greed, in their ruthlessness, in their disregard for human dignity, they are one."

"No . . ." I begin to contradict him, but I'm interrupted by the sound of an explosion, then footfalls clattering down a staircase. "Ethan! They're coming." This new voice is foreign, low and commanding, lilting, dangerous.

"Thank you, McCann. We're almost ready," says the first voice, and just then the voice's owner—Ethan, it would seem—steps forward into the light. He's younger than I expected. Thirty years old, maybe, with fine features and a trim, compact body. He'd be downright handsome, except that the shapeless brownish hair that falls into his almost indolent blue eyes gives him a look of being somehow unfinished.

The other man, McCann, comes to Ethan's side. The quivering lamplight etches the fine lines of his dark-skinned, muscular arms and his square jaw. Through the shadows, his fierce brown eyes shine.

"Ethan, we can't hold them off much longer," he whispers.

Ethan turns back to me just as gunshots resume above us.

"Time is up," Ethan says, leaning close to my face, his ice-blue eyes almost sharp enough to cut me. "You have to choose."

"Choose what?" I say.

He holds up the knife.

"You helped Clair and you could be very useful to our cause."

My head is spinning. I might or might not puke.

"Ethan . . ." says McCann.

"May, the people of America, the people of the world, need you."

"I don't understand. Who are you?" I ask.

"We are not the Godless anarchists the Company would have you believe. We are a secret order, a fourth branch of the United States government, started by the founding fathers of this country."

"Fourth branch of government?" I say. Bewildered, dizzy, terrified, I can hardly remember the first three. That stuff is ancient history.

"Ethan," says McCann, blinking at the crackle of distant gunfire and brandishing a huge white machine gun I somehow never noticed before.

"Our order was started for one purpose and one purpose alone, May. In the event that the people of America should lose their democracy at the hands of a tyrant—"

"Let's go . . ." Clair says, appearing from a shadow-strewn corner.

"If the army, the CIA, the militias should all fail—"

"Ethan . . ."

"—we are charged with leading the revolution."

"They're here!" McCann shouts.

There's a flat *crack* and a puff of dust from the stairwell. McCann, Clair, and two other men I hadn't noticed before, all wielding huge white guns, take aim at the open doorway.

"I'm taking her!" Ethan shouts. "Cover the rear!"

He pulls me to my feet, holding me up, and we flee.

Though I will later learn I have a concussion and three broken ribs, though it feels like every joint in my body is sprained, somehow I run.

Through a long, long tunnel with white-tiled walls, Ethan leads me by the arm. A timid flashlight beam blazes our trail, augmented after a moment by the flash of gunfire from behind us. I wince, slow, look back, but Ethan drags me on.

As we pass a cross tunnel, I fall. Pain shoots through me. Sprawled on the ground, I look to my left. Three squadmen, all in black, are coming toward us. They train their guns on me.

My eyes squeeze shut.

Then the reports, the million echoes of gunshots, deafening, terrifying. They must've gotten me. I must be dead. They were too close to miss.

When my eyes open, Ethan is standing in front of me, the barrel of his gun smoking. Looking down the tunnel between his widely set legs, I can see the bodies of three squadmen sprawled on the concrete floor.

And I'm alive.

Ethan pulls me to my feet.

"Come on," he says.

"You—you just saved my life!" I stammer, stating the obvious.

"Don't fall again," he replies.

As we run, he pulls the knife from his belt.

"Choose."

"Choose what?" I wheeze.

"Who are you going to give your allegiance to? The Company—or the ones who will destroy it?"

I almost laugh. "Destroy the Companies? Why? They give people everything they have."

"They give people what they want them to have, and in exchange, they ask for everything."

Still running, our path is riddled with sundry debris: a bundle of clothing, an old beer bottle, a basket of some kind, a discarded doll. My head is pounding. My ribs feel like there's a red-hot poker jabbing them with each step.

"Nobody's forced to work for N-Corp," I say. "They don't like the Company, they can leave."

"There's a lot you don't know, May," he says. "Take the knife."

I take it. He grabs my arm, pulls me to a halt. We both crouch on our haunches, our backs against opposite walls, eyes locked, breathing hard in ragged unison.

A moment passes.

Gunshots, which we both ignore.

Looking at the knife in my hand, I say, "I could kill you now."

He smiles, "No you couldn't."

"Why do you trust me?"

"I don't. I don't trust anyone. But you could help us."

"Why would I?"

His eyes smile at me through the half-light. "Because I've seen you in the shopping plaza, May. You're different."

I don't have to ask; I know what he means. The pants.

"You really think you have a future at the Company, May? Your father won't be around forever."

So he doesn't think I could make it without my daddy's help? I look at the knife clenched in my fist and think of stabbing him after all. Except deep down, I know he's right. Take my dad away, and I'm one bad ad campaign away from being an unprofitable, just like everyone else.

From down the corridor come the sounds of more gunshots and yelling. Ethan allows himself one glance back, but it's enough for me to see he's worried, and not just for us.

"What do you want me to do?" I ask.

He looks back at me. There's an urgency in his voice that wasn't there before. "Cut the cross out of your face."

I don't answer. I don't know what to say. It's my life he's asking. He's asking me to take my own life. My name, my credit, my credentials, my accomplishments, all recorded in the cross, all will be wiped away.

"That's impossible."

"We've all done it," he says. He points to his cheek and tilts it toward the light. Instead of the cross, there's just a ragged scar.

"I'd be giving up everything I have to destroy everything my father helped build," I say.

"Not destroy," he says. "Commerce will still thrive. All the wealth the Company controls will still exist—many companies will remain, but we must divide and disarm the *two* Companies. We aren't anarchists, May. We don't want to destroy society. We want to reinstate the rightful, democratic government of the United States and return sovereignty to the people."

In other words, they want to bring back the same corrupt, inefficient government the Company managed to replace.

But what if he's right? What if it was because of the Company—and the people behind it—that the government became corrupt in the first place? I shake my head to clear the confusion. Even if I weren't suffering from a concussion, the whole thing would still be too difficult to process.

I look at the knife. Scintillations of distant gunshots play across its deadly sharp blade.

From somewhere behind comes the sound of a muffled explosion.

"No time, May," Ethan says again. "Choose."

Yes, choose. Cut the cross out, or stab Ethan and run. Either way, I have a feeling my life will never be the same.

Suddenly Ethan's head snaps to the right, toward the direction from which we came. Footfalls.

"It's us," yells a woman. I think the voice must be Clair's, but it sounds more resonant, more powerful now.

McCann is with her, and one of the other men. The fourth man does not appear.

"The stairway's collapsed, but they'll get through the debris soon," says McCann, as he runs past us.

And now we're all running, single file, McCann then Clair then me then Ethan.

"Did she cut it out?" yells McCann.

"She was about to," says Ethan.

"They'll just track her right to us with that bloody cross in her face," Clair shouts. "Let's leave her."

"They can't track the cross underground," says Ethan. "The satellites aren't that powerful yet."

"There are no tracking devices in adults' crosses," I wheeze. "They only put tracking devices in kids' crosses, in case they're abducted."

"They put them in everyone's," says Ethan.

"That's not true," I huff. "I'd have heard about it."

"Blackie," Clair says, "what you don't know could fill a warehouse."

Shadows jump and squirm against two blinks of light as, behind me, Ethan squeezes two shots off over his shoulder.

And we run on through the dark, through the earth, and my mind reels as I wonder where the tunnel will come out and who I'll be on the other side.

—CHAPTER Ø0̷6—

This is the Fourth of July. Company Day.

I know it by the smell of grilling in the air: barbeque sauce, grease, and delicious-smelling smoke. Somewhere, a marching band plays.

This must be a long time ago, because I still believe my father's promises. He says he will meet me in the park and we'll eat ice-cream sundaes together, just like old times. The fact is, we have never met in the park and eaten ice-cream sundaes. Those "old times" are completely fictional, existing only in the deluded depths of his mind where he's the greatest father in the world.

Today, I walk at the bottom of a canyon of skyscrapers. Distant fireworks crackle, but nobody in sight is celebrating. A tangle of faceless people hustles past me, their eyes downcast. Above, on a balcony, a woman is grilling, flipping a piece of chicken with metal tongs. She blinks the smoke from her eyes. She frowns. She doesn't see me. Nobody sees me. A child somewhere laughs. Ahead, on the next block, the green expanse of the park beckons, but an endless blur of passing cars separates me from this oasis. There is no crosswalk; instead, there is a set of concrete stairs leading down to a tunnel that comes out on the other side of the street.

I descend.

Smells of puke down here, but I don't notice it much. I'm wracking my brain. By Friday, I have to figure out how to make twenty million people think they need a tiny, dancing robot. An assignment for my marketing class. Even now, at only fifteen years old, marketing is my life.

I walk along, lost so deep in thought I don't see what's waiting for me until I'm upon it.

My gaze snaps up from the concrete at my feet and I find three sets of ferret eyes blinking at me. It's three squadmen, hats cocked, legs set wide in various stances of macho aggression.

"Hey D. D! We got an even younger one."

Then I see the fourth one, further away in the shadows. A woman is pressed up against the wall in front of him. Greasy hair falls across her face.

The man holding her there—D, he must be—turns and looks at me. We make eye contact, and he smiles. He shoves the woman away, down the tunnel. She stumbles, adjusting her skirt, and I see the sheen of tears on her cheek.

"Get the hell out of here," D barks at her.

"You've been relieved of duty," one of the other guys shouts, and everyone cackles. Her footfalls echo back to me as she runs away down the tunnel, interspersed with the sound of her sobbing. I'm already backing up, but not fast enough.

Here they come. Their movements, their tense, over-energized gestures, their forced, nervous, almost demonic laughter, all fill me with increasing fear. The stairway I came down is perhaps ten yards behind me; I can't make it there before the nearest one catches me—all I'd succeed in doing by running is turning my back on my attackers. So I stand my ground, take a deep breath. One very young squad man with a serious face hangs back. Something—maybe the fact that I'm not running, maybe a twinge of conscience—clicks in his mind, and he slows, but the other three are already on me. The nearest one, the one they called D, reaches for me.

"Don't worry, baby," he says. "We won't hurt you much."

As his hand comes close, instinct kicks in and I snatch two of his fingers, one in each of my hands, and jerk them apart like a wishbone. The snapping sound echoes loudly in the underground, as does D's ensuing howl. He cradles his hand and stumbles back, falling against one concrete wall.

The next one is on me instantly. He grabs my arm in one hand and my hair in the other, picks me halfway up off the ground, then throws me backward. As I fall, I use the momentum he's given me and kick upward as hard as I can. My foot hits his crotch squarely, so hard it hurts my ankle. The squad member collapses, huffing and moaning, and I land hard on my back on the moist, dirty cement, scraping both my elbows and bruising my tailbone.

Two squadmen remain uninjured, the final attacker and serious boy, and both are now hanging back, unsure how to proceed. I scramble to my feet.

In my brain, a worried voice tells me I should run now, that the luck I've had so far was only luck, after all, and will run out fast. But it's too late; the attacker has decided not to let me go.

"We got a feisty one," he says, and lunges at me.

I slap him across the cheek, and he instantly retaliates, punching me squarely in the face. The blow is sudden and knocks me over against the wall. Stars sparkle across my vision. My eyes well up with moisture, and I feel my nose start to drip. I regain my composure just in time to see the other punch coming at me. I duck it, and his fist slams against the cement of the tunnel with bone-splintering force. He staggers backward, mouth open in silent agony. From the sound, he must've broken his hand.

As he falls to his knees in the throes of pain, I begin backpedaling as fast as I can away from him, until a single word interrupts my flight: "Stop."

I look to see the last squad member, the boy, the serious one. He stands a few paces away from me, looking very pale. In his hand, a gun. It's just me and him, our eyes locked.

"It's alright," I say soothingly. "I won't tell anyone. You won't get in trouble, okay? Just let me go."

I take a step to leave and he shouts again, "Stop! Lay down on the ground."

D scrambles to his feet now, snarling like a dog. The guy I kicked in the crotch is up too, and limping toward me.

"On the ground, now!" the kid says. The black pistol in his hand trembles. One twitch of his trigger finger and I'm dead. There's no other choice. I lie down.

It feels like a trap door has opened beneath me, and I'm falling. I don't know who the girl is who lies on the filthy concrete while D climbs on top of her, but I'm a thousand feet underground, falling away from her.

"My father's the CEO," I hear myself say with all the boldness I can muster.

"Sure," D chuckles. "So's mine"

The whole world is growing dim. My breath is chugging in and out of my lungs, faster and faster. This can't be happening to me. My dad is the CEO. I'm going to be a Blackie.

D glances to one of his comrades. "You get her legs."

I open my mouth to scream, but D clamps a hand over it. I thrash and fight with all my strength, but their hands, their bodies are too many. The last thing I remember is the grit and filth of the tunnel floor against the side of my face and D on top of me, his breath reeking.

"Who's the CEO now, sweetie? Huh? I am."

The rest, thank God, I black out.

Half an hour later, I stand between the band shell and the Ferris wheel in front of the ice-cream stand waiting for my father, my mascara streaked, skirt torn, knees trembling. No one looks at me or asks if

I'm okay—they just gave me a wide berth as they passed me by.

The clock in the tower strikes two o'clock. I stand there, unmoving as the tears dry on my cheeks. After what seems like only a few minutes, the clock strikes three.

My father never shows up.

The blindfold falls away from my eyes. For some reason, my first impulse is to look up.

Birds wheel above. I don't know the name of their species— sparrows, maybe—but I watch them turn as one, and I envy them. Their freedom. Their thoughtless unity. Beneath the wood-raftered ceiling of almost heaven-like girth, they turn and turn and flitter away.

Ethan stands watching me, his arms folded, an odd, wry grin playing across his lips. The blindfold still dangles from his hand. As soon as they were confident they'd lost the squadmen pursuing us, he and his rebels made me put it on.

"Don't want you giving us away, do we, Blackie?" Clair had whispered into my ear as she cinched the blindfold tight, a new harshness in her voice.

Now, as I blink and look around, letting my eyes adjust, Clair and McCann stand a few steps away, whispering to one another. Behind them, scattered across the cracked concrete floor of the old warehouse, crumpled shapes move ever so gently, breathing the deep breath of sleep. There must be hundreds of people here. Some are obscured beneath tents or hidden by makeshift lean-tos. Some figures are large, probably comprised of whole huddled families, and others are small, single, and fitfully roll and rustle beneath their blankets. A dozen glimmering campfires dot the expansive space, lending the room an air of warmth, casting the whole scene in a tremulous light that makes it all oddly beautiful.

"What is this place?" I ask.

"Our camp," Ethan says, "for tonight, anyway." He turns and, with a gesture, leads me onward, picking his way through the sleeping bodies. McCann and Clair follow.

As we walk, I stare down at the sleeping figures in utter confusion. Who are they?

A tattered, camouflaged blanket covers a bearded old man. His head rests on what looks like a backpack. Next to him in small, orderly stacks rest a deck of cards, a pack of chewing gum, a chrome butane lighter, and a white pistol.

That can't be right. I squint through the dark. Only squadmen are allowed to carry firearms. For anyone else, it's a breach of Company policy punishable by termination. But Clair had one, didn't she? All of them do.

Ethan notices me staring.

"Ceramics," he says, gesturing to his own gun. "Company metal detectors don't pick them up."

Beyond the old man, I see another sleeper. He or she rolls over and the sole of a boot pushes out from under the corner of the blanket. Next to the figure, within easy reach: a white rifle. "Who are these people?" I ask.

"The unemployed. Drifters, dreamers, scholars, misanthropes. Rebels." Ethan glances back at me, as if gauging my reaction. No doubt, even in this light he can see the color draining from my face.

"The Company would call them unprofitables," Clair says. She does not look at me.

"Unprofitables. . . ." I repeat, feeling suddenly dizzy and sick with fear.

Unprofitables are the people we are warned never to become. They lack the capacity to be productive. They lack respect for the good of the stockholders. They are filthy, worthless, useless, idiotic, insane, and criminal, leeches stuck to the underbelly of society, stealing its productivity, draining its resources, undermining its order. They are the cancer that refuses to be excised from our world. They are selfish sinners who lack the moral strength to do what the Company requires of them. If it weren't for the drain people like this put on the economy, the Company could be perhaps 15 percent more profitable, at least according to what I learned at N-Academy. I stand up straighter and walk faster. If I could, I would hold my breath to avoid breathing this air, polluted as it is with the breath of these slothful wretches.

Ethan glances back at me. Seeming to read my thoughts, he says, "Not everyone is meant to be a tie-man, May. Surely you've realized that by now."

Certainly not. There are also positions for receptionists, mechanics, construction workers, transportation experts. But there is no place in the world for an unprofitable. As Jimmy Shaw says, laziness is the father of all sins.

My mind races to figure how I can escape this den of unprofitable, anarchist murderers.

Clair picks up on my uneasiness. She gives me a sidelong glance and a bitter smile, then spits on her hand and swipes it across her face. Before my eyes, the cross on her cheek smudges and streaks. Shocked, I look down at a sleeping face, then another. Both have scars on their cheeks, and no crosses. My eyes snap back to Clair.

"How did you get into Headquarters?" I demand. "You have to have a cross to get in."

But she only rolls her eyes and walks on.

Suddenly, a shape emerges from the shadows and races up to us as quickly as a darting cat. "Da! You're safe!" A little boy no older than six sprints toward the one called McCann, leaps onto him, and clings to his neck. McCann laughs.

"Always. And you, were you a good boy while I was away?"

The boy suddenly turns sullen. "No," he says reluctantly. "I broke Ada's jar with the soccer ball." He winces after speaking, perhaps in anticipation of punishment, but McCann only laughs.

"Well then," he says, "I guess you'll have to find her a new one."

The boy seems hardly to hear his father's words; his attention has wandered to me. "Who's that?" he asks, pointing in my direction.

"I'm May."

"This is my son, Michel," McCann says, introducing the boy.

"She's a Blackie, Michel," Clair says, making no effort to disguise the disdain in her voice. "I bet you've never seen one of those before."

Michel squints at me and wrinkles his little nose.

"A Blackie?" he says. "But she's so . . . white!"

Ethan and McCann laugh loudly. Even Clair lets a smile slip.

"No, no," McCann corrects, still grinning. "It means she's her own person, not owned by the Company. It means she's not in the red. She has no debt."

"Well, I'm not quite a Blackie yet," I murmur. I don't tell them the rest, that I'm only about five years and a few million dollars away.

Little Michel still seems perplexed. "What's debt?" he asks.

"Don't worry," Clair says, giving me a pointed glare. "When we're finished, all the debts will be settled." Her eyes linger on me for a moment longer, then she turns and makes her way across the room through a maze of blanketed bodies.

"Don't mind her," McCann tells me. "She's an angry person. Sometimes I think after she's done fighting the Company, she's going to declare war on everyone else. Don't worry, she'll be back by the time dinner is served."

McCann laughs and Michel does, too, but Ethan just watches me.

From another direction, a kind-faced, middle-aged woman with large hips and squinty eyes approaches, wiping her hands on an apron. She smiles, but shakes her head with disapproval.

"You've been fighting again," she says.

"Yes, ma'am," Ethan says with a smile. "How are you, Ada?"

Ada shrugs the question away, as if it is of no importance. "Dinner's ready," she says. "You all must be starving."

In the middle of the massive warehouse, Clair, Ethan, McCann, Michel, and I all sit around the fire burning in the cut-off bottom of a steel drum. We eat sandwiches of wheat bread, dried beef, and mustard—silently.

Mostly I stare into the fire, but when I look up at the others, I sometimes catch them exchanging glances. The tension is almost palpable. Other times, they gaze at their sandwiches as a gypsy would at tea leaves. I wonder if it's my fate they're looking for, or their own. Sometimes, one of them pretends to look past me, but I know they're actually checking me out, sizing me up. Maybe they're just trying to discern the differences between themselves and me, the only Blackie-to-be they've probably ever seen.

My mind is a tangle of confused, fearful thoughts. It's good that they're feeding me. It might mean that they aren't planning to kill me right away. Unless, of course, this is to be my last meal. If it is, I'd have preferred Italian. . . . I should escape, but I have no idea where I am, and I'm surrounded by people with guns. If only I could contact someone. . . . I manage to glance at my IC, but it shows that there's no wireless here. Either we're out of satellite range, or they've blocked the signal somehow. I have no options. I'm powerless. All I can do is enjoy my sandwich, try to ignore my throbbing head, and hope that if they kill me, they'll do it quickly.

It's McCann who finally breaks the silence: "I like having the fire," he says, and the music of his African accent brings a smile to my face. "A man needs a fire."

"Yep," his son, Michel, agrees.

Clair snorts. "Enjoy it now. When the next-generation sats are up, they'll be able to detect the heat even inside the building. If we want a fire then, it'll have to be in the deep underground."

"N-Corp doesn't have any satellite programs like that in development," I say around the last bite of my sandwich. "I would know about it."

McCann trumpets a laugh. Clair looks at me dismissively, and then back at Ethan.

Just then, a broad-shouldered, ruddy-cheeked young man approaches. He stops at the edge of the firelight and gives Ethan a stiff salute.

Ethan returns the gesture. "Well?" he prompts.

"It's like we thought," the young man says breathlessly. "The Headquarters explosion targeted our people. The only operatives we have left on the inside are—"

Ethan gives the young man a look, and then tilts his head toward me. When he sees me, the young man instantly clams up.

"What did I tell you?" Clair says, shaking her head bitterly. "Three years they worked to stop the final consolidation, what did they get? Murdered, all of them. It can't be changed from the inside. I told you that."

"It seems you were right," Ethan says dryly.

"Wait," I say. "Are you saying that the Company was behind the explosion in the Headquarters building? That's insane."

Everyone ignores me.

"And now—the financial loss," Clair continues. "What are we going to do?"

Ethan stares into the fire.

"We can't let it happen, Ethan!" Clair shouts.

"Can't let *what* happen?" I ask.

Clair still turns on me with fire in her eyes, but McCann answers my question.

"The Company won't allow a financial loss to take place," he says patiently. "The entire world system is based on the Companies making a continuous profit. A loss hasn't happened in thirty years, and they won't let it happen now." He glances at Ethan, then back to me. "They have a plan in place to prevent it."

"They have a plan, alright," Clair snorts.

"What do you mean?" I ask. "What's the plan?"

"What do you care?" Clair growls. "It won't affect you. You'll go about your life, shopping, feasting, going on vacation, and you'll never even know it happened. None of you Blackies will." She shakes her head and chomps into her sandwich, like it's a small animal she's trying to decapitate with her teeth. "We've got bigger problems than her, Ethan," Clair continues after a moment, nodding toward me as she chews. "Someone outed our people. We've got a rat to kill."

"She's right," McCann agrees. "If there's a traitor, we have to find him."

"Or *her*," Clair amends.

"The lives of everyone in the Protectorate could depend on it," McCann finishes.

Ethan only nods.

From behind, I hear footsteps. Startled, I look over my shoulder. It's just a middle-aged man, no doubt picking his way through the camp toward the latrine. It's too late, though. Clair has already noticed my jumpiness.

"What's the matter?" she says with a cynical smile. "Too many uprofitables for you?"

"No . . . I just . . ." Not knowing quite what to say, I feel my voice die out. I look to Ethan to speak for me, but he doesn't. He just watches me with his blue cat's eyes. I feel almost dissected by the intensity of his gaze.

"We have to do something about her, Ethan," McCann says, nodding toward me. "The sats will pick up her cross soon, if they haven't already, and when they do they'll be on our doorstep."

Ethan nods pensively. "What do you say, Clair? What do you think of Miss Fields?" Ethan says, with a slightly amused expression on his face.

She shrugs. "I just used her to get out of the building. You're the one who wanted her."

Ethan stares at me for a long, silent moment, and I fight to hold his gaze. Finally, his hand goes to his belt and draws out the knife. He offers it to me again.

"Cut out the cross, May," he says gently. "Stay with us."

I look down at the knife. Strangely enough, part of me longs to take it. Despite my fear and distrust of the unprofitables surrounding me, I have to admit that I do feel strangely drawn to them. Even this tense camaraderie I've felt around the campfire is more genuine human interaction than I've had in months. I can almost imagine myself staying here, living happily among these outcasts. As bizarre as it is, sleeping in their dirty blankets with a white gun at my side and campfire at my feet seems far preferable to wandering my immaculate apartment alone for the rest of my life. Surely here they wouldn't care if I wore pants, or if I kissed a woman. Maybe Clair, even . . . if I could persuade her not to kill me first.

But of course, such thoughts are insanity. Sure, there is something that thrills me about these people, but what I don't understand is the nature of their cause. The Company is good! Credit limits go up every year, and the product lines just keep getting better. Every imaginable luxury is just a shopping trip away. Crime is dropping. Faith in God is through the roof. And anyone, if they just work hard enough, can be a Blackie one day! Why would somebody want to rebel against a world like the one we, the Company, have created? That's what I can't fathom.

No, the idea of living here is just another dream, another ridiculous, unrealistic utopian fantasy.

I am a Fields. I live in a penthouse. I will be a Blackie. When all these anarchists are wasting away in Company prisons, I will be tanning myself on a two-hundred-foot yacht off the coast of Fiji.

And the Company, it will be expanding still.

Ethan still watches me, and I can see disappointment on his face as he guesses my thoughts. Without a word, he slips the knife back into its sheath.

Clair stands, finally smiling. "What did you expect?" she says to Ethan. Then she stalks off into the shadows.

"You all seem really nice," I say quickly, apologetically, "but I can't understand—"

"We don't have time for you not to understand, May," Ethan stands, nodding to McCann, who rises, too. "Take her," he says.

Without warning, McCann grabs me from behind.

"No! Please! Listen! Let's talk! My father—we can negotiate! He'll pay you—please—" I shout, in a panic.

Ethan doesn't respond. He merely stands there in the firelight with his arms crossed, watching as McCann drags me away. I scream until I lose my voice, but McCann doesn't stop, doesn't answer. He moves with the inexorable gait of a robot, dragging me away, into the darkness.

—CHAPTER Ø∅7—

McCann leads me to a heavy, rusty-hinged steel door. When I open my mouth to speak, he jams a gun in my back, urging me through the doorway and into the darkness beyond. A set of metal stairs. We clang our way downward endlessly. The suspense is too much. I could puke at any second. The silence is killing me. I have to speak.

"What's going to happen to me?" I ask, glancing over my shoulder at him.

"You and God will decide that. No one else." The humor that filled his voice earlier has fled.

We continue the rest of the way in silence, trudging down the stairs, flight after flight, until I imagine we must have reached a level at least five stories lower than that of the rebel warehouse. At the bottom of the stairs is a doorway, and I hold my breath as we step through it and into a small, twelve-by-twelve-foot room with walls of unadorned concrete block.

Inside the room, now. The door through which we entered is at our backs. Ahead of us is another door, this one a little lower, a little narrower, made of steel and shut tight. The door behind us swings shut as well. One dying, fluorescent tube flickers above us, providing the only light.

I turn and face McCann. A knife blade protrudes from his fist, deadly and evil-looking. We are alone in a place where even the most pitiful death scream would fall to silence before reaching any living ear. I struggle to remember the prayer of Jimmy Shaw, the one he closes each sermon with, but although I have heard it a million times, only a few phrases remain in my memory: *Give me the grace to bear my burdens, the will to work hard . . . let me obey the Lord Jesus and His mother, Mary, honor my family, devote myself to my Company . . . forgive my sins . . .*

My heart sinks. Surely, these scraps of drifting words will never form a solid enough raft to float me to heaven. Still, paradoxically, in this moment I feel God all around me as never before. Maybe even without Jimmy Shaw's words, He is here with me after all.

The knife.

My eyes close. Despite all the anger, all the frustration I have wrapped around myself for years, I would still, in this moment, cast it all off and live.

McCann takes a step toward me. In the wavering light, his eyes seem to quiver. The scar on his left cheek stands out in livid relief. He smiles or snarls, I cannot tell which.

"McCann," I say, making sure to use his name, hoping it might elicit some measure of mercy. "Am I here to die?"

"We're all here to die," he says. "The question is, how will we live?"

What I meant to say was, *Have you taken me here to kill me?* My mind reels as I try, without success, to articulate my fears.

He holds up one large hand, hushing me. "Listen," he says, "we don't kill no one if we can help it, but especially not you. We need you. The best way to kill a chicken is to take off the head, right? If the Company is a big, evil chicken, you're closest to the head, you see?"

I shake my head. "No, I still don't get anything. People have more luxury than ever before. Billions of people all over the world have accepted Jesus. Thousands of people are raised out of poverty every day because they work for the Company. You're telling me all that's suddenly meaningless? That the Company is just evil?"

McCann pauses. He breathes deeply, as if drawing words up from a deep well inside his chest. Finally, he speaks.

"You know, I used to work for N-Corp," he says. "Back in my home, in Africa Division. I loved the job. They gave me a small, clean place to live, and food, new clothes—decent credit. It was like a dream. So I tried to get my countrymen and tribesmen to work for N-Corp, too. But they didn't trust the putting of the cross in the face or the way the Company made people abandon the old ways. Some villagers protested. They fought to take back the lands the government had sold to the Company. The spirits told them the Company was bad, they said. . . . Well, on this day hundreds of tribal leaders gathered in my village to discuss ways to resist the Company. I went to change their minds, to tell them how good my job was, and I brought with me an imager camera, purchased with my new Company credit. It turns out, you will see, I was wrong about the Company. The spirits were right."

The light flickers above us, casting trembling shadows, like black, capering demons, across the walls. McCann holds out the knife.

"After what I am about to show you, if you decide to join with us and fight the Companies, you will cut the cross out of your face and come back through this door, the way we came in. If you decide to stand with the Company, then you will go out the far door. The tunnel it leads to will take you back to the industrial arc. That door will lock behind you once you pass through it, and by daybreak this camp and every person in it will have scattered like smoke in a wind, and you will have made your choice."

When he stops speaking, the silence is complete. Still, I can find no words. I stand holding the knife, staring dumbly.

McCann retreats to the door. He does not smile now.

"You're leaving?" I ask. A moment ago I was terrified he'd kill me; now I'm terrified he'll leave me alone.

When he turns back, a bottomless sadness seems to inhabit his eyes. "Forgive me, but I cannot stay and watch," he says. "Already, my dreams are polluted."

He opens the door, steps through, and then turns back once more. "I like you, Miss Fields," he says to me. "I hope you will choose well."

He seems about to say more, but a distant, haunted look comes over his face, and he nods at me and says nothing. The door closes behind him with a clap deeper than a peal of thunder, and I am alone.

The light above flickers to darkness.

Then all around me, the nightmare begins.

In that tiny underground room, perhaps only a few hundred feet above hell itself, white light leaps onto three walls. From the light, images come forth, indistinct at first then solidifying. And I suddenly realize: this room is a 3W3DI, just like the one I have at home.

The audio system crackles to life, and the sound of laughter echoes eerily against the barren concrete walls. I glance over my shoulder, half expecting to see McCann standing behind me (for the laughing voice is his), but the steel door is shut tight, and I am alone on a narrow, dusty road somewhere in Africa Division. The road stretching out at my feet is skirted by dry, wind-rustled grass. Against the horizon, a few small huts and piecemeal shacks rise from the barren landscape under a majestic, cloud-swept sky. My world jostles as I/McCann move up the road amid the faint cloud of dust kicked up by our feet.

In the next instant, I see what has elicited his laughter—a group of children run up the road toward us, screaming, laughing, and shouting greetings in a language I don't understand. They swarm around us, skipping, jumping, and kicking a tattered soccer ball back and forth. From our pockets we take out little pieces of candy, which the children receive with elation. We laugh with them. They clamor to take our hands and pull us toward the village, leading us home.

A few chickens hasten out of the road as we pass. The children chase one another around us in circles. Several of them speak to us quickly, excitedly. Part of me yearns to know what they're saying but another part of me already knows, for children are children the world over, and excitement is universal when a favorite uncle comes to town.

Up ahead, two women wearing long, colorful robes approach, and next to them comes a thin man with long arms and a bright, toothy smile not unlike McCann's. He wears blue jeans and a sweat-stained button-up shirt. When we meet, we all exchange handshakes, hugs, jokes, and exclamations of joy. Amongst the children, we walk on. We have reached the outskirts of the village now, and we pass a tiny, windowless shack with a tarp for a front door. Two old tires and a rusting motor scooter stand next to the house.

For a moment, my heart swells with pride to know that through my work at the Company, these destitute people are probably now living in clean, comfortable conditions.

The narrow, dusty road curves toward the crest of a hill. The rest of the village—perhaps only a few more scattered huts—must wait on the other side.

The most eager of the children, a young boy of perhaps seven with fast legs and no shoes, has already reached the hilltop. There, against a feathery wisp of cloud draped in the blue of the sky, he stops short. At first, I think he must be waiting for us to catch up. As adults often do, we are lagging behind. But instead of looking back at us and shouting "come on" in his tongue, instead of doubling back, grabbing our hands, urging us forward, he simply stops. He stands very still and shades his eyes, watching something intently. Then he slowly extends one small finger and points.

For a moment, we ignore him—many other children vie for our attention, and the adults surrounding us engage us in lively conversation. But soon, as the hilltop grows nearer, the boy draws our full attention. We follow his finger into the distance. At first, there's nothing to see: only the blue of the sky and, to the east, the still-low disk of the morning sun.

But gradually, out of the distant blue, dark specks come into being. A flock of birds approaches. At first, they are distant. An instant later, they are close. They are birds—must be birds—but they are birds of singular purpose, for none of them wheels; none darts down to alight on a branch. And the sheer number of them is awe-inspiring. This migration must be unprecedented, for the black specks gush over the horizon by the hundreds. In the next moment, these straight-flying birds are nearly upon us, their wings rigid, their movements fluid and marked with almost supernatural speed. Now the people next to us are pointing too, speaking in hushed and fearful tones.

And I realize, in a wave of nausea and foreboding, that nobody in this village has seen a flock of these strange birds before. Ever.

The little boy on the hilltop lowers his pointing hand slowly and backs up a few steps, his eyes fixed on some unseen thing waiting just below the line of the horizon. The world is thrown into tumult as we run toward him. The little boy's fear is thick, palpable, spreading like blood through water. The sound of footsteps is all around us—everyone is running, the adults, the children, all hurrying toward the fear-stricken little boy. We, McCann and I, reach him first.

He stands face-to-face with a bird that nature would never have allowed to take wing. From here we can see it is actually a two-foot-long aircraft, a black-painted triangle of metal. It hovers maybe four feet from the ground, issuing a barely audible, mechanical purring sound.

The boy points at it and says one word. I can only imagine he's asking us what this thing is. He swallows his fear for one instant, allowing himself to glance away from the thing and turn his hopeful brown eyes on us. He even forces a smile. We say something—tell him not to be afraid, perhaps—but his eyes snap back to the flying triangle. He backs up a step.

Something inside me screams, *Don't trust it!*

And then we hear the sound, a tiny expulsion of air like an over-enunciated T. At first we don't see what's happened. The black bird's purr raises a few notes in pitch, and it darts away. It's already just a speck in the sky again by the time the little boy hits the ground. We've reached him in two steps, but by then his gaping eyes have already glossed over. His arm is still extended, his finger still points, but now it points heavenward. In his neck: a tiny dart.

The little boy is dead.

Then the sound again, more unnatural purring, more T sounds. We turn to see the children all around us falling, one by one, like a set of dominoes.

T-T-T-T-T

They all fall down, ringed by hundreds of hovering black triangles.

We snatch up a child, the only one who hasn't fallen—a sobbing little girl—and run over the hill with her in our arms, screaming warnings that aren't words, screaming in the most primal, most universal of tongues.

Over the hill, in the village below, among the dry, brown grasses, inside the huts, piercing the canopy of the sky at every turn, the metal birds swarm like locusts. We run among them through the village, screaming our warning as, around us, men carrying spears and guns, women bearing babies, children with dolls and playing cards, all fall, one by one, into the dust.

Perhaps the most horrible thing of all is that, I, we, can still hear the wind. We can still hear a distant radio. The black triangles make no sound except their murmured purring and their staccato exhalations of death. We run through the horrible quiet, searching for a weapon, for a refuge, for a way to turn the tide of annihilation, but in the next instant, it's already too late.

The black birds are gone. We spin and spin, looking for the last one, the one that will put death in *our* throats. But the flock has flown away. We watch them diminish, like the smoke of a dying fire, and soon the distance and the blue have absorbed them again. It's over. I look around.

Everywhere, I am watched by the staring eyes of the dead. And that's when I notice: none of these corpses has a cross in its cheek.

I drop to my knees and set down the little girl I have saved. For now, after this horrible judgment of God, it is my duty to dry this little girl's tears, to root out the answer when she screams at night and asks why her parents, her friends, her teachers, and her cousins were all killed. I must raise her. I must love her. Through her, I must make things right.

I set her down. She smiles at me, her teeth shining and white. Catching my breath, through shuddering tears, I speak words to her. Is she okay? Is she alright? She mustn't be afraid, mustn't cry (although I am crying) she mustn't, mustn't—

Her smile doesn't flinch. Her eyes cannot blink.

I, we, roll her over find the dart in the back of her neck.

We look up, our view unsteady with the shaking of sobs, but the only thing that still moves in the once-vibrant village is the wind through the dry, dead grass.

Across the road, between two squat, mud-brick huts, I see something so strange that at first I think I must be imagining it. There, looking as out of place as a spaceship might in this peaceful, primitive place, stands a billboard from the last N-Diamonds campaign.

I—we—turn away, and in the dusty side window of a broken-down pickup truck, we catch the reflection of the Company cross in McCann's cheek.

And the viewer goes dark. The room goes dark.

There is no sound except my own moan, no feeling except the slow bleed of tears down my face.

I finish screaming and sit trembling, staring at my knees beyond the hem of my sweat-soaked nightgown.

It's March. I'm sixteen. And I wish I were dead.

The nurse comes to my bedside with a smile on her face and a tiny, slimy, screeching person in her hands. There's another woman there, too, holding a large IC and entering data into it through the touch screen.

I cover my ears to silence the baby's screams, but I hear the woman's questions anyway.

"You want to hold her?"

"No."

"It's a healthy baby girl. What are you going to name her?"

It is a girl. My girl. My daughter. Dad was hardly concerned when I told him. *N-Ed has wonderful new programs to take care of problems like that,* he said.

"Young lady? What are you going to name her?"

"Rose."

"Rose Fields. That's nice. I see here that you've chosen N-Care for her, is that right?"

"Yes."

N-Care, another great perk of being an N-Corp employee—or the daughter of one. The Company will take your child and raise it for you, using the latest scientifically proven methods, for a reasonable monthly fee. Visit the child as often as you want—or, in my case, never.

It's a much more cost-effective way to raise children according to all the studies, and parents who don't have to worry about raising their children are an average of 22 percent more productive in the workplace. But I'm not thinking about efficiency now. Even with all the pain meds, it feels like a bomb went off between my legs.

"It looks like there's no father listed—" the woman says, frowning down at the screen of her IC.

"There is none," I whisper through my parched, cracked lips.

The woman's frown deepens. "We need to put something in the 'father' box, Miss Fields."

"Make something up," I say, and I close my eyes, ending the conversation.

"Are you sure you don't want to hold little Rose before we turn her over to N-Care?" the nurse's voice says from the darkness beyond my closed eyelids.

I don't answer.

Before long, I hear the nurse's footsteps as she walks away, taking the screaming little person with her. And I can finally breathe again.

A mile beneath the rebel warehouse, I stand in darkness. From the churning shadows all around, the sightless eyes of dead African children stare at me.

At some point, the quivering light above is rekindled. I realize I have been staring at the knife in my hands for untold minutes, but I cannot find the will to move. Tears pour down my face.

The only words that reverberate through my brain make no sense to me: *I can't.*

I don't know what it is I can't do. Can I not face what I have seen? Can I not stomach the sight? Can I not believe this could really have taken place, that the Company is really responsible? Can I not fathom that my closest friends and family, everyone I know, may have somehow been complicit in making it happen?

I can't.

I can't leave behind everything I've ever known, loved, strived for.

I can't.

I bring the knife to my cheek, shivering at the chill of the steel. The cross under my skin feels burning hot against it. I try to press, but the blade slides harmlessly off my tear-slicked skin.

I can't. I can't.

I feel my destiny building, hovering over me like a black, thunder-racked storm cloud, ominous, terrifying. In my heart, I know I can't run from it, but I still crave shelter.

Then a revelation hits me with all the desperation of a tidal wave: those images might be fake! Those might have been actors, dying on that lonely roadway! The flying triangles might have been toys or computer-generated images instead of real weapons. Anybody who's ever watched *N-News Tonight* knows how deceitful unprofitables are! Jimmy Shaw has preached about it countless times. This is just a trick, an elaborate ruse these anarchists are employing to get me to spill Company secrets to them!

A new wave hits me, this one of anger. I wheel and throw the knife at the door through which McCann exited.

"You can't fool me!" I scream. "You damned unprofitables! Anarchists! *You can't fool me!*"

My heart pounds. My hands tremble. Tears mar my sight.

Two doors. One leads to McCann, to Ethan, to Clair and Michel, to a cause I still don't fully understand and a life spent in the shadows of want and fear and probably death. The other leads to every dream I've ever had, every plan I've ever made, every person I've ever held dear, every luxury, every comfort the world has to offer, and every hope for a peaceful life.

Who says the Company made those black metal birds? Maybe it was some insane inventor. Or B&S. Or the anarchists!

I swallow, catch my breath, dry my face with the palms of my hands, then pull open the heavy, heavy door that leads back to my life. With each minute, with each hurried step I take through these lonely industrial arc tunnels, the thunderheads of my fate seem a little less threatening.

It's decided; it's over. I'm going back to the Company, back to my life.

I'm going home.

CHAPTER 008

Kali's gonna buy you a mocking bird. . . .

As a child, I swore I would be a writer. And that's not even the kicker: of all things, I wanted to write romance books.

A handsome, young, orphan pirate who was really a prince would fall in love with a powerful, impetuous heroine. After grueling, heart-wrenching tribulations, they would wind up in each other's arms, drifting into a firework sunset on the crest of the majestic, swelling sea. Nothing in my dreary, schoolwork-and-macaroni life could compare to the vivid fantasy-scapes that lived in my imagination. I was sure that a great love story awaited me, that I would be a worthy and beautiful heroine, that once I found my true love and determined which battles I was destined to fight, my life would at last take on the radiance that lived only in my mind.

Then, there was Kali.

All my life, throughout my imaginary wanderings, in every class-room at school, behind every smile I forced onto my face, a shadow had lurked, stalking me. I turned every light on in my mind like a scared child left home alone: I learned to play the piano, studied French, played sports—especially basketball and soccer—and I excelled at N-Academy. But lightbulbs burn out. The sun must set. And then the shadows come out. God, the darkness became ominous, all-consuming. I loved girls. I wanted to taste their lips. And no amount of distraction could keep that truth at bay. Denial was impossible.

Now, suddenly, there was no sanctuary for me, no future. How could I hope to live a beautiful tale of romance when instead of blushing at the sight of the brave, young pirate, I was reduced to tatters at the thought of kissing the princess? And the Company, the Church, my friends—they gave me no comfort, either. As Reverend Jimmy Shaw said many times, "God blesses the love between man and woman, but the unnatural love between man and man, woman and woman, is against God, science, and Company policy, and earns as its reward an eternal swim in the Lake of Fire." Hallelujah.

Here I was, twelve years old and already damned.

Here I was, lost, alone, empty, with no hope for a future and nothing but hate for the lie of my past. My mother was long gone, and my father seemed entombed in his own ambition, locked in a chamber of anxiety, exhaustion, and endless labor where I might never reach him. There was nobody to turn to, nowhere to run.

Then came Kali. I was fourteen the summer we met. On break from school, I wandered my father's house, tired of piano, tired of my N-Ed programs, tired of the magnificent view, tired of my own problems and the sight of my own face. In a rare moment of acumen, Dad noticed how depressed I was and made a few calls. He hired an eighteen-year-old girl to come and watch over me—a poor, low-level tie-man's daughter. Her name was Cecily. She was a huge bitch. But Kali, her fifteen-year-old sister . . . Kali was divine.

"I need to see Blackwell."

The hours spent in the long walk back from the industrial arc have done little to untangle the confusion in my mind. A thousand contradictory voices seem to shout each other down inside my skull. But as Jimmy Shaw always says, *When in doubt, report it.* So here I am.

The kid behind the desk looks like a thirteen-year-old pumped up on steroids. His body seems far too big for his childish face. His eyes, however, negate any chance that one might mistake his youth for innocence. They narrow, watching me closely.

I probably look like a maniac to him. My hair is still matted with blood from the jump into the river. My clothes are torn and filthy, and I'm so exhausted I can hardly stay on my feet.

There's a familiar beep, and the young squad member looks down at the monitor of his IC, where my identity information will have just popped up. He scans it dubiously.

"Sorry, Miss," he begins, "Mr. Blackwell isn't—"

I decide to help him out. "Fields. As in Jason Fields. I'm his daughter."

The kid's eyes snap up from the IC instantly and he mutters an apology.

Two minutes later, I'm pacing in Blackwell's office. The guy from the front desk mans a computer terminal near the door and Timothy Blackwell, VP of Human Resources, Director of the Security Squad, leans back in his chair, both feet propped up on his desk, hands behind his head, as if I were finding him in a hammock on some tropical island.

I'm already talking: "There were unprofitables—hundreds of them!"

"Is that right?" Blackwell says.

"They tried to get me to join them. They told me horrible lies about the Company!"

Blackwell sits up, reaches into his desk drawer, and pulls out something long, wrapped in wax paper. "Go on," he says.

"They—one of them—said that the tie-men killed in the Headquarters explosion were actually their people, their spies, who had infiltrated the Company."

"That's true," he says, as he unwraps a fat submarine sandwich.

I stare at him, baffled. "You know about it?"

"We know about everything, May. Always," he says, in a tone drenched with self-satisfaction. He takes a huge bite of the sandwich.

I watch the muscles of his jaw flex as he chews. "I've been tracking this group of anarchists for years. They're a particularly malignant bunch, responsible for the deaths of hundreds, maybe thousands of squadmen."

"Why haven't we stopped them?"

He wipes some mayonnaise off his chin with a napkin. "We did," he says, his dark brown eyes gleaming.

"I don't understand," I say.

"That explosion killed exactly seven people, May. The seven unprofitables who infiltrated the Company. What those anarchists told you was absolutely correct."

"*You* were behind the explosion," I say, horrified at the realization.

Blackwell nods, smiling. "Absolutely."

The look of confusion on my face prompts him to continue. "I'm sure you understand, this discussion is completely confidential. We have a very important project taking place right now at the Company. This new initiative hasn't been rolled out yet, but believe me when I tell you, it's big. And now that you were kind enough to point out the impending financial loss, the stakes are even higher."

"What new initiative?"

Blackwell swats my question away and takes another bite of sandwich.

"I'm not authorized to tell you that, May. Suffice to say that these unprofitables were planning to disrupt it, and it was imperative that we disrupt them first."

"But the explosion—innocent people could have been hurt."

"That was Shaw's idea," Blackwell says. "He's always one for theatrics. An explosion during a board meeting—that's one good way to keep the public outrage boiling. And a public that's outraged by the anarchists isn't likely to join them, is it? Don't worry. Damage to

Company property was minimal. The board room is being repaired as we speak."

My head is reeling, and it's not just from my concussion or the sleep deprivation.

"It was a localized explosive device, set up near spies' assigned seats," Blackwell explains. "It killed them and only them. Of course, one of them changed seats at the last minute and escaped our little trap. . . ."

Blackwell nods to the huge young man sitting at the computer in the corner, and he presses something on the touch screen. An imager wall behind Blackwell comes to life, and there's Clair and me in the stairwell, then Clair on the rooftop, holding her white gun on me.

"She escaped with your help, I might add," Blackwell points out as he stuffs the last bite of sandwich in his mouth and licks his fingers. I don't like his accusatory tone.

"I don't know if you noticed," I snap, "but she had a gun on me. Hey, aren't you the one in charge of keeping guns out of the Headquarters building?"

Blackwell chuckles, a low, rumbling sound. He wipes his mouth with the napkin again.

"That's not the first time the two of you have been together, May. "Blackwell nods to his lieutenant, and another picture appears on the imager: me, in the shopping plaza. Clair is a few steps behind.

"She was following me. . . ." I say.

The image changes, and there she is on another day, following me. Then on another day. And, of course, in two of the shots I'm wearing pants and a suitcoat.

Blackwell swivels in his chair and points to the imager, to my pants. "I see a few handbook violations there, Miss Fields. No wonder these anarchists thought you might be a good target to recruit."

I do my best to look outraged. "That's insane. My father *made* this company."

Blackwell leans over his desk. "So you don't have any sympathy at all for their cause, Miss Fields?"

"No. Of course not." And I mean it. But the words come out a whisper.

Blackwell looks over at the young man in the corner. The lieutenant looks down at the screen in front of him, and then almost imperceptibly shakes his head. Blackwell smiles darkly and looks back at me. *What was on that screen?* I wonder. But there's no time to ask.

"Of course, May. You're no anarchist sympathizer," Blackwell says. "But still—I'd be very careful if I were you."

For a second, I'm taken aback that he actually has the gall to threaten me; then I'm just furious. His eyes bore into mine. I've hated Blackwell for years, but at this moment it's all I can do to refrain from jumping over the desk and choking him.

"I should go," I say, my heart pounding. "I just wanted to make my report."

"We appreciate it," Blackwell says with a smile. "Give my regards to your father."

I turn and walk out of that place faster than if it had been on fire.

Simmering beneath my anger toward Blackwell is something much worse—fear. He has always been an unnerving presence, hovering in the wings during board meetings, accompanying my father on secret business trips. Then, there's our less than cordial personal history. . . . But today, something about his demeanor is positively terrifying. Perhaps it was the way he looked at the young squad member when I lied to him—the way the kid looked down at the screen then shook his head so slowly—that disturbed me so much. Or maybe deep down, part of me feels guilty for my time with the rebels, for the fact that I don't quite hate them the way I'm supposed to. Either way, the urge to run from Blackwell is overwhelming—which only probably incriminates me further.

Now, hustling down the empty night-darkened street, my head throbs. My stomach burns like a furnace. I need to know. I need answers. And there's only one man in the world who can give them to me.

In my car now, switch from auto-nav mode to manual drive and race between stoplights, watching the streetlights paint themselves across the shiny hood of my N-Jag. This beautiful car accounts for almost a quarter of my debt—and it's my pride and joy. I long to hear it growl and purr under the pressure of the accelerator like Dad's Lamborghini did when I was a girl, but the only cars that still sound like that are old collector's items now, banned from street use. Instead, my ear is met only with the rush of the wind and the almost imperceptible hum of the battery-cell power plant. Not very satisfying. It also breaks down all the time. But what does the Company care? They can crank N-Jags out all day and sell them at a 300 percent profit. It's not as if you have any other makes of car to choose from.

At least now, in the middle of the night, I can drive at a decent speed. During the day these streets would be so choked with traffic it would take half an hour to drive ten blocks, but at this late hour everyone is sleeping in preparation for the workday ahead and the roadway is practically deserted.

I look up, through the moon roof. There are no stars here, only streetlights and illumination from the giant, ad-flashing imager screens lining the roadway.

At a stoplight, I pull up next to a huge black vehicle with massive chrome wheels. On the door the security squad star is painted. The bass from the SUV's stereo makes the car seat vibrate under me.

From every window of the huge vehicle, sharp eyes glare at me from beneath the cocked brims of their HR baseball caps. One squad member spits, and the heavy, mucousy wad lands just short of my open window. The others laugh. I feel a tide of fury rising within me, but before I can act the lights atop the squad truck blink on, the siren wails, and the big, black vehicle lurches through the red light. On the other side of the intersection they shut off their siren again and take off with a screech of tires. The only sound left behind is the echo of their laughter.

Full of indignant anger, I watch them speed away. When the light turns green, I take off speeding down the street, too, ripping around every corner and squealing off from every stoplight.

Finally, I arrive at an elaborate gate.

I stare at it, my car idling silently. The throbbing in my head has become a dull ache that draws my eyelids together, toward the sweet darkness of sleep. I smell rank, whether from the river water or my own sweat, I can't tell. My muscles are sore, my ribs explode with pain at each breath, and my back feels tweaked from the fall out of the helicopter. But I can't rest until I get answers.

Surely, if anybody should put aside his own agenda, his own self-obsessed crusade, and be honest with me, it should be him. He's a great man—a genius, most would agree. He's been my protector, my mentor, my distant benefactor for all of my life.

Surely, my father will give me the answers I need.

A sensor reads my cross and recognizes my identity. When the gate swings open, I squeal my tires again, racing around the curve of the driveway, and come to a shuddering halt only a few inches away from one of my father's prized Italian fountains.

I jump out of my N-Jag and cross the lawn (the grass is short and soft as carpet fibers), then jump up the front steps (which are made of German crystal and lit from within) and up to the massive mahogany door, where Eva's spectral voice greets me: *Welcome, May Fields. Your father is not accepting guests at the present time. Please call him on his IC, or try back tomorrow. Have a great night.*

I'm already pounding on the door. Eva says her spiel four more times, and each time I only knock harder. I pound for maybe twenty minutes, until I'm pretty sure I cracked a bone in my hand. Finally I hear the lock turn, which is good because I was about to break in through a window.

The door swings in, and there's Dyanne, standing in the doorway, regarding me through half-closed eyelids. My stepmom: eight months older than I am. Her breasts look like a pair of motorcycle helmets inside my father's dress shirt, which she wears without pants like a nightie. Her sleek, muscle-etched legs extend for what seems like miles before they hit the floor. Her professionally sculpted face (I seem to be the only one who notices one of her eyes is bigger than the other since her last surgery) is framed by perfectly highlighted blond hair. Last time I saw her, she was trying to quit smoking because the substance her lips were made out of is flammable. Seriously.

"Maaay," she whines, "it's laaate."

Maybe it is, but I don't think that's why her eyes are half closed. I shoulder past her, in no mood to chat.

"Dad!" I call. "Dad!"

My voice echoes over and over again, bouncing off the fifty-foot cathedral ceiling of Dad's foyer and the sparkling fountain in its center, across the imported marble floor, and back to my ears.

I look up the huge, winding marble staircase. After a moment, my father's grizzled head peeks over the banister.

"Dad, we have to talk."

"Oh, May, look, listen . . . if it's about the loss projection don't worry—it will all work out. Okay? Goodnight."

He goes to turn around, but I shout up at him: "It's not about the financials, Dad. I need to talk. Now."

"Now? But . . . Well, we were just settling down for the night. . . ." He blinks with exaggerated slowness. His hair is a tousled mess.

I look at Dyanne again. She smiles at me dreamily.

"Maaaaay," she says.

"What's wrong with you two?" I ask, unable to mask my disgust.

At first, she makes a face like she's offended, and then she laughs the musical laugh of a carefree little girl (a sound that God knows I've never uttered) and leans against one of the marble columns.

"May," my father admonishes, reaching the foot of the stairs now, "it's a bad time. We were just getting into bed—or the hot tub. And I—did you notice the fountain in here? It's a new one. It's not too big? The other one seemed too small."

No doubt about it, my father is acting very, very strange.

"I'm here to talk about work, Dad."

He straightens up suddenly. "Of course," he says. "Is it gonna take long?"

"It depends on whether you let me start or not. . . . Are you two alright?"

"Perfectly," says my father.

"Purrrrfectly," says Dyanne.

"Okay," I say. "I'll try to make this quick for you—"

"Wait," says Dad. "You want some coffee?"

Before I can answer, he's tilted his face toward the ceiling and pressed two fingers to each temple, like a B-movie psychic. He squeezes his eyes shut, nods, and then opens his eyes again.

"What are you doing?" I ask.

He grins and puts his arm around me, leading me from the foyer.

"That was the future, my dear," he says. "I just ordered three coffees to be brought to us in the North study!"

"That's how you order coffee?" I ask, skeptical.

"That's how *everyone* will be ordering coffee!" he says. "And operating imagers and driving their cars. N-telekinesis! Cross/brain interface isn't just going to be for ICs anymore. It will work with every appliance in your house and workplace!"

It makes sense, I guess. It's just another use of the cross/IC technology. Still, something about it gives me the creeps.

"Watch!" Dad says eagerly.

A wheelchair waits in the hallway. Dad sits in it and closes his eyes, concentrating. Immediately, he starts rolling forward alongside me.

He holds up both hands for me to see.

"See, no hands! All operated by the brain. This is the next big-ticket item, I'm telling you!"

"That's great Dad, but listen . . ."

"Everyone's going to have their apartment outfitted with the system," Dad continues, ignoring me. "No more remote controls, no more light switches, no more touch screens, just the brain itself! And the technology isn't that expensive, I'm telling you. Profit margins will be huge. We're talking big money!"

We've passed down the ornately decorated hallway and entered Dad's office. The room is massive and full of books—mostly unread—and periodicals—mostly pornographic.

"We'll make a ton of money on the serving robots, too," Dad continues. "Did I ever show you the new 'bots? We're rolling them out next year, May. I'm telling you, they're fantastic. Nobody wants to work, especially not at home."

"You're right, as usual," I say. "But listen. I have to talk to you about the Africa Division expansion program. You said it received a *warm welcome.*"

"Sure," Dad says. "Profits are up thirty-four percent out there!"

Dyanne sits in a wing chair by the fireplace (the fire sprang to life automatically when we entered the room and now blazes cheerily). She sprawls in the chair with her legs half open, and I get the distinct feeling she's situated to give my dad a show. It's a disconcerting thought, but I press on.

"That's not what I mean," I say. "What I'm saying is, did some of the African people refuse to work for the Company. Did we—?"

"Aaah!" Dad says. "Look!"

A robotic butler with a rubbery-looking face enters, walking with a fluid yet utterly unnatural gait. On a serving tray, he has three coffees. He bends at the waist and offers them to my father, graciously.

"*Your drinks, sir,*" the robot says, its voice a digital approximation of a stuffy butler's drawl.

Dad takes his drink and hands me mine.

Dyanne only responds with a muted snore when my father goes to give her hers, so he puts it back on the robot's tray.

"Take this one back," he says. "Dyanne doesn't want it."

"*What?*" the robot butler says. "*I didn't understand your instruction.*"

"See," Dad mutters to me. "Here's the problem. Now I have to remember the right command."

He places two fingers on each temple and squints at the ceiling. The robot does not move.

"Return to the kitchen," he says aloud.

"*What? I didn't understand your instruction.*"

The robot is still bent over, offering the drink.

"Go back to the kitchen," Dad says. "We don't want the G. D. drink. Take it back!"

"Dad, listen. About Africa Division—"

"What? I didn't understand—"

"Oh, for crying out freaking loud!" Dad shouts at the butler. "Stand there and rot then!" He turns back to me. "I'm telling you, May, the bugs are almost worked out, and we can sell them for huge money. I'm talking starting out at five. It's the next car or apartment—the next big-ticket thing we can get people for. And it's going to be a necessity. See, and I want to build them in Africa, that would be perfect, but the stinkin' rustics there don't know electronics. It's going to take decades to get a good class of worker there...." As he speaks, his eyes wander to Dyanne, who still sits spread-eagle in the wing chair. "Most of them are so undereducated, heck, undernourished—that they can barely string a few beads together, much less do high-end robotics."

"Dad," I say, losing my patience, "that's what I was going to talk to you about—"

"See, that's where B&S has us by the balls—the Asian worker is just a better class of worker than the f—pardon me—stinking Africans. Better consumers, too. But of course, B&S is mostly a Chinese outfit anyway, always has been."

"Dad," I say, "did we—did the Company—"

The robot suddenly jerks to an upright position, sloshing latte all over his tray.

"If you won't be needing me, sir, I'll return to the kitchen."

"Bout time," says Dad.

"What?" the butler says, *"I didn't understand your instruction."*

"Dad!" I shout.

"I wanna get in the hot tub!" Dyanne whines, suddenly wide awake.

"Baby—" Dad coos to her.

"Stop!" I stand, furious. "Everybody shut the hell up! N-Corp killed a whole African village! Women, children, everybody! They did it with little flying robot machines! I saw it. Now you explain it to me!"

Everyone's suddenly silent, even the robot butler.

"May," my father says, "such language. As Jimmy Shaw says, your mouth should belong to God, and hence—"

"Dad," I say. "Please! When I was growing up you cussed like a sailor. Don't lecture me, just answer the damn question."

"I've never been a cusser," my father says, indignant.

"Baaaby, the hot tub!"

"Please," I beg, "please, I don't want to argue. Just tell me, did we wipe out a village in Africa Division?"

Dad stands from the wheelchair, suddenly indignant.

"No!" he says. "There are six fundamental principles N-Corp was founded on! One: we strive to earn and deserve the trust of the community; two: we pursue excellence and success for our shareholders, our customers, and ourselves; three: we commit to making our community and our world a better place by prioritizing good service and neighborly conduct. Three . . . Wait. Three? Or four? Was it? What was it? Place ourselves on a path to success by—? Huh, dammit . . ."

"Dad, forget the principles! No one cares about the principles. I'm talking about—"

"That's exactly the problem with the modern debtor-worker, May! No principles! In my day—aha!—five: to achieve the maximum potential by working together as a team in all aspects of our . . ."

My father's thought is derailed as his eyes wander to Dyanne again. I wheel on her.

"Would you stop it! I can see in the window what you're doing!"

She pulls her shirt-nightgown down and crosses her hands over her chest. "Heeeeey!"

"And you!" I say to my father. "You should be ashamed of yourself! You're a seventy-five-year-old man!"

"Ah," says Dad, "but with our newest medical advances, aging is a thing of the past! I could conceivably stay like this forever. Just like this, at this age. Denny assured me the product is ready for market. I've been taking the treatment for months now! It's gonna be huge!"

"Baaaby! Hot tub!"

"Please!" I scream. "Please, Dad. People died. Many people. I saw it. If the Company has all these principles, they shouldn't—couldn't be doing this. If we have all these principles, it can't have been us, right? Can it, Dad? Just tell me it wasn't us!"

Dad stares at me, suddenly lucid. "The Company would never hurt innocent people, May. You know that."

I stare at my father.

"And who decides who's innocent and who's not?"

He doesn't answer. He doesn't look at Dyanne. He sighs. For a moment, I think I've actually gotten through to him.

"Promise me," I say. "Promise me the Company would never kill innocent people, even if they stood in the way of expansion. Or profits. Even if they stood in the way of everything."

"I promise. But . . . it's a big Company, May. Nobody can know all its dealings.

I nod. "And do we make little flying things that shoot poison darts?"

"No," he murmurs and sinks back into the wheelchair, suddenly somnolent. "I mean, not that I know of . . ."

He sits back down in the wheelchair, looking suddenly weary. "Let's get some ice cream," he murmurs.

"Yeeeeaaah!" says Dyanne.

Dad slumps. His chin is almost on his chest. His eyelids are almost closed.

"What the hell is wrong with you two?" I ask.

"Neeeeew pills," says Dyanne. "They do work well, they do, do, do."

Dyanne's chirps seem to wake my dad, and he rallies for a minute: "We have to break down the barriers to worker productivity, one by one, May. Depression, restlessness, despondency—these attitudes can ruin a worker's productivity and negatively impact the attitudes of those around him. With our new line of N-Meds, we not only meet this problem head on, but we also meet it with a product on which we can make an over five hundred percent profit. And it's virtually side-effect free. Virtually. Some headaches, dry mouth, disorientation, vertigo, mild dementia—but, so what? It's not like the old days where we had to worry about lawsuits, thank God! With these meds, work can be sustained for longer periods of time, with fewer breaks, and the debtor-worker's overall mood stays high. After taking the pills for only a few months, Dyanne and I are already feeling in much higher spirits. Talk to your HR rep; I'll send a memo to Blackwell, make sure he approves a sample pack for you. Seems like you could use a pick-me-up. . . ." Dad says. By the end of his speech, he's wound down again. His eyes close.

Dyanne, in her chair, has suddenly fallen asleep.

I watch my father for a moment as he dozes peacefully. "Things may not have always been great between us, Dad, but you always had my respect," I say, then shake my head sadly.

I take a throw blanket from the back of the couch and drape it over him before I leave. As I pass the robot butler in the hallway, I pick up the latte on its tray and dump it over its head.

After the encounter with my dad, exhaustion descends on me like a crushing weight, and I nap. Now, a few hours later, I'm wide awake again, out of bed, and showered. Amid all this chaos, all this confusion, all these questions, what I want, what I need—is distraction.

Standing in my massive closet, I scan the racks. I bypass all the black, brown, or gray skirts, all the little striped tops, all the tailored blazers that mark my—and indeed every N-Corp tie-woman's—wardrobe. Instead, I reach out and part the hanging clothes, right at the spot where the shirts meet the skirts. There, hanging against the back wall of the closet on a nail, is my father's suit, one from the skinny days of his youth. It fits me perfectly.

My head, already hurting from the fall from the chopper, throbs a little harder now in response to my fast-beating heart. Without another thought, I pull on the pants, button up the white shirt, and put on the jacket. Last, I take out the tie, a shiny red one, and slowly tie the knot.

I step up to the mirror and see myself. Perfect.

Cross-dressing has been a proven source of decreased productivity, and the Company has made it its mission to stamp out any such behavior in the workplace. Since all land and all facilities are owned by the Company, any place could be considered a Company workplace—so the policy extends everywhere. Technically, I could be fined for being dressed like this in my own apartment. Where I'm going, the risk is many times greater. But it doesn't matter. There's no way I'm staying home tonight.

N-Dance, the neon sign above the door reads.

A few years ago, places like this were absolutely taboo. Then some new study came out touting the benefits of dancing for people who spend their days crammed behind desks in uncomfortable swivel chairs. Apparently, it improves these people's spirits. Who'd have thought? So the board grudgingly allowed a few test dance clubs to be built. Judging from the tremendous revenue they bring in, N-Dance clubs are probably here to stay, unless they're found—as Jimmy Shaw expected they might be—to be dens of nefarious activity, in which case they'll be shut down again. High-credit-level workers like myself are strongly discouraged from patronizing N-Dance clubs anyway, just on general principle, and every time I round this corner of the alley I fear I'll see the neon sign dark, the sidewalk empty. As I round the corner this time, I'm relieved to find the sign still intact, for tonight at least.

A few pale, meek-looking youths stand out front, chatting and stirring their fruit-juice cocktails nervously. Alcohol, of course, is forbidden.

Suddenly, my attention is ripped away from these teenagers. There, beneath the doorway, bathed in the red light of the neon sign, stands one of the most beautiful women I've ever seen. Her strong, smooth legs are revealed by a slightly-shorter-than-dress-code-length skirt. Her hair falls around her tanned face in dark ringlets.

She stands there, looking bored, next to a muscular guy in a cheap suit.

The minute I step into the streetlight, her eyes snap to meet mine.

Something passes between us, some primal message, an energy so powerful that if it were harnessed it could probably power a fighter jet.

She says something to her beefy companion, and he glances at me, too. Then, without a moment's hesitation, she turns, still watching me until the last moment, and disappears into the club.

I'm reminded of the story of Odysseus—the part where he passes the sirens, those beautiful women who live in the middle of the ocean and sing pretty songs to draw sailors onto the rocks, where they die. Someone in my position should be very careful going out in public dressed like this, much less pursuing forbidden relations. I know that. But this girl has the allure of one of those sirens. Somehow, the thought of drowning with her doesn't seem half bad.

I follow her inside at something just short of a run.

Thank you, May Fields, a three-hundred-dollar cover charge has been added to your account. Have a blessed day, Eva says.

Lights slash across the walls, rending the darkness. Murmuring men crowd the bar, leaning too close to distracted-looking women. On the dance floor, couples turn and gyrate. There among them is my siren, looking exquisite, dancing alone. She sees me, gestures for me to come to her. And I do.

Welcome, Miss Fields, a one-hundred-dollar dancing fee . . .

God knows I'm no dancer, but for this girl I'll try. Her eyes seem to flicker in the strobe light as she watches me, as I watch her. Her body moves like mercury. Her hands trace my lapel, pull me toward her. Now, she moves against me.

She brings her lips to my ear.

"I knew you were different," she says, and takes my hand.

She could lead me into a meat grinder now and I'd follow her. Instead, she pulls me into the ladies room, into a stall. It's all too perfect to imagine. Here, where the light is better, she's even more beautiful that she had been in the darkness of the club. But my eyes close. Already my lips are on hers. Already, my hands are moving, down her side, to her hip.

I can feel her heartbeat against me. Her breath. Her hips moving against mine. I feel her lips on my earlobe, then the words: "I'm sorry."

Of course, that makes no sense. "What do you mean?" I ask breathlessly.

That's when the stall door swings open. Five squadmen stand there, laughing. Behind them, I see the muscular guy, my siren's friend from earlier, grinning smugly. The siren steps out of the stall, straightening her skirt.

"I told you it was a woman," she says to her friend.

One of the squadmen pulls out his IC, which beeps as it reads my cross.

Sorry, May Fields, Eva's electronic voice says, *a five-hundred-thousand-dollar depravity fee has been added to your account.*

The squadmen, still chuckling, begin to file out. I hear one of them as he turns to my siren: "Nice work. The HR credit will be in your account by Monday," he says.

HR credit: the money you make for turning someone else in.

Everyone is gone now, and the bathroom door slams behind them. I'm still standing there, stunned. As the stall door drifts toward me, I realize the cross commercial is playing on the imager screen embedded in it. In the heat of the moment, I hadn't even noticed.

Face it, the voice-over says. *It's your identity!*

I punch the screen as hard as I can and watch it shatter.

—CHAPTER 009—

Darkness. Chirping.

My body feels as heavy as cast iron. My eyelids might be slabs of lead. I could sleep here forever and that would be just fine with me. In sleep, there are no decisions to make, no mysteries to unravel, no moral conundrums to face. If only I were to stay asleep for the rest of my life, I might never have to remember last night's humiliation or yesterday's confusion. In sleep, I could forget about Clair and Ethan, my father and Dyanne, Blackwell and that damned siren at the dance club. God, I would love to sleep forever.

Except last night, I dreamed of black triangles coming out of an African sky.

Chirping.

Slowly, my eyelids drift open.

Sunlight, deliciously warm but painfully bright, floods my ninety-fourth-floor apartment. I'm sure birds are singing somewhere, but not up here. Even if they were to fly this high, you still couldn't hear them through the thick, blast-proof windows. Whatever is chirping isn't them.

Then I realize: someone's calling. I grab my IC off the bedside table and think *Answer*.

"This is Fields," I croak.

"May! Are you okay? I've been worried." It's Randal.

I throw my N-Mystique series goose-down duvet over my head in frustration. I love Randal, but I'd much rather be passed out right now.

"I'm fine," I say.

"You're on the imager. Turn on the news."

Instantly, I throw off the duvet and look at the far wall of my room.

I think the words *Imager, on. News.* The imager in the wall responds to my thoughts, and there I am on its premium 3-D holo-display. I'm on the rooftop of the Headquarters building with Clair, her white gun pointed at me. Cut to us, jumping out of the helicopter. Cut to me, looking determined, walking down the hall toward Blackwell's office. I wait for the next cut, the one that will show me at N-Dance, getting humiliated in a bathroom stall, but instead, they cut back to Patty Patrone, the news anchor.

"Miss Fields, of course, is the daughter of legendary N-Corp CEO Jason Fields." The abundance of curls on her head bounce with emphasis on each syllable. "Mr. Fields couldn't be reached today for comment, but VP of HR Timothy Blackwell had this to say . . ."

They cut to a shot of Blackwell at his desk, looking more serious than a snowman at the equator. "Miss Fields is a loyal employee of this Company, as her father has been for many years before her. If she did help this anarchist murderer escape, she clearly did so under coercion. In any case she's safe now, and HR is conducting a full investigation." He stares down the camera after the last sentence, letting the full weight of his words sink in before they cut back to the news studio.

"In other news . . ." Patty continues without pause, and I think *Imager, off.*

The screen obeys and goes dark.

So, someone at the Company wants the world to know that I was involved with Clair and the bombing. This isn't like the old days Dad used to tell me about, when reporters ran around town trying to dig up stories to report. That would be laughably inefficient. N-Media simply decides what they want people to think, then they report stories that will make them think it—without the burden of having to worry about the facts. There are no other news organizations to contradict them anyway. What they say is the truth is the "truth." I always knew that was how it worked, and it never bothered me much before. After all, what reason would my own Company have to lie to me? That, of course, was before I saw McCann's imager footage. And before N-News started doing stories about *me*.

"May? You still there?" Randal says. I completely forgot he was still on my IC.

"Yeah," I mutter. "I'm here."

"They've been running this stuff for the last few hours," he says. "I tried to call, but you didn't answer. Are you at work?"

"No, I decided to rest this morning," I say. Tardiness carries some major financial penalties, but what do I care? Let them send me to a work camp if they want to; I can't be expected to concentrate on a stupid ad campaign with everything that's happened.

What's going on? Why did those anarchists kidnap you?"

"I've got to go, Randal."

"B-b-b-but, May—"

End call, I think, and the IC disconnects.

I inhale deeply, and then expel the lungful of air, trying to steady my shaking hands. It doesn't work.

With no other options available, I do what I do best: go to work.

Two hours after Randal's call, I sit in a meeting room with my team as Miller plays several rough vid sketches of the new IC campaign.

"Well, what do you think?" he says eagerly as the last one finishes playing.

Before anyone responds, they all look at me. Of course they do; I'm the boss. Everyone likes to pretend it's not because of my dad, that I'm really that good at what I do—and I *am* good—but as I sit in that chair with all their eyes on me, the truth becomes painfully obvious. They all despise me even more than they envy me. And they despise me because they're afraid. Afraid I could select one option on my IC and have their credit level downgraded. Select another one and have them repossessed. And as their boss, I suppose I could. Which is why no one dares to give their opinion of the presentation before I do. The problem is, I didn't see one bit of it. All I saw were images of Clair, Ethan, McCann, Randal, my dad, Dyanne, Kali, all swirling in a carousel of confusion around me.

"May?" Miller prompts.

When confused, I've always found it best to respond with anger.

"Am I the only one in this entire building who has an opinion?" I shout. "What the hell are you all being paid for?"

Everyone's head droops and they become incredibly interested in their ICs. I've just opened my mouth to berate them further when I see *him* walk by through the glass wall of the conference room. He wears a cheap-looking suit. His hair is slicked back and the black cross on his face stands out in stark contrast to his pale skin. It happens so fast that I hardly recognize him; he could be any one of the millions of tie-men I've met wandering the halls of the Headquarters building, except for his piercing blue eyes, which catch mine for a half second as he passes by. They're familiar. Then I realize, this is no tie-man.

It's Ethan.

Without slowing, he continues on his way, disappearing down the hall.

Suddenly, the world seems to spin. My head feels light.

Carter is saying something about keeping the campaign cohesive, when I stand, mutter, "Excuse me. Let's take lunch," and bolt out of the conference room.

My calves ache as I rush down the hall in my high heels, moving as fast as I can without breaking into a run. The hallway curves, and for a moment I'm afraid I've lost him, but after a few minutes, I catch a glimpse of him, hustling away from me in the distance. My heartbeat quickens.

Fifty yards ahead of me, he turns down a side hall and I turn too, then he turns left down another corner. Jogging now, I glimpse him slipping through a wood-paneled door near the end of the hall.

When I reach the door, I notice that unlike all the other doors in the Headquarters building, which bear signs that say things like Conference Room K3 or Media Room H14, this one is unmarked. I take a quick glance over my shoulder to be sure no one is watching me, then place one hand on the knob and turn. Cool air wafts from the hallway beyond, brushing over my face.

I go to take a step forward then hesitate.

This guy is a dangerous criminal, I remind myself. An unprofitable. An anarchist. If I were smart, I'd call Blackwell right now and have him dragged off to prison, so I could collect the HR fee. Who knows, on a big anarchist like him, it might be big enough to buy that new speedboat, the N-Aqua Thunder.

But no. That's not why I'm following him. It isn't *want* that's compelling me toward him; it's *need.* A need as compelling as a starving man's need for food or a lonely woman's need for love. I need to know the truth.

So I step over the threshold and close the door behind me, finding myself in a long, windowless hallway. To the left, to the right, it extends interminably, but there's no sign of Ethan. So, I pick a direction and start walking.

At first, I just hurry forward, listening for the sound of footsteps, staring ahead, hoping to glimpse Ethan around the next corner. But gradually, I begin to notice my surroundings—and I'm shocked. I've never seen conditions as bad as these except for the few times in my life that I strayed into the low-low-credit-level housing. The paint here is drab. The carpet is threadbare and stained. Above, water leaks from a black, mold-stained ceiling tile into a bucket. Paint peels from the walls. The carpet is worn, unraveling. This corridor, I surmise, must be for cleaning, maintenance, and security services—though in all the years I've been coming to the Headquarters, I never knew this passage existed.

When I turn the corner, I almost run into a man in an N-Service uniform pushing a trashcan on wheels, and my guess is confirmed.

"Excuse me, did a tie-man just go down this way?"

The man nods, giving me a strange look. Whether it's because he's never seen a woman like me in this hallway or because he recognizes me from the imager—who knows? I press onward. For about a hundred yards, there's nothing. No windows, no turns, no doors, no signs of Ethan.

When I finally come upon a door, I poke my head through and find myself looking into a hallway, B hall, not far from my office. There's the triple-thickness carpet, the diamond-pane glass, the titanium-composite office chairs—all the beauty modern design can muster. I've walked down that hallway a thousand times, immersed in sunlight and enamored with the spectacular view, never knowing that this shabby, windowless world existed on this other side of this thin wall the whole time, like a parallel dimension.

I watch a few tie-men and women hustle past, but there's no sign of Ethan, so I pull my head back into the drab maintenance hall and continue my search. After a few minutes, I come upon a bank of elevators. The digital display above the doors shows that one of the elevators is going up—and Ethan might be on it. I push the call button but am too impatient to wait. Instead, I hurry through a stairwell door nearby and charge upward. After ascending three stories, I find myself in front of a door labeled rooftop access. I open it, and sunlight splashes across my face.

I've probably lost Ethan now, but what does it matter? With one more step, I'm among the clouds. The view takes my breath away. An ethereal landscape stretches before me, grand mountains of mirrored glass and steel rising from a valley floor made of puffy, gray cloud.

This is what I've been looking for. This place. This peace. Heaven.

I look left, then right. No Ethan. I could almost believe I never saw him at all. In this place, he and the conflict he represents seem like nothing more than troubling dreams, dissipating in the morning sun. Why couldn't I forget them? Forget everything, and just live?

Suddenly, a daring thought enters my mind: I'll walk toward the edge of the roof. To the very edge. My body shivers with excitement. It'll be like standing on the prow of a ship sailing on an ocean of cloud. . . .

There is no sound but the scuffing of tiny roofing pebbles under my polished pumps. The wind fills my lungs, infusing me instantly with its life. I realize that I've been holding my breath and wonder for how long. My heavy brow feels lighter and the knot of tension I didn't even realize I was holding in my stomach unclenches. Approaching the edge of the roof is like discovering a brand-new country. I'm Columbus on the shore of America, Alan Shepard on the moon. The wind tugs at my N-Elita blazer, and it snaps like a banner in the breeze.

At the roof's edge now, I stop and look down. Suddenly, my feet tingle violently and my knees feel like toothpaste. Dizziness washes over me, and I panic. The N-Corp Headquarters stands over 207 stories high. One gust of wind and I'd be gone. . . .

But I don't step away from the edge. I don't let myself. Below, through the tendrils of cloud and smog, I can see tiny people milling about the courtyard below, looking like grains of sand tussled by a gust of wind. What would it be like to fall from this here? For a second, you'd almost fly. . . .

"You're breaking Company policy," a voice says, almost in my ear.

I start so badly, I almost tumble off the edge. My balance regained, I wheel on the owner of the voice. Already, my face is flushed with rage and embarrassment.

There, smiling, is Ethan. "This area is off limits," he says.

My heart pounds from the scare he gave me. "You bastard! I almost fell off! Are you trying to kill me?"

"If I wanted to kill you," he says calmly, "I'd have just given you a little push."

He seems pleasant enough—even happy to see me—but adrenaline from the fright he gave me is still coursing through my system, filling me with a jittery anger. I look around the rooftop, making sure there are no HR cameras there.

"Did you want to talk to me about something?" I ask him gruffly, "or you just get a kick out of scaring the shit out of people?"

Ethan paces away from me, gazing out from the edge of the rooftop. "Language, May. Company could fine you for that, too. Plus your little stunt at N-Dance. . . . At this rate, you'll never end up a Blackie."

I was irritated before. With that comment, I'm furious. "What do you want?"

He grins. "Your autograph. You're a celebrity, May. You've been on the imager all day. I wonder why."

"Because you had me kidnapped," I almost shout. I take a deep breath, trying to regain my composure. "Why are you here?"

"To give you answers. Isn't that why you went to see your father last night?"

Okay, so Ethan knows I went to see my father. He had me followed after I left his camp, just like he was having me followed before I went there. Fine. Clair told me in the helicopter that he was trying to recruit me, so the fact that they were scoping me out makes sense. But my mind returns to the first part of his statement. About getting answers.

"Why did N-Corp kill those people in McCann's village?" I ask him. He raises his eyebrows.

"That's an interesting question, May," he says, gazing at me against the backdrop of blue sky. He takes a deep breath before he begins. "Imagine a beast. A monster. Imagine it cares nothing for children or trees or animals. The only emotion it knows is hunger. Let's say, a hunger for gold. It will keep a man alive as long he brings it more gold, but as soon as the man stops, it will burn him to ashes and collect the gold in his teeth. Anything that stands in the way of the monster's mission to collect every last scrap of gold in the world will be destroyed. Now imagine there are two of these beasts, May, and they rule the world."

I can hardly repress a smile at his silly fairytale analogy. "So now the Companies are monsters?" I ask.

"That's right."

"Have you seen my penthouse? My car? My imager? Not very monstrous. They're quite nice, actually."

"The most dangerous monsters are often the most beautiful."

I roll my eyes. "We're talking about a public corporation here, not some *creature*! It's made up of people—people like my father. People like me."

"An organism is nothing more than a collection of individual cells," Ethan says patiently. "A huge group of people, working together, form a larger entity. Individual morality fades. The new being develops its own macro-consciousness. In this case, a mind of infinite hunger."

My father's words from last night flash through my mind: *It's a big Company, May. Nobody can know all its dealings.*

Ethan leans close to me, not threateningly, but in earnestness. "It's not your fault, May. It's not anyone's fault. Corporations exist to make money. Greed is what they are. It's their nature, their soul. Decades ago, that greed used to drive innovation, to breed excellence, to inspire hard work. But now, now that there are only two Companies left, there is no more competition, no innovation . . . all that's left is the greed." He shakes his head. "Don't delude yourself, May. The Company will make its profit goals, no matter the cost."

"What do you mean?" I whisper. Despite the golden sun on my face, I'm suddenly feeling numb. "What cost?"

Ethan steps closer to me. "May, what if I told you the Company is planning to murder over one million of its own employees?"

"I'd say you're a lunatic."

"The Company won't stand for a loss. Plans for an N-Corp–B&S merger were already in the works. Since you gave your report, they've moved up the timeline. When the consolidation happens, over a million workers will become unnecessary."

I stare at him. "You're lying."

"Am I?"

"What you're saying is ridiculous! First of all, I'd have heard about the merger, second even if it were happening, we wouldn't kill all the unprofitables!"

Ethan leans even closer to me, his eyes scalding. "Who will pay to keep them alive, then, May? Not the Company. The cost of feeding and clothing them would ruin the profit margin. Think about it."

I do think about it. Suddenly, I feel like I might throw up.

"You don't believe me, look into it for yourself," he says. "The downsizing is to be carried out by a division called Black Brands."

"Black Brands," I whisper, suddenly dizzy as well as sick. *Where have I heard those words before?*

"But don't take too long, May," Ethan continues. "You have to go to your father. Get his help. The Company has to be stopped before—"

Suddenly, there's the sound of a door opening. I turn to see two squadmen in the stairwell doorway, looking at me.

"Hi," I mutter lamely. "I was just . . . getting some air with my—"

When I go to gesture to Ethan, he's gone, disappeared—as if he'd evaporated and wafted off into the clouds. I look around, bewildered. Where could he have gone? Around the side of that air-conditioning unit? Over the edge of the building? I don't have time to speculate. The squadmen approach. They look me up and down with palpable disdain.

"This area is off limits, ma'am," one of them says.

"What are you doing up here?" the other spits.

The first one looks down at his IC screen. There's a beep. When my identity appears on his screen, his demeanor changes entirely. He plucks at the sleeve of his comrade and shows him. They both smile at me, as shy as schoolgirls.

"Terribly sorry, Miss Fields," the first one says. "We didn't know."

"There are a lot of things you don't know," I tell him.

This seems to confuse him, and he glances over at his friend.

My thoughts have wandered back to Ethan's words. They sizzle through me like a powerful acid, filling me, burning me, leaving me hollow. Though my logical mind works feverishly to discredit or dismiss his claims, there is a deeper part of me that simply cannot.

"Miss Fields?" the squad member says, watching me closely. "You alright?"

I look up at him, at his eyes, dark-ringed and tired, at his face, furrowed with stress. The name Chavez is embroidered on his uniform.

"Chavez," I tell him, "you're a slave and you don't even know it."

And I brush past him and his friend and hurry toward the staircase, toward Black Brands, and a swarm of questions that won't go away.

I'm elsewhere now. All the changes leave me dizzy, bewildered. The blending, falling from one scene to the next is disconcerting, but I always know where I am.

This is my life. . . .

"Your room is so stacked, Randal," Kali says, looking around. "Not as nice as Blackie May's, but . . ."

She gives me a playful glare. I stick my tongue out at her. Randal laughs.

This is not the same Randal of later years. No, this is the beautiful Randal, the quiet teenager with dark, serious eyes and high cheekbones. This Randal is my confidant. Two years ago, he was my first kiss—though now, despite his good looks, that thought is repulsive. He's the only kid in my class smarter than me, and therefore a cherished study partner. He's polished—even stylish—good at playing pool, loves comic books, cracks dirty jokes, and has a goofy dog with one ear shorter than the other. He is, in a word, utterly lovable.

Randal is my best friend from N-Academy, and Kali is my best friend outside of school, so, of course, I wanted them to become friends, too, and the few times we've all hung out, they seemed to get along well with each other. Normally, they both hang out at my house, since it's so palatial, but it's nice to be at Randal's for a change.

His parents are both mid-credit-level, so his room is decent—furnished with a large bed with a couple of cool, comfy chairs at the foot of it and a small single-wall imager with an N-Game system, which was the object of our visit.

"Alright, who wants to play first?" Randal asks, holding up the two "mind clamps," helmets with sensors in them to pick up the player's thoughts. The mind-clamp system is a forerunner of the cross technology that allows players to control the game with their minds, and it instantly made regular, handheld video-game controllers and body-motion technology obsolete. The new system was all the rage when it hit the market last year, and Kali was pretty impressed when she found out Randal had it. Of course, I've had mine for two years now, and I'm scheduled to have my cross implant in three months, which will be way better than the mind-clamp junk—but I don't tell them that.

"I'll play," Kali says excitedly.

"Sure," I say, taking the other helmet. "Why not?"

The game is Metal Death Six, a game of skill and strategy in which, basically, you and your partner are both huge robots that try to pummel the hell out of one another. Right now, I'm pummeling Kali.

"Ouch. May, you're pretty good at this," Randal observes when he comes back from downstairs with a tray of N-Cola and some snacks.

"Don't let her pretty exterior fool you," Kali quips. "She's totally a metal death robot on the inside."

"Damn right I am," I say, as my robot rips Kali's robot's head off and punts it off the imager screen. With the imager's 3-D hologram technology, it looks like it's flying right toward us. The timing is perfect, and we all laugh.

"Here, can I play?" Randal asks.

"Sure. Avenge me," Kali says, and hands him her helmet. He puts it on, sits down next to me, and gives me the meanest-looking scowl he can muster. With his pretty green eyes and adorable dimples, however, he looks more like a male model with a migraine headache.

"Alright, Randal," I say, "let's see what you've got."

I hold my own, but in the end he winds up beating me. And Kali is cheering for him the whole time, which—although it shouldn't—pisses me off.

"Okay, okay," I concede. "You're tougher than me. At video games, anyway."

"Not in real life, though?" Randal asks, amused.

"Of course not," I boast.

Randal and Kali both laugh, which only eggs me on.

"You don't believe me?" I say. "Let's go. I'll wrestle you right now."

"Where?" Randal asks, amused but incredulous.

"Right here," I say, shoving the chairs out of the way and assuming a ready position.

"You really want to wrestle me?" he asks.

"Looks like she does," Kali says. "Watch out. May is a wiry one."

What Randal doesn't know is that my dad wrestled in college, and he taught me a few things. The minute we start, I shoot in, grab his legs, and take him to the ground with a double-leg takedown.

On his hands and knees now, his body shakes with laughter.

"Yeah! Go, May!" Kali shouts.

But despite my superior skill, Randal is still stronger than me. He manages to rise up into a kneeling position then pivots to face me. We're forehead to forehead when our eyes meet.

"You're in trouble now," he says, and surges forward, pushing me to my back.

His body is pancaked against mine, his chest crushing my breasts, his hands at my wrists, holding me down. I arch my back, bucking violently to get him off me, but his weight is too much. Suddenly, Kali is on the floor next to us, beating out the count on the carpet with the palm of her hand: "One . . . Two . . ."

I can smell Randal's cologne, feel the warmth of his breath on my cheek. I look up to find his eyes on mine. Am I imagining the desire I see in them?

"Three! Randal wins!" Kali shouts.

He lingers before getting off me, his lips coming nearer to mine, and for a terrifying second I'm afraid he's going to kiss me. I give him a little shove to hurry him along and we both sit up, catching our breath.

"Randal wins. Nice work," Kali says brightly.

"It wasn't easy," Randal concedes. "You're right; she's stronger than she looks."

"And meaner," Kali jokes. We're all sitting on the floor now, close together, our knees touching.

"Good effort," Randal says, giving me a gentlemanly handshake.

"Yeah," I grumble, squeezing his hand. "Everyone's bound to get lucky once."

My two friends laugh at my feistiness.

"Aw, somebody's a bad loser," Kali teases, and she leans forward and gives me a slow, lingering kiss—a pretty good consolation prize. When she pulls back, Randal is staring at us, wide-eyed.

"Are you two . . . ?"

"A couple?" I ask, taking Kali's hand. "Yep."

"But you can't tell anyone," Kali amends, a note of alarm in her voice. "Promise?"

The look of surprise on Randal's face ebbs, replaced with a smile. "Of course. We're friends, remember?" he says, and he snatches up the mind-clamp helmets. "Come on, let's play again."

—CHAPTER Ø1Ø—

The Cranton Facility.

This is the place they call Cranktown. Morning light pools on the shiny marble floor beneath my fast-moving feet. The lobby looks like a palace anteroom, full of huge, ornate, gold-gilded pots overflowing with fake flowers. I weave around countless fountains. Classical music trills softly around me, emanating from some unseen source.

This is the home of the Peakers, the brightest minds in the Company. Engineers, electronics wizards, technological visionaries, and computer geniuses all live, sleep, and work here, surrounded by every luxury N-Corp has to offer. The place is filled with huge imagers, state-of-the-art stereos, and the latest video-gaming technology. Top Company chefs man the kitchens twenty-four hours a day, preparing gourmet food that can be delivered to the Peakers at any time of the day or night. The geniuses who live here are given some of the highest credit limits of any Company employees and are allowed to take several weeks off per year to enjoy exotic vacations (unlike most N-Corp employees, who are only allowed one week of vacation per year, in addition to the standard one-day-a-week weekend).

In exchange for these privileges, the Peakers are expected to produce staggering amounts of research and develop thousands of new products and technologies every year—only a few of which will actually make it to the public. To help them meet the extraordinary demands of their work, one team of Peakers a few years back developed a drug, which, for its extraordinary properties, has been a required part of the Cranktown regimen ever since. Accumenzaphrin is the name of it, but the world has come to know it as *Peak*, since it has the effect of raising those who take it to their peak mental capacity. Test subjects experience a 30 percent increase of mental function across the board. The best analogy to describe Peak's effect is that it soups up the mind the way a mechanic in the old days would have souped up a car.

Randal calls it synapse grease.

Good old Randal; he's the quintessential Peaker and an ideal poster boy for the remarkable effects—both positive and negative—of the drug for which his tribe is named. He has a staggering capacity for mental mathematics and produces an impressive number of inventions and innovations every year. He has the entire periodic table of elements memorized, along with formulas for estimating the load-bearing capacity of various structures and materials, the gravitational pulls of most known celestial bodies, and the tensile strength of the seventy-seven most common aluminum alloys. He has memorized the name of the director from nearly every episode of every television and imager show going back to the 1950s. He can recite—and will, if you don't stop him—the DNA code for most shared human characteristics, along with the abnormalities that cause Alzheimer's, MS, Crohn's disease, diabetes, and male-pattern baldness. Any task you can conceive of doing, he can tell you a better, more efficient way of doing it. And probably will.

For these abilities and many others, he and his comrades are well rewarded by the Company. A few of them have even become Blackies over the years.

But their gifts also exact a price. Randal has told me that he sleeps only a handful of hours a day, often at strange times. Sometimes he finds it difficult to sit still and focus on conversations; other times, it is almost impossible to rouse him from a contemplative stupor. He can rarely stand to spend time in the Company of non-Peakers, because their lower mental speeds make the conversations seem maddeningly slow. As a result, Randal and most other Peakers can't help but look down on "normal" people and tend to separate themselves from regular society as much as possible. In fact, the only reason Randal probably picked up our friendship again is because of our long history together—and because my dad's the CEO of the Company.

Male Peakers are almost universally impotent, an unfortunate side effect of the medication, although they often enjoy the company of women because of their favored position in society. And of course, there's the stuttering.

Lastly, and perhaps most disturbingly, most Peakers find themselves incapable of mustering real emotion. Sympathy is foreign to them, as are love, jealousy, rage, and delight. Most are vaguely despondent and aloof, but full of an almost superhuman, vital drive that is invariably directed toward the abstract world of their intellectual and scientific work. As a result, Cranton's lavish imagers often go unwatched, the spa goes unused, and much gourmet food goes uneaten while its residents busy themselves in their labors of the mind.

Because of the drawbacks of the drug, N-Corp decided long ago that it should be administered only to an elite few. An entire workforce cranked up on Accumenzaphrin, while it might be more productive, would be uninterested, for example, in producing children—hence population growth would falter, and Company growth would soon follow. Worse, a "peaked" public would have little interest in consuming the products and services they had worked so hard to create, and the Company certainly has no desire to create a society like that. Therefore, though a large and ever-expanding pantheon of pharmaceutical deities are available for public worship, Peak is available only to an elite caste of perhaps four hundred people Company-wide.

This is their home.

Skirting another fountain, I pass pictures of famous old paintings displayed on several massive imager screens hanging on the walls on either side of me. I walk on, through a maze of velvet couches, glittering lamps, fake flowers. Finally, the reception desk.

The pale woman behind the desk stares back at me emptily, as does the white cleavage between her massive fake breasts.

"I'm looking for Randal Watson," I say.

The woman only gives me a vapid glance then looks down at the screen of her IC. I stand there in an uncomfortable silence until a blip from the computer announces that the scanner has read my cross. Numbers, letters, an old photo—all the bits of data that are somehow construed to denote my identity—appear in front of the woman.

"Oh, Miss Fields, welcome!" her demeanor changes entirely when she realizes I'm from Headquarters. "Yes, Mr. Watson was stepping out, but I'm not sure if he's left the building yet—"

Out one massive plate-glass window, I see something dart behind a tree. I stare, fixated. Was it a bird, a squirrel—or a flying metal *something* . . . ? I shiver with horror, staring out the window, waiting to see it again, to see a flock of them. Maybe Blackwell knows what I'm doing. Maybe they know why I'm here. . . . But whatever it was outside, it doesn't reappear. I finally tear my eyes away from the glass, but my brow remains slick with sweat. Of course, I'm just being paranoid.

"May!"

I gasp and wheel around, one fist balled up and ready to strike.

Instead of punching my assailant, I let out an embarrassed breath and slap Randal on the arm. "Bastard!" I say. "You scared me."

"Wound a little t-t-tight, huh?" Randal says with a wry grin. "What's wrong, being a hero doesn't agree with you?"

I give him a confused look.

"It's been on the imager all day," Randal continues, his confusion mirroring my own.

"The last thing I saw, Blackwell was thinking I helped some anarchist escape and he was vowing to investigate me," I say.

"That was this morning," Randal says. "Now they're reporting that you gave the Company the information they needed to catch that anarchist. The woman who bombed Headquarters."

It feels like the ground drops out from under me.

"What?"

"They caught her," Randal says. "Pretty lady. Too bad she'll f-fry."

"What?" I say again.

"You didn't hear about this? Didn't you lead them to her?"

"Clair?" I ask, disbelieving. "The woman who kidnapped me? They captured her?"

These are the type of repetitive questions Peakers can't stomach. Randal groans and looks away from me. His eyes dart and linger in unnatural ways. I watch as the drug drags his mind in a thousand different directions at once. I've seen him like this before, but never this bad—he must've taken a high dose today. But it's not him I'm worried about—it's Clair.

"That can't be right," I say.

Randal shrugs, sniffs, rubs his face with his hands, looks impatiently over at the receptionist, who's watching us a little too closely. The last thing we need is an HR watcher recording our conversation.

"Randal," I say. "Come here." I grab his sleeve and drag him a few yards away, behind a gigantic pot containing a fake-flower arrangement. "Listen to me. I have an important question for you, and you have to tell me the truth, okay? It's very important. Randal?"

He's looking all around, now glancing at his shoes, now glaring into the skylight above.

"Triangles," he murmurs, "the strongest shape. For the bio-adhesives, maybe that's what we need on that nano-engineering project, yes . . . manipulate the molecules into triangular formations. Probably nothing, but worth trying . . ."

"Randal, look at me," I say. "Remember when you were talking about all the money that's being bled from the Africa project budget?"

". . . And I have to tell Shawn the idea about the triangular arrangements for digital d-d-d-data, about the processor that runs in three dimensions."

Randal keeps looking over his shoulder, glancing back and forth, up and down, all around us, as if gripped with a terrible case of paranoia.

"Randal, what have you found out about where that money went?"

He cranes his head and looks around the edge of the plant at the skinny, pale receptionist, and I look over at her, too. We both catch the woman staring, and she quickly averts her eyes and busies herself with her IC.

"Randal, I'm afraid something terrible is happening. I have to know what the Company's doing with that money."

"I don't know. But, hey, if everything can be reduced to d-digital data, and believe me, it can be—assuredly, as terrifying as that is, it can—the whole world reduced to all ones and zeros, forever and ever—maybe it can be reduced even further. Think of that! Say, to only zeros, but different arrangements of them, th-th-three-dimensional arrangements of them, signifying everything around us, everything that is, everything that was, everything that is yet to be, all reduced to its common denominator, its simplest form, a single symbol repeated infinite times. That's the universe decoded. But reduce it further, and you realize that if that's the real root of the c-coding—and it is, it pervades everything, this huge 'O'—this gigantic ring—is the shape of everything. If space, t-t-t-time, life itself curls back on itself and repeats, then that's what it reduces to: a huge, universal, unified . . . zero."

"Randal. You're creeping me out. Just answer the question—what's that money being used for? Have you ever heard of a division called Black Brands?"

Randal's eyes snap to mine and his gaze steadies. For a terrible instant, he is utterly lucid.

With eerie slowness, he raises one hushing finger to his lips. Trembling, he makes his hand into an "o" shape. I wonder just how haunting the voice of genius is, ringing inside his skull. Randal doesn't say another word, but with his eyes he bids me to follow him.

"Tell me where the money's going, Randal."

As we enter Randal's apartment we pass two massive, carved-stone replicas of ancient Chinese lion sculptures. Randal locks the door behind us then squints at the windows, and they instantly go from clear to an opaque black. Hurriedly, trembling, he looks in the coat closet, slams the bedroom door shut, and then peers suspiciously under the couch.

"What are you doing?" I ask. "You're acting like a lunatic."

He doesn't answer. With his mind, he turns on the imager—Jimmy Shaw is there, standing at his familiar gold-and-pearl-inlaid pulpit with the N-Corp logo on it, warning us about hell and reminding us in his strident, lilting voice that the best cure for restlessness is a hard day's work and a good read of the Bible. The N-Corp translation, of course.

Randal jacks the volume up in a bone-shaking crescendo.

"What are you—?" I start.

He comes over to me, close. I smell in his sweat the faint, nauseating odor of Peak. He cups his hand and talks into my ear. I can barely hear him over the shouting imager.

"This is the only way we can talk without somebody overhearing. There's no p-privacy."

"Who's going to overhear?" I ask, and then I remember the woman at the front desk.

"Just listen," Randal says. "Black Brands is a division of the security squad. I've been looking into it and you're right—that's where the extra m-m-money from Africa Division expansion project is going. To them. How did you know?"

I only shake my head, dismissing his question.

I cup my hand and whisper into his ear, "Black Brands. What do they do?"

We switch, Randal whispering into my ear again. "They develop new t-technologies—mostly weapons and space systems, I think. A few of the guys here have been tapped to work on the program, but it's secret."

"Do you think they make little planes? You know, like flying drones that shoot poison darts or something? Could they make something like that?"

Randal shrugs. "Of course. I've heard rumors of all k-kinds of things: drones, submarines, neurotoxins that kill on contact. I even heard there's a satellite that can drop lightning bolts on p-p-people. But why are you asking me? When I told you about the missing money, you d-didn't even care."

"Lying," says Jimmy Shaw on the imager, *"is the Devil's specialty. So is deceit. The Devil wants you to agree with him, so he's going to say things you want to hear, simple as that. He's going to show you the easy road. But the path to righteousness is an uphill slope. . . ."*

I shift on my feet, take a deep, steadying breath. My headache is starting to come back now, seeping from the top of my head down through my neck and shoulders.

"What's g-going on, May?" Randal asks with almost child-like curiosity.

I put my hands on his flabby biceps, making him face me. "I'm worried about Black Brands, Randal. The Company was supposed to be about making money, giving people everything they want, making their lives better. There should be no reason to make weapons like that. I have to tell my dad about this. But first, I need proof. Where are the offices of these Black Brands people?"

Randal fidgets, sniffs, scratches his head, looking uncomfortable. "They're here," he says finally.

"Here? Now?" I look around in fear, Randal's paranoia infecting my mind.

"Here," he repeats. "This building. B-bottom floor, Z hall."

I nod. Cranton is the most secret and secure N-Corp facility in the hub. It makes sense that Black Brands would be located here. "Okay," I say. "Let's go."

Randal smiles that strange, Peaked-out smile. He counts something on his fingers, rubs his face. When he looks back at me, there are tears in his eyes. He motions me to him and says into my ear: "You're on your own."

Heavy autumn leaves burden the horizon. The sky is a sheet of homogenous gray, dark with the threat of impending rain, but there's a strange stillness in the crisp air. I'm fifteen, wandering home from school, thinking of Kali.

"May," a whisper turns my head. Seventeen-year-old Randal steps from behind a tree trunk. He nods me over to him, off the path, and leads me away from the crowd of students heading home from N-Academy.

"What's up?" I ask when we're out of earshot.

He glances over his shoulder. The movement is smooth—not like the jerky, bird-like movements of the later Randal. He speaks softly, with no stutter: "You have to come with me," he says. "There's someone who wants to talk to you."

"She'd better be pretty," I say—though I love Kali and Randal knows it. Besides Kali, Randal is the only one in the world who knows I like girls. He usually jokes around with me about it. But apparently, not today. The look Randal throws me is meant to squelch my attempts at comedy. It doesn't.

"Or is she one of the ones you like? Fat and hairy, with a hunchback and a peg leg?" I do my best impression of Randal's fictional lover, limping along next to him and making a grotesque face.

He smiles in spite of himself. "Stop it, May." He quits walking and turns to look at me. "You know who I like," he says quietly. Our eyes lock for a moment, but he looks away before I can get angry with him. He's professed his love to me twice before. Twice, I've told him it's never going to happen. He cracks his knuckles, a nervous tick he started because he played piano. He was a beautiful pianist in those days, before he had to give it up. Peak makes your hands shake.

"We better go," Randal says. "We shouldn't keep him waiting." He seems so serious that I'm afraid to ask who it is we're meeting, and we walk the rest of the way in silence.

We pass out of the school grounds, into a park filled with sickly looking, pollution-stunted trees. We pass in silence down a slippery, muddy path between the groping branches of overgrown shrubs. After a moment, the foliage falls away, revealing a clearing.

Ahead, a fountain. Sitting on its rim, a man.

He looks up but does not rise as we approach. Though he's not very old—forty, at the most—his hair is already tinged with silver. The bulk of his black overcoat betrays muscular shoulders. His jaw is square, his face handsome, his gaze unflinching.

"May Fields," he says, but instead of tipping his head as you would expect one to do with that type of greeting, he merely stares.

"May," Randal says (in those days he was unfailingly polite), "this is Squad member Blackwell."

Then I recognize him. This man had haunted the fringe of my life for years, passing in and out of my father's offices, standing in the corner during important press conferences, and dropping by the house late at night for unexpected briefings. He isn't one of the sniveling, pitiful tie-men who usually fawn over my dad, though—far from it. And he's not one of those last few rogue government agents who had to be rounded up a few years ago, as I had momentarily feared. No, Mr. Blackwell is none of those reprehensible things. There's no need to fear this man; he's one of the good guys. A good Company man, an N-Corp HR agent, a member of the security squad. I smile at him, and he smiles back.

Randal looks at his shoes, sniffs the cold air.

"I'm a friend of your father's, May," Blackwell says. "Do you remember me?"

"Yes."

"Good. Because I'm here on his behalf."

If I'd had a different father, this might have raised a red flag. Most fathers would never send a surrogate to do their work where their daughters are concerned. But not my dad. A secretary brought me to my baptism. I have the pictures to prove it.

"There's a very important matter that your father—and the Company—need your help with. I'm sure you've heard of HR watchers?"

"Yes."

"And you know what they do?"

"Yeah. They spy on people. Turn them in for cursing and stuff."

"Well," Blackwell says, "sometimes. Sometimes they do more important things than that. They help squadmen enforce Company HR policy. For example, if somebody were going to steal your dad's car, you'd tell someone, right? And if, say, somebody was going to sabotage a Company product—like an imager—you'd want to stop them, because what if a bunch of people bought the sabotaged imagers and they were defective? Think of how disappointed they'd be. Or if somebody burned down a Company building, then people would have no place to go to work."

"But why would somebody do something like that to their own Company? That's stupid," I say.

"Of course it is. But there are bad people out there who want to hurt the Company, because they don't understand how many good things we do. Unprofitables. These people are very sick, very confused, very dangerous. And I'm afraid you might know one of them."

"Who?" I ask, shocked. I glance over at Randal for some hint, but he doesn't look at me.

"He's the father of one of your friends."

"Who?"

A swirl of falling leaves mirrors the confusion in my mind.

"Kali." It's Randal who speaks. I look at him.

"What?"

"You're going to help us find out what he's doing," Blackwell says, "and then we're going to apprehend him."

"What? No!"

"No?"

"I can't do that to Kali!"

"But you'd be saving Kali," Blackwell says. "And your father. And yourself."

"What do you mean?"

"I'll show you."

Blackwell reaches into the pocket of his jacket, pulls out an IC, and touches the screen. There, suddenly, are Kali and me, in my bedroom. Kissing. The blush in my cheeks burns until I think it will sear my skin. Kissing a girl is a major breach of N-Ed policy, and I know it. With an image like that, I could be kicked out of school—and the Company—forever. I could become an unprofitable myself. And so could Kali.

"Put it away," I say weakly.

"You know," Blackwell muses, "footage like this could fetch a pretty penny in the right circles."

"Put it away!"

This time, something in my voice makes him comply. The IC disappears into a pocket of the big coat. He shakes his head.

"May Fields. Such immodesty. Think of how that scene could shame you. And now of all times, when you're about to start applying for your Company position. You'd never pass the morality check, not with this floating around. Think, you could wind up on the cleaning service—or worse. And with your father's position as CEO up for review, something like this becoming public could ruin him altogether."

For a moment, Blackwell and I lock eyes. I'm caught somewhere between crying and punching him in the face.

"You're threatening me," I say, my voice tremulous with anger. "I'll tell my father."

"Your father won't be able to do much about it, after he's been thrown off the board for raising a pervert. Remember, May, upright moral conduct is a cornerstone of N-Corp "

"My father is a great man. You could never get him fired."

"Little May. Your father might be a big fish, but he doesn't control the ocean."

"I'll tell the Company. I'll go to your superiors."

"This errand is on behalf of the Company, May."

"I'll tell . . . I'll tell . . ." And that's just it; there's no one else to tell. Blackwell stares at me.

"Welcome to the life of a watcher, May. Don't be so upset. Everyone has to do it sooner or later. And if you do well today, you might go far. I can promise you this, you'll get your position in the marketing department. And this kid—" he nods at Randal, "he'll get to go and play with the geniuses."

"Cranton?" I say. "He hasn't even tested yet."

"It's been decided," says Blackwell, rising. "It's all been decided. Next time we meet you'll tell me what you've seen. And this—hide this someplace in your friend Kali's apartment. We'll take care of the rest." He hands me a tiny metal object, no larger than a breath mint. "God bless you both," he says, and just like that, he leaves.

Raindrops start falling, huge and frigid. Blackwell's footfalls clatter away along the water-darkened pavement. For a moment, there's no sound but the patter of rain on leaves.

"I know what you're going to say," Randal begins. Without another thought, my hands shoot out, striking him in the center of the ribcage, and I shove him to the grass.

"It was a secret, Randal! I thought you were my friend!" I shout.

"He said they were going to take you down, May! You and your dad. I had to give them something; I had no choice."

The only answer is the rush and tick of the rain. I stare at Randal, trying to set him on fire with my eyes.

"You'll get to train for the marketing department, May. And I'm gonna be in the tech development tier! I'm gonna be a Blackie," he continues. "Everything's working out like it should. And Kali . . . Kali is no good for you anyway."

"Go to hell, Randal." I say, and stalk off into the downpour.

I won't see him again for weeks. He'll train for the next two years at the tech development school in N-Hub 3 before finally taking up his position at Cranton. I'll only see him once more before he leaves. After that, he'll try sending me e-mails for a while, telling me about how much he loves his new school, telling me about his new best friend—some guy training for an HR psychology position. He'll try to convince me that what we did was for the best. I'll delete the e-mails without replying. Years later when we happen to get assigned to the budget presentation together, the allure of a familiar face will be strong enough to make me forgive and forget.

Today, though, I wander in the rain. And tonight, I'll see my Kali for the second to last time.

CHAPTER 011

The elevator plummets, and I descend into the bowels of Cranton. On the lowest floor, I hurry past hallways: X hall, Y hall, and finally Z hall. Here, a thick black door that looks as if it's made of carbon fiber stands closed. I step toward it, hoping to hear the familiar chirp as the door reads my cross and slides open. Instead, Eva consoles me: *Sorry, May Fields. Clearance denied.*

I grit my teeth in frustration and weigh my options. I could try to get clearance, but that would raise all kinds of red flags. I could bring my father down here—as CEO, he has access to all Company doors. But who knows where he is now? He might be halfway across the world on business for all I know. One thing is certain: I have to get in here, and I have to get in now.

Just then, I hear the voices of two men coming down the hall. I silently slip behind a marble column and listen as the Peakers approach.

"The levels of d-dark matter are negligible," the first one says.

"It's still enough to disrupt the experiment if we d-don't neutralize it."

They're close. I hold my breath, waiting to be discovered, but instead the electronic door voice pipes up: *Mr. Reyes, Mr. Mason, welcome to Black Brands.*

Then comes the whoosh of the door sliding open and the clatter of footsteps as the Peakers pass inside and down the hall. Without a second thought, I dash out from my hiding place and shoot through the doorway.

"I just don't see how it's going to work . . ." one of the Peakers is saying, as I slip behind them and take cover next to another large fake plant.

The door whooshes shut again behind me. The Peakers' footsteps fade away down the hall. I'm shocked and strangely concerned at how easy all that was. For better or worse, I am now inside Black Brands. I step out from behind my plant and head down the hallway, trying to walk with purpose so as to not appear out of place.

This hall is no different from the others in Cranton: rich-looking red wallpaper and strange paintings adorn the walls. Big fake plants are everywhere. Classical music murmurs from the ceiling. But something is different. I can feel it.

Now, on my right, I approach a heavy-looking paneled door. With one hand on the door-handle, I take a deep breath, then push it open and poke my head in. If the rest of Black Brands were to be judged by the contents of this room, it must be a pretty benign place. There's a big conference table, a bunch of chairs, and an electronic chalkboard full of mathematical equations.

I proceed to the next door. This room is as strange as the last was boring. It appears to be a medical exam room of some sort. White walls surround a ceramic medical table, on which the body of a middle-aged man rests. I look up and down the hall to be sure no one is coming, then step inside the room. Slowly, I approach the exam table.

The cadaver is wrapped in a white sheet with only his waxy-looking face exposed. The cross that was in his cheek has been pulled partway out. Wires run from the cross and appear to be connected deep inside the dead man's face. On the wall, an imager screen hangs. Ones and zeros flit across a black background. All is silent here save for the distant whir of the air conditioner. Suddenly, the sound seems to surround me, and I get the disturbing impression that I'm at the center of some giant, humming machine. The dead man's eyes stare emptily toward the ceiling. I lean closer to him, staring in fascination and disgust at the slit in his cheek.

Suddenly, he blinks.

I gasp and stumble backward until my back is pressed against the door. My hand fumbles for the handle, then in an instant I'm back in the hallway, my heart thumping wildly. But there's no time to catch my breath. Up the hall, two patrolling squadmen hear me burst into the hallway. I watch in horror as they turn toward me—but already, I'm ducking into another door, slamming it shut behind me.

When I turn to face this new room, I'm shocked to find five people seated at a conference table, blinking at me expectantly. Two of them are the men I followed into Black Brands. The other three are woman. Then all smile at me strangely as I hold my breath, calculating my next move.

I'm even more surprised when one of the men stands and extends a hand.

"You must be Doctor Mullins," he says. "I'm Walter Reyes. Thank you so m-much for coming all the way from Cranton West to join us. Please, sit."

This is all too strange, too surreal. Who the hell do they think I am? What am I supposed to do? But I have no time to think, no chance to form a plan. If I go out into the hall, the squadmen will snatch me up for sure. All I can do is muster a smile and take the chair I'm offered.

"Nice to meet you," I say, casually wiping at the sheen of sweat that's suddenly appeared on my forehead.

"First, let me just say we're all big fans of your work," Reyes says. "We've read all your memos."

"Thank you," I say.

"So let's get right down to it," Reyes says, and they all stare at me expectantly. Several of them have their ICs out, ready to take down notes on whatever it is I'm supposed to say. I shift in my seat, clear my throat.

"Why, uh ... why don't you start?" I suggest.

Reyes seems taken aback for a second then nods. "Oh, you mean start with what we know of your work?"

"Exactly."

Reyes glances at his colleague, Mason, who begins. "Okay, maybe we should start with your nano-poisons. You've developed over two thousand different varieties, each of them completely programmable and able to attack a d-different type of cell."

Flashing before my eyes, I see an image of the little boy on the Africa Division hilltop, his arm extended, finger pointing, as he falls to the dust. I see the dart in his neck. A dart that, I suspect, must have been filled with nano-poison.

"Why?" I ask, my voice quivering.

Reyes and Mason glance at one another, perplexed.

"Excuse me?" Reyes says.

Mason turns to him with disdain. "It's Socratic questioning, moron," he says, then turns back to me with a confident grin. "Right, Doctor. I understand. We use the nano-p-poison because it's more humane than other poisons. And undetectable. And when we get quantities up, it'll be cheaper than bullets, right?"

Everyone laughs except me.

"Sorry," I say, trying hard to keep my voice steady. "Humor me while I play devil's advocate here. What I'm asking is, why are we making these poisons in the first place?"

Reyes looks at me, mystified. "Because," he says, "it's our j-job."

To that, I can make no response. I sit there, frozen, mortified, until from behind me I hear the sound of the door opening. I turn to see a silver-haired woman entering.

"Terribly sorry I'm late," she says, and introduces herself: "Edna M-M-Mullins."

Instantly, all eyes are on me.

"What—?" Reyes blurts, rising to his feet.

But I'm already halfway to the door.

"Excuse me," I mumble, shoving my way past Dr. Mullins and out into the hallway. Then, I run.

Hundreds of paneled doors streak past on either side of me, but I lack the courage to open any of them. All I can do is run, faster and faster, until I've fled this place and all the horrible meaning it contains. Ahead, the hallway dead-ends at two heavy, metal doors. I blast through them and find myself in a warehouse of unbelievable scale. The walls could be a mile distant. The ceiling seems a thousand feet away. I sprint down aisleway after aisleway and am surrounded at every turn by horrors:

Crate after crate of strange, black guns.

Rows of large, flying drones.

Ranks of fearsome-looking robots.

And racks and racks of small, black, triangular aircraft, the same ones from McCann's video. The labels on the racks read: *Ravers*. Next to that, the N-Corp logo.

Even in repose, the aircraft are terrifying to behold. Small, dark disks—probably infrared sensors—seem to watch me as I hurry past. I half expect to see the Ravers rise one by one, hover slowly but inexorably toward me, then fill me with a thousand darts full of nano-poison death.

I run, faster and harder than I've ever run before. After sprinting for what seems like hours, I reach the outer perimeter of the warehouse, find a bank of elevators, ride them up to the main level, then pick my way through the maze-like corridors of Cranton. By the time I finally make it out, tears have already risen to my eyes and then dried again. I stumble down the Cranktown steps and linger at the edge of the street, watching the traffic lurch and stop, lurch and stop, staring at the taillights like some lunatic unprofitable.

In this moment, I feel utterly hollow, empty enough that the wind could blow right through me. My hands tremble. My head pounds. Across the street, a huge sign reads: N-Shopping.

I don't so much walk as drift toward it. I have no sensation of my feet touching the ground. I can hardly hear the cars honking all around me. The slogans blaring from the imagers wash over me as imperceptibly as the faintest breeze. All I feel is my brow, knotted, furrowed, heavy, as the weight of my thoughts presses down on me. I imagine that the weight, the pressure, will either crush my spirit completely or temper it, harden it, turn it into something new—as coal under tremendous pressure becomes a diamond.

Welcome, May Fields. A fifty-dollar entry fee has been added to your account. Have a blessed day.

The chaos of the shopping plaza mirrors the confusion in my mind. Dazed, milling shoppers choke the great marbled halls. A handsome young man pauses to swallow a handful of pills. Squadmen patrol the area, moving slowly and deliberately through the crowd like sharks through a school of fish. Store windows showcase the new fall line. It's just the same as last year's—only twice as expensive. To my left, I notice a woman arguing with a retail manager.

"N-Corp is very sorry, but there are no refunds," the manager says. "Next in line."

"The thing was broken when I got it!" the woman protests.

But the manager has already forgotten her. He cranes his neck to see the rest of the waiting customers. "Next in line!"

A moment later, two sweaty tie-men duck out of a storefront labeled N-Surance and hustle toward me.

The taller one shouts: "Hey! Miss! We got the best deal around on health insurance!"

"You can't pass this up," the shorter one says. "Just let us show you some numbers."

I push my way past them, but they hurry along with me.

"Two hundred K a month, full coverage!" one says.

"Today only: free luggage when you sign up."

I double my pace, suddenly ill, but the taller one grabs my arm, desperate to detain me.

"Come on, just give us five minutes!" he says. "We got a quota to hit!"

I pull away from him and keep walking as his pleading fades into the murmur of the crowd: "Please! Come on, please!"

Ahead, an unspeakably handsome man stands at a kiosk, with his equally adorable little son. Suddenly, a shrill beeping sound emanates from the checkout.

"You have exceeded your credit limit, Mr. Blanford. Prepare to be detained."

The man backs away, but before he can run three squadmen have laid hold of him and are dragging him away.

The little boy stands frozen in place, watching as his dad disappears behind a pair of steel doors set into the shopping plaza wall. "Daddy?" he calls.

But the doors are shut. It's as if his dad never existed at all. The boy's head swivels as he looks around in confusion, searching for something or someone—his mother, maybe. Instead, his eyes find mine. They're brimming with tears.

Suddenly, I'm running again. *I can't be responsible,* I think over and over again. Not for the little boy. Not for the Company. Not for Kali.

Not for any of this. It's not my problem if these stupid tie-men can't hit their quota, or if Dagny outspent her productivity and got repossessed. It's a competitive world. Hard workers win; lazy people fail. That's the natural way: it's called justice. So what if a few weak losers end up suffering to pave the way for the rest of us to live in luxury? Why should strong, successful people like me waste five minutes worrying about unprofitables? They aren't my responsibility.

These are the thoughts I've consoled myself with my entire life, but now, for some reason I can't fathom, they fill me with a nameless horror. *Because they're lies,* a voice inside me says. *They've always been lies, and you know it.*

Nauseated, I make my way to the nearest wall and lean there. Sweat covers my forehead. My legs shaking, I slide along the wall to a corner, where a cherry panel meets a marble column, and take out my IC.

Ethan's words ring through my head: *You have to go to your father. Get his help. The Company has to be stopped. . . .*

As I pull up my father's number on my IC, I glance over my shoulder. Is it my imagination or are those tie-men following me? And if they are, who do they work for, the Protectorate—or the Company?

My IC connects.

Dyanne's voice sounds shrill and strange when she answers.

"Hellooo?"

"Where's my dad?"

"Who is this?"

"Who do you think? I need to talk to him."

I glance over at the tie-men who were following me. They've disappeared—for now.

"Well," Dyanne drawls, "your father's in a board meeting right now. . . ."

"Where?"

There's a slight pause. "It's a closed meeting, May."

"That's perfect," I say. "Where?"

N-Corp Cathedral.

The polished steel panels of the walls intertwine. Their shapes evoke a feeling of movement, almost seeming to swoop like soaring angels around the grand, stained-glass windows before ascending to an expansive domed ceiling almost as high as heaven itself. Many skylights stare up at the nightfall. The carpet underfoot is plush, my steps silent. I pass between suede-covered pews—each with its own row of small, square imager screens, all dark. The immensity of this space can only be compared to that of a football stadium or a large combat arena. But there is no crowd here tonight. Only me.

I hurry down one of many aisles, toward the point where they all converge: it is the decadently ornate pulpit familiar to every N-Corp employee, perhaps to every person in the world. *The Jimmy Shaw Hour in Christ* films here.

Behind the pulpit, a three-story-tall cross rises from the floor, huge and gray. Without warning, it startles me by coming alive with a swirling, beautiful array of light. After a moment, the various shapes and hues finally coalesce into the form of a crucified Christ, complete with bleeding wounds and slowly blinking eyes. The image—that's all it is, of course; the cross itself is just a huge 3-D imager screen—is startlingly, disturbingly lifelike. The activated cross now bathes the whole darkened sanctuary in eerie light.

I rush forward to a small door near the base of the cross. I have never been behind the scenes of Jimmy's show, so I don't know where the hallway leads. All I know is that my father is here somewhere, and

I have to find him. The staircase behind the cross is completely dark, its shadows stirred to life only by the flickering of the cross above.

I descend. My footsteps carry me down the staircase for what must be two, three, four stories. At the base of the stairs, one lone squad guard steps out of the shadows. Behind him: one more door.

"Stop," he says to me. He asks for no explanation, and I offer none. I watch him in the tenuous light, staring down at the screen of his IC. After a moment, it beeps.

I fully expect to be arrested, detained, fined, demoted. Instead, the squad member nods to me. "Welcome, Miss Fields. They've been expecting you."

That's disconcerting, since I wasn't expecting to be here myself. . . .

He opens the door for me, and I pass through. The room I enter is large, but still ringed in darkness. At its center, an overhead light shines down on a conference table. There's Yao, Jimmy Shaw, my father, and several other people whose names escape me. Leaning against the far wall, his arms folded, stands Blackwell.

At first, no one notices my presence.

Yao leans forward and places a data stick in the center of the table.

"This is the list," she says. "Black Brands division will handle the processing. For both companies combined, the number will be one million thirty-seven thousand."

The others nod slowly. That's when Dad notices me.

He half rises, alarmed. "May? What are you doing here?"

I step forward into the light. Blackwell approaches the table, too, from the opposite side.

"It's okay," Blackwell sooths my father. "Welcome, Miss Fields. I'm glad you made it. We were just discussing the red slips."

"Red slips?"

"Terminations of employment," Jimmy Shaw offers. He notices my bewilderment and adds, "What, didn't you get the memo?"

Several men at the table laugh. My father does not. He clears his throat. "We're merging with B&S, hon. It's gonna be huge. We'll be able to cut a lot of useless jobs. Bring in low-credit-level workers from places like Africa Division to phase out some higher-credit-level folks. Cost savings will be in the hundreds of trillions. Gonna be great for the bottom line." He smiles that charming old salesman's smile, but there's a note of weariness in his tone. "Sorry I couldn't tell you sooner."

"What happens to the workers who get terminated?" I ask, my voice so low even I can hardly hear it.

"What's that?" my dad asks.

Blackwell's dark eyes stare into mine. "They'll be released from service as efficiently as possible."

"How?" The word is like a stone dropped into a deep well.

"This merger will be one of the greatest events of our time, Miss Fields," Shaw says. "And you have a role to play."

Yao nods at Shaw, who rises and approaches me. My dad starts to stand too, but Yao puts a hand on his arm, stopping him.

Shaw puts his arm around my shoulder and leads me out of the room.

I look back at my father, but he stares down at the table, his face veiled in shadow, refusing to meet my gaze.

"Come, my dear," Jimmy Shaw croons into my ear. "I'm going to let you in on our little plan."

Shaw leads me out into nave of the church, bathed in the muted light of the Company cross.

"Thank God I got you alone, Jimmy," I say. "You're the only one I can trust."

Jimmy, my father's oldest and most trusted friend. My lifelong moral compass. My spiritual leader. Surely if anyone will understand my concerns, it will be him. He nods, a sad smile plastered across his saintly old face.

"Of course, my dear," he says. "Mr. Blackwell analyzed your viewing habits. It seems you're quite a fan of my show."

He's right. I hardly miss an episode. In the plastic, shallow, material world that surrounds me, Jimmy Shaw and the idea of God have sometimes been the only things that seemed to keep me afloat.

"I love your show, Jimmy," I admit. "Sometimes I feel like you're the only one in the Company who's actually sincere."

He pats my hand gently then releases it.

"Of course, my dear. Of course. . . . Girls!" he shouts.

From a door on the far left side of this stage, three women enter. They wear frocks of blue, not unlike the one Jimmy Shaw wears during his televised sermons, but these are cut short, exposing lean, smooth legs and high heels. All three women have long blond hair and fake breasts, which seem to struggle to break free from the confines of their religious habit. These altar girls stop at the edge of the stage and stand still, presumably awaiting instruction.

I take a tremulous breath. At first, Shaw's presence was calming me, but now I'm getting nervous again. "So, Reverend Shaw . . . the plan?" I say.

Shaw only smiles. He steps over to a basin of holy water, dabs some on his fingers, then walks over and presses his wet, age-gnarled fingers to the cross on my face, tracing it tenderly. "Little wandering sheep," he says, looking at me with a stare so probing I can only stand it for a second before having to avert my eyes. "Do you have a confession for me?"

I nod.

"Jimmy," I begin quietly, "I think something terrible is going to happen to those terminated workers."

Shaw nods thoughtfully. "That is serious, indeed," he says. "We'd better have a good talk." He glances toward his altar girls. "Bring us a chair, honey," he says to one of them, "and a bottle of wine."

I look at him, startled, but he's already walking away from me, to a huge, bejeweled throne at the foot of the cross. He sits with a heavy sigh, and then glances up at the towering Jesus.

"Looks bigger on TV, doesn't he? I mean, on the imager?" he says, and laughs.

I nod, glancing around the room. "This whole place is beautiful," I say. "I haven't been here in a long time."

One of the buxom altar girls approaches with a chair, and I go to sit.

"Bring it closer, closer," says Shaw with that familiar, endearing-yet-commanding drawl with which he addresses the worldwide masses. "I want us to have a good talk, and I don't want anything, not even a few feet of air, to come between us."

I pull my chair closer, and he motions me closer, then closer still. When my knees bump into his, he closes his eyes and nods. I sit.

"You seem so distressed, dear," says Jimmy, laying one big, soft hand on mine. "Don't you remember when old Uncle Jimmy would come over for meetings with your daddy and bring you candy canes?"

It's been years and years ago now, but . . . "I remember."

"Well, today is no different. Not a bit. I'm here today as your loving uncle once again, and though my duties have kept me very busy and far away from you, don't ever think I forgot that willful little girl with that sassy mouth and those big, dark eyes."

"I'm still a willful girl," I say. "I guess that's why I'm here."

Jimmy laughs. Above him, Jesus disappears and the cross roils with swirling color again. "I never expected anything else from a child of your father's, believe you me!" he says. "Take your little indiscretion at the N-Dance club the other day. Oh, yes, Blackwell told me all about it, my dear. Could have been quite an embarrassment for your father, May. Quite a few people were surprised by your . . . unusual passion. But never old Jimmy. It takes a good deal more than that to surprise me. No, I've always known you were different and have always been your champion, though I bet you never knew it. Your father and I, we have great faith in you. I've always said, the further a person has to fall, the better their balance!"

Jimmy chuckles until it devolves into a bout of coughing.

One of the women comes back with a bottle of wine. Shaw gestures to her and she hands me a glass and begins pouring.

"Oh, I . . ." I begin. "I don't drink."

Shaw laughs again. "Why, because it's against Company policy? Don't worry about that here. You're in the house of God! Here, wine is Christ's blood, and believe me, we drink our sacrament by the case, don't we, ladies?" His altar girls giggle.

The woman fills a glass for me and for Jimmy, then sets the bottle down and withdraws.

Shaw takes a long, slurping sip then wipes his mouth with the back of his hand.

"Where was I?" he asks. "Oh yes, I was your champion. I promise you, May, there were many *many* folks, some of them on the board, who feel a woman with your . . . secret proclivities . . . deserves no place in the high-executive ranks, much less a shot at rising to the board or becoming a Blackie. Frankly, I think some of those men are just jealous that a delicious young morsel like yourself is permanently off their menu. And you can tell me truthfully, you do like women, don't you?"

I don't answer. I look down at the wine glass in my hand. A sickening realization barges into my head: this might be a trap. If I have a drink, or if I admit to loving women, they could use it against me. One slip could mean the end of my life with the Company—or worse. But Jimmy wouldn't betray me like that—would he?

"Drink some wine," says Shaw, almost without pause. "You look so pale! That nasty unprofitable woman who kidnapped you the other day must've really frightened you! You look positively shaken up!"

I feign a smile.

"Fortunately," Shaw says, "we caught her fairly easily, God be praised. She was foolish enough to be caught at a shopping plaza trying to buy food—probably provisions for her anarchist buddies. My PR team and I spun the story to make it sound like you were responsible for the arrest. No need to thank me."

My mind is on Clair and what's going to happen to her, and Shaw seems to realize it.

"Don't worry about your anarchist friends, May. We'll catch every one of those rats soon enough and hang them all, I promise you that. But they aren't the only ones I'm worried about. As impossible to comprehend as it is, there may be enemies of the Company even among our employees and shareholders. Shocking, I know, and hard to imagine. But let's think about it. Let's put ourselves in the shoes of these anarchists. You're a smart girl, May. A good God-fearing girl, though you're a homosexual and hence cursed in God's eyes. You tell me. Why would anybody want to hurt the Company?"

"Do you know about Black Brands?" I ask him. "What they really do?"

"I know about everything," he snaps, rising to his feet. "Now I asked you a question. Why would anyone want to hurt the Company?"

Jimmy Shaw isn't going to help me, I suddenly realize with a horrible, plummeting sensation. Nobody is.

"I don't know," I mumble.

"May Fields, do not mess with me, do not trifle with me, do not dream of concealing even an ounce of yourself from me while you're here, in God's house!" he shouts, jabbing his trademark cane toward me like the barrel of a gun. "God sees everything. And you know what? I am his eyes, his ears, his mouth, and sometimes even his teeth.

"I ask you again," he says, pacing the stage. "What reason could you imagine for anybody to want to hurt the Company?"

It takes me a moment to muster words, for the muscles of my face feel frozen with emotion. "Because," I say, "the Company hurts people."

"What?" says Shaw, full of fire and brimstone. "Speak up!"

"Because," I say, "I imagine, because . . . people never really own anything they have. It all belongs to the Company. They can only learn the things that the Company wants them to learn, and see the things the Company wants them to see. They can only eat the things the Company gives them, and in exchange, they have to work for the Company forever, even until they're old, until the day they die. Then their kids inherit their debt."

Shaw nods a big sarcastic nod. "That's true," he says. "God as my witness, all of it is true and more. But one thing you forgot, little sister—it's been that way since the beginning of time. Somebody rules, everyone else is led. But the Company has been the most generous ruler in the history of the world, hasn't it? Twenty-one percent of the population of America Division has been to the moon on vacation. Doesn't that strike you as generous, even extraordinary? Most people have fast, sleek cars. They can afford surgery to make themselves beautiful, medicine to make themselves healthy, happy, and eternally young; they have gadgets, imagers, and robots to entertain them at every hour of the day or night. We have taken the garden God gave us and tamed it, replaced the poison apples with sweet, nutritious health bars, made all the wonders of creation available to anyone willing to sign on to the Company payroll. Is that wrong?"

Shaw builds up steam, sometimes turning his burning gaze on me, sometimes calling his words out to the ceiling, as if speaking to God Himself. "We have united the world—not under two flags, but under two logos—ours and B&S's!" he shouts. "And until that ugly incident at Headquarters, we had brought peace to the human race. We have carried nearly every single employee of both Companies to Christ. Do you know how extraordinary that is? We have created the perfect world God envisioned. We have rebuilt the Garden of Eden! All we ask in exchange is a little hard work!"

Jimmy suddenly approaches me, his nose an inch from mine. "Is that your problem? You don't think people should have to work? Well, May—truth be told, we don't need them to work. We have machines and computers that can accomplish almost everything society needs done. We don't need the people's labor; it's the other way around. It's the people who need the work, because idle hands belong to the Devil. Constant work is among the greatest gifts the Company gives its people. We want them occupied, because hardworking people are too busy to commit crime, too busy to be discontent, too busy to be unhappy. And all we really want here at the Company is for everyone to be happy. Is that too much to ask, May Fields? I'm asking you. Is it?"

The old man is red-faced when he finishes his speech. The beautiful women, standing in their robes at the edge of the stage, nod in approval. One of them claps. Shaw takes one last look at me, to be sure I have no rebuttal, then grins, turns to the cross, points his cane at it, and yells, "Hallelujah!"

"Amen," the altar girls respond in a dissonant chorus.

"Uh . . . one thing," I say.

Shaw looks back at me, still smiling, eyebrows raised.

"What about Black Brands?"

"Excuse me?"

"What about the people who disagree. People who, say, quit. Or are terminated. What about the people who can't work, or who refuse to buy only what the Company sells, or who disagree with Company policy, or who violate the HR handbook? What about people who are good and capable and hardworking but just aren't suited to the job the Company wants them to do?"

Shaw's smile fades. He looks at me hard. "They're transferred to other locations."

"Where?"

"To other, various Company locations to which they might be more suited. Or to work camps."

"And what happens to people in work camps who break the rules? Or people who . . . who . . . I'm talking about—"

"Yes, May, what *are* you talking about?"

"People who don't want to be in either Company, who don't want to be in any Company at all?"

Shaw moves toward me slowly.

I continue, "In the history of the Company, especially in the beginning, there must have been people who opposed the Company, who didn't want to be a part of it. People who wanted to start their own businesses or something. Even now, someplace, there must be people who just refuse to be told what to watch and who to worship and what job they can do. Why don't we ever hear about them?"

"You must be referring," says Shaw, "to devil worshipers and anarchists. Unprofitables. Yes, they exist. Most are in jail, or dead. Eventually, they all will be. They are of no concern to the hardworking, God-fearing, Company-loving people of the world. You see, Company people live in bliss, working hard, knowing that the harder they work,

the more their credit will go up and allow them to have all the beautiful things their hearts desire. A few might even become Blackies. Most
will not, but hey, it's a dream. And what greater gift can you give someone than a dream? An anarchist, on the other hand, has no dreams.
He simply lives in misery, with no Company to protect him, no way of
getting the things he needs, no pride, no joy, no pleasure, no God. The
anarchist will die young and hungry while the Company tie-man lives
on, grows fat, and dies old and happy, drenched in luxury, saturated
with pleasure, smiling, sucking from the tit of abundance until the last
sweet drop. Do you prefer the ways of the anarchist? Do you want to
cast yourself out of the Garden? Do you think, May, that your twisted
desires would be accepted among those cursed few who live outside
the light of the Church and the walls of the Company? Because if you
want to be an anarchist, you can be one. I'll simply snap my fingers
now, and we can hang you like an anarchist right this minute."

Movement above catches my attention. Up in the balcony, several
squadmen linger. Rifles in their hands glint in the feeble light.

Shaw smiles at me. "There have been many, many, who've said that
a woman like you has no place in this Company except at the lowest
level. And, of course, those who betray the Company are punished
with death. On the other hand, there are some, like me, like your father,
who are quite fond of you, who see your potential and who might be
inclined to clear your way to a higher station in life. We might even
be induced to support your bid to become CEO one day. In light of
recent events, you could be positioned to come across as a hero. The
media campaign has already begun. We could make your life quite
divine—if, of course, you were willing to do us one small favor."

"What?" I whisper.

"You see, that foul rebel Ethan Greene and his rabble trust you.
That makes you the only one who can help us catch them."

Silence hangs heavily around me as Shaw's words sink in.

"Are you willing to help us?" he presses. "Are you willing to serve your Company?"

I hesitate, glancing once again at the riflemen up on the balcony.

"Yes," I murmur. "Of course."

Shaw's eyes narrow. "But you harbor reservations."

"No," I lie. "I love the Company. And I watch your show all the time, I really do."

"No reservations?" Shaw leans close to me. "Make sure you're honest with me, May. No reservations at all?"

"No," I say. "None."

Shaw's stare pierces me; then he smiles.

"Let me show you something," he says. "I think you'll like this."

Stepping over to his pulpit, he takes out an old-fashioned remote control and presses a few buttons. Suddenly, the swirling colors that had engulfed the massive cross give way to blackness. He presses another button, and the lights of the sanctuary dim even further. Shapes become indistinct. The gigantic room feels suddenly, eerily like a cavern. I shiver.

A shape condenses in the darkness, moving toward me. It's Shaw. He leans close to me and whispers, "Watch."

He presses a few buttons on the remote control, and on the great cross, tiny white figures appear, trickling back and forth against a field of black, like lines of marching ants. There must be millions of them, filing across the massive imager. At first, I can't tell what they are, but as I squint and lean forward, I realize what I'm seeing—ones and zeroes, thousands of them. I stare in wonder.

"Do you know what that is?" Shaw whispers.

"No."

"Well," he says, "I'm no scientist, mind you. But the boys at Cranton assure us that everything in the world, every color, word, idea, even every emotion, can be codified with two figures as simple as ones and zeroes, the digital language. Take brain function, for example. I don't know much about it, myself, but they tell me that most brain cells aren't good for much but making an electric charge. It's like a light switch—there are two settings, on and off, charge and no charge, and they can be represented by two figures, in this case one and zero. It's probably much more complex than that, but that's how they explained it to this ignorant old man. The code you see in front of you represents the brain function of an individual, an employee of N-Corp, as a matter of fact. And our brilliant Cranton boys assure me that they've figured out how to codify and record the thoughts and emotions of an entire human brain with figures just like that. Ones and zeroes. I think it's pretty amazing, don't you? And they can decode the meaning of the thoughts, too—tell exactly what people are thinking at any time of the day or night. Isn't that something? Now whose thoughts do you think those are, up there?"

The huge cross: cloaked in drifting pieces of a human mind. I open my mouth to answer Jimmy's question, but my thoughts scatter like sand in the wind. All I can do is sit and watch the numbers stream past. Then, a horrible idea hits me, and as it does, the stream of numbers changes. They are still moving, but the pace has slowed. I can hardly breathe.

"Is it . . . do those thoughts belong to . . . ?"

"Yes?" prompts Shaw, and I feel him smiling at me through the darkness.

"I want to say . . . are they from . . . ?"

And Jimmy Shaw says it: "From . . . you?"

I'm mesmerized by the numbers—zero, one, one, one, one, zero, one, zero, zero, one, zero, one, zero, zero, zero, one, zero . . .

"Of course they belong to you," Shaw says. "Didn't you recognize your own thoughts?"

He starts chuckling, then laughing loudly. When I say nothing, he laughs even harder.

"I told you not to lie to me in the house of God, didn't I? But I'll tell you, May, it doesn't matter where you are, we can read you from anyplace! We know you're queer. We know you spent time in the anarchist camp, and we'd have tracked them down because of you, too, but it took some time to recover your thought data because you hit your head so hard jumping from the chopper. We also know you sympathize with those rebel mongrels, deep down in your pathetic, misfit heart. Well, out of respect for your father, instead of tossing you in jail and throwing away the key, we're going to allow you one last chance at redemption. All you have to do is infiltrate the rebel ranks again. We'll track you to their refuge and exterminate them. And if you refuse? Well, remember when you asked what happened to all the people who disagree with the Company? You see those numbers up there? It's as easy as changing a few zeroes to ones or ones to zeroes, and suddenly—voilà—a person's outlook changes. They go from being a queer, masculine, rebellious misfit of a girl to being—well, maybe even to being the CEO of the Company one day, who knows? And if that doesn't change your crooked ways, we can always cut your throat and let God sort you out. It's all up to you, sweetie pie."

Jimmy Shaw leans heavily on his cane as he straightens up.

"You'll go to find the rebels tomorrow, and you'll go alone. They trust you. They'll let you in, and we'll trace you to them using your cross. Just get yourself into their midst and we'll take it from there."

I stand, trembling. I feel the blood beating through my veins. My flushed face burns. Tears are running down my face, although I hardly notice. I take a few steps down the aisle, then turn back. There's something else, one other thing I have to know before I leave this place.

"Jimmy," I ask quietly, "do you believe in God?"

He looks over at his altar girls, and with a nod of his head sends them away. In a flutter of blue robes, they disappear into the shadows. There's the sound of a door closing, then Shaw turns back to me and smiles. His eyes glitter wickedly. "I believe God-fearing workers work harder, May," he says. "And if you want to sit on the board one day, that's all you need to know."

His raucous laughter follows me as I turn and stride down the aisle. "Welcome to the Company, May," he calls after me. "Welcome to the inside!"

Outside the church, everything looks the same as it always has: throngs of fashionable people pass on the sidewalk, streetlights burn, and imager screens flash my ads for the new IC.

But nothing is the same.

—CHAPTER Ø12—

The rain has stopped, but dark clouds still linger.

My fifteen-year-old self walks fast. The steel of the moving sidewalk buzzing beneath my feet is perfectly clean. Looking around, one might even think this a pleasant place to live. At first glance, the low-credit-level arc seems to represent one of my father's great achievements: every one of these buildings is owned by N-Corp, and everyone who lives here owes his livelihood to the Company. But passing through it today, for the first time I begin to see the differences between this area and the Blackie arc where I've always lived. Here, instead of mirror and marble, the buildings are faced with mildewed stucco. Windows are cracked. One of the crosswalk signs is broken and stares at me, dead. All around: the faint smell of urine, but no hint of the animal or person who made it. Why did I never notice these things before?

It's not a long train ride to where the mid-level tie-men live, but those few miles make a world of difference. I step off the moving sidewalk and onto the cement. At my feet, I see a solitary soda can, the only piece of litter in sight, and I give it a good kick. Seemingly out of nowhere, an old man—probably eighty years old—steps forward, stoops down with a breathy *humph*, and snatches up the can. He tosses it into a plastic trash bin and walks on, pulling the bin behind him. I look for the name under the N-Corp logo on his shirt, but I can't make it out. He smiles at me as he passes, a nearly toothless jack-o'-lantern grin. He must not have earned enough credit privileges to afford a dentist, I muse. But bless him; he's on the right track. If he keeps on working so diligently, in a few years they'll raise his credit limit and he'll be able to get some dentures.

Ahead, the door to Kali's building waits beneath a great banner bearing the N-Corp logo and the words: Eat N-Soy, taste the health!

When I reach out to press my thumb to the security scan, I see the door is broken and hanging open. So much for security. I stroll in. The elevator screeches and shudders its way upward and finally deposits me on the third floor. There, with a heavy heart, I knock on Kali's door.

In most ways, this is almost a normal evening. Kali's mother is out working. She's been pulling double shifts all week, which means she's only home around eight hours per day. Kali's wench of an older sister is off wherever she goes—some sort of job, I guess. And Kali's father is nowhere to be seen. Probably, he's at work, too.

Even though I'm young, I already know enough to realize they'll never be Blackies, although ostensibly that is the goal every lower-credit-level worker sacrifices almost every waking hour to achieve.

All I care about is the fact that they're never around. Kali and I get to sit on the couch alone and relax. Pure heaven. But when I suggest she turn on their new imager, she shakes her head.

"Doesn't work."

"What do you mean?"

"What do you think I mean? It's broken."

"But," I say, "it's brand new."

She shrugs. "Dad was trying to get it fixed, but they spent the last credit they had on it. Then they got charged the support fee when he called to report the problem, then he got cut off, then he was charged another support fee to call again. You should have seen how pissed off he was! He was cursing up a storm. If a watcher had been here, he'd have been fined a month's credit privileges for sure. Anyway, after all the fees there was nothing left over to get it repaired."

She laughs at my expression. "Why do you look so shocked?" she says. "This isn't like the premium products Blackies get. It's a low-credit imager. They break."

"What about the warranty?"

"What the hell's a *warranty*? . . ."

"Never mind," I say.

"Whatever."

A moment passes in awkward silence. I can't help but look over at her, her ruddy cheeks, silken hair, the smooth skin of her shoulders. She, however, makes a point of not looking back at me.

"I love you," I say, tentatively.

"I love you, May," she says, like it's a tremendous burden.

Reaching out, I place my hand on hers. She looks over her shoulder at the door. I wish she wouldn't do that. Why is she so paranoid, I wonder? Then I remember Blackwell's little movie, and I realize she's right to be afraid.

"May," she says, "would you do anything for me?"

"Of course," I say.

"I mean really, *anything*?"

"Of course. Why?"

"Well . . ." she sighs, "Dad has been saying that . . . we're almost at the end of our credit. With my sister's appendix rupturing last fall and everything . . . he says unless he works more hours, he's going to get shipped to a work camp."

"So," I say, "he can pull a few double shifts "

"He already does," she says. "He works triple shifts sometimes."

Her eyes are shining now in the lamplight, not with their normal radiance, but with tears.

"That's impossible," I say. "Triple shifts?"

"It's not impossible," she says. "People do it all the time. Honestly, May, for somebody so smart, sometimes I think you don't know anything."

I pull my hand away from hers.

"Oh, don't get all pissy," she says. "I'm just saying . . ."

"What? What are you saying?!" I shout. "So your dad has to work all the time. Big deal. My dad works all the time, too. I never even see him. If you want to watch an imager that works, come over to my house. Mine's as big as your whole apartment . . . What? What's the problem now?"

Kali is standing now, furious.

"You don't get it, May! My father's going crazy! He's snapped. He cries for no reason. He hit my mom the other day; he's never done that. Right now he's in his bedroom. He hasn't come out for hours. And on top of it all, now he might get sent to a work camp."

I wonder if Blackwell's tiny listening device, nestled in the pocket of my skirt, is picking all this up. I hope not.

"So what?" I say quietly. "Your dad'll work there for a while, pay down his debt, then come back home."

"When was the last time you heard of anyone coming back from a work camp, May?"

A moment passes.

"Maybe you can pick up a shift after school or something and help out."

Kali shakes her head in disgust. "It won't help."

"Or we can help you," I say quickly. "I can talk to my dad."

But she's already walking away. "You don't get anything, May," she says. "Of course you wouldn't; you're a Blackie!"

"Wait. Where are you going?"

"To pee," she says. She disappears down the hallway and a door slams.

Silence. Until the upstairs neighbor decides to walk to his closet, that is. Then his footsteps rattle the whole apartment. My hand snakes into my pocket and finds Blackwell's listening chip. My first thought is to hurl it out the window, smash it under my foot, or toss it into the garbage disposal. It sits there in the palm of my hand, a tiny metallic capsule. Maybe I should swallow it, crap it back out in a couple days, and have it delivered to Blackwell with a note saying, *Here's what I think of your blackmail attempt.* The thought almost makes me smile.

But what if Blackwell is right? What if Kali's dad is plotting against the Company? Then I'd have a duty, to God and my Company, to make him pay. Kali even said he was acting crazy, right? From what she says, it's sounding more and more like he really is an unprofitable. If he were allowed to harm the Company, thousands, even millions of people could lose their jobs, their homes, their livelihoods. As Jimmy Shaw always says, anybody who's against the Company is an enemy of the people.

Heck, even I'm a stockholder, and I'm only fifteen. An attack on the Company is an attack on me. Rising from the couch, I cross to the hallway. From the ceiling comes the sound of the upstairs neighbor opening his refrigerator. I hear Kali blowing her nose in the bathroom. Beyond, the hallway is dark. But Kali's dad isn't sleeping. Already, his voice drifts to my ears. A slim blade of light shines from beneath his bedroom door. I creep toward it now, press my ear against it. Through the hollow wood, his words are broken, barely audible: "... Atrocity! ... all over South America ... the workers ... holocaust—mass graves ... unconscionable, reckless, immoral policies, man. All over the world ... tell everyone, *make* them see ... stop this damned Company, in the name of God, in the name of ... murders!"

The bathroom door opens behind me, and I choke back a gasp.

"What are you doing?" Kali asks.

"I—just—was waiting for you to come out. I was worried."

She squints at me suspiciously. "Why were you standing in the dark like that?"

"Uh..."

"Oh, my God," says Kali.

I hold my breath.

"We're not that poor," she says. "Turn on a light!"

Back in the living room, the storm of Kali's anger seems to have blown over. We make out for a while, brainstorm names for all the babies we're (somehow) having together one day, eat a bag of instant popcorn I brought over, and make out some more. Kali doesn't mention our previous conversation, but the worry never quite leaves her eyes.

When it's time to leave, she goes to walk me to the door. On the way, she stops and stoops to tie her shoe. I watch her. The way she pushes her hair back behind her ear, the way she chews her gum; God, I love her.

Still, while she's busy tying, I drop the little metal listening-pill into a vase of dried flowers. Even though I love Kali and Kali loves her father, the Company must be protected. Because without the Company, how will Kali and I support our eight kids, Katherine, Jase, Ky, Josette, Daniel, Zach, Nigel, and Noreen?

Whispers:

"I love you, baby."

"I love you more than anything."

And before I step out the door, I kiss my Kali goodbye—not knowing that I've kissed her goodbye already.

Dawn.

I wake with a smile on my face, sure that yesterday's events—the descent into Black Brands, the meeting with Jimmy Shaw—were nothing but a bizarre nightmare. But when I sit up in bed and ask Eva to tell me my schedule for the day, she replies with one word: *"Vacation."*

Jimmy Shaw's mission to track down the rebels still stands. Worse than that, it's my job now. I sit up, my legs dangling off the bed, my head cradled in my hands.

"Fine. I'll do it," I murmur. But, it occurs to me, there's someplace I have to stop first. I pack and re-pack my bag. At first, packing seems an almost impossible task. How do you pack for a journey from which you might never return? Everywhere I look are little sentimental items, scattered shards of my life's meaning, begging to be included. I start off packing some of these things—the dried flower Kali gave me long ago, the necklace with the big diamond heart my father gave me on my sixteenth birthday, the tiny headband my mother made for me to wear on my first birthday—the year before she died. But in the end, I take all of them out of my bag again.

Though my thoughts are still obscured behind a heavy cloudbank of confusion, tiny rays of truth are beginning to break through, and one of these truths is that on the path I will soon be walking, wherever it might lead, things will be irreparably changed and the trappings of my former life will only hold me back.

I remove from the bag my lotion, my favorite pair of high heels, my electric toothbrush—all the things that have no bearing on the stark task ahead of me.

I pack a flashlight, two changes of clothes, extra socks, a few cans of tuna fish, a bottle of water, and a loaf of bread. I put on athletic shoes and wear pants beneath my skirt, rolling the pant legs up so they won't show. I tie my hair back tight and leave my makeup on the vanity. I take a long carving knife from the kitchen, an old compass from my dresser drawer, and my grandmother's rosary.

My packing finished, I take one last look out at my executive-credit-level view. From here, the Headquarters Hub (What was it called once? Chicago?) glitters in an aura of golden stillness. I shoulder my pack. Who would have thought that everything a person needs to survive would feel so light on my shoulders? I look around my apartment for anything indispensable, anything I might miss too much if I leave it behind, but there is nothing. I take a few steps toward the door, stop, and take the IC out of my pocket. The first impulse is to call my father, but I'm so completely at a loss for what to say to him that I cast the thought out of my mind entirely. For all I know, he's the one sending me on this terrible errand. Carly, my secretary, will she miss me when I'm gone? Wonder where I went? I doubt it.

And Randal? Poor chaotic mind—despite his misgivings about the Company budget, I doubt he'd understand what I have to do. To call him would endanger him by association. Better just to disappear. I toss the IC on the couch.

I shut off the lights in my lonely apartment, cross the first radiant beams of sunrise, and pass through my door for what might well be the last time.

"*Goodbye, May*," says Eva's eerie, computerized voice.

"Goodbye," I say, and smile because I mean it.

I will never come back here again.

It's only a short train ride to N-Academy 13, fifteen minutes at the most, but this is my first time taking it. Visitations at the academy are discouraged and are considered disruptive to the students' learning process. That's always been fine with me. Between work, shopping, and dreaming about members of the fairer sex, there hasn't been a lot of time for chitchat with family members I don't even know. The front doors are emblazoned with the N-Corp logo and the motto of the N-Ed division: *Effective, Efficient Education.* The woman at the front desk doesn't even look up at me until her computer recognizes my cross implant.

"Here for a visit?" she asks tonelessly.

"Yes."

"Name of the student?"

"Fields. Rose Fields."

"Your relationship to her?"

I start, but the word sticks in my throat. I cough, then try again. "Mother."

Finally the woman looks up at me, brushes her stringy blonde hair back from her shoulder, showing the N-Ed badge on her chest. Her eyes widen as she takes in my strange appearance—the backpack slung over my shoulders, the bunched-up pants beneath my skirt, the lack of makeup. Her expression drips with judgment, and I bite back a sarcastic retort.

Thank God kids are taught by imager these days, I think. The thought of this person educating anyone gives me the creeps.

"All the way down. Last pod on the right, chamber fourteen twenty-one," she says. "Rose is a wonderful child. I'm sure you'll enjoy your visit." She speaks with all the sincerity of a crow cackling, and I'm certain she has no idea who Rose is. Her little speech was just that: a speech she was trained to say. But I can't really criticize her for it. I don't know Rose, either.

A set of glass doors slides open, revealing a hallway painted with brightly colored stripes—red, yellow, green, orange, purple. On my left and my right I pass an endless parade of doors—wide, octagonal things outlined in black with small, round, porthole-like windows in them. The first dozen or so doors I pass without hesitation, but soon my curiosity gets the best of me, and I stop and cup my hands around one of the portholes. Inside is a little boy—or a little girl with short hair. Who can tell from the back? He sits dangling his legs off the end of a cot, staring at a three-walled imager. The scene is of a country road, shaded by an arch of high, windblown treetops. From somewhere up the picturesque dirt road, a set of numbers appear. They zip toward us, growing larger and larger, until they take up most of the screen.

7 x 3 =

I can't hear the little boy's answer through the glass—but the imager screen blinks in swirls of yellow and purple, and the answer flashes across the screen:

21, that's right!

I walk on.

Perhaps a hundred yards down the seemingly endless hallway, I pause to look in another window. There, I see a nearly identical scene, except that it's a little red-haired girl sitting on the bed, gazing at her imager. Words stream across the screen, and as they do the background image changes. When the story talks about a happy fish, there's a smiling cartoon tuna. When it talks about an angry pelican, there he is, glowering down from a pastel sky. There might be audio, too, but the thick door muffles any sounds coming from the chambers, leaving the hallway eerily silent.

I walk on. By the time I've reached the end of the hall, I've gone so far my feet are aching. I stop and stare at the door, the number 1421, the little porthole . . .

And I turn and start to walk back the way I came. This is the most efficient way to raise kids, I remind myself. Not only is it cost effective, it gives them the most enriching environment possible. Complete safety. A perfect education. All the knowledge they need to be successful contributors to the Company. There's only one thing could possibly mess up a kid from a high-level N-Academy like this: their parent.

Still, I might die—today, tomorrow, or next week. My mind isn't completely made up yet about what I'm going to do when I reach the rebel camp, but there's plenty of danger either way. If I betray the rebels as Jimmy Shaw told me to, they might kill me. If I join the rebels, the Company might kill me. Or they might show my picture on the imager screens in the schools: May Fields, the famous traitor. Shouldn't my daughter meet me once in person before that happens?

I stop and stand completely still, staring down the endless hallway, gazing back the way I came. I swallow. I take a deep breath and exhale through my teeth, then turn around.

I have to meet her. Even if it's just for curiosity's sake. The minute I step forward there's a beep and the octagon before me slides upward like a garage door. Before I can back up, before I can think, I force myself to step through the opening, into the chamber. The door hisses down again behind me.

I'm standing next to the bed, now. A little girl sits on it, cross-legged, in a perfectly clean and pressed blue dress, her shoulder-length hair a mess of curls, her eyes big and dark gray. There's another little girl there, too. She wears a red plaid dress and has two blond pigtails and a sprinkling of freckles on her cheeks—except this second girl isn't real. She's on the imager screen.

"And so I learned it all and got all As," the real girl on the bed tells the girl on the imager, before my entry cuts the conversation short.

Then, Rose turns to look at me, and all I see is her.

She has dimples. A perfect little nose. She gazes up at me demurely, as if I were a newly arrived guest at a tea party she'd been planning all along.

"Hello," she says, her voice high and crystal clear.

"Hello," I say. Compared to her, I sound like a chain-smoking fifty-year-old man.

"This is my best friend, Annie," she says, gesturing to the girl on the imager.

"Hello, Annie," I say.

The girl on the screen waves at me, and for the first time I notice that her movements are slightly unnatural. She's not some real girl teleconferencing with my Rose; she's just part of the N-Ed program. Lesson number 621: how to have friends.

"I'll leave you to talk with your guest, now. Bye, Rose," Annie says, and just like that she pops like a bubble and, in a sparkle of holo-plasma light, disappears, leaving me alone with my daughter for the first time in either of our lives.

Rose looks at me from head to toe.

"You're not in your uniform," she observes. "Everyone who works here wears a uniform."

"I don't work here."

The girl—Rose—my Rose—frowns.

"You must be a visitor, then," she says. "Some of the children get visitors. It usually makes them cry."

"It makes them cry?" I repeat.

She nods in an adorable boinging of curls.

"Why?"

"Because. It's usually their parents, and they usually want to go home with them, but they can't. So, they cry." She says it so matter of factly, and with such maturity that I have to do some quick math in my head to confirm her age. Yep. She's still only nine. So maybe there's something to be said for the N-Ed Academy after all. Little Rose already seems to be smarter than I'll ever be. Maybe I shouldn't have come....

"So, are you a visitor?" Rose asks me.

I take a slow breath, in through my nose, out through my mouth. When I speak, the voice doesn't seem like my own: "Yes, Rose. I'm a visitor. I'm your mommy."

She nods, but she doesn't seem impressed.

"I know about you, you know," she says. "You're May Fields. You're already a marketing executive. You're going to be a Blackie. My grandpa is Jason Fields. He already is a Blackie. He's the CEO of N-Corp. They teach you all that stuff in the lesson on 'family.'"

I nod. "That's right, honey. All true."

She frowns again. "But—who's my daddy?"

In a flashback, I see myself in that tunnel on that long ago Fourth of July, the squad member D on top of me, his sweat dripping down on me, his friends watching, laughing. Laughing . . .

"You don't have a father, sweetie," I say.

This really confuses Rose. "But I learned that everyone does."

"You don't, honey." All I can think to do is lie. I can't tell her the truth. I can barely stomach it myself.

Thankfully, she only shrugs. "What's in the bag? Are you going on a trip?"

"Yes, I am," I say. "I'm going far, far away."

"To Australia Division?"

I nod. "Somewhere like that, yes."

"Are you ever going to visit me again?"

I stare at her. All this time I've been standing a few feet from the bed, my feet frozen in place, but suddenly I want to go to her, to embrace her. Nine years she's been alive and I've hated the idea of her existence. But now, now that she's in front of me, something in my heart snaps. And I love her. I love her, just like that. And it hurts like hell.

"I don't know if I'll visit you again," I say, tears clouding my vision. "I don't know if I'll be able to."

Rose nods. "It's better if you don't," she says. "Children in here perform an average of eleven percent better when their parents don't come visit."

I glance around the room, as I wipe my eyes, trying to get myself together. For the first time, I notice how incredibly tiny it is. Five feet by seven feet, at the most.

"Is that what you want, Rose?" I ask her, my voice gravelly with emotion. "You want to do well in school?"

She nods. "Oh, yes!" she says. "I'm going to be just like you, Mommy! I'm going to be a high-credit-level executive, and I'm going to have a penthouse apartment and an N-Rolls car and N-Elita series clothes, and someday I'm going to be the CEO of the Company, just like my grandpa Jason Fields."

I look at her and force a smile onto my face, while a gaping chasm of horror opens up beneath me. This is not a school. It's a jail cell. It's not an education; it's efficient, effective brainwashing.

I stoop next to the bed. "Just remember this, Rose," I say quietly. "Things are not always what they seem. There are things in life that are more important than credit. More important than work."

From the expression on her face, I can see she's confused, but I press on. "Someday Mommy might do something you don't understand. People might tell you things about me that will confuse you. But I want you to know that—even though I just met you—I'm fighting for you. Everything I'm doing is for you. And . . . and . . . I love you."

Tentatively, I reach out and put my large hand over her tiny one. She looks down at it, uncomfortable.

"You should go now, Mommy," she says after a moment. "I don't want to get behind on my studies."

I gaze at her one last time, drinking her in, soaking up the sight of her, then nod.

"Okay, sweetie," I smile through my tears, "Do your best. Make Mommy proud."

Before I leave, one last thought occurs to me, my father's benediction. I turn back. "Rose. Don't let the other kids give you crap about being different, okay?" I whisper.

Rose looks at me uncomprehendingly. "I'm not different, Mommy," she says.

My journey out of the Headquarters district and out of the hub flits by now as nothing but a collection of surreal slideshow images:

Here, a little boy throws a fit on the sidewalk in front of an N-Toy store.

There, a woman jogs, her huge fake breasts bobbing in front of her and her eyes fixed on some indefinable point in the future when she'll finally be thin enough to taste the happiness she's been starving for.

Here, a lone tie-man walks past, fiercely talking business to someone through his IC. A vein on his forehead throbs as he gestures desperately. Was I him, just last week?

Above, great glass buildings surround me, reflecting disjointed pieces of the beautiful, purpling sky. I wonder what the sunrise would look like without man's achievements cutting it to shreds.

Finally, I descend to a lonely subway stop where the air is stale and the concrete is worn and gray, but very clean. Even when I was a little girl, I remember when bums, unprofitables, used to haunt this place. The air in the train stop was pungent then with the smell of piss and echoed with harmonica and guitar music and raspy singing voices as strange street folk sang for their bread. Now, the stop is silent and I wonder where the homeless unprofitables have gone. Have they joined Ethan and his band of doomed rebels? Or did Jimmy Shaw wave his great God-wand and remake them into happy worker bees in the N-Corp hive? Either way, I grieve for them. When I was a child their dirty skin, haunted eyes, manic mirth, and unclean scents made me feel uneasy, but now I somehow miss them.

There's a rush of air on my face as a train rattles up and squeaks to a halt.

Its door opens and I step through to the sound of a beep, and Eva's ever-present voice, saying, *"Welcome, May Fields. A fifty-dollar transit fee has been added to your account."*

Only a few solitary men populate this train, for it leads to the industrial arc. The first shift out in the factories has already started, so these men must be the last few tardy stragglers. These days, even at the start of a shift, the trains on this route are only half full. Most industry has, by now, been shipped either to South America Division or to the new Africa Division factories, and the industrial arc is mostly ghost land.

I look around at my fellow riders, at their big, coarse hands and their downturned faces. Each of them keeps his own council. I take a seat near a window and watch the dark tunnel walls slide past faster and faster.

I fight not to think of Rose. Rose, who I don't even know. Still, somehow, what I'm about to do is all for her.

The black walls blast by. The train rattles violently on its tracks. This is the feeling of exile—terrifying and intoxicating. Three, four, five stops come and go. I await the seventh.

When the train's hisses and sighs give way and the doors finally open, Eva's strange and familiar voice drones from the ceiling: *"Blue station: outer industrial arc. Please watch your step exiting the train. Enjoy N-Corp Cola; drink the N!"*

After the voice cuts out in a staticky *click*, the quiet is so complete I almost have to hold my breath. I rise, one hand gripping the smudged steel rail above my head, and sling my pack over one shoulder.

Ahead of me, two riders lumber silently out of their seats and out the doors without the slightest glance at me. I follow them onto the platform, into a waft of canned, sterile-smelling air. The two men ride up the escalator a few steps apart, neither acknowledging the other, each staring at his feet in exhausted detachment.

Seeing them at a different time, perhaps only a few weeks from now, my mind might flood with questions: why are these two men strangers, who seem in every way as if they should be kindred spirits? Why are they not brothers, united by all their common bonds, instead of depleted, lonely souls blind to each other's existence? Who erected the wall between them, and what would happen if that wall were to be torn down?

But this morning, no such thoughts enter my mind. This morning I think only of myself. And Rose.

The escalator whisks my fellow riders upward and away, and the train chimes and chimes, closes its doors and rattles off, leaving me alone. I stare down at my feet—they've always been an embarrassment to me, being large and awkward—and past them, to the inky puddle of my reflection in the polished tile floor. I hike up my skirt, revealing the pants beneath. I pull down the skirt and step out of the beige ring the discarded garment makes as it crumples to the floor. I kick it down onto the tracks, then stoop and unroll the bottoms of my pants.

My transformation is nearly complete, but one task remains.

I walk around the empty platform for a few minutes before I discover the bathroom, tucked away behind the escalators. I place one hand on the door reading women. The picture on the door shows a little white outline of a woman in a skirt. Grinning, I remove my hand. No skirt here.

I go into the men's room instead.

It isn't a clean place. Toilet paper is strewn everywhere. Dirty, wet footprints range all over. But somehow I like it. It lacks the pretense of the ladies' room—no little sachet of potpourri here, no fake plant in the corner. There is no mistaking this room for anything but a place to piss, and this rare glimmer of honesty comforts me.

But my business here is not excretion—at least, not the typical kind. I walk to the row of white, ceramic sinks, unsling my bag, and toss it into one of them. Then, I step up to the vanity and confront myself.

I'm no beauty queen, that's for sure. Dark half-circles cling under my eyes. My face looks ashen. The buds of crow's feet are almost imperceptible at the corners of my eyes, but they're there all the same. My lips look thin and pale, my hair dark and plain, with a few ethereal wisps bristling from my otherwise slicked-back, pony-tailed mane. And of course, there's the standard blemish: the black stain of the cross on my cheek. Despite all of it, I can't quite shake the disquieting feeling that I'm sort of pretty.

I run the water over my hands, as hot as I can take it, until steam fogs the mirror and hides my reflection. I try three different soap dispensers and finally find one full. I rub my hands together, washing them slowly, enjoying the scald of the water, the thick breath of the steam, the smell of the dirt and piss and emptiness all around me.

In one unfogged patch of mirror, I catch another glimpse of the cross under my eye, dark as a bruise beneath my pale skin. I take the knife from the waistband of my pants and hold its blade under the blistering-hot water. My hands, now removed from the heat, tremble.

With the slowness of a high priest at a sacrificial ceremony, I raise the blade before me, eyeing its length, measuring its sharpness, fearing it and refusing to fear it. This is what must be done, so that the rebels will take me as one of their own, so that Blackwell and Jimmy Shaw can't track me. So all I have been will die. So Rose might one day emerge from her Company cocoon into a new world.

This is my choice.

I bring the knife to my face, feeling the heat of the blade on my skin before the bite of its edge.

Now, the pain—God, it hurts more than I had imagined it would— I have to finish fast.

Push harder.

Oh, God. Ow.

At least the knife is sharp. As it passes through the skin of my cheek my stomach turns mightily. I hear myself whimper. Now that I've loosed the flap of skin, I have to cut underneath the implant to break the wires.

Breathe, breathe, steady . . .

I push the point of the blade under the edge of the cross, aiming for the place where the four arms meet. I push slowly, carefully; if I move too fast, I might go too deep and cause irreparable damage. I cut underneath the cross then try to pry it free; I lift its edge and watch in disgusted fascination as the skin of my cheek rises with the tilt of the blade. But I can't break the wires.

Dammit!

The nausea is so bad I'm gagging; my head throbs, my brow pours sweat. I wiggle the knife blade, seeing stars pass before my vision with each movement, and finally give one last hard, upward jerk. There's a sickening, metallic *snap*.

The first thing I'm aware of is the taste of puke in my mouth. I roll over and spit. I open my eyes, but they're too clouded with tears to be of any use. My stomach feels horribly hollow, empty, twisted. As I slowly rise onto my hands and knees on the dirty floor, only now do I realize that I must've blacked out.

With one blindly groping hand, I find the knife, just a few feet away. With the other hand, I find the sink and pull myself upward, with badly trembling limbs, to an upright position. Finally, I rise from my knees to my feet. Blinking, squinting, I look at myself in the mirror. Blood has stained my face, my shirt, my jeans. It's smeared on my hands, and drizzles down my face like rain from an overflowing gutter. I reach into its source, not bothering to wash my hands or clear the blood away to see what I'm doing. I reach beneath the loose flap of skin, grip the hard, thin, metallic edge of the cross, and pull as hard as I can.

At first, there's nothing—hardly even pain—then, slowly, the cross moves, and agony swells behind it like a tsunami. There's a sound like the tearing of fabric, mixed with a beastlike scream that must have—but surely couldn't have—come from me.

And the cross comes free.

I toss it into the sink and it clatters there unimpressively. I lean forward, my face in my hands, leaning against the white ceramic, and cry like a child. Tears mingle with my blood against the slick, smooth surface of the basin, and slide together into the devouring black maw of the drain. As I listen to myself wail, noticing how the sound echoes in the dirty little restroom, I feel strangely detached from the whole scene, as if I were not myself going through this horrible ordeal, but somebody else entirely.

After a few minutes it occurs to me that if I don't take action soon, I'll lose enough blood to pass out again and will probably bleed to death before somebody finds me. Slowly, delicately, I raise my head toward the spinning lights of the ceiling. Slowly, delicately, I turn on the water and take some into my cupped and trembling hands. I wash the blood from my face, trying but failing to avert my eyes from the mirror and the cavernous wound under my left eye. When I've washed it out as well as I can withstand, I rummage through my bag—realizing I neglected to bring bandages—and pull out one of my spare shirts. I tear it into strips, fold some of it into an absorbent patch, and tie it in place with some thinner strips, as tightly as I can tolerate. Gingerly, I remove my bloodstained shirt, leaving it in the sink, and replace it with the last clean one from my bag. Despite my planning, my stock of clean clothes is already gone. I fish the small, black cross out of the sink in front of me, wondering at how light it is, walk over to the nearest stall, and hold it over the commode.

My apartment, my car, my career, my life—everything I've ever desired is right here in my hand. It's amazing how good it feels to be throwing it all away.

Looking back, it seems incredible how long it took me to understand the ways and means of deception. After all my time working in marketing, how could I not have known? Of course the Mark of the Beast would be a cross.

Drop. Splash. Flush.

And I'm finally, finally free.

This is where the revolution begins.

Somewhere inside the hot womb of the earth, through what must be miles of tunnels, I wander. The harder I try to retrace my steps, to find my way back to the rebel camp, the more lost I become. Now there is some kind of track under my feet, but whether it was made for a subway system or to haul some kind of ore out of the ground, I do not know.

I feel I've been swallowed by a python and am passing through his narrow bowels, waiting to be shat out or reborn or . . . at the thought of the word *shat*, I almost laugh. It's been a long time since I was capable of humor. I realize now how much I've missed it. Already my exile, as terrifying as it is, has lifted a grave weight from my shoulders.

As I walk, though, the insanity of my situation strikes me. The fact is, I have no idea how to get back to the warehouse headquarters Ethan and his rebels took me to last time. And even if I did somehow stumble onto it, there's no guarantee they'll be happy to see me . . . quite the opposite.

Still, I press on. Concrete walls weep with moisture as I pass. Dizzy, lost, delirious, I step into a place where the tunnel widens into some sort of small, underground station. I pass a large set of gears, now rusted to stillness. Chains hang from a ceiling obscured by darkness and distance, braided with cobwebs and frayed electrical wires. Somewhere, the rustle of a rat. I've grown used to the sounds of the rats by now, the whisper of silence, even the—

Click.

Behind me. Not a rat. Not my imagination.

"May Fields. You've come back to us."

I turn and my flashlight finds Ethan Greene, his strange, handsome face looking somewhat tired, somewhat amused. His white gun is trained at my head.

"The light," he says, gesturing for me to shine my flashlight away from his face. I aim the beam at his shoes, but not away from him completely. I want to be able to see the expression on his face. My fate, my future, and even my life depend on how he reacts in the next few minutes.

The barrel of his gun never wavers for a second; it remains locked on my forehead. Now, he shines his light on me. Even through the glare I can see the strange look register in his face. Still, when he speaks his voice is even.

"Take the bandage off."

With the involuntary deliberateness of one who's lost too much blood, I remove the makeshift bandage, wincing as I pull the last layers free from the already-drying gore.

Ethan stares into the chasm of flesh on my cheek, his expression unreadable. He could put a bullet into that open wound right now, I know. The hole is already begun; his aim is steady. And why shouldn't he? What am I to him but a spy and a tie-wench, a life-long Company hack, born into its inner circle? Suddenly it hits me: he has no reason to trust me, no reason not to shoot me. I was foolish enough to think that by cutting the cross out I would prove my devotion to the Protectorate. It could just as easily be interpreted as an act of loyalty to the Company, as proof I'd be willing to mutilate myself in the service of the great corporation and in doing so make myself their perfect spy, the perfect candidate to infiltrate and expose the "anarchist rebels." If Ethan's thoughts take this tack, he kills me now.

Blood runs down my face again. Suddenly, my eyelids grow unbearably heavy.

"Why are you here?" Ethan asks.

"Jimmy Shaw sent me."

His nod seems to say, *Good, at least you're honest.*

"Why?"

"So I could lead Blackwell to you. To wipe out the camp."

His eyes narrow. "And so you're here for that reason? To lead them here?"

"No," I say. "I cut out the cross so they couldn't track me. I came to warn you that they're coming for you."

"To warn me," Ethan seems to taste these words as one might a sip of questionable wine.

"And to join you," I say.

Ethan's snorted laugh is not exactly derisive. "You already rejected us once. That seemed like a pretty good choice. So tell me, why would a future Blackie want to join a bunch of miserable unprofitables?"

"Because," I say, searching for words, trying to pin down the elusive thoughts slipping through my mind. "Because you're free."

"Nobody's free," Ethan says.

The barrel of his gun gapes at me. I'm waiting for the bullet, almost hoping for it. I'm too tired to endure any more questions, any more thinking or walking or working or searching, and I'm struck with the deep and overwhelming urge to lie down and sleep for a thousand years. The gash in my face pours blood like a great, weeping third eye. *Let me live or die,* I think, *just no more questions.*

And suddenly, as if he heard my unspoken thought, Ethan holsters his gun.

"No one came with you?"

"No."

"No one followed you?"

"I don't think so."

"They probably counted on tracking you with the cross . . . I'm sure they never imagined you'd have the guts to cut it out. You know if you betray us, I'll have to kill you? I'll have no choice." He approaches and takes my face in his hands, makes me look into his eyes. "You know that, right?"

"Yeah," I say. "I know." I'm about to fall like a tree under an ax.

Out of a bag I hadn't noticed, Ethan produces a device like a magic wand. He passes it over my head, my arms, my legs, my body. It emits a small humming sound.

"We'll check you over closer later, but it looks like you're clean," he says. "Sometimes they bug people and they don't even know it. Alright." He produces a strip of cloth from his pack and begins passing the blindfold around my head over and over, until I'm wrapped in a cocoon of deep darkness. "Let's go," he says.

I feel him put an arm around me, guiding me, steadying me.

"I'm fine," I say. "I can walk." But the words come out slurred.

Ethan laughs. "Sure you are," he says. We travel down the tunnel for a few minutes before he continues, "Maybe I'm an idiot to trust you, but I have to hand it to you, you're tough as hell."

We might have walked for minutes or days; time, like so many other things that once seemed indispensable, has become a worthless commodity. At first, I try to rely on his strength as little as possible, but soon I'm leaning heavily on him.

Finally, Ethan tells me to stop and steps away from me for a moment. I hear the guttural grinding sound of a heavy door reluctantly swinging open, then his hand is on my shoulder again, leading me on. As I step through what I imagine must be a doorway, I feel, for the first time in what might have been miles of walking, fresh-smelling, cool air on my face. The space around me seems to open up, ringing with echoing voices, laughter, droning music. Without ceremony and without a word, Ethan pulls the blindfold from my eyes. I blink, surprised.

This is not the warehouse Ethan took me to last time.

Surrounding me is what can only be described as a subterranean village. Two rowdy, pale-faced boys brush past me, chasing a ball. To my left, two men and two women crouch next to a tiny, gas-powered stove, frying what smells like bacon. They laugh together.

Ethan starts walking, and I follow slowly, my legs feeling leaden.

"Look up," he says.

Above, a great domed ceiling soars, its vast, yellowish glass face swirled with amber. It's lit from behind and glows down on us like a great glass sun. The light it casts over everything is pleasant if some-what dim, the color of melted butter, and it lends the stark concrete walls and floors an air of comfort and hospitality.

Everything we pass seems perfectly ordered. Tents have been pitched in precise rows. A pack of what look like old gasoline-pow-ered motorcycles stand perfectly polished in utterly straight columns. In one cordoned-off area a huge blanket is laid out. Upon it sit what must be thousands of white guns like the one Ethan carries, each placed a uniform distance from its neighbor. Two narrow-shoul-dered Asian men kneel in front of different guns, both working with nimble hands as they snatch various tools from leather belts at their waists, pull a gun apart, clean it, inspect it, reassemble it, put it back in its exact place, then move on to the next one. The men glance up at us as we pass, and I expect they will call out a greeting to Ethan or give some utterance to the questions that cross their faces as they notice me, but they look back to their work without a word. Ethan leads me on.

"This is your headquarters?" I ask.

"Isn't that what Shaw sent you to discover?"

"What's it called?"

"We won't be here long enough to name it," he says. "Soon, the squads will discover us—even without your help—and we'll be forced to abandon it."

"I'm sorry," I say, not knowing why. It isn't my fault they have to live this way. Not exactly. . . .

We're passing down another long row of tents, nearing the far wall of the chamber that, I imagine, must've been an underground train station once upon a time.

Something dawns on me. "How did you know I was coming?" I ask.

"The squadmen aren't the only ones with eyes and ears," he says with his mysterious, lopsided grin. "Besides, some of us have been hoping you'd come back. Most of us felt that once somebody's declined to join us, they shouldn't be given another chance, but others thought we should make an exception for you."

"What do *you* think?" I ask. "Your decision is the most important one, isn't it?"

He throws me a sidelong glance, a look half admonishing and half amused.

"It's true that I'm the general of the Protectorate's fighting forces, but we have no leader here. There is an elected governing council, twelve members. On our tiny scale, we might be the last democratic government on earth. And as for what I think of you . . ." his lips move, as if chewing his thoughts before spitting them out. "I don't believe a person's soul can change, and you've been a tie-girl all your life. But I do believe a person's circumstances can change. I believe things can happen to bring them closer to their true, maybe dormant selves. And I believe in a brutal thing called destiny that's been known to make kings into slaves and vice versa. In other words . . ." He stops walking abruptly, turning back to face me with flinty, amused eyes, "I'm still making up my mind." Then, he calls over his shoulder, "Ada!"

The kind-faced, middle-aged woman who brought us our food last time I was in the camp appears from a narrow doorway in the curved concrete wall so quickly she must've been watching us from there, perhaps waiting to be called.

"Stitch her up, would you?" Ethan says absently, not looking at the woman but still eyeing me.

Ada walks up to me with quick steps then stops abruptly, taking me in with a motherly yet business-like glance.

"Jesus, Ethan! Were you going to let her bleed to death on her way here? Poor dear," she says to me. "I'll stitch up your face very well; you're so beautiful, we don't want a nasty scar to ruin you."

Ethan snorts. "You might be doing her a favor if you let it heal ugly. I suspect beauty is a burden Miss Fields might not mind being relieved of." He looks at me and smiles, half conspiring with me, half mocking. "In any case, she won't need her looks here."

Ada gives him a reproving frown, takes my thin hand in her soft, plump one, and leads me toward the narrow doorway from which she appeared.

"Be quick, the council is waiting," Ethan calls after us. "I'll send word when we're ready for her."

Ada waves his words away as if swatting at a fly.

"Come here, poor girl," she whispers. "We'll fix you very well."

In my delirium, she's the mother I hardly knew, and I release myself into her care with relief, almost with tears.

The room we enter is a dimly lit kitchen with cinder-block walls and clean, sparsely appointed countertops. To one side of the kitchen stands an old, cheap-looking table with a pale, laminate top and four greenish vinyl chairs surrounding it. Ada gestures to the table and helps lift me onto it, manipulating my long frame with surprising strength and ease.

"Forgive me," she says. "This may not look like much of a hospital, but I promise it does the trick. There've almost been miracles per-formed here." She pulls open a drawer in a cabinet I hadn't noticed and takes out some gauze, a bottle, a small plastic box, and several white towels.

"Lay back," she says, and eases me down, placing one rolled-up towel under my head. Next, she picks up the plastic bottle, begins to uncap it, then stops, remembering something. She crosses to the door and closes it. "Don't want the children to hear this," she says.

I wonder, fearfully, what sounds the children aren't meant to hear. Before I can ask her, she's at my side again. Above, one bare light bulb hangs from a wire, and in its glare I can see a shiny, raised scar on Ada's face, just under her left eye. She must've undergone the same trial I'm facing. This knowledge helps to steel my nerves, and I wonder how many others have walked down these tunnels and torn from them-selves the mark of civilization.

In the next moment, Ada is obscured; she's thrown a towel over my forehead.

"Close your eyes."

Cold, the alcohol on my face. I hiss in pain, bite my teeth together so hard I'm afraid they might break. Ada removes the towel from my eyes and blots my wound. Next, from the plastic box she takes a needle and thread and, placing one hand on my forehead to steady me, begins stitching. The pain comes in pricks and tugs and a general burning and throbbing, but I'm so deep in shock and so low on blood that I can muster no response to the pain but to lay there and take it.

I stare at the slightly swinging light bulb hanging above me, watch it become a twin of itself as my eyes lose focus and I fall toward uncon-sciousness. Somehow, the sight reminds me of the duality of my life: the dutiful worker versus the irreverent dyke, a life of wealth versus a life of banishment, the Company versus the Protectorate, God versus

Satan, good versus evil. Now, these distinctions blur in my mind like the light hanging over me. All these reciprocal elements, these warring factions in my life; what if—if—but sleep erases these thoughts.

In my dreams, I am somehow aware that I will awaken a new person, reborn, resurrected like Lazarus. In my dreams, I am a warrior.

Kali has a hammock. We sit in it and play truth-or-dare. This is what fifteen-year-old girls do. This is what everyone expects. They don't know what we dare each other to do when no one else is around, how those secret dares make every minute of every day an excruciating journey through fear, anticipation, and rapture, in an ever-repeating, ever-divine cycle. They don't know how I love her, how my love for her permeates every moment of my life, how since I met her every fiber of my body aches, burns, screams with agonizing, electric longing.

They don't know I would die for her.

It's a few days after I planted the bug in Kali's apartment, and I've almost made myself forget about it. Almost. Now, in the hammock, we drink N-O orange soda. Her bare foot rests on top of my bare foot.

Both her parents are at work. Still, she looks over her shoulder before kissing me. In the tension of her body I can feel her fear. Now, that fear no longer offends me. In fact, I share it. After Blackwell showed me his movie of us, it seems only a matter of time before everyone discovers our love, and forces us—God forbid—to live our lives apart.

If this ever happens, I have decided, I will go to the top of my dad's office building, over two hundred stories high, and jump off. I will proclaim my love for Kali as I fall, so the whole world can hear.

I love Kali. I vow I will never stop.

As years pass, I will eventually become ashamed of almost everything about myself: the privilege I was born into, my bony shoulders, my masculine-looking jawline, and especially my perverse and sinful desires. But my love for Kali—of that I will never be ashamed. Today, I'm just glad her sister is at the shopping plaza and we're alone.

I creep a finger up the bottom of Kali's tank top, along her belly. She takes a sip of her soda and stares at the ceiling of the patio. I slide my hand up the skin of her stomach. My fingers are trembling; I can't help it.

"May," she says, "don't you ever get tired of making out all the time?"

Of course I don't.

"Sure," I say. "Sometimes."

This is a first. Normally, Kali will submit to me without a word. She might start by acting uninterested—she might keep reading her magazine or pretend to be watching a show on the imager (though not today; the imager is still broken), but soon she will turn her lips, shiny with sweet-tasting lip gloss, to my own. Never before has she protested my advances, and my mind is spinning with rage, fear, and nameless jealousy.

"What's wrong?" I ask.

She doesn't answer.

"I know you're pissed off about something," I say.

She doesn't answer.

"Seriously, Kali, what's wrong? I love you. You can tell me anything. Tell me to jump off a cliff for you and I'd do it."

She looks at me and smiles sadly. I've never seen a fifteen-year-old smile like that. Her smile speaks of long-submerged sorrow, of knowing things that neither children nor adults should ever know. I don't know what to make of it, so I smile back, but inside I'm terrified.

"Tell me what you're thinking," I say. "Please."

She looks at me for a moment before finally beginning. "I'm sad," she says, "because . . . you remember what I told you the other day? About my dad? Well . . . May, I believe in God. I believe God makes things the way they are for a reason. And . . . he made me love you and he made you love me . . . even though it's wrong. I've been thinking about that a lot. About what Jimmy Shaw says, how things are the way they are because that's how God wants them. Then that means God wants a lot of terrible things. He wants you and me to be horrible sinners. He wants my father to die so young—"

"Your father isn't dying," I say.

She shakes her head. "You should see him. He's always working or hiding in his room when you're here, so you don't know. May, his hair falls out in big clumps, more and more every day. Sometimes he wakes up and his pillow is covered. And it's getting gray."

"There are drugs against aging," I say. "My dad is over sixty and he doesn't even have gray hair."

"It's not his age," she says, looking at me with those big, mournful hazel eyes.

"What's wrong with him, then?" I ask.

"It's his work," she says. "He has nightmares. He can't sleep. Sometimes he never comes home from the office."

"He's a distribution manager for retail stores, right?"

She shakes her head. "He does other things. He won't talk about them, but I know something is going on, and it's killing him—there's something horrible they make him do at work. Last night, he woke up screaming and all I heard was 'black brands.' He screamed it, May. But that's the way God wants it. And I'm a queer sinner because I love you, and I'm afraid that when Dad finds out, it will kill him. You know, like the straw that breaks the camel's back? And it'll all be my fault. And I'm afraid that's how God wants it. And I'm afraid . . . you and me will stop loving each other." She's crying now. "I couldn't take that.

Because then I'll be alone. I mean, I have no parents—they're always gone—and my sister is such a bitch . . . I'd be alone. And I know I'd die alone. I'm afraid I'll lose you. I'm afraid that's how God wants it."

Of course, I have no idea what to say. I touch her arm, feeling the heat of emotion under her skin, coursing through her blood.

"You won't lose me. And your dad will be okay. That's not what God wants; he doesn't want everything to end up all tragic. He wants . . ." My mind scans through every Jimmy Shaw sermon I've ever heard, looking for the answer. "He wants everybody to be rich," I finish.

"But you and I will never really get to be together," Kali says, "and if we can't be together, I'll die. I know I will. And if my father goes crazy and my mother is gone working all those triple shifts . . . and we're always in debt, deeper and deeper—"

"Just work hard," I say, "and you'll be a Blackie some day, too." This is the mantra of our Company—although I've already begun to recognize it's a lie.

Kali smiles the sad smile again. She kisses me. She lets me take off her shirt. And at that moment, the unthinkable happens; her tragic prophecy fulfills itself: her father walks in.

My memory of what happened after that moment is flawed, like scar tissue. Here's her dad's face, livid and red as he screams at her. There's Kali, just sitting on the hammock, crying and crying. And here's me, afraid to stand up for her.

That is a wound that will never heal, that will forever bleed: knowing that I did not stand up for her and for our love that day. I just wait until her father stops screaming, then walk out the front door, my head hung low, lips quivering as I hold back tears. Kali and I don't even say goodbye. How could I know that I'd never see her again?

And Kali's prediction about her father comes true, too: A few months after he walks in on us, the rest of his hair falls out. Soon, he gets reclassified as an unprofitable. One day, he goes for a walk and disappears forever. Repossessed.

Me, I get an HR watcher credit for leaving that bug in their place. Fifty thousand, with a letter from Blackwell: *The Company thanks you for your service.*

My father, when he finds out about me and Kali, sends me away to an expensive, prestigious, N-Corp boarding school. When I come back to visit, I almost feel like a different person. I'm more considerate, more God-fearing, more self-loathing, more intelligent. Back home on Christmas break, I stop by her apartment and learn that Kali has run away. No one knows where she's gone. Except for her family, hardly anyone even remembers her.

I don't throw myself off the building when I get the news, but some piece of me does fall into oblivion that day. Part of me is still falling.

A yellow field with a rattlesnake coiled at its center. Beneath it, the words: *Don't Tread on Me.* The flag hangs on the far wall.

"As you can see, she has undergone the baptism of the knife . . ."

There are nods, but nobody speaks.

"That alone should make her one of us."

A strange trick of my imagination: Ethan seems taller now, standing before the eleven assembled members of the governing council. They watch him, taking in his words in measured silence. The twelfth council member—Clair—is still in Company custody.

A woman speaks up, "If her daddy weren't one of the founders of the Company, and if she hadn't come to us as an admitted spy, then, yes, the fact that she cut out her cross would make her one of us." Five of those seated before me are women and six are men. The woman speaking now has short, curly gray hair, glasses, strong arms, and a low but cutting voice. She is perhaps fifty years old.

"What kind of a spy comes announcing that they've been sent to spy on you?" says an older man.

"A stupid one," a stocky, bearded young man says with a laugh.

"Or a very clever one," says the first woman, eyeing me with unconcealed disdain.

"So what do *you* say we do with her, Grace?" asks Ethan.

"She's admitted to being a spy. We have to try her as one and punish her as one."

Those words elicit many furrowed brows among her companions. I can only imagine what the penalty for spying is around here, but I doubt it's good.

The small assembly takes a collective breath, everyone watching me. Despite the overwhelming urge to run, to go back and hide in my own apartment with the shades drawn, or to spit at them all for judging me, to curse them out in embarrassment and frustration, I swallow my fear and stand tall, shoulders squared, making eye contact with every one of them just as Ethan advised me to before leading me into what he called "the hearing." It's hard to do when I know they're probably thinking about condemning me to death.

"McCann," Ethan says, "you're never this quiet. What do you think?"

McCann! In the stress of the moment, I hadn't noticed him there at the end of the council table. Now, seeing his familiar face is a much-needed relief. He chews on a plastic straw, leaning back a bit in his chair, arms crossed at his chest and seething with muscle, like two intertwined snakes. His eyes are narrow as he looks at me. He sucks on the straw for a second, then takes it from his mouth.

"It's a right and good rule that a person only gets one chance to join us—at least now, while our safety is so fragile," he says in his exotic accent. "But . . . it is also a right and good rule that if somebody takes the baptism of the knife and leaves the Company—especially her, who is almost a Blackie—it's right and good that they should be let in. She's given up much to get back here."

"Might gain much, too, by betraying us," mutters the woman— Grace—under her breath.

"In my mind, it's a tied game for her," continues McCann in his thick accent. "And to break the tie, I'm interested mostly in why you think we should accept her, Ethan."

There are some assenting murmurs.

Ethan clears his throat. He's been pacing back and forth during his exchange, and now he stops next to me.

"The Reapers and I have watched May for a long time," he says. "She's strong, she's in the inner circle, and she knows how the Company works as well as anyone. But most importantly, she has the seeds of hatred for what the Company stands for. She's different. She loves women. She's wearing pants, you can see, and we didn't give them to her. She came wearing them."

Even the curly-haired woman raises her eyebrows at this news.

"She cut the cross out of her face herself, with no help," Ethan continues. "And as McCann can attest, she saved Clair's life by helping her escape after the Headquarters bombing. Jimmy Shaw didn't tell her to do that. Nobody did. I want her here because I think she's one of us. Because she has the potential, I believe, to be one of the greatest among us."

His words hang before me like a curtain, one that might rise to reveal a death sentence, or perhaps a new life.

"I have a proposal," Ethan continues, with new energy now as he senses the tide turning in his—and my—favor. "We've received intelligence that Clair is being held in the prison at Work Camp 5, along with some other Protectorate sympathizers. I will take a small force and rescue them. May will fight with us, as a test."

The council reacts, mostly, with stares. A few people shake their heads.

The curly-haired woman, Grace, speaks up: "First, how do you know where Clair's being held?"

"I have my ways, Grace," Ethan says.

Grace snorts. "Fine. Again, being mysterious. That aside, does Miss Fields know how to fight? Does she even know how to fire a gun?"

"I'll teach her," Ethan says. "I taught you, didn't I?"

Grace, rebuffed, loses her resolve, but still manages to say, "I don't like it. It's too great of a risk for you to take, General. We can't lose you."

"You won't," Ethan says. "May will keep me safe. Isn't that right, May?"

He looks at me, eyebrows raised in playful expectation. I feel my mouth gaping. My voice cracks as I try to speak, then I clear my throat. The burn of my blushing cheeks makes my wound throb, and the pain hardens my resolve. All eyes are on me.

"I . . . I want to help you," I say. "If the Company has wronged people, I am partly responsible and I want make it right. Besides . . ."

My mind whirrs, searching for the right words to express the doubt, the loneliness, the ever-present, ever-growing sense of unease that has haunted me year after year. But how can I express to them what was wrong with my life inside the Company? In what must seem to them the rose garden of my life, how to point out the thousand stinging thorns? I have had all the luxury in the world, all the opportunity. I have never trembled in cold or sweated in heat, never lived in fear or moaned in hunger. Still, I was bound. Bound to work I did not love, to morals that were not my own, and most horribly to the sovereign will of the Company, which forced me to place myself and all I loved on the altar of their insatiable God of Money. And all I can think of is: I want to write poetry. I want to kiss women, and tell the world about it. I want to lie in grass unwilted by the Company's pollution. I want to go to a place where my name and my debt and my work history and my million plastic possessions cannot follow. The revelation hits me like an exploding grenade: I don't want to go back. I truly do want to join the Protectorate.

All I can think to say is, "I want to be free."

A smile rises in Ethan's eyes. He turns back to the council.

"I'll take approximately two weeks to train May and plan the raid," he says. "After that, we strike."

He looks around the room for objections, but there are none.

"God bless America, and God bless the Protectorate," Grace says, and clacks a small gavel on the table, ending the meeting.

McCann smiles, but his thoughts seem far away. "God bless America," he murmurs, "and bless our bullets, too."

—CHAPTER 014—

The next morning, Ethan shakes me into wakefulness hours before dawn.

He does not say good morning or offer me coffee. He simply pulls me to my feet and orders me to stand at attention.

Humans, he tells me, are composed of three parts: mind, body, and soul.

I want to tell him this is a pretty esoteric discussion to have at four-thirty in the morning, but the gravity of his demeanor silences me.

If any of these three facets of a human being are deficient, he continues, then that individual will be unable to enter the Order of the Protectorate. Conversely, every Protectorate member must keep each of these aspects of himself honed and balanced, so as to be prepared for any possible test. Since I already put myself through the baptism of the knife, it stands to reason that my spirit is firm. Therefore, since I must be prepared to fight in only two weeks, my accelerated training schedule will focus on my body and my mind.

Standing here at four-thirty AM, drowsy enough to nod off standing up, I very much hope we'll start by working on my mind. Doing crossword puzzles, for example. But no. We spend the next two hours running through miles upon miles of tunnels.

I do pull-ups until my arms tremble, sit-ups until my stomach spasms, and push-ups until I'm afraid my meager breasts will fall off. Then, we run some more. The workouts are so hard that I don't even notice the throbbing ache of the wound on my face, because the pain in my muscles is even worse.

At lunch, Ethan and I sit apart from the others. While they laugh and dine on pasta and sausage, I choke down four boiled eggs and a banana. Then, Ethan tells me with a grin, it's time for fight training.

I learn stomp kicks and jabs, takedowns and sprawls, arm bars and chokes, left hooks, elbow strikes, eye gouges and head butts. Each new lesson in pain Ethan first demonstrates on me, so that by the time an hour has passed, I feel as if every inch of my skin should be purple with bruises. Probably, I would have quit within the first hour of running, before the sun even rose, except that Ethan endured each of these trials right along with me. During the runs, we went together, step for step. For every push-up, sit-up, or pull-up I did, he did three.

He ate the same lunch as me: four boiled eggs and some fruit, each and every day. By the third day of fight training, Ethan's letting me use the moves I've learned on him.

I give him a black eye.

The third evening of my training, Ethan leads me into room full of books. The air is rich with the smell of their musty pages. We are at another camp now—this one is larger than the last, pitched inside an old oil refinery.

"Remember," he tells me as he leaves, "body, mind, and soul."

Alone now, I stand among piles of books higher than I am tall. A few of the titles I've seen before: *Treasure Island, The Complete Works of William Shakespeare, The Three Musketeers,* the Bible. Most of them, though, I'm unfamiliar with. There are multiple copies of many titles—especially those dealing with American history, philosophy, and warfare. The sight amazes me. I've never seen so many books in one place—ever. My dad has a few shelves full of them in his office, but nothing like this.

Over the next few days, I read as much as I can.

At first, I read very slowly, almost painfully, having to stop every few minutes to walk around or look up from the page. I hardly read during my school days—N-Ed has much more efficient ways of teaching than merely having kids read books—and since then I haven't done it at all. For adults, it's easy to download a copy of the few dozen Company-approved books on your IC, but who has time to read when you have to work sixty-five hours a week? Even when I was in school, I mostly listened to audiobooks. The ability to absorb the words and let my imagination fly free takes time to re-learn, but soon, just as one develops sea legs onboard a ship, my eyes and mind once again acclimate to digesting the written word.

After a few days, Ethan no longer has to direct me to go into the room; I race there myself when my training is done. I spend hour after hour sprawled on the floor or leaning against stacks of moldering paperbacks, poring over biographies of Martin Luther King Jr., Benjamin Franklin, and George Washington, the writings of John Locke, the Dalai Lama, and Karl Marx, novels by Kurt Vonnegut, Ernest Hemingway, and George Orwell, and books with titles like: *1776, Self-Defense for Dummies*, and *The U. S. Army Field Manual.*

Occasionally, Ethan stops by to check on my progress or to suggest a title for me to read. Sometimes, we get into long discussions about philosophy or religion, about the nature of life or love or mankind itself. Every book I mention, he's read. Often, especially if we disagree or if I am particularly adamant in opposition to one of his arguments, he pulls a book from the middle of one of the stacks and hands it to me.

"You're still thinking Company thoughts," he says, his face serious but his eyes smiling. "Look deeper."

Once, during one of his brief visits, I ask him why I've never seen so many of these wonderful books before. "What happened?" I ask. "Did the government make them illegal? Did the Company round up copies and burn them?"

Ethan shakes his head. "No," he says, "They didn't have to do anything as dramatic as that. They just stopped printing them. They stopped promoting them, and they removed the downloadable copies from the Company network. Most of all, they distracted people with other, more flashy, less substantive forms of entertainment so that pretty soon nobody had the patience to read. And they keep everyone working so hard, nobody has time anyway."

He's right. I'm ashamed to think of how many nights I wasted staring at my imager, playing video games, or working at the office until well past midnight.

"The Company isn't our real enemy, May," he continues. "It's complacency. Apathy. Fear. We destroy those emotions in the hearts of the workers and the Company won't stand a chance."

Now, I feel myself changing. Between chapters, I do push-ups or sit-ups. I do pull-ups on a dripping pipe that runs across the hallway just outside my little library. I feel myself getting leaner and stronger, feel my thoughts getting sharper, like I'm an image that's coming into focus. I feel my entire self expanding, not just the lean muscles of my arms and shoulders, not just my mind, but my soul. My energy feels too big to fit inside me any longer. I take up more space than my physical body occupies. The other rebels, at meals or around the camp, smile warmly at me but give me a wide berth as I pass. One night, I find Ada and ask her to do me a favor—she finds a set of shears and cuts off my hair for me. The resulting hairstyle is a short, uneven, unfashionable mess that makes me look even more awkwardly masculine than usual. And I feel more like myself than I ever have in my life.

After the first seven days, Ethan expands my training, teaching me to shoot, to strategize, to wire explosives. He takes me to the hundreds of underground locations used as camps by the rebels and shows me maps and blueprints of tunnel networks all over the land that was once America.

"We're always in danger," he tells me, "but when we're above ground, where the sats can see us, we're completely exposed—like a mouse in a field with a hawk circling above. You have to know the underground."

He tells me the history of the Protectorate, the fourth branch of the American government, formed in secret by George Washington himself. After playing a key but unpublicized role in the first American Revolution, the group that would become the Protectorate lay silent for years, training their leaders, staying few in number but never losing the collective knowledge of their forefathers. Often, posts were handed down from father to son to maintain the secrecy and integrity of the Order. For hundreds of years, the other three branches of government checked each other's power, as the Constitution had envisioned, and there was no need for the Protectorate to come forward. Always, Ethan explained, the fear had been that one of the other branches of government would become too powerful, overstepping its bounds and forcing the Protectorate to rise and reestablish equilibrium. A few times in history, the executive branch became power hungry and managed to gain almost complete domination over the other two branches, to the point where the Protectorate elders were forced to convene and consider stepping in, but always balance was restored naturally, without their needing to take action.

Nobody envisioned that the sanctity of the government would be broken not by a power-hungry faction in the government itself, not by the army or the CIA or a fanatical political party, or even by an invading foreign state, but by the corrupted capitalist system itself.

"We should have seen it coming," Ethan says with a sad shake of his head. "As soon as the big corporations took over the government

and started writing their own regulations, it was over. The natural out-
come of the rigged market they created is one Company, controlling
everything."

But they didn't see it—not in time, anyway. The consolidation of
power happened too gradually for anyone to notice in the beginning,
and later, the Company's usurpation of all government function happened too fast and was too complete for any effective reprisal. To make
matters worse, many of the Protectorate elders were also major Company stockholders, either in N-Corp or B&S, and resisted any action
that might hurt their own financial well-being until it was too late.

The result, eventually, was a schism in the Protectorate itself, which
left Ethan—its youngest member at the time—along with a handful
of others, the only ones able to organize any meaningful resistance.
Still, even with all the resources, the knowledge, and the training of
the Protectorate at his disposal, Ethan found fighting the Company
nearly impossible.

"George Washington and the others, when forming the Order of
the Protectorate, believed that all forms of society, no matter how well
organized or well-intentioned, would eventually fall into domination
by a calculating and self-serving few. They were right. But there was
one area in which they were wrong: they assumed that people would
have the capacity to realize when they were no longer free. The Companies, in their genius, have manipulated and bribed the people into
submission. They give them fancy toys to play with, expensive clothes
to wear, luxurious places to live. They occupy them with jobs that eat
away their time and their mental energy, wasting their days with endless menial tasks. The media division fills their minds with confusion,
not by telling lies, but through a series of half truths, omissions and
rhetorical tricks that slowly warp the public consciousness until even
the most basic principles of the society are distorted. Perhaps most

importantly, they give them stock, so the workers believe that they and the Company are one and the same. They hold out the examples of a few powerful people who've become Blackies—like your father—to perpetuate the false notion that if they work hard enough, they too can become a Blackie one day. They put their words in God's mouth, so that even *goodness* and *righteousness* are commodities they control and benefits they can dole out or withhold as they please. They completed a centuries-long campaign of vilifying the government, so that in the end, the people were glad to see it go. And now, most of the fortunate ones are grateful slaves, happy to have lost their freedom, content to be cogs in the machine that converts human dignity into cash."

"Wow," I say. "Nice speech."

"But do you understand?" Ethan presses.

"Yes . . . but . . . my father used to brag to me about all the good the Company was doing for people, you know? How much more they had now than when he was a kid, how technology was better and work was easier and life was safer and . . . I was proud of him. Proud to be a part of it."

"People do have a lot of toys," Ethan agrees. "They've mortgaged their lives for them."

"What's a mortgage?" I ask. Like every other debtor-worker, I rent my housing from the Company.

"I'll wake you up early tomorrow," he says. "And show you what I mean."

The next day Ethan wakes me, shoves a protein bar into my hand, and leads me, blinking, out of our basement encampment and into the fresh morning light. We travel for quite a ways on foot—perhaps a mile—before coming upon what must've been a handsome, modest house at some time in the not-too-distant past. Now, the roof has fallen in and a stray dog, bone thin and mangy, watches us from the hole where a few splintered shards of a front door still hang from broken hinges. Ethan takes me into the garage attached to the house, where we find a motorcycle.

"Motorcycles are less likely to be spotted by the sat-watchers than larger vehicles," he explains. "Still, we're taking a risk where we're going, so pay close attention to everything you see. I won't be able to take you back there again."

I have no idea what he's talking about, but I nod anyway. Mostly, my attention is taken up by the motorcycle. It's impossible to tell how old it is, but it must be many years, since as far as I know neither N-Corp nor B&S make motorcycles any longer. The bike is sleek-looking and painted flat black, with no logos or placards to identify its maker.

Ethan fires up the engine. It gives a throaty roar that instantly subsides to a grumble.

"Come here," he says, and paints a cross overtop the incision on my cheek with some dark gray, strangely metallic paint. "If anyone asks about the incision, tell them that your old cross implant stopped working and you got a new one a few days ago. Here, put this in your pocket." He hands me a tiny, plastic chip, flat, smooth and small, like a dog's tag.

"This contains your electronic identity code for this mission. When the squadmen try to scan your cross, they'll get this instead. Don't lose it or we're as good as dead. Your name is Elizabeth Ono. You work in retail, selling shoes. My name is Mike Prescott and I'm your boss—and your boyfriend. Got it?"

"Sure, baby."

Ethan laughs. "Let's go."

I climb on behind him, arms around his waist, and in a spray of dirt we're off. I quickly lose track of what direction we're traveling. My mind is tangled in the serpentine curves of the road and blown to excited tatters by the wind in my hair. For this one fleeting instant, life is good.

The danger and gravity of our position hit hard again when we reach our destination, however. Ahead, over the leafless tops of stunted trees rise thick columns of black smoke. A second later, the scrawny foliage gives way to a vast area of brown, dry grass. Beyond, a high chain-linked fence with barbed wire looped at its top extends to the limits of my sight in both directions. The area enclosed here is much, much larger than any of the other secured complexes I've seen in America Division. This is an entire city.

In front of us, squadmen mill about, their black guns brandished and ready.

We approach them fast, then stutter to a stop.

"Slow down there," says one of the squadmen, squinting at us as he steps out of a metal guard hut. He pulls a large, outdated-looking IC out of his pocket and it beeps twice.

"Ono and Prescott? Is that right?"

"Yeah," says Ethan, "we're consultants for the shoe division of N-Sport. We're running late for a production meeting."

The squad member blinks at his IC, scrolling through several screens, presumably.

"Alright," he says. "You're on the list. Head in and take a right on the first street. Follow it all the way around and the factory will be on the left. They'll scan you there and let you in the gate. Just make sure you stay on the main road—this place is full of animals. Wouldn't want anything to happen to your pretty friend."

He shoots me a lecherous glance.

"Thanks," says Ethan, revving the motorcycle impatiently.

"Where'd you get that bike?" asks the guard. Though he's chewing gum, I can still smell the reek of contraband alcohol on his breath from six feet away. As usual, these squadmen are above the rules. "I haven't seen one of those in ten years."

"Family," Ethan says, and he revs the motor again, rendering the guard's response inaudible.

Realizing the conversation is over, the squad member slips his IC back into his shirt pocket, adjusts the rifle slung over his shoulder, and sits back down inside his hut.

Ahead, an electric motor buzzes to life and the corrugated steel gate pulls back. We sputter past it but are stopped by another, identical gate, this one maybe forty feet past the first. When the one behind us has closed, the one in front of us opens, and we lurch through it, the engine of our bike buzzing like a gigantic insect.

I lean forward to Ethan's ear. "What is this place?" I whisper.

"Used to be called Indianapolis," says Ethan. "I'll explain later. Just keep your eyes open."

Ethan shifts his weight, pulling us off the main, four-lane road (on which we are the only vehicle) and onto a narrow side street between two sagging apartment buildings.

The sights here are haunting. Clotheslines crisscross yards littered with old, rusting appliances. The houses all wear dingy coats of peeling paint. Hardly anywhere is a window unbroken. We pass a few men walking in a group. They wear red jumpsuits and stare at the ground, hardly even glancing up as we roar past. Their shoulders are hunched, their steps slow, their feet heavy, their limbs spindly, and their cheeks sunken. Even from a distance, I can tell they are broken men.

We pass children standing barefoot and still in a few dirt yards. They stare at us with eyes as sharp as nails, then disappear behind us.

Sometimes, we pass whole blocks of buildings that seem to have been burned to the ground; only charcoal outlines of their ruins remain. On and on the hellish vision continues. Other than the knot of sullen men, we pass no other adults and only a few children, but block after block, the desolation and squalor extends unbroken.

Finally, Ethan brings us around to another large street—or it could be the one we were on before, I have no way of knowing—and we speed off. We pass over a set of weed-choked railroad tracks and a brown, murky-looking river before at last approaching something familiar: this area looks like the industrial arc. But unlike the industrial arc in the Headquarters hub, this one is teeming with workers wearing red jumpsuits. Some face away from us. They're lined up in cues that extend for hundreds of yards down both sides of the street and terminate in a complex of huge, menacing-looking factory buildings larger than any I've ever seen. In between the two lines, massive groups of workers spill out of the factories, heading toward us. I don't know how many of them there are, but they must number in the thousands. There are so many of them that they choke the roadway and force us to kill the motorcycle's engine and continue on foot, weaving our way upstream through the mass of milling bodies.

"Shift change," Ethan explains.

Nobody will look me in the eye. They must see us, for they clear out of our way as soon as we approach, but none of them acknowledge our presence in any way. They simply wander past us, like reeking, exhausted zombies.

Above, I hear a deep roar and look up to see a huge airplane pass low overhead, descending toward a landing strip that must be very close by. To our right: a concrete guard tower filled with squadmen and bristling with guns.

"What is this?" I whisper to Ethan.

"Just watch," he says. "Save your questions for later."

The next hour blurs in my mind: we enter the gates and pass from factory to factory. In each one, men and women are lined up as far as the eye can see, performing all sorts of jobs, from painting vases to stitching footballs. We pass through a foundry, filled with the stench and heat of hell. There's a slaughterhouse the size of seven football fields, a fish cannery, and of course, the airstrip, where all kinds of goods are loaded, unloaded, and sorted. There are plants for extracting gold from ore, for creating diamonds from carbon, for making all sorts of plastics, resins, paints, and solvents (here, even more than in the rest of the city, the air tastes of poison, and we move along quickly).

Every area we pass through is filled with throngs of workers, all of them intent on the task at hand and heedless of our presence. Some of the factories are filled with elaborate machines, but others are just packed with tables where the workers perform tasks by hand. We enter one such room in the shoe factory, and Ethan leans over to me.

"We'll talk to one of them briefly, but only one. You pick who."

I look around, not knowing exactly what Ethan meant or what I'm supposed to be looking for, but I finally see an old fellow with a friendly-looking face. His dark skin is withered, but his eyes are edged with laugh lines. His fingers work quickly, weaving white laces into the newest athletic shoe, the N-Hoop 6. I point to him, and Ethan leads us over.

"Hey," Ethan says to the man.

"Yes. Yes, sir," the fellow says, putting down the shoe and standing fumblingly. "How can I help you?"

"Just answer a few questions," Ethan says.

"Alright," says the man. "Sure." His gaze lingers at our feet, looping back and forth like one who is dizzy and on the verge of fainting. He is very old, and sickly thin.

"How did you get here?" Ethan says.

"Well . . . bus took me," the man says with a shrug.

"Okay," says Ethan, "but I meant—"

"I don't do nothing wrong, I lace 'em up as fast as I can, sir . . ."

"I'm not worried about that," says Ethan. "You're not in trouble. Just tell us how you ended up here. Why were you taken to this place, do you know?"

"Oh, you know. It's an old story," the man says, his sick, yellowish eyes smiling at us. "I wasn't working like I was supposed to. Was more interested in playin' the trumpet and singin' songs than working a real job, truth be told. Then I threw my back out and couldn't work no ways. My debt was getting big; real big. Same reason as everybody else is here, pretty much. I wasn't workin' enough to pay back the debts, so m'credit got froze. I couldn't buy nothing. Couldn't go anyplace. Got put outta my apartment and got m'car taken away. Had no food for my wife and kids. You know how it is. . . ."

"So what happened?" I ask. "You got repossessed and taken here?"

The man laughs. "Oh, no, no. Never got repossessed or nothin' like that. I begged to come here. Otherwise I'da starved and my kids woulda starved and my wife woulda left for sure. The Comp'ny was good enough to take me in here, after I did a lotta beggin'. I said, 'Please, please, God! I ain't no unprofitable! I'll work! I'll work!' And they took me to this here work camp. Now I got food and a place to live and they make me work; don't let me get lazy or nothin' like I used to be. I'm grateful, I tell you the truth, I thank God, Amen!"

"Isn't this a bad place to live, though?" I ask, mystified.

"Well . . . people do get killed here. Lazy people get tired of workin' and get mad and the squad puts 'em down, or otherwise people find out somebody's got something they want, and one guy steals from another one, you know, and pretty soon they're stabbing each other or raping each other's wives. But mostly when that happens the squad finds out and puts 'em both down, so that way the problem ends. Sure, people get killt. But no, not me. I'm one of the good ones. I'm grateful to the Comp'ny, for sure I am."

"Are they erasing your debt, then, as you work?" I ask him. "I mean, since you aren't buying things?"

He shakes his head. "I don't think so," he says, thinking. "I don't remember mucha what they said when I came in, but it was something about fees . . . it costs to live in the camp . . . and plus food and all . . . so I think my debt is gettin' a little bigger . . . but the Comp'ny's good about it. They ain't mad—long as I keep on workin' hard, they'll let the debt run, so just my kids'll pay it later on instead of me. But . . ." He glances dubiously at the pile of shoes stacking up next to his table. "Maybe you want me to get back to work? I shouldn't get behind."

I open my mouth, but Ethan speaks first. "Yes, do get back to work, but one more question first: how long ago were you brought here?"

The man scratches his head for a moment. "Truly, I don't know. It's been so long."

"If you were going to guess?"

"Well, to guess, I'd say . . . fifteen years, maybe. Pretty close to that." He glances again at the pile of shoes.

"That's all," says Ethan. "Thanks for answering our questions. God bless you."

I'm about to speak again, but Ethan gently takes my arm, "We don't want to get him in trouble. And we should go, too. It'll be dark soon."

I turn to thank the old man, but he's already too involved in his work to notice me, his shoulders hunched over the big sneaker in his hands, his head bobbing to a beat only he can hear.

We make our way out of the factory quickly. If Ethan's pace is any indication, he's feeling the same urgency to leave this bleak, soul-crushing atmosphere that I am. But when we round the corner and step into the alley where the motorcycle is parked, we find the squad member from the gate sitting astride it. When he sees us, he smiles, climbs off the bike and starts walking toward us.

"I checked with the N-Sport people," he says. "It looks like you missed your meeting. And it's a funny thing, no one at the N-Sport office had heard of either of you."

I hear a shuffle behind me, and two squadmen with large machine guns step out of the shadows behind us. I'm on the verge of screaming, but Ethan's breathing remains even.

"I think this is my lucky day," the squad member continues gleefully. "I always wanted a motorcycle."

"Well, I'll just get you the keys," Ethan says, calmly, and he reaches inside his coat.

I hear the crack of the shot before I even see the white pistol in his hand, and the squad member by the motorcycle drops face first to the pavement. Ethan is wheeling toward me now, and I instinctively duck out of his way and cover my ears as three more gunshots ring out.

Ethan's eyes scan the alleyway once more, shifting from one end to the other then flitting up to the rooftops. Satisfied, he spins the gun like an Old-West gunslinger and slips it back into his coat, adjusts his tie. I suddenly realize I'm staring at him, my jaw dropped. I close my mouth quickly and clasp my hands together to halt their trembling.

"That was . . . " I whisper, searching for the words. For the second time, Ethan has saved my life. He's a scholar, an athlete, a master of disguise, and now a gunslinger. If I could ever be interested in a man, it would be him.

A grin crosses his handsome features. "You can pat me on the back later," he says. "If HR catches us here, the squad will execute us before sundown."

Once again, a protest forms in my mind: all HR punishments are doled out only after three meetings with your department review board, and capital punishment is at the sole discretion of the divisional HR head.

Yeah, I remind myself, *and work camps are humane, temporary opportunities for workers to "get back on track...."*

I hurry back to the motorcycle, climb on behind Ethan, and wrap my arms tightly around his waist as the engine thunders to life. I will hold on to him, I decide. I will follow him—wherever the road might lead.

The ride back to the Protectorate camp, through the deepening night, seems to take forever. Questions buzz in my mind, angry and fighting to come out, but I can't shout them over the rush of wind and the growl of the motorcycle. Finally, like an island in a sea of darkness, the little house emerges in our headlight, and next to it, the garage from which we began our journey so many hours before.

We pull in and stop. With the engine silenced, the quiet seems as thick and sticky as molasses. Ethan pulls the rattling garage door closed and we start walking down the footpath, retracing our steps from the morning. I have so many questions that I don't know where to start.

Ethan senses my reticence and begins: "The kind of extravagant luxury the Company provides can only be built on the backs of the impoverished. That's the way it's always been, in all of human history. All Company workers are slaves, but the people you saw today are the most wretched ones of all."

"But why?" I ask. "I don't understand why it has to be that way.

Instead of everyone buying gold-plated hairbrushes and brand-new, three-million-dollar ICs every six months, why can't we give something to help those people? I know the Company has the means to do it."

"Of course they do," says Ethan, "but it would come out of their profit."

"It makes no sense, though," I say. "What good is profit if nobody benefits from it?"

"A few benefit," says Ethan. "The rest is just wasted, or used to perpetuate and expand the Company's power even further. But the Company is a machine, May. It's not a thinking entity in the normal sense. It doesn't operate on logic. If it would increase the Company's profits, everyone would be sent to a camp like that. There is no logic in a Company, only greed. If somebody tries to do something for the good of the world that hurts Company profits, they'll simply get fired. It's the nature of the system."

Night sounds envelop us. I've grown to love nature—what remains of it, in this poisoned world. Twigs crackle under our feet. Stars glimpse us through the tree branches. At least, I hope they're stars and not satellites.

"Why do you take the time to show me so much?" I ask. "Teach me to fight and help me understand the Company and everything?"

Ethan sighs. "There are a couple reasons. For one, you've grown up closer to the Company than anyone. I guess I figure if I can make you understand why it has to be destroyed, then I can convince anyone."

"What's the other reason?" I ask.

He stops, turns to me. "Because you're a leader," he says, "and I may not always be here."

We walk the rest of the way back listening not to our own words, but to those of the owls and the crickets and the breeze.

—CHAPTER Ø15—

The prison raid.

The team and I leave the underground village at dawn, rising from the earth at almost the same moment as the sun. Already, the day grows hot. We trek through a long tunnel, climb up a ladder, and come up through some sort of storm drain set in the cracked, decaying foundation of a long-fallen building. This is the outer industrial arc, where nature has almost reclaimed most of America Division's former manufacturing might.

Ethan leads us single file under cover of trees down a long dirt footpath, and despite my nerves, I begin to feel good. The throbbing pain of the wound on my cheek has diminished almost to nothing. I notice strength in my legs, feel the sun on my skin—and there's something else, something new: the weight of the white gun on my hip.

There are twenty-six of us, including me. Ethan walks in the lead with McCann, the only other member of the ruling council to volunteer for the mission besides that bitch Grace, who takes up the rear. Twenty-six seems to me a tiny number for such an undertaking— even I know that Company prisons are heavily fortified and armed with elaborate electronic defense systems. Judging from the whispers I heard in the camp before our departure, I wasn't the only one who thought the idea of this mission was pretty foolish. But nobody asked my advice, and if they had, I doubt if I'd have said anything. I, like the twenty-five rebels now walking with me, face the coming danger with the sort of calm only claimed by the truly blessed, the stupid, or the doomed.

After a short hike, we descend a small hill and find the path ahead opening up into a narrow dirt road. There, in among the trees, sit five large, black, off-road vehicles, identical to the security squad trucks. If anybody else is surprised to find them sitting in the middle of the grove, nobody shows it. We all draw up in the center of the sandy clearing and look at one another. I'm amazed and delighted by the fact that ten of the twenty-six-member crew are women. Some of them look at me now with hard, patient, unreadable expressions. I'm thrilled by the strength they exude and by the thought that one day I might be like them, with the same wrinkled, sun-battered skin, the same sharp eyes, the same quiet, implacable strength. I meet their appraising gazes with what I hope is a friendly but measured smile.

Ethan crosses his arms and scans our ranks with pursed lips and narrowed eyes. Something looks a little different about him today. It's not just the strange, bulky sunglasses pushed back against his forehead or the gauntness of his face; everything about his bearing is slightly different—no less commanding than usual, but a little strange, as if he's channeling a spirit with different mannerisms from his own. I wonder: *Could it be fear?*

Nodding to himself, apparently satisfied with us, Ethan points to McCann, then to a short, hefty woman, then to a broad-shouldered young man, and then to Grace. "The four of you will each drive a squad truck. Follow me," he says. "When we get there, I'll do the talking. When the fighting comes, run fast, shoot fast, and stay close to your leaders. You all know what to do."

I have no idea what to do, but I nod anyway.

As the vehicle doors open, I head toward Ethan's car, but McCann calls me back.

"Miss Fields," he says. "You'll ride with me." Then, perhaps reading the expression on my face, he adds, "You'll see why soon enough."

This is one of the few times in my life I've actually been on the ground beyond the industrial arc. I ride, watching the countryside streak past, watching abandoned houses, gas stations, and stores appear in my window then disappear again. I still remember when N-Corp enticed the last stragglers from the countryside, where they were unproductive and difficult to police, and into the cities. First, they cut all jobs that existed outside of the hubs, so most people had to move into town in order to make a living. Some proud country folk were resistant, but once the Company cut electricity to all rural areas (for the sake of efficiency, of course), country life completely died out. Rumor has it that there are still a few mad hermits here and there who live off the polluted land and attack people who wander near their homes, but for all I know, these stories may have been started by the Company. The tales are just scary enough to keep people inside the hubs, where HR can keep an eye on them.

Now, I'm struck by the beauty of these lost and forbidden places. It's fall, and this empty world seems golden. The polluted air has been cleansed by the cooling weather and smells of things old and sweet and ripe.

As I watch it all pass out my squad-truck window, my mind wanders to Clair. During my training, I fought hard to keep any distracting thoughts of her out of my mind, but now, on this long drive, it's impossible. A few weeks ago, I would have assumed the Company treated their prisoners well, but after seeing the work camp, my worry for her has steadily increased. Now I know they'll treat her in whatever way is most cost-effective for them. Which could mean they won't feed her. And if you have to pay prison guards by the hour, it's more efficient to torture a prisoner than to wait weeks for a confession, isn't it?

I thrust these thoughts from my mind. I'm jittery enough as it is—there's no need to get emotional. Around me, my fellow passengers are checking and re-checking their guns, peering into their clips, and patting their ammo pouches, all with the perfect calm of people about to go fishing and making sure their tackle boxes are in order.

McCann presses a button in the dash and music blasts forth with enough force to make me jump. He laughs good-naturedly around the plastic straw hanging out of his mouth and yells over the din.

"You mustn't startle that easily, Miss Fields, not where we are going."

"Call me, May," I say. "And I won't be scared."

Although I am already scared—shaking, in fact—I somehow know that I'm telling the truth. I will be brave. He only nods, then gestures to the radio.

"This was my music," he says. "I played the drums."

I pause, listening to the sounds blaring from the speakers. Galloping drums pound over a twanging sort of instrument that I can only liken to a mouth harp tinged with distortion, and behind it all, a distant voice chants. The sound is beautiful, savage, stirring.

"I love it," I tell him.

"I was a big star in my village, back in Africa Division. Can you believe that? I went into the hub city to make this album. I did everything when I was young, anything to get ahead. When I left my village and went to the city, my people were starving. So I did any work I could to help them. I sold drugs, guns, guitars, even dolls!" he laughs. "I sent half of the money back to the village elders, to help my starving people. All the money from the music concerts I sent back. When I met my wife and we made Michel, there was less money to send back. My wife, she was beautiful. I loved her very much. But she was a woman who liked nice things. Perfumes. Silk. Dresses. She wanted us to save money to send Michel to a private school when he was big enough. I had to work harder to make her happy, and now there was nothing left to send back to my village. Then, N-Corp came to the city with posters offering jobs that seemed too good to be true. I was one of the first to sign up. I wanted the people in the village to join the Company, too. Then, they would have everything they needed. Maybe it was just me being selfish. If they all worked for the Company, they wouldn't need me sending money to them every week, then I would have plenty of credit and my wife would be happy. . . . " He shakes his head.

"You know the rest," he says. "After what happened in the village, I knew I had to fight the Company. I stopped chasing money and started chasing God. I joined this holy fight. I won't even tell you what it was like for me and Michel, smuggling ourselves into America Division. It was hard. But I wanted to cut off the head of the dragon."

"Where is your wife now?" I ask warily. "She's dead, isn't she?"

"Oh, no. At least, I pray she isn't. I pray she has all the perfumes and chocolates and pearls she could want." He pauses. "She still works for the Company. She's a manager in Africa Division."

He pauses, then goes on: "Me and Michel, we'll slay the dragon for her. We'll give her that, instead of diamonds. You can't take diamonds into heaven, but good deeds will follow you everywhere. He misses her very much."

His sparkling eyes go watery for a second. I begin to ask him another question—it seems like there are so many questions I need to ask— then stop. Instead, I take out my ceramic and pretend to check it over like the others are checking theirs, though I hardly know what to look for. Next to me, McCann presses a button on the stereo and a new track of music comes on. Driving percussion and distant-sounding guitar fills the truck.

"This is what we like to sing before battle," McCann says, then begins to sing words overtop the drums. He starts with a whisper, but soon his voice has grown to a full-throated call.

O say can you see,
By the dawn's early light,
What so proudly we hailed
At the twilight's last gleaming?

One by one, the others join in.

Whose broad stripes and bright stars,
Through the perilous fight
O'er the ramparts we watched
Were so gallantly streaming . . .

Their voices rise together as strong and as powerful as any sound I've ever heard. Their song drowns out all other noise, even the simpering whispers of fear in my own gut, and soon I'm fortified, electrified, and ready to fight, to conquer or die. A tear comes into my eye as the song ends. Everyone sits solemnly, ready for action.

Against the silence of my companions and the rumble of the truck's engine I whisper, "I've never heard that song before. It's beautiful."

"We're close," McCann says. "Prepare yourselves."

The sporadic, nervous conversations and jokes of the previous hour dissipate, replaced by a taut silence. Around me, the brows of my comrades have lowered, their jaws have set. One woman in the back produces a tube full of the dark, inky makeup and begins painting a cross over the scar on the cheek of the rebel next to her. When the process has been repeated on everyone's cheek and a layer of powder is applied, the crosses look remarkably like real implants. Next, the woman reaches behind the rear seat and produces a security-squad uniform for everyone in the car—everyone except me. As I look around, confused, I notice that on the far side of McCann's cheek, the side that had been hidden from me, a cross has already been painted as well. In the back, my comrades wriggle into their uniforms.

Nobody offers to paint a cross on me.

McCann catches the look of concern on my face. "Alright, May," he says. "It's time for you to learn the plan. You are lucky to have a place of special honor in it."

I fight the urge to roll my eyes. In my experience, whenever somebody tells you you're lucky, it's always the kiss of death.

"Now listen close," he says. "You will be our ticket into the perimeter of the prison. You're going to be our prisoner. You will be handcuffed, and when we arrive, the squadmen will take you from our custody. Ethan will go in with you, and once the two of you are inside, he will set you free. When that happens, an alarm will sound and the entire facility will go into lockdown mode, which means all doors in the prison will automatically close and lock until the emergency is over. You and Ethan will then be sealed inside, but more importantly, each quadrant of the prison will be sealed off from the others; all the guards will be stuck in the quadrant of the prison they're in when the alarm sounds. This will cut by one-quarter the number of armed guards we'll have to deal with at any given time. The doors will remain sealed until the alarm has stopped, and by then, God willing, we'll have freed Clair and the others, and will be on the road with them already. For your part, you'll simply have to play the prisoner, keep silent, and fight like a lion when the time comes. Remember, until we can break in to join you, you and Ethan will have to hold off all the squadmen in the quadrant by yourselves. One advantage you will have is that the electronic defenses inside the prison should be neutralized. Even so, it will not be easy. This is your chance to back out of the role you've been assigned, if you choose. Somebody else could go in your place, although Ethan feels you'd be best for the job."

McCann looks over at me, studying me slyly, probing for hesitation, for any sign of weakness. I draw a deep breath to steady my voice before I say: "How many squadmen in the quadrant?"

"A hundred and fifty, by our best estimates."

A moment passes as the enormity of the situation dawns on me. This is my first battle and it's going to be me and Ethan, alone, against a hundred and fifty squadmen. What the hell have I gotten myself into?

"Okay," I say finally, "But I'm going to need another clip."

McCann grins.

As I go over his words again, my mind roils with questions. The plan seems riddled with holes and pitfalls too numerous to contemplate. Even if we—who only number twenty-six—are able to defeat one hundred and fifty fully trained and equipped squadmen, what if the electronic defenses aren't neutralized, as they are expected to be? We would be decimated by the auto-defense systems. And what if the prisoners have been moved to another quadrant, or if they attempt to take me to a different quadrant than the one Clair is in? Then we'll have to break into that second quadrant, releasing another one hundred and fifty squadmen, bringing the number of adversaries to a completely insurmountable three hundred. Most obviously, what if Ethan and I can't hold off the guards long enough for reinforcements to break through and help us?

I am no fool. I see our odds clearly enough. But for some reason, there isn't a doubt in my mind that I'm going to go anyway. It strikes me that this is a new kind of faith, one deeper than the brand that the

Company peddles, and I bow my head in prayer. Unbidden, Jimmy
Shaw's heretical words march through my mind: *I believe God-fearing
workers work harder.*

Maybe his confession should have strangled the faith within me, but
somehow, as I finish my prayer and gaze at the brambles and scraggly
pines out the car window, I feel God near me more clearly that I ever
have. The immediacy of the feeling strikes me almost hard enough to
bring tears into my eyes.

Who would have imagined, as I step into the world of everything
forbidden by the Company church that I would find God there waiting for me? Not the God of old, dusty books or tired, threadbare
admonishments, but the living God, the one that dwells in adrenaline
and breath, in the present, inside me, not in some far-off cloud city but
in the electric blue of the sky hanging above.

I will go. And I will set Clair free.

Though trembling, I am calm. There's no doubt I will fight like hell.
I do not fear that I will crack under the pressure of gunfire. For the
first time in my life, I do not even fear death, perhaps because it no
longer stalks in the shadows but stands clearly before me, expectant,
inexorable.

Half a mile later, a small guardhouse comes into view. McCann
murmurs a few orders—which I hardly hear, as wrapped up in my
thoughts as I am—and I am shuffled to the backseat. One of the men
back there, a strapping fellow with big, brown doe's eyes, whispers an
apology as he squeezes the shackles tight against my wrists and takes
my gun from my hand. I do not grimace or utter any response. I simply
wait for what comes.

In front of us, Ethan's vehicle halts before the guard gate. He leans
out, says a few sharp words and gestures toward the prison impatiently.
The guard, who even from here looks very young, very slow-witted,

and utterly confused, gives a conciliatory shrug and speaks into his IC, presumably calling some higher-up inside the prison. Finally, after a few tense moments, the gate swings open and we roll through, following Ethan's lead.

We pass down a long, asphalt driveway, on either side of which an expanse of parched lawn stretches almost to the horizon. Soon, we reach another checkpoint. This one consists of a steel gate set between two concrete guard towers that rise from the bare plain like a couple of gigantic fangs. From each of the guard towers, a wall of razor wire makes a wide arc around the perimeter of the prison, which itself is an unremarkable-looking edifice of water-stained concrete and scant, black windows.

We are stopped at this gate, too, and as I glance over at McCann, I see sweat beading up on his brow. Ethan explains something to another guard, and after another brief delay, this gate, too, opens. As we roll past the guardhouse, I hear the computer inside reciting a list of names: *Nancy Hernandez, squadmember third class, John Bell, squad captain, Will Pence squad member fourth class.*

As they scan us, my fingers snake into my pocket and touch the tiny encoder chip there, just like the one Ethan and I used to fool the cross-reader at the work camp. The implant ID system is supposed to be infallible. Fortunately for us, it's not. And I suddenly wonder how Ethan and his team were able to figure out a way around it.

"How—" I begin.

"Shut up, prisoner," says the man who'd handcuffed me. His voice is sharp as flint, but when his brown eyes meet mine, I see they're filled with sympathy, even apology. He points to one ear, and I understand: they could be listening.

Now we've entered the open square in front of the prison. Some of the rebels in the car with me exchange glances, and I can feel us collectively holding our breaths. The vehicles pull around a large, circular driveway and stop. To my right rises the citadel of the prison. Set in the wall directly before us stands what looks like a thick, steel garage door.

Before I can think, almost before we've completely stopped, my friendly captor leans over me, opens the door, and shoves me out onto the pavement. The breath is almost knocked out of me as I land hard on one shoulder.

"Up."

It's Ethan, standing above me, yanking me to my feet. At the same time, it's not Ethan at all. The familiar charm, the humor, the quiet, good-natured power, all have drained from him. Everything about him is completely different now, his voice, his mannerisms, even his facial expressions. The transformation is creepy, even scary. He doesn't look at me once I'm on my feet, but grabs my shoulder and pushes me along ahead of him so hard I almost fall over again. I wonder, with a sense of rising dread, if I've been betrayed. If, in fact, the rebels have not elected to accept me at all, but instead have struck a deal with the Company to turn me in. Worse yet, perhaps there was never a rebellion at all: perhaps it was all just an elaborate ruse, a test of my loyalty to the Company, which, after having failed it, necessitates the forfeiture of my freedom.

But there is no time for speculation. Already, the huge door before us has risen and three men walk out to greet us, moving almost as quickly as we are. Each wears the familiar HR squad uniform complete with the white star on the cap, but atop these stars is stitched the insignia of a black padlock, the mark of the prison division.

The squad member in the middle, obviously the commander, has a thickly muscled neck, popping with veins, and small, dark eyes. "What is this?" he says as he approaches us. "We haven't gotten any communication whatsoever about a prisoner coming in today."

"It's an anarchist informant," Ethan says, in a voice unlike his own. "We caught this one, and she pointed the way to the nest where the rest of 'em are hiding. Blackwell ordered us not to talk about it over the airwaves or the net—those damned anarchists have big ears. Blackwell doesn't want to tip them off."

The prison commander is sucking on his upper lip. "So what am I supposed to do with this one? I don't have a cell arranged, I don't have a prisoner number. . . ."

"I don't care what you do with her, but do it fast. We're expecting a nasty fight when we catch those damned unprofitables, and we'll be needing every gun we can get. I'm under orders to haul tail back down there as soon as the prisoner is dropped off. And if you can spare anybody, they're to come with me. Send 'em to the garage in the west quadrant. We'll pull around and they can fall in behind us."

The commander is shaking his head. "I didn't hear a word about any of this. . . ."

My heart is sinking. It's not going to work; he's not buying it.

"Look," Ethan says. "I don't have time to hold your hand here. You don't want to spare any of your men, fine. Explain it to Blackwell when you see him. Just take this prisoner off my hands so I can get back where the action is."

"I'm just gonna call headquarters and confirm all this," says the commander. His nostrils are flared, like a bloodhound trying to sniff out the truth.

I'm shaking with tension. This isn't going to work. . . .

Ethan doesn't seem worried at all. "Do whatever you want," he says with a dismissive shrug.

Now the commander steps over to me, takes my jaw in his hands and raises my chin up, studying me.

"It's an anarchist, alright," he says, his sour breath reeking against my face. "Cut out its cross and everything. A woman, too. I thought she was a man when you were bringing her up. We'll have fun with this one."

"Great," says Ethan. "Well, I'm going to be getting out of here. . . ."

The commander nods, still eyeing me. I stare at the ground, refusing to meet his gaze, playing the role of the prisoner, afraid to let him see the gleeful foreknowledge of vengeance seething inside me.

"Take her in and strip her down," the commander says to one of his men. "Have Baz get her in oranges and assign her a cell."

"Alright," says Ethan, affecting impatience. "She's your prisoner now. I'm outta here—right after I use your john. Where is it?"

"This way," says the commander. "I'll show you."

And we all walk toward the big, steel door.

My heart beats like a struggling captive in my chest as we step inside. Behind us, the door closes with a low *bang* of terrifying finality.

Here it comes, I think to myself, *this is where the revolution begins.*

Our footsteps echo from the polished concrete of the walls, the ceiling, the floor. One squad member behind me pokes my ass with the butt of his rifle and another one stifles a laugh. Lights hanging above, bare bulbs housed in plain, steel shades, cast strange shadows as we pass by—one, two, three, four of them.

Then a word, slowly and clearly spoken, breaks the monotony of footfalls. "Sigma," Ethan says, and I see his hand fall to his gun an instant before the lights above click out. In the blackness, the guards around me are too startled even to make a sound.

I hear the commander in front of me mutter in exasperation, "Okay, what's—"

And an ear-splitting report cuts his voice down to nothing. Two more muzzle-flares, two more *cracks*; I feel the heat of the shots as they speed past me, and I know the guards on either side of me are dead, though I can't see them fall.

I feel Ethan's hands on my wrists, hear the tiny *clok* as he unlocks my cuffs, feel the grip of the ceramic pistol as he presses it into my palm.

"Put these on," Ethan hands me something else—some sort of glasses. I put them on and instantly the darkness around me burns with strange, iridescent shapes. I see Ethan in front of me, his features all intact but somehow without detail. On his face, he wears the strange sunglasses that had been on his head earlier.

"Fire at any movement," he says, "and stay close."

He leads me back the way we came, perhaps twenty yards. On my left, I make out a door I hadn't noticed coming in.

Voices behind it: *"You think it's a drill? Where's the back-up power?"*

Ethan knocks, and as the door swings open he steps through, gun barrel already flashing. Three squadmen fall before I'm even through the doorway. The target I see first is a small-looking man who is either trying to cower behind a desk or looking for a gun in a drawer. It takes me three shots, but he falls, howling like a wild animal.

Only one of the squadmen in the room gets a shot off, firing at Ethan's head and striking the steel door behind him with a deep metallic *clung*. Ethan hits him in the throat, and even with my strange, truncated vision I can see the blood erupt from his neck. Ethan shoots two more guards and I get one, clipping him in the shoulder, the shot spinning him around so he drops his gun. Ethan steps up to him and shoots him once in the face, finishing him off, and I thank God I am spared the details and can only see the shape as his head distorts in the darkness. I know that I should be scared—or sad, perhaps—but the adrenaline makes any emotion impossible. All I feel is an overpowering, exhilarating drive to survive.

Now, back to the main hall. We enter three more rooms in the same way; one is empty and the other holds a few squadmen that we quickly dispatch. I replace my clip. This time, before we step back into the main hall, we can hear squadmen amassing there, their voices hardened and brittle with forced bravado. Taking cover in the doorway, Ethan pushes me to one knee and presses me to the doorjamb as he takes position standing.

We start shooting.

Maybe six guys in the hallway die before anyone can even return fire. Those who do resist look for us desperately, their flashlight beams raking the dark, their guns firing blindly, but the shots ricochet uselessly off the door frame behind which we hide, and in a few moments, most of our assailants are cut down.

Some of the survivors drop to the ground and try crawling away. Others dash for cover, diving into one of the many doorways off the main hall.

"Watch our back," Ethan says. "I think there's another entrance to this room."

Sure enough, just as I turn I see a door behind us opening up. Tracer rounds rake the wall off to my left, and I take cover behind a desk, firing as I go. I must've hit somebody, because the machine-gun fire ceases for a minute and I hear soft, guttural muttering from across the room. Peeking over the desk, I see one squad member stooping, attending to his companion. Still, he's too well concealed behind the doorway for me to have a clear shot. I look around the room for the advantage, and spy an alcove inset in the wall to my left. Concealed by several filing cabinets, I crawl over and stop, leaning against the wall. I poke my head over the cabinets, half expecting to have it blown off. From my new position, I see my enemy clearly. He fires a few useless shots at the desk I was crouched behind a moment ago, then turns back to his friend.

I smile cruelly and level my ceramic, feeling the tension of the trigger against my finger. But I hesitate. I drop to my knees again. Don't know how many shots are left. Better change the clip. I rise again, looking over the filing cabinets at my unsuspecting adversary and open fire. Of the five shots I unleash, at least one finds him, for he falls back, dead.

My heartbeat pounds in my ears.

"May," hisses Ethan from across the room.

"Here," I say.

"You alright?"

"Fine."

"Then come here."

Ethan is leaning just slightly out of the doorway, angling for a better view of the main hall. "Look," he says, trading places with me. I lean out into the wide passage, and stop breathing. Something's coming. My first thoughts are absurd: that it's a huge, many-legged monster stalking us, or that the entire hallway has come to life and is boiling with movement, folding in on itself, collapsing toward us. Of course these ideas are foolish. It's just difficult to differentiate shapes with the night-vision glasses on. What looks like one massive form approaching must be a mass of men—easily a hundred—and from what I can see, they seem to be concealed behind giant shields.

"Riot gear," says Ethan into my ear.

As the men draw rapidly closer, small groups of them break off, firing into side corridors and storming the rooms adjoining the main passage. I suddenly feel ill. There are too many of them. No way we can hold them off.

"What do you think?" Ethan whispers. "Can we take them, or should we call for help?"

I'm so incredulous at the question, I almost yell my response. "Call for help!"

Ethan laughs, and for a moment I'm gripped with the fear that he's actually gone mad. He checks his clip, fills it, replaces it, and surprises me by leveling it not at the mass of rapidly approaching squadmen, but in the opposite direction, at the huge, steel door through which we entered the prison.

One, two, three—he squeezes off the shots with an interval of perhaps one second between them, and with the strike of each bullet, the steel door belches forth a knell like a great church bell.

Next, Ethan is pulling me back from the doorway. Seeing the muzzle flare from his shots, the squadmen direct fire at us, and in a moment's time, the doorjamb we were leaning against is reduced to a jagged, crumbling ruin. The air hangs thick with cement dust. We pull back deeper into the room and Ethan yanks me behind the desk again for cover.

"Watch that door," he says to me, nodding toward the back entrance by the file cabinets where I had dispatched the two squadmen only a minute before. The fire outside intensifies, blended with the terrifying footfalls of countless heavy-booted feet. Still, no reinforcements seem to be coming.

"Dammit," Ethan says. "Come on, guys. . . ."

The footsteps grow nearer. Suddenly, I'm falling back against the wall, my arm stinging. Shots blink like Christmas lights from the doorway I was supposed to be watching, and the top of desk we're hiding behind splinters before my eyes. Ethan wheels toward our attackers, rattling off six shots in quick succession, and just like that, the doorway empties.

"I said watch that door!" Ethan shouts. And his gun barks again, this time casting lead toward the main door leading to the passageway, which is now crowded with bodies and bristling with gun barrels.

Bullets swarm around us like hornets. I shoot, reload; Ethan shoots, reloads. Below the din, I become aware of a low sound, like the beating of a great drum. It comes only every few moments, but when it does it seems to rattle the very foundation of the prison, the two-foot-thick block walls around us, and the desk against which we lean. My eyes squint at my doorway; now it's a rectangle of black, but from behind the tangled limbs of fallen men lying across its threshold, I see furtive movements and tremble with anticipation, knowing that any instant now more men will appear there, gunning for my life.

"You okay?" hisses Ethan. "You get hit?"

"I think it was just a splinter of the desk. I'm okay."

"Keep it that way."

At that moment, another deep crash rattles the structure around us, and I allow my eyes to dart over to Ethan's doorway, behind which the passageway has suddenly been flooded with the light of day. I see a few black-uniformed squadmen dashing away, and the sparks of tracer bullets following them, stinging them with death. A moment later, one of the black squad vehicles rolls past, moving fast with guns blazing from each open window and I understand: the rebels have used the vehicle to batter down the steel door and breach the perimeter of the prison. Reinforcements have arrived. Another vehicle rumbles past, close behind the first.

"Come on," says Ethan, leading me toward the wide passage, "but keep watching that door; cover our backs."

"KAPPA!" he says when we reach the ruined, crumbling doorway, and the lights above blaze to life again. Ethan removes his glasses and so do I, blinking in the newly rekindled light. He pulls what looks like a scarf, striped with red and white, from some unseen pocket and waves it over his head as he runs down the passage with me in tow. "It's us!" he yells.

As we run, I keep one eye trained over my shoulder, watching our backs just as Ethan ordered, and I see another of our vehicles stopped at the entrance to the prison, just past the twisted, fallen hulk of the steel door. It's positioned across the entrance like a blockade, and I see several rebels standing close to it, using it for cover as they fire with massive, roaring machine guns over its hood and out across the grassy courtyard we traversed on our way in.

I glance ahead again just in time to avoid running into Ethan, who's already stopped next to one of the vehicles.

"Christ, you took long enough to signal us," says Grace, sliding out of the driver's seat with a big, smoking assault rifle hanging from her fist. Behind her, more rebels pile out of the personnel carrier. "We thought for sure you were dead."

"Not yet," says Ethan. Leaning into the backseat, he pulls out two white machine guns, slings one over his shoulder by its strap and hands the other to me. I'm shocked at how light it is. "Here," Ethan says as he passes me a bag, which I hang over my shoulder. "Extra clips. This is how you drop a clip out to reload; this is how you clear the chamber if it jams. Got it?"

"We gotta go," says Grace, out of breath and frowning. "It's pretty hot outside. We could only take out one of the guard towers, so they're taking a lot of fire from the other one. We don't have much time."

"Put this on first," Ethan says, handing me a garment rather like the jerseys I remember wearing in school gym class. It has no armholes, only a neck hole and a bib-like swatch of cloth hanging down over the chest and the back. It's covered with stars and stripes, the old American flag. Ethan puts one on, too; I realize it's the object he had waved over his head a moment before, the one I had taken for a scarf. Grace, glaring at us impatiently, already wears one, too.

This, I realize, will allow us to tell our comrades from our enemies.

"Come on," says Ethan.

We step over many bodies; dozens of squadmen were mowed down by gunfire when the vehicles came in, and scores of others died under the crushing wheels. The other guards have scattered, fallen back into the hallways and side rooms. These hiding, sneaking, probably terrified squadmen, I realize, could be very dangerous. At any moment, from any conceivable hiding place, we could face enemy fire. And we do.

There are maybe fifteen of us, running at a shuffling jog down the dim hallways, firing at anything that moves. The rest, I imagine, are still fighting at the entrance or going door-to-door in the main passage, just as the squadmen had been doing a few moments before, killing any lingering enemies so they can't strike us from behind.

Soon, the narrow hall widens and the ceiling soars; we've reached the cellblock. All around us, the yells and curses of the prisoners rise in a strident cacophony. Though I had expected we would find the greatest resistance here, I am relieved to see there are no squadmen at all. Evidently, they had all been ordered to defend the main entrance. A few yards away, I notice Ethan standing very still in front of one of the cells. In his hand, he holds a red paper tag.

Looking out across the cellblock, I can see that perhaps half of the cells here bear the same mark. I approach one of them and pull it down from the bars.

Notice of Termination, it says.

Ethan's voice cuts the through the prisoners' shouting.

"May, Grace—to me."

We rush to him.

"Clair is being held in a lower level. You two will come with me. Blake?"

A young driver with an acne-scarred face, one of Grace's soldiers, steps up to Ethan and salutes.

"You know which prisoners to rescue. Get them loaded onto the trucks. We'll meet back at the entrance. If we're not there in ten minutes, leave us."

Ethan nods to Grace and me, and we fall in behind him. I ignore the suspicious glances Grace gives me as we cross the cellblock and descend down a stairwell on the far side. The further down we go, the hotter it gets, as if the staircase might deposit us in the middle of hell's foyer. In fact, we reach the bottom of the stairs, pass down a long hallway, and then arrive in a long, low-ceilinged room at the far end of which a gaping furnace burns.

There is one door on our left and another on our right.

Here, Ethan pauses and speaks into an IC. "Come in, R. Which way to Clair from here?. . . . got it."

I tug on Ethan's sleeve. "Who's 'R'?" I whisper, but he ignores the question.

"Clair is behind this door," he says. "I want the two of you to wait here and secure our escape."

Grace starts to protest, but Ethan's already disappearing through the doorway. Left alone with me, she glowers. The good thing about me is that I can take a hint. I wander away from her, toward the swirling flames of the furnace.

"What is this place?" I wonder aloud.

"How the hell should I know?" Grace grunts.

I lean closer to the flames. This furnace is much deeper than a regular fireplace or kiln, and the enclosure seems to be made of some sort of special, heat-resistant ceramic. Stranger yet are the logs, or rather the log, that burns in the space. It's very long, almost as large as a person. In fact—of course it's my imagination—but it's almost as if I can make out a human form hidden among the ravenous flames. There are the legs, the arms, the torso, the head.

Suddenly, I'm sick. My head spins. Sweat drenches me. I dash for the door—not the one Ethan disappeared into, the other one—poke my head through and puke until there's nothing left of my stomach but a single, throbbing cramp. Only then do I raise my eyes to take in the room I've discovered. What I see turns my stomach all over again.

Bodies. Thousands of them, stacked against the wall like firewood. The room must be as large as a football field, and it is completely filled with tangled arms and gaping mouths, staring eyes and twisted legs. They all wear orange prisoner jump suits. They all bear red tags tied around their ankles. I can read the words on the tag closest to me: *Notice of Termination.*

"Problem and solution," I whisper, suddenly feeling utterly numb.

Everything the Protectorate says about the Company is true.

A second later, Grace appears in the doorway next to me. "My God," she murmurs.

Suddenly, Ethan appears. His hand is strong on my shoulder.

Grace has tears in her eyes. Clair is there, too, leaning heavily against Ethan. Even in the shadows, I can see both her eyes are blackened. Her nose is broken. Blood is crusted at the corners of her mouth. Ethan stares past me, into the carnage of the room beyond, the thousands of dead, twisted bodies, the Company's efficiency turned deadly.

"This is it," he says quietly. "It's beginning."

—CHAPTER Ø16—

Back at the camp, I wander among the blanketed, sleeping forms. The smell of so many bodies pressed in together no longer bothers me. The fear that my fellow unprofitables once elicited in me has vanished, replaced by camaraderie, even love. The camp is already beginning to feel more like home than any home I've ever had. Still, I am far from content.

Images keep splashing through my mind of the squadmen we killed during the prison raid—and, worse, of the countless dead bodies stacked in that horrible underground room. But what I'm about to do now is more frightening than those memories could ever be: I'm going to go and talk to Clair.

After taking three circuits around the massive room, at last I get up the courage to find Ada. She sits in a metal folding chair outside the makeshift hospital—in this camp, it's an old ticket office. She hums a happy tune to herself, staring down at her hands as she busily knits an orange scarf. She must be the only person in camp who sleeps as little as I do.

"Well, hello there, May," she greets me with a friendly smile. "Here to visit one of our patients?"

I nod. There were several people injured in the raid. At least four of us were killed. But the only one I'm here to see is Clair.

"Go on in," Ada says. "Just go quietly. Some of them are sleeping." And she goes back to her knitting.

The medical room is lit by candles. There are four shapes at the far end of the room, lying on several stacked sheets and covered by threadbare sheets. All of the sheets rise and fall in the easy rhythm of sleep except for one, whose owner seems to be panting because of pain or a nightmare, I can't tell which.

Clair, however, is awake. She sits cross-legged atop her blankets, playing solitaire with a deck of ragged playing cards. Her eyes flick up to me as I enter, then back to the game.

"Hey," I whisper. "How you feeling?"

"How does it look like I'm feeling?" she asks, slapping a card down in front of her. It looks like she got hit by a transport truck, but that's no reason for her to give me attitude. Not after I just risked my life to rescue her.

"Why do you hate me so much?" I ask.

She chuckles, still intent on her game. "Why do you think everything is about you, Blackie? I just spent two weeks in that God-awful Company dungeon, being tortured and choking on the smoke of burning human flesh night and day, and all you can think of is yourself?"

The intensity of her attack confuses me, then makes me angry.

"All I'm saying is that I risked my life to try to help you, and obviously you still despise me. I'd like to know why."

"I don't despise you, May," she says, looking up at me at last. "I just don't trust you."

The idea that she still thinks I might be a traitor after everything I've gone through makes me bristle.

"I cut out my cross, Clair. I gave up my life. I fought and bled for you." I gesture to my shoulder, freshly bandaged and still stinging from the shrapnel Ada dug out of it hours before. "So why can't you trust me? Why?"

She gazes up at me now, the hardness in her eyes replaced with something like wonder. "You really don't know me, do you?" she asks, shaking her head in disgust.

Of course I don't know her, I want to shout. She hasn't given me the chance; we hardly met before she decided that I was the enemy. But before I can answer, the door behind me swings open. The next thing

I know, Ethan is at my side. Instantly, Clair's countenance brightens.

"Well, how are the two loveliest soldiers in the revolution doing tonight?"

The compliment makes me wrinkle my nose in mock repulsion, but Clair smiles. And, as I watch, Ethan falls to his knees before her, and Clair presses her lips to his. Twin revelations wash over me in that moment, the second more nauseating than the first. One: I have feelings for Clair. And two: I'm already too late. She's in love with Ethan.

"I'm going to get some sleep," I mutter, and turn on my heel.

Their "goodnights" are lost in the clatter of my footfalls as I hurry out of the room, out the door, across the sleeping camp, angrily wiping tears from my cheeks as I go. It's fine that Clair hates me, I think to myself. I hate her, too. And Ethan. And myself. And this whole pathetic, miserable revolution. I think back to my lonely apartment, my job, my life, my Company. But I hate those things even more. There is nowhere and nothing for me. My heart feels like a volcano, ready to explode.

I had foolishly convinced myself that once I escaped from the Company's repression, the love I'd been needing for so long would magically materialize. But no. There is no home for me. No love. There is only the fight.

In the Company, it was a fight to succeed and win power and be respected. In the Protectorate, it's a real fight, a war, a battle to the death. And right now, in this dark and lonely watch of the night, death doesn't sound half bad.

What follows are three days of waiting. The first day I spend mostly asleep, recovering from the physical and emotional exhaustion of the battle. The second day I hardly eat, and I don't talk to anyone. I merely walk around the camp for hours, staring at the faces of the honest soldiers around me as they go about their work, and trying to get used to the idea that my former life within the Company is truly and completely finished.

Twice I find myself standing outside the door to the infirmary where Clair lies recovering, but I don't have the courage to go inside again. I just stand there staring at the closed door for a few minutes like a moron, then move on.

Before dinnertime arrives I'm exhausted again, and go to bed. As I wrap myself up in my privacy tent, beneath my Protectorate-issued holey woolen blanket, I wonder to myself which was more exhausting: the battle I fought in the prison block or the war I feel going on within myself when I think of Ethan and Clair enmeshed in each other's arms?

The third day I wake up starving. Before half the camp is even awake, I head to the mess area and eat two and a half bowls of N-Chow— cheap, nutritionally fortified food pellets that N-Corp markets to low-credit-level workers—stuff my dad always called "human dog food." I never had it before, but it's actually not quite as bad as I thought it would be, at least in my ravenous state.

I spend all morning in the mess area, watching N-News on the portable imager there:

Another relic found on the Sinai Peninsula; this one is a scroll, perhaps written by Moses himself, listing an eleventh commandment: Thou Shalt Relish Hard Work. N-Corp scientists have confirmed that it is, indeed, authentic.

Authorities have revealed that anarchists attempted a prison break two days ago at a facility seventy miles southeast of N-Corp Headquarters. All involved were either arrested or killed (here's some altered video footage).

And now, for more on our top story: Today, N-Corp CEO Jason Fields announced the merger of N-Corp with longtime rival B&S. In one result of the merger, thousands of debtor-workers at both companies received red slips this week, informing them they'll be required to transfer to another location within the Company as part of the reorganization process. (On the screen: long lines of workers stand, holding red slips of paper.) *Despite these minor inconveniences, experts agree that debtor-workers across the globe stand to benefit greatly from what's being called the final consolidation. If all goes according to plan, the merger will be finalized a week from Friday, according to sources in both Companies.*

Sitting a little further down the table from me is a tall, bearded man with dark, mirthful eyes. He nods knowingly and points his spoon at the imager.

"Ethan's not going to let that stand," he says. "Wait and see."

"What do you think we're going to do about it?" a sallow-faced man sitting across from him says. "We can't even feed ourselves properly; you think we're going to be able to stop a merger if that's what old Fields really wants?" He pushes his bowl of N-Chow away in disgust.

"I think we'll be on the move before next Friday, I'll tell you that much. The general's got something up his sleeve, guaranteed. The offensive is finally going to begin."

The other man rolls his eyes peevishly. "Christ, you can't see any further than the end of your own freaking nose, can you? If we could do something, we'd have already done it! That murderous butcher Fields is going to have us slaughtered, and I'm sick of sitting here waiting for it to happen."

The man shoves away the table and rises to his feet. I'm on my feet, too. In an instant, I've grabbed his shirtfront and stand nose to nose with him.

"Jason Fields is not a murderer," I say through clenched teeth.

The man's eyes are wide with surprise at first, then narrow.

"Look, honey, if you're a Company loyalist, I think you must have taken a wrong turn."

He tries to extricate his shirt from my grasp by pushing me away, but I push him harder. He stumbles back a few steps and the expression on his face goes from one of irritation to one of fury.

"I'm no loyalist, and I'm not your honey," I say.

The man looks from me to his bearded friend, apparently viewing us both with equal contempt. "You know what? Screw Jason Fields and screw General Greene, too. Screw all of you. You're all nuts. I'm getting out of here before we all get slaughtered."

"Screw me?" I shout. My famously short fuse already sizzled down to nothing, I charge him.

From out of the shadows, a figure emerges and steps between us— Ethan. "Stand down, soldiers," he says with his usual calm.

My adversary takes a step back, stands up straight and salutes. "Sir. General. I'm sorry if—I didn't mean to say . . ."

Ethan gazes at him, and the man's words fade into an uncomfortable silence.

"That's alright, soldier," Ethan says quietly. "Worse has been said about me. And I'll bet worse has been said about CEO Fields, too." He finishes with a glance at me. "May, could you come with me, please?"

Ethan and I step into the makeshift council chamber to find the twelve-member council (minus the still-recovering Clair) assembled and waiting for us. They rise as we enter the room, and Ethan immediately urges them to take their seats.

Since I don't warrant a seat at the council table, I sit in a metal

folding chair by the door. The emotions I felt the last time I was in
this room, when the council was deciding whether or not to have me
executed, come flooding back to me, and for a moment I'm afraid that
they've changed their minds and decided to shoot me after all. But
everyone in the room ignores my presence completely, instead focus-
ing expectantly on Ethan.

"So, the reason for our meeting today," he begins placidly, "is that
the merger date has been announced. By any measure, it's an important historical event for the world. Although the two Companies have
been working in concert for many years now, it will be the first time in
the history of humankind that every man, woman, and child on earth
is ruled under one single governing entity. And I don't need to remind
any of you of that entity's true, immoral nature."

"Of course not," Grace agrees, "but what do you intend to do
about it?"

Ethan touches the screen of the IC in his hand and the imager on
the wall behind him flares to life with a map of a city on it. "N-Hub
2," he says. "Formerly New York City. Back when there were hundreds
of companies, their stocks were traded here, at the New York Stock
Exchange."

He presses a button and the image changes to one of a beautiful,
old-fashioned stone building with huge columns and, above them, an
elaborately carved pediment.

"Most people are unaware that this structure, in the district formerly known as Wall Street, is still the place where the computer that
tracks the two Companies' stocks is actually housed. And, our intelligence tells us, this is one of the locations from which N-Corp Media
will be broadcasting as they celebrate the merger."

Ethan touches his IC again, and again the imager changes, this time
to a feed from *N-News Live*. A news anchor prattles away, but the

sound is muted. At the bottom of the screen, a ticker slides past—the stock price of the Companies, N-Corp and B&S. Naturally, the average worker doesn't care much about the daily fluctuations in stock price, and for a while there were discussions of getting rid of the N-Media ticker altogether, but my father fought tooth and nail to keep it.

"Of course it's basically a meaningless, arbitrary number now that all the capital in the world is tied up in Company stock that no one can buy or sell," he remarked once, "but it gives the people something to root for, by God! Something to work for. 'Come on guys, let's get this stock price up!' they'll say to each other, and they'll work harder. It's a motivator."

And it was. From then on, the stock ticker remained at the bottom of every N-Corp Media program. More times than I can count I overheard conversations about people wistfully wishing the stock price would go up, or dolefully debating about why it had dropped, or dutifully working an extra half hour, in the interest of fulfilling Jimmy Shaw's admonition: "Productiveness is next to Godliness—let the stock price be your guide!"

Truly, millions in the Company were obsessive ticker-watchers. And, I realize, Ethan is right. The merging of the two ticker-numbers into one will be a momentous event, the most immediately tangible demonstration of the new, unified Company.

"Destroy the Wall Street mainframe," Ethan finishes, "and the ticker stops."

"So what exactly are you suggesting?" the grizzled Grace asks, eyeing Ethan warily. "Aside from the headquarters, the Stock Exchange has to be the most heavily guarded location in the most closely controlled hub in all of America Division. And on the day of the merger, with a live worldwide broadcast going on, the security is going to be tighter than ever. Obviously you're not proposing a direct attack on the Stock Exchange building on that day, are you?"

"Actually," Ethan replies, "that's exactly what I'm proposing."

Ethan and I walked into the council assembly before 8 AM , and the debate lasts until well after midnight. The council was split into three factions: McCann spoke vociferously in favor of Ethan's plan, expressing his opinion that in light of the upcoming merger, a decisive opening blow had to be struck immediately. The coverage of the merger would be live, and with an attack on the physical computers that ran the stock trading, the ever-running ticker was sure to stop. Such a disruption was something that the Company couldn't explain away by claiming it was executed by a handful of disorganized anarchists. Risky though the attack would be, it was the necessary springboard required to bring the Protectorate movement into the open at last. Four other council members, two men and two women, seemed to agree with McCann.

The second faction was led by Grace, who claimed that an attack on such a prominent Company target, in the middle of a heavily armed hub, was simply too dangerous a move. Besides, she said, the military importance of the target was questionable. If they were going to risk the lives of hundreds or thousands of Protectorate soldiers, she argued, it should be to take out a squad member barracks or a weapons facility, not to participate in a symbolic gesture of defiance.

A lone man, Dr. Le Grande, who I later learned had a Ph.D. in agriculture from Cranton and left when Peak came into fashion, proposed patience. First and foremost, he was concerned about potential innocent casualties that might result from an attack on the Exchange. When Ethan assured him that every measure would be taken to ensure that only armed squad members would be injured in the raid, he still wasn't convinced.

"We should watch and wait," he said. "After all, I'm still not convinced that it's impossible to reform the Company from the inside."

The rest *were* convinced. Apparently reform efforts had been made for years, with the result that those who proposed the reforms either disappeared, died mysteriously, or were somehow induced to rethink their position—a change of heart that was usually followed by either a large increase in their credit level or a mysterious case of total amnesia.

Of course, I thought of my father. If only there were a way to get through to him, to make him understand what was happening and put a stop to it. . . . But after my visit to his house, I doubted whether he was in any mental condition to tell right from wrong. And even if I could get him on our side, did he really have the power to effect a change? Or was Jimmy Shaw the Company's true master? Or Yao? Or Blackwell? Or someone else I'd never even met?

No, Ethan argued. There could be no falling back on strategies that had already failed. At this stage in the conflict, he claimed, no target was more important than the Stock Exchange.

"A symbolic victory is exactly what we need," he argued. "Our real enemy isn't the Company, it's complacency. People need to understand what's happening and get inspired to take action. The Protectorate Education Initiative is what's going to change the tide of this war. R almost has it finished. And what better way to set the people up for it than by disrupting the merger ceremony? I'm telling you, if we show the people that the Company isn't infallible, they'll come flocking to our banner."

"But how, Ethan?" Grace nearly shouted. "What's your plan? I understand the Protectorate Education Initiative and I know it's important, but this . . . I can't see how this is anything but a suicide mission."

For the next four hours, Ethan laid out his plan in incredible detail. He showed 3-D maps of the tunnels beneath N-Hub 2, architectural drawings of the Stock Exchange building, and even provided the names of the squadmen who would be assigned to security that day. If anyone else wondered how he got his information, they didn't show it, and I vowed to ask him myself after the meeting.

Ethan laid out what sounded to me like a brilliant plan, but the moment he finished, Grace and her faction set about attacking it.

"What if they employ drones?" a barrel-chested, redheaded man asked as he stroked his goatee.

"Won't happen," Ethan said. "The Company has never brought out any of its lethal technology in any of the larger hubs. It would terrify people. They won't do it. It's bad P.R."

"What about the escape plan?" a slight, middle-aged woman with long, gray-blond hair asked. "That's what worries me."

"Sorry, that's the one part of the plan that I have to keep confidential," Ethan said. "As you know, our security has been somewhat compromised lately."

It was hard not to notice a few of the council members glancing at me.

"I agree with Leon," Grace said with a shake of her head. "It sounds wonderfully dramatic, but in practice I just can't see it working. There are too many things that could go wrong. All it would take is a thunderstorm with some gusty winds and the whole second team would be finished."

"What would you propose instead?" McCann asked, finally getting annoyed.

"I propose we find a target that's slightly less ludicrous!" Grace shouted.

Ethan broke in to explain why the exit plan for the second team was sound, but he still refused to give away the details of how our soldiers would escape the island of Manhattan. The debate went on.

The whole time I remained uncharacteristically silent, listening to the arguing, reasoning, pleading, and discussing with an odd mix of exhilaration and foreboding. It was certainly an incredible-sounding plan, and if Ethan was able to pull it off, it would be a huge victory for the Protectorate—and a major black eye for the Company. But it would be incredibly dangerous. I couldn't help but wonder if I would have to take part in it.

Now, at forty minutes after midnight, the final vote is tallied: six in favor of Ethan's plan, five opposed, with Clair, of course, not voting.

Grace stands, shutting off her IC and shaking her head. "Well, I hope you're right, Ethan—for all our sakes."

"One more order of business," Ethan says, and the council, most of whom were already heading for the door, sigh as one and turn back.

"I have a tremendous number of preparations to make if we're going to get ready for the mission next Friday," he begins. "With Clair in the infirmary, I'm going to need some help."

"What? You want Major Blake from second battalion?" Grace asks.

"Captain Hernandez has an excellent mind for strategy," McCann suggests.

But Ethan, for the first time all day, looks at me.

"Fields, the Blackie spy?" Grace growls, incredulous. "You've got to be kidding me, Ethan! When the troops find out about this they're going to be calling for a no-confidence vote on your leadership. It's insane enough that you even let her sit in on this meeting, but I managed to bite my tongue."

A few of the other council members are nodding and glowering at me. I glower back, even though I have no idea what's going on.

"I'm the one commanding this operation and I'm the one planning it," Ethan replies coolly. "If it's going to succeed, I'm going to need all the help I can get. And Fields is the woman for the job. I propose we immediately bestow on her the rank of first lieutenant, under my command."

Everyone stares at me like I have six eyes and a hand growing out of my forehead. Fortunately, I have the good sense to keep my mouth shut.

"You didn't see her fight at the prison raid," Ethan continues. "I did. Before reinforcements arrived, she stood by my side for ten minutes holding off the enemy. If it had been anyone else, I probably wouldn't be standing here today. She's a fighter. And she's my choice."

Ethan and Grace glare at one another for a few awkward moments, then Grace finally shrugs. "God, I hope you know what you're doing," she says wearily. "All in favor of promoting Private Fields to first lieutenant under General Ethan Greene's command?"

"Aye," they all say.

"Nay," Grace says, but she's the only one. "The ayes have it. Congratulations, Blackie. Meeting adjourned."

Without further ceremony, the council files out of the room, except for McCann, who approaches and claps Ethan on the shoulder.

Ethan smiles tiredly. "Well, the hard part is over," he says with his usual dry humor, "Now all we have to do is execute a precise, highly dangerous raid in a heavily guarded urban area."

"Piece of cake," McCann says, smiling.

I turn to Ethan. "You did that deliberately, didn't you?" I ask. "Bringing up my promotion at the end of the meeting, when they were all too tired to argue about it."

Ethan only winks at me.

"Never underestimate our general, Miss Fields. He has the finest mind for strategy around," McCann says, then gives me a hearty pat on the shoulder, "Congratulations, First Lieutenant."

I hardly know what the promotion means, but I feel a swelling of pride anyway.

"Don't congratulate her yet," Ethan says. "If we get out of the Stock Exchange alive, you can congratulate her then."

CHAPTER 017

My promotion comes with a new shirt with some stripes on the shoulder and a crapload of work. Basically, my job is to follow Ethan around and help him make all the preparations for the raid. We spend the first morning reviewing stores and provisions. One hundred of the Protectorate's finest soldiers will be taking part in the operation, and they'll need enough food, supplies, and ammunition for three days away in the field.

Ethan takes me to a blocked-off section of tunnel where we're met by the two young Asian men I saw checking guns the first time I came into camp. Supply officers Wang and Monroe, as Ethan introduces them. He hands them each a paper with the words "requisition sheet" at the top. The two men look at it, exchange a few quiet words and nod.

"The packs and food will be fine, but I'm not sure about the sniper weapons. We have a few of them here and more coming soon, but we've been having trouble getting a hold of the lenses for the scopes."

"I'll check with R on it," Ethan says. "It's imperative we have them by Thursday morning at the latest."

"We'll try," Monroe says, sounding a bit dubious.

"We'll get it done, sir," Wang asserts.

Just then, a sound in the tunnel behind them draws their attention, and the two men excuse themselves. There's a strange, rhythmic clacking noise I've never heard before. I put one hand on my sidearm, ready for the worst, but Ethan seems unfazed. He steps over to a rack of ceramic rifles and begins examining one. Wang and Monroe, too, seem relaxed as a shape coalesces out of the darkened tunnel and approaches them. My heart beats faster when I realize what I'm seeing. It's a horse, pulling a wagon!

"Ethan!" I nearly shout.

"What?" he asks, sighting down the barrel of the rifle.

"There's a horse pulling that wagon!" I exclaim. I've never seen one before in my life—except in movies.

"Very good," Ethan agrees dryly. "Ninety percent of our supplies come from Company shipments. We break into the computer network, adjust the shipping quantities, then our people on the inside take what we need—and nobody in the Company is the wiser. It works for food, clothing, medicine, almost everything. The only things we manufacture ourselves are weapons and ammunition. We have a small factory in a secret location that produces them for us. And we grow some limited quantities of food, too. N-Chow might keep an army alive, but it won't keep it happy."

"But why the horse?" I ask.

"Getting a hold of gasoline is tricky and the Company is pretty good at monitoring their electric grid, but there's plenty of grass out past the industrial arc for a horse to graze on."

Ethan sets the rifle back down on the rack as I watch Wang, Monroe, and a couple of burly men who must've been on the cart unload large sacks of N-Chow and stack them on pallets against one wall of the tunnel.

"Let's go," Ethan says, "They'll take care of the requisitions. We've got work to do."

Over the next few days, I learn more about the Protectorate than I ever thought possible.

I learn that so far, 523 Protectorate members and 711 squadmen have been killed in a secret war that has been simmering for years, unknown to nearly everyone in the Company.

I learn that five years ago, N-Corp added facial recognition software to their security cameras, so every Order operative who wants to go back in and perform clandestine missions is required to get plastic surgery to alter their appearance.

I learn that the Protectorate has an elite division called "The Reapers," whose job it is to comb the countryside in search of wandering unprofitables or any people living outside the Company, assess their mental state, and, if appropriate, recruit them. Some Reapers even infiltrate the Company and try to recruit select high-level tie-men and women—like me—from within its ranks. Grace was the commander of this division for five years before being elected to the council. Clair served with them for a six-month stint, too. Because the Reapers are more likely than any of the other branches of the Protectorate to be engaged by the enemy, they are the most highly trained and battle-tested unit in the army.

I learn that the Protectorate has no less than twenty different campsites throughout America Division. Most of them are manned by only a handful of soldiers, who keep the area safe and secure in case the main army arrives. This force, of which I am now a part, numbers just under two thousand, and it moves at least once every six months to avoid enemy detection, a process they call "migration."

Spies and traitors to the cause are shot. Thieves are locked up until the next migration and then are expelled from the community.

Ethan has been the commander in chief, the head general of the Protectorate, for as long as anyone can remember, although the ruling council has the right to relieve him of command at any time with a majority vote. Grace has been on the council for five years, McCann for two, and Clair for one.

Though many of my fellow soldiers still call me "Blackie," since the prison raid it has become more an ironic term of endearment than an insult. My close association with Ethan seems to have earned the trust of some of them, and dozens tell me their stories, tales as varied as the faces of those who tell them. People from all credit levels, all backgrounds, and all parts of America Division and the world have come to the banner of the Protectorate, some because of Company injustices, some because they didn't fit into the Company system, and some simply because they were sure there had to be something more than working their lives away just to get the next new IC.

The only thing I don't learn is who or what "R" is, although from all the functions it accomplishes I determine that it must be a vast computer system. R adjusts the Company supply numbers when we steal food or medicine. R supplies the new identities and wireless security codes that mimic the cross implants when we go on missions within Company-controlled sectors. R provides maps and aerial views for the planning of missions. R alerts us of squad activity in our area. In short, R does almost everything, but the one time I ask Ethan about it, he blows off the question.

"Don't worry about R, May. Worry about the mission."

By the end of a week, I've learned almost everything about how the Protectorate operates. Though I repeatedly push the thought out of my mind, the fact is that I could return to Shaw and Blackwell now with enough information to wipe the Protectorate out forever. I'd be a hero within the Company. I'd get an immediate credit level raise, an even bigger and more luxurious apartment. And my future, as bright as it was before, would be blinding.

But now I know for certain that there's no way I would ever go back. As I get to know more and more of the Protectorate's members, I'm amazed to find that most of these "vile unprofitables" are actually wonderful, intelligent people. I'm amazed by their industry, their bravery, their fidelity, their ability to live so cheerfully under such hardship, and all right under the nose of the squadmen who would like nothing more than to see them all dead. Then there's Ethan. He's unfailingly kind and patient, and he shares so much with me that sometimes I get the feeling he's deliberately sharing Protectorate secrets in an effort to demonstrate his trust for me. His ingenuity, patience, and faith astound me. And as more and more of his Merger Day plan takes shape, I can hardly wait to see how it will come off.

No, there's no way I can leave and go back to the Company. Not now, not ever.

"Deeper, deeper," calls McCann. His son steps warily back, pushing further into the woods. Finally satisfied, McCann throws the ball. It strikes his son in the chest and knocks him on his butt. Michel sits there for a second, not knowing whether to cry or laugh. When at last he decides on the latter, we all join in, me, McCann, and Ethan. Little Michel stands, picks up the ball and hurls it back to his father. It falls ten yards short.

This is only two days before the Merger Day operation. Preparations for the mission have filled almost my every waking hour, but all week, while eating, sleeping, and working out, my mind has unfailingly wandered back to Clair. Even now, playing football on this perfect, sunny day, I can't help thinking of her. About her face, her skin. About the strange, almost familiar way she'd brush her hair out of her eyes. According to Ethan, she'll likely be well enough to participate in the upcoming mission, but so far she hasn't left the infirmary. And I haven't gone back to visit her again, either. I'm probably more afraid of seeing her than I am of going into combat.

"May!" Ethan gets my attention just in time for me to catch the ball that was speeding for my head.

McCann is still helping little Michel off the ground.

"He's not the sportsman his father is," says McCann, shaking his head but smiling.

I roll out a few yards and rocket the ball at Ethan, who expels a little *oof* when it drills him in the gut.

"Now, May, she can throw!" McCann laughs. "Look at that arm, boy! That's how I was telling you to do it!"

The kid nods dutifully.

"Oh, McCann," I say, "lay off him."

Ethan throws to McCann, who catches the ball gracefully with one hand.

This began as a scouting mission. Someone reported seeing footprints around here that looked like they belonged to a squad member, and Ethan decided to scope out the report. Turns out, the footprints were nothing. But we decided to play football, just in case.

This grove stands on the edge of a small lake. A few old, rotting beach cabins sit lifeless on the shore. A few others have already collapsed to the pine needle–laden earth. Once, this must've been a wonderful place.

I jump up and snatch a wildly errant pass from Michel.

"Good throw," I say, and pass to Ethan. As he catches the ball, a question occurs to me. "So, Mr. General, Sir, were you an athlete in your school days?"

He glances at me and sidearms it to McCann. Right on the money.

"Can't you tell?" he asks.

"Did you like school?"

"I've always loved learning."

"Have you always hated the Company?"

Michel bobbles a pass. He picks up the ball and dusts it off daintily before throwing it to me.

"I always loved people," says Ethan, "above any institution."

It suddenly occurs to me that, as much as he's shared with me about the Protectorate, he's told me next to nothing about himself.

"Come on, Ethan," I say, "do you always have to be so damned vague? Can't you give me one concrete fact about yourself? I mean, anything! I don't even know your favorite flavor of ice cream!"

Ethan only gives me his usual, inscrutable smile.

McCann laughs, juggling the ball from one hand to the other. "Give up now, May," he jokes, and throws the ball to me.

I catch it, then press on: "Seriously, Ethan. You expect us to follow you to hell and back, and we don't even know the name of your high-school crush, or what kind of a job you did before you became a rebel, or what kind of music you like!"

My throw hits Ethan in the chest. He catches it and passes to Michel.

"I like all kinds of music."

"Tell me about your training," I say. "How did you learn everything about weapons and tactics and fighting? What was it like, being trained by the Protectorate?"

"The same as how I'm training you."

I grab Michel's wobbling pass with my fingertips.

"Don't take it personally," McCann tells me, "he doesn't trust anybody. Not even me, and I've saved his life. Three times."

"Twice," Ethan says, with a sidelong glance at McCann. Then, to me: "I prefer to remain mysterious."

"Mysterious my ass," I say. "Go deep. Deep, General. Come on, El Capitan, go deep! What, you think I throw like a girl? Come on!"

Ethan is backed up nearly to the lake and is still going. I cock back, take two hopping steps forward, and hurl the ball with all my might. It shoots into the sky in a great arc, passing miraculously through a mass of tree branches, and comes to rest—*splash*—ten feet past Ethan, in the lake.

"You do have one hell of an arm," Ethan says with his amused grin.

"Come on, Michel!" yells McCann. "We'll get the ball, come on!"

The boy and his father race to the water.

"Last one to the ball is a baboon's ass!" says McCann. He kicks off his shoes, yanks off his shirt, drops his trousers, and yanks down his underwear. I gasp. Father and son, both naked, both laughing, splash into the water.

"Oh, my God, McCann!" I say, walking up to join Ethan at the shore.

Ethan looks at me, laughing. "He loves to do this."

"I don't know why you America Division people are so worried about clothes," McCann shouts to us. "In my home, this is how we would always swim. Who brings a bathing suit everywhere?"

"What about pollution?" I ask, still laughing.

"If the world is polluted, we are polluted. If the world dies, we die anyway. I don't pretend to be separate from the world. If she is poisoned, I jump in and be poisoned with her."

Michel, giggling, splashes his father in the face. McCann splashes him back, then they both plunge deeper, chasing the drifting football.

I'm still laughing so hard tears are in my eyes. It's so beautiful, father and son playing together like that. If only I could bring myself to jump in there with them.

"Catch!" yells Michel. He heaves the ball at us. It splats into shallow water at our feet, splashing Ethan and me.

We both laugh. With one hand, I reach down and touch the gun on my hip, making sure it's still dry, then fish the ball out of the water. I dry it off on my shirt as Ethan and I stand there together, watching McCann and Michel wrestle in the water.

"By the way," Ethan says, his eye catching mine, "Rocky Road."

—CHAPTER 018—

On September 2, the day before the attack, we set off before dawn. There are twelve vehicles total, ten squad trucks crammed with ten soldiers each, and two more vehicles filled with supplies. Per Ethan's plan, the vehicles depart in pairs, at half-hour intervals, with each pair taking a different route. If any trucks in our scattered convoy are stopped by the squads before reaching N-Hub 2, we are to attack the squadmen with everything we've got, then fall out heading south, so as to lead them away from the rest of our forces.

Everyone I know well in the camp, except Ada and Michel, agreed to take part in the battle. As during the prison raid, I am once again assigned to McCann's vehicle, which is a relief; the idea of riding with Grace or Clair is more daunting than the thought of battle. And Ethan, to my surprise, opted to drive one of the supply trucks, so he's riding alone.

Dawn finds the world in much the same state as it was before the sun rose. A leaden shroud of clouds hangs above the pollution-choked countryside, casting everything in a muted pallor. It seems like a depressing omen—until I realize that in addition to screening out the sun, the clouds are obscuring the view of the Company sats, too.

It reminds me of the history books in the Protectorate library detailing stories of the first American Revolution. Several times when the rebel army seemed on the verge of being destroyed by the superior British force, they were able to escape or gain the advantage because of drastic changes in the weather, a fact that General Washington attributed to "divine providence." I hope we have some of that, too. We're going to need it.

We ride uncomfortably for hour after hour, our bodies pressed together, legs overlapping, hip against hip in the overcrowded SUVs.

We're dressed in squad member uniforms just as we were during the prison raid, only this time I'm wearing a uniform, too. Maybe it's the material or the fact that we're all crammed in together, but I feel like I can't stop sweating. Ethan has warned us that once we enter combat, we might not get the chance to sleep for days, so those who are able to get comfortable enough are dozing now. The rest sit in a tense silence, watching the faded beauty of America Division slide by us: abandoned farms, empty towns, pollution-stunted trees, fields full of dead grass surrounding ponds of acid rain.

As midday approaches, the flatlands of the land formerly known as Ohio give way to hills. Remembering the maps Ethan showed me during the planning phase of the mission, I surmise that we must have been assigned the northern route, which passes through old Upstate New York rather than old Pennsylvania. Here, the pollution is slightly less severe, and the natural beauty of the countryside fills me with an awe that borders on the spiritual. For the first time since leaving the Company, I utter a silent prayer.

Dear God, thank you for this day. I ask that you give me the courage to serve bravely. Please, be merciful to our soldiers tomorrow. Help us to find success. And if I should die in the battle tomorrow, try to forgive me for . . . for everything. Amen.

The prayer seems oddly incomplete, and after a moment I realize what it's missing. There's no mention of gaining more credit or getting a promotion. No begging for a bigger apartment or a better car. This new simplicity of my desires feels good. And I realize that this might be the first time I ever prayed because I wanted to, rather than because Jimmy Shaw and the Company expected it. And the funny thing is, the minute I open my eyes, a small ray of sunlight pierces the clouds and bathes the road ahead of us in a golden glow, a gesture that almost seems to say, *I'm here, and I hear you.*

At last, I'm able to fall asleep. When I open my eyes again, it's dark out. The truck has come to a stop. It takes a few moments before I realize what's happening. We've reached N-Hub 2. The battle is upon us.

The time between 5 am, when we arrive in N-Hub 2, and noon, when the official merger broadcast is to take place, is perhaps the most difficult part of the ordeal. We spend most of the time in our cramped squad truck, crunching on little packets of N-Chow and stirring only to relieve ourselves in an alleyway.

Through communication on the Protectorate's encoded IC network, McCann learns that the rest of the teams are in place, except one. Apparently, one two-truck team was stopped for questioning at a checkpoint outside N-Hub 256. A gunfight broke out in which several squadmen were killed, and then the team broke south as their orders required. That was four hours ago, and they haven't been heard from since. So our numbers are down from one hundred to eighty. The news seems to unnerve several of our team members, but not McCann. He sits in the driver's seat, listening to music and drumming a syncopated dance rhythm on the steering wheel. Meanwhile, I'm trying not to throw up from my mounting nerves.

I was with Ethan during every step of the planning process, and it's hard to say whether it's a blessing or a curse. The advantage is that, unlike most people on the team, I know exactly what's going to happen today down to the most minute detail—everything up to our top-secret escape plan. The bad news is, I also know everything that might possibly go wrong, and as I sit there waiting, an endless array of potential disasters parade through my mind.

It seems like days pass before the alarm finally goes off on McCann's IC, indicating that it's 11:15 AM. The minute the chirping sound stops, he checks his white pistol then slips it back into its holster and the rest of us follow suit.

"Who's ready for glory?" McCann asks with his usual, wide-mouthed grin.

"I am," I say. A few others answer, too.

"We all know what to do?" he asks, and everyone nods. "Good, then. History is waiting."

We all get out. Two of the men open up the tailgate of the truck and take out a large, black trunk, then fall into line behind us, carrying it along.

We move single file down the street behind the Stock Exchange building, up to the back door. There are barricades set up outside and several squadmen in riot gear standing guard. I sense the tension from my team members, but McCann's pace doesn't falter as he approaches them, and his men follow him confidently.

As we pass, I catch a glimpse of Clair's face behind one of the squadmen's helmets.

At the door, the men are met with another surprise. The squad member running the IC that scans everyone's fake cross implant is none other than General Ethan Greene. With each man that passes, the IC in his hand beeps and he gives a small nod of encouragement. When I pass, he speaks softly to me: "When we get inside, stay close to me," he says.

And I pass through the barricade with the others. Seconds later, we're in a small maintenance room—Ethan, Clair, McCann, me, and the eighteen other members of my unit. Someone opens the trunk and everyone pulls out their white machine gun, checks the chamber, checks the clip. On the wall is an imager: Jimmy Shaw sitting in the boardroom back at Headquarters, my father and Bernice Yao next to him.

"We thank God for this day of marvelous unity," Jimmy says in his grand, booming voice. It's amazing how phony he seems to me now. "Truly, a new era of abundance is dawning—Amen."

My father takes the podium. "And with that, ladies and gentlemen of the Company, stockholders, employees, friends, the moment is at hand. We take you back to the Stock Exchange in N-Hub 2, where the merger will officially be final in . . ."

A countdown begins on the screen. *Ten, nine . . .*

Ethan moves to the doorway now, and I follow him like a shadow. His IC beeps, and he looks down at the screen. The message reads: *All clear. GO. —R*

Ethan surges forward through the doorway, with nineteen soldiers a step behind him.

The sound of the loudspeaker system reverberates the countdown through the walls:

. . . eight, seven . . .

Down a long maintenance hallway to a set of double doors.

. . . six, five . . .

We pull the American-flag jerseys from the prison raid over our squad uniforms. My heart is pounding so hard I'm afraid it might crack my ribs.

. . . four, three, two . . .

We're through the double doors in an instant, barging into the vast, empty floor of the Stock Exchange. There are no more than five squadmen in the room, and Ethan's shot three of them before I'm even through the door. I wound another, and McCann shoots the fifth, killing him instantly. None of them even have a chance to get a shot off.

In researching the raid, I saw pictures of the Stock Exchange as it used to be—filled with hundreds of computer monitors, packed with scores of traders. It's a completely different scene now. Aside from the dead squadmen, there are only a few other people here, members of the imager crew, I guess, and a few high-credit-level VIP types, standing along one wall. They raise their hands in terrified surrender. The rest of the huge room is basically empty. Its only purpose now is to house a single large, outdated computer mainframe. A handsome young Asian man, who I recognize as Bernice Yao's grandson, William, stands in a stiff-looking tuxedo in front of the computer, looking completely dumbfounded. Apparently he was supposed to be the onsite imager correspondent.

"What are you doing? What's going on? Who are you?" he demands, but no one answers.

The cameraman who was filming him has already run away and joined the throng of prisoners against the far wall. Ethan wastes no time. He hurries past Yao's grandson directly to the mainframe and plugs a data stick into it.

There are several imager screens around the room, and on one of them I see the scene cut back to the boardroom, where Jimmy Shaw has once again reclaimed the podium.

"Terribly sorry, folks. It appears we've run into some minor technical difficulties over at the Stock Exchange. Nothing to worry about, of course."

But at the bottom of the screen, the ubiquitous stock ticker that was to bear the unified N-Corp/B&S stock price now reads:

DEMOCRACY FOREVER, OLIGARCHY NEVER. THE PROTECTORATE IS FIGHTING FOR FREEDOM. THE PROTECTORATE IS FIGHTING FOR YOU.

*SQUADMEN, LAY DOWN YOUR
WEAPONS NOW AND YOU WILL
NOT BE HARMED.*

These words are being read by every person on earth. Even if we die now, we've won a stunning victory today.

"Come on!"

Five other soldiers and I follow Clair up a series of marble steps, then burst into the open air. A cool wind blasts me instantly, almost taking my breath away as I rush out toward the colonnade at the front of the building. Two squadmen are up here, shouting down to their comrades on the street below. One hears us coming and tries to draw on us, but Clair shoots him dead. The other, more wisely, throws down his gun and gets on his knees. And just like that, we've secured the third-floor balcony looking down on Wall Street. Each of us takes cover at the base of one of the columns.

Below us, a line of squadmen in riot gear is forming up.

"Fire!" Clair shouts, and the deafening report of our machine guns echoes among the skyscrapers. Civilian tie-men and women scream below and run in a frantic stampede, but they have little reason to fear. The Protectorate's marksmen are extraordinarily accurate, and we're not aiming for them. Within seconds, several squadmen have been wiped out and the rest have taken cover behind their vehicles. More squad trucks full of men, however, are arriving by the minute—just as Ethan anticipated.

I continually scan the sky for Ravers, but thank God, they don't appear.

The squad force below seems to be stunned, awaiting orders, which leaves us to amuse ourselves by shooting at the bullet-proof windows of their vehicles.

After perhaps ten minutes, the signal must come through from Blackwell to attack. The dozen or so squad trucks below have multiplied to no less than forty, and they open fire on our positions. We return fire. The whistle of passing bullets is surreal, as if the air around us has come alive and become deadly. The guy at the column next to me gets hit, and I start to go over to drag him back to safety. One glimpse of his gaping head wound, however, convinces me that he's a lost cause.

Just when the fire from below becomes so heavy I'm thinking we might have to retreat, our artillery kicks in with five explosions in quick succession on the street below.

Knowing Ethan's plan as I do, I can't help but smile. Rebels with rocket-propelled grenade launchers must have made it to their assigned positions atop the adjacent buildings. Now, they drop a rain of thunder onto the crowd of squadmen that had amassed to attack us. I hazard a glance from my cover to see that the street below has been demolished, transformed into a hell of mangled vehicles, flickering flames and black smoke. There's no time to gloat, though. The attack from above is our cue to retreat, and Clair is already holding the door open.

"Fall back!" she shouts. "Move, move, move, move!"

Down the steps, back into the echo chamber of the Stock Exchange. There were six of us when we went up; four come back down. We find Ethan standing where we left him, near the computer's mainframe, still holding Yao's grandson at gunpoint. The rest of the civilians have their hands bound by plastic zip-ties and are sitting on one side of the room in relative calm, guarded by ten or so rebels. Outside, the fusillade of rocket-propelled grenades continues, until Ethan speaks into his IC.

"B team, hold your fire. Begin phase two."

Instantly, the explosions outside stop. "Leave them," Ethan shouts to the men guarding the prisoners.

Yao tries to take a step toward them, but McCann sticks his gun barrel in his back. "Not you. You're coming with us," he says.

Ethan hurries to the front door of the Exchange. Over his shoulder, he shouts, "Fall in. We're getting out of here."

"Out the front door?" Clair asks, incredulous.

Ethan ignores the question. "Keep up a steady fire throughout the retreat," he says. "You see a squad member, take him out, but be careful not to hit any civilians. If anyone gets separated from the group, continue south and rendezvous in Battery Park."

Without hesitation, Ethan pushes through the front doors, and we all follow outside. Some of the smoke from the grenade attack has dissipated now, and the carnage on the street is apparent. Hundreds of squadmen lie dead or dying, some of them crushed beneath the twisted remains of their blasted vehicles. A few straggling survivors open fire on us, only to be taken out. Others simply run or take ineffectual potshots from their covered positions.

Ahead, the great, gothic spire of Trinity Church rises before us. As we turn left down Broadway, heading south, I catch a glimpse of movement above and look up to see our air force in flight. Clair follows my gaze upward and gasps in wonder.

The same seven rebels who perpetrated the surprise attack with the rocket-propelled grenades have launched hang gliders from their rooftop positions and are now following us, covering our retreat from above. The wings of the gliders are red, white, and blue in a pattern of stars and stripes. Curious faces peer out the windows surrounding us and point upward at them, their eyes wide with amazement.

At Morris Street, our ranks swell with twenty or so rebels who were

stationed there to cover our retreat. So far, resistance has been meager—half the enemies that came to oppose us have already been taken
out by machine-gun fire or grenades dropped by our makeshift air
force. But as we approach the intersection of Broadway and Battery
Place, I can see the flashing lights of squad trucks ahead, forming
a blockade. Worse, the chugging of helicopters becomes audible and
grows steadily louder.

At the head of our column, however, Ethan doesn't slow.

"Keep moving!" he shouts. "We have to break through their position."

We weave through a gridlock of mostly abandoned cars as we
approach the enemy, hoping to keep some measure of cover, but when
they open fire, it seems like a wave of lead is washing over us. The men
on both sides of me fall dead before they even get off a shot. Several
others try to stop and take cover, but Ethan shouts, "Keep going!" and
redoubles his pace, and the rest of us follow suit.

Several rocket-propelled grenades from our air force zip down on
the blockade ahead of us, but one misses altogether, and the other two
are only partial hits that don't completely destroy their targets.

"C team! Now!" Ethan shouts into his IC. At first, it seems like
nothing happens, then I see a dozen or so rebels stream out from
behind a building ahead and to our right and open fire on the squad's
position from behind. Instantly, the enemy fire lessens considerably as
the squadmen turn to face this new attack.

But we have another problem. Two helicopters race up on us from
behind, their cannons thundering, blasting small craters in the street
behind us. Two gliders get hit by fire from the choppers and come
tumbling from the air to the street below.

Still, Ethan keeps up his relentless pace. I change my clip on the run
and continue firing as we overtake the line of squad trucks and meet
up with the C team on the other side. Ahead is the grassy expanse of

Battery Park, and I race toward it on aching legs. The once-green park is now a wasteland of brown grass and dead trees, but I hardly see anything except the ground before me as I try to rush ahead at full speed without tripping and falling on my face.

Another glider flitters to the ground on my left, its wing aflame. One of the choppers races ahead of us then wheels around, ready to open fire and head off our escape, but one of our glider-borne soldiers slams it with a rocket-propelled grenade, a direct hit, and it drops out of the sky. We skirt the burning wreckage, running faster than ever now, as, from behind us, the gunshots of squadmen pursuing us on foot ring out.

Fortunately, our destination is just ahead: Castle Clinton, a former fortress from the War of 1812 and our rendezvous point, awaits. My legs are burning with exertion, my heart aches in my chest, and my legs are cramping, but my yearning for survival outweighs my need for rest. Above, there are three helicopters now strafing us with their machine guns, and a woman to my left takes a shot to her thigh that almost takes her whole leg off. Per Ethan's orders, I don't stop to help her. With a wound like that, she'll bleed out in a matter of minutes anyway.

As we near the fort, a new barrage of rocket-propelled grenades erupts from atop its brick walls, and two of the pursuing choppers fall in flames. The third wheels around in retreat. A dozen or so rebels stationed on the rooftop of the fortress cover our retreat, their withering machine-gun fire causing the squadmen still pursuing us to fall back. Only one of our glider troops remains, and as I watch, he descends gracefully inside the walls of the fort.

In a matter of minutes, we are all assembled at the edge of the water, staring at a white, wooden ferryboat tied up at the breakwater.

"You're kidding me, Ethan," Grace growls, aghast. "You expect us to escape in *that*?"

I'm feeling the same way. Ethan never told me his plan after this point. We were to escape to the water, to the southern tip of Manhattan, that's all I knew. But how we're supposed to outpace a bunch of helicopters in a ferryboat, I can't imagine.

"Get on the boat or stay here," Ethan says dismissively. "Your choice" and he embarks, followed by McCann, who's still holding William Yao at gunpoint. One by one, the men follow him across the gangplank. Grace groans and follows too, and in a matter of seconds we've pushed off from shore and are chugging into the open water. But the battle isn't over. I can see three more helicopters already coming over the horizon, and in the distance, a squad boat approaches.

Ahead, I can see an island with a square structure of brown stone standing upon it, and I remember my dad, on our only visit to N-Hub 2 together, telling me that a statue of Lady Liberty used to stand there—until the Company had it melted down to reuse its valuable copper.

As we press out into the open water, I go to stand near Ethan and McCann at the stern of the boat. We're all watching another wave of deadly squad choppers approach when Yao addresses me.

"You're May Fields," he says, a mixture of astonishment and disgust in his voice.

"That's right," I say.

"You're one of them," he says. I can't tell from his tone if it's a question or a statement.

"I am," I say. And I can't deny the pride I feel. I'm telling the truth; I am one of them. Somehow, I always was. And I always will be.

"You have to be the dumbest woman alive," he mutters, shaking his head.

The choppers are making a pass at us, and Ethan and McCann engage them with their machine guns.

"Yeah," I say. "I'm dumb? Why's that? Because I don't want to live my life a slave?"

"No," he says, grinning now. "Because your revolution is going to fail."

The next second seems to happen in slow motion. Yao reaches into his jacket pocket and comes out with a small pistol. Ethan and McCann, distracted by the helicopter, don't even notice as he levels the gun at the back of Ethan's head. I've already set my machine gun down—there it is, sitting in a chair three feet away.

"The Company always wins, May," Yao says, and his eyes flick from me to his target.

What happens next is pure reaction. Hardly a second elapses, hardly a thought crosses my mind. In one fluid, flawless motion I draw the white pistol at my hip and pull the trigger, just like Ethan taught me. Red explodes from the young man's head, and he falls backward against the stern rail in a heap.

Ethan and McCann both turn back to face me, looking from me to Yao.

"He pulled a gun," I explain. But there's no time to talk about it. The choppers are making another pass.

"Up to the bow, now," Ethan shouts to McCann and me, and he herds us forward, to a staircase that leads below deck. The rest of the force, apparently, descended while I was distracted by our prisoner. It seems a little strange that the lower decks of a wooden ferry would be made out of steel, but I don't think too hard about it—until Ethan turns back and closes a huge, steel hatch behind us and seals it by turning a metal wheel.

Above deck, I can hear the ferry being rattled by machine-gun fire and a single rocket blast.

When a light above the door glows green, Ethan shouts, "Dive!"

The sound of the engine changes and I can tell that we're moving.

The roar of the helicopters fades, then disappears. Finally, I understand what's happening, and when I ask Ethan he confirms it. The upper part of the boat was just a shell, made to conceal a submarine beneath. Right now, the squad thinks they sunk the boat and killed us. By the time they learn the truth, we'll be long gone.

"Where did we get a submarine from?" Clair asks.

"That's the fun part," Ethan says. "We stole it from Black Brands."

"Who pulled that off?" Grace asks. "Oh, let me guess, *R*."

I'm beginning to surmise that whenever Ethan doesn't want us to know how something was accomplished, he just tells everyone that R did it.

"That's right, it was R," he says, "but R isn't the hero today. All of you are. This is a victory that will be remembered for generations to come, and it was your bravery that made it happen."

We all celebrate differently—some with laughter, some with tears, some with an intense, contemplative silence. The sole-surviving glider pilot, Aziz, drinks a bottle of champagne he found on board and passes out. Many don't crack a smile until after we've made it safely to our pick-up point somewhere on the shore of the former state of New Jersey, where the supposedly missing team of twenty soldiers awaits with another set of squad vehicles in which to drive us back to camp.

Me, I'm smiling until we do our head count. Of the one hundred souls that embarked on our mission, seventy-three will be returning alive, and six of those are wounded. Still, the battle was much more costly for the Company, Ethan reminds us. In his estimation, the squadmen probably took one hundred casualties or more, while no one saw any civilians who were hurt or injured.

When we return to camp, we are greeted as heroes, showered with wine and champagne (what little the Protectorate has of it, anyway) and treated to a feast. Ethan is lifted on the shoulders of his army and carried around the camp while guitarists and fiddlers play him a happy tune. With the music, my exhaustion and sadness fade away. The strike was a triumph. We all behaved with incredible bravery. And Ethan, our kind and brilliant leader—I'd be willing to follow him anywhere.

—CHAPTER 019—

Ethan stands facing the wall-mounted imager screen in the council room, the American flag and the flag with the coiled snake hanging on the wall at his back. He wears an impeccable blue military uniform Ada apparently sewed for him. Standing there, his shoulders back, head held high, he looks distinguished, dashing, and thoroughly ready to be inaugurated the president of a new United States of America. But if the man Ethan is teleconferencing with on the imager has his way, he'll certainly die first.

"I'm sure we can come to some peaceful accommodation," Blackwell says, managing to sound both cordial and irritated at once. "You're not the first person to express discontent with the Company, Mr. Greene. But this is a business, not a government. We don't participate in wars. When we see an enemy, we don't fight them. We propose a merger. That's what the Company is willing to offer you today. A competitive compensation package in exchange for laying down your arms."

"It's General Greene," Ethan corrects, "and I have to disagree with you. The Company certainly does participate in wars. It participated in a good many of them before it took over half the world, and it's participated in even more of them since. Just because nobody knows about a war doesn't make its victims any less dead, Mr. Blackwell. And as for your offer of a merger, I'm afraid we will remain, now and forever, independent."

McCann and I, pressed to one side of the room with the rest of the council, grin at one another, thrilled with Ethan's eloquence.

Blackwell merely scowls. "I think you owe it to yourself, if not to your people, to at least come in and meet with me to discuss it, *General.*" There's a note of condescension in the last word, but Ethan ignores it.

"Thank you, but again I'm going to have to decline," he says.

"Then what exactly do you want? Everyone has a price. Name yours and let's be done with it."

Ethan nods. "Of course. My price is the dissolution of the Company into no less than one hundred thousand individual, competing businesses. My price is the reestablishment of the democratic government of the United States of America, and the disbanding of the security squads. In short, Mr. Blackwell, my price is your unconditional surrender."

Blackwell shakes his head. Clearly, it's all he can do to keep his anger in check. "Your precious government didn't work before. What makes you think it will work now?" he says.

"We've learned our lessons, Mr. Blackwell," Ethan replies. "We won't take it for granted this time."

Blackwell sits up straighter at his desk. "Of course, the Company utterly rejects your ridiculous demands. You leave me no choice but to come and wipe you out, Greene. Certainly you know that I can do it. The only reason we haven't done it before was the expense. It wasn't in the budget. Now it is."

For the first time in the conversation, a chill of fear rises up my spine.

"I expected no less, Mr. Blackwell. Please pass a message along to your squadmen for me. Any of them who quit now will be spared. The Protectorate has no desire to harm people who are simply trying to make a living within the tyrannical system you've created. But anyone who takes up arms against the free people of America can expect to forfeit his or her life."

Finally, Blackwell erupts into laughter. "Lord, man. You must've been an actor before you turned unprofitable," he says. "Do you seriously think you stand a chance against us?"

When Ethan doesn't reply, Blackwell leans in. "We've infiltrated your outfit, you know. I have a spy ready to serve you up to me on a silver platter."

Ethan glances over and motions for me to come forward. My heart racing, I hurry to his side and face Blackwell, trying to match Ethan's calm, regal deportment.

"Well. May Fields," Blackwell says dryly.

"She's not going to turn on us, Blackwell," Ethan says. "You have no spy. And soon, you're going to be out of a job, my friend. On this day, the Protectorate, on behalf of the United States of America, officially declares war on N-Corp."

Blackwell is no longer smiling, but he doesn't exactly seem intimidated, either. "Alright," he says, glancing from me to Ethan. "But don't say I didn't warn you."

The rest of the afternoon the imager drones on, showing re-edited clips from Ethan's conversation with Blackwell, making Ethan look like a moron rather than the brilliant leader we all know him to be. More often than anything else, they show the part where I enter the scene, looking thinner than usual, with the ugly cross scar on my cheek. My expression on the imager screen is a strange mixture of defiant bravery and green-faced nervousness. Overall, it's pretty embarrassing.

Fortunately nobody in the camp is watching it now; we're all too busy. Packs are being stuffed, bedrolls rolled. Crates of guns are readied for transport. Our miniature city almost buzzes with the kinetic energy of hundreds of rebels, all working to strike camp as quickly as possible.

I was to receive my official commendation today for shooting

William Yao and saving Ethan's life, which was to include a solemn and secret ceremony. Instead, Ethan simply hands me one of the Protectorate's trademark white pistols with my name etched on one side of the grip and the word "heroism" etched on the other, shakes my hand, then unceremoniously orders me to start stacking boxes of ammo.

There's no time to be disappointed, though. The revolution is finally beginning.

When I corner Ethan later and press him for details of our strategy going forward, his answer is typical Ethan: cryptic. "All-out war," he says.

From what I can gather, the plan, which has been in place for over a year now, is actually nearly as simple as that. In every hub city, members of the Protectorate have secretly been building up strength. Now that the final merger has been announced, they have four days to organize and gather their forces. At sunset of the fourth day, they are to strike a list of pre-selected targets. Some squad-related sites such as satellite control and relay stations are so heavily fortified that it's unlikely they'll be successfully destroyed. Other targets, like imager studios and power stations, will be easier to hit.

On the fifth day, all the groups of rebels will meet our main group at a predetermined location to make preparations for the larger battles to come. The primary objective of this mission is to create enough of an impact on Company operations that they will have to at least acknowledge that some damage has been done, and thereby inspire workers around the world to take action. All this must be accomplished while avoiding catastrophic numbers of casualties. And, as always, innocent lives are to be spared.

There's another key part of the plan that I've heard mentioned on several occasions: the Protectorate Education Initiative. No one seems to know what it is exactly, but from what I can tell, it's a secret effort that's somehow meant to get word out to everyone in the Company at once and inspire them to take action. Ethan seems to have high hopes for this part of the plan, but rumor has it that whatever it is has been under development for months and still isn't finished.

Regardless of what our plans are, it's clear that months, probably years of arduous and deadly struggle lie ahead.

"It's hard to say what will happen when we confront the Company directly," Ethan confides to me. "But the time to strike is now, before the two Companies' forces are completely consolidated. With any luck, we'll be able to capitalize on some confusion while they merge their security systems. Even so, it's a huge gamble. If they have half the weapons they're rumored to have, it could be very bad for us. It's a tough plan, but it's all we've got."

I nod and smile. "I'm in," I say.

But, in his uncanny way, Ethan sees through me.

"What?" he says.

"Nothing, it's just . . ."

I can't tell him what I really think. Despite our victory at the prison and the triumph on Wall Street, I can't help but remember McCann's imager footage, a whole village dead. I can't help but flash back to the catacombs of Black Brands, stuffed with thousands of wicked weapons that the Company hasn't even used yet. The truth is, I spent last night awake, thinking about our prospects for victory, and they don't seem very good.

When I did sleep, my dreams were disturbing. In them, I went back to the Company. My father embraced me and gave me a promotion. Jimmy Shaw interviewed me on an imager. I went back to the comfort of my apartment—my divine shower, my heavenly bed. And I was happy. I watched on the imager as the squads raided the rebel hideout, burned it down to nothing, while I sat on my N-Lux suede couch eating sushi. And I was happy. Happy I went back to the Company. Happy I was alive. Because in my dream, I always knew the Company would win.

My waking self is just confused. Of course, I can't tell Ethan all that, but he is my friend, and I feel compelled to tell him how bleak I feel our chances are.

"Ethan," I sigh. "You know I've always been the biggest fighter around. I mean, back when I was with the Company, I was so miserable that I spent most days fantasizing about beating the hell out of somebody. But lately, since I've been hanging around with these things all day . . . " I hold up a book I'm reading. "I don't know . . . I've been reading about Martin Luther King Jr. and his nonviolent methods of protest, and about the labor movement, which sometimes was very violent but was still rooted in just standing together, being united, and I was thinking . . . "

"You think we could change things without fighting?" Ethan says.

Yes. Because there's no way we can beat them in a battle, Ethan. No way on earth. Instead, I say, "I don't know. I wish there was another way. What do you think?"

He puts a hand on my shoulder. It's my nature to recoil at any touch, but I force myself to stay still.

"I feel the same way you do, May. And perhaps there was a time when everything could have been changed without violence. But I'm afraid that time has long passed."

"You're right," I answer grudgingly.

"You know, May," he says, "I like you." There's nothing romantic or sexual in the way he looks at me—if anything, his demeanor is fatherly, though he can't be much more than seven years older than me. "If you think of an easier way, let me know, alright? I would love to hear it."

His dry humor makes me smile, and my smile makes him laugh. In a second, we're both cracking up. It feels good to laugh, even in the face of Armageddon.

I'm fifteen years old. In the last few months, I've been raped and I've betrayed the love of my life. I've been sent to boarding school, and I've been raped. My mother is dead and my father is an absent workaholic. In my loneliness, in my pain, I turn to the only person I have left: Randal.

I show up at his door at eight o'clock on a stormy Wednesday evening. Even though his apartment's IC system should have alerted him that I was outside, he still looks wide-eyed as he opens the door and finds me standing, drenched, on his stoop.

"Hi, May. What—?" he begins, but stops as I nearly fall toward him through the doorway. He flinches, clearly expecting me to punch him in the nose, but instead my arms encircle his neck. I bury my face in his shirt.

"She's gone," I sob. "She's . . . she's gone."

"What do you mean? Who's gone?" he says, putting his arms tentatively around me. But he knows very well who's gone. Kali.

"We did it, Randal. It's all our fault."

He leads me inside, and after taking a quick glance out in the hallway for any HR watchers who might be lingering nearby, he closes the door. I let him lead me toward his bedroom.

Thank God, his parents aren't home to see my meltdown. They're at work, as usual.

He sits me down on the bed.

"It's okay, May. We did what we had to do."

I shake my head, sending a shower of tears across my lap. "No," I whisper. "No, no. We destroyed her."

Only now do I glance around the room. Everything is all packed up in a series of plastic boxes and shiny, silver garbage bags. In my distraught state, it takes me a moment to comprehend what all the boxes are for, and then I realize. He's packing for Cranton. The opportunity of a lifetime. The opportunity he betrayed Kali to get. Suddenly, my hatred shifts from myself to him.

He seems to sense the change and puts both his hands on my shoulders, gently keeping me from rising to my feet. "May," he says softly. "We didn't mean to hurt her."

Violently, I shrug out of his grasp, push my way back further on the bed. "But we did," I hiss. "We did hurt her. And her family."

Randal is shaking his head. "It had to be done, May. Blackwell told me everything. Her dad was part of some rebel group. He wanted to destroy the Company."

My sadness and fury suddenly abates like the stillness after a storm, leaving me utterly empty. Outside, a constant rain patters against the windowpane, a lulling sound.

"It had to be done, May. If we didn't do it, someone else would have."

Randal is close to me now, his handsome face inches from mine. He tenderly brushes one strand of drenched hair out of my eyes. And suddenly, I understand. I understand why he's been calling and emailing me, ever since he realized I was mad at him about Kali. I understand why he's been my most persistent friend—the only one who would put up with my fearsome moods for the last three years. I understand. He really is in love with me.

And, I realize, he's the only one. Even if Kali reappeared, she'd never forgive me if she knew the truth. My mom is gone. Dad might as well be. Randal is it—the only one. I'm crying again, so lost in thought that I hardly feel his lips on mine, hardly notice as he slips my shirt up over my head.

Randal isn't like Kali, my beautiful goddess of fire. He isn't like the squadmen, either, brutal, violent, and demeaning. He's gentle. Sweet. Still, I don't look at him as he kisses my neck. I watch the raindrops trace their way down his bedroom window and wonder if I'll ever feel happy again.

For a week after that night, Randal calls me every day, and every day I ignore him. The messages and e-mails he sends me talk about us dating, about him being my boyfriend. Yeah, right. Even after he ships off to Cranton, I get the occasional message from him, but I never, ever write back.

With the final merger announced, the Protectorate's end game, for better or worse, has begun. After two days of marching through tunnels and across endless, dead forests under the cover of night, laden down with heavy gear and under constant threat of attack, we've succeeded in moving the camp into an abandoned city once called Detroit.

From all over, those sympathetic to our cause gather here, in this old, crumbling convention center. I meet so many people; their faces parade before me in an almost unending line: there's Antonio Russo, a carpenter; Joaquin Clay, a distribution manager; Christine Ahearn, a (hot) makeup artist with two small daughters.

I had imagined that anyone who would come here and risk so much for our cause would have a specific grievance, a family member who the Company dragged off to a work camp, maybe, or a lover killed by the squads. At the very least, I expected our new recruits would have firsthand knowledge of an atrocity like what happened in McCann's village—a horror which, I learned, had been repeated all across the globe. But no. To my surprise, many of those I meet are like I once was:

intelligent, good-hearted people who are cognizant only of a feeling that something in the world has gone awry and the Company is somehow to blame. They're normal Company workers, regular tie-men and women, blessed with brand-new high-speed ICs and spacious, luxurious apartments, who've decided to trade in these extraneous toys for a shot at regaining their human dignity.

It's a beautiful sight, these faces. Never, when I was a wildly whirling cog in the Company machine did I take the time to really see the people around me, to notice the lines on their faces or the shape and shade of their eyes. Among the rebels, there are relatively few plastic noses or sculpted bodies, but in the ugliness, the plainness, the dumpiness of the forms passing before me, there is a singular majesty that surpasses false beauty by far. These are God's real creations: imperfect, fallible, unromantic, beautiful creatures. It makes me wonder how the false idols of youth and empty beauty ever eclipsed the honest humanity that used to pass before me, unnoticed.

Small camps are set up a few miles away from the city, where new recruits are required to go for screening and cross removal; a spy in our midst at this stage would be disastrous. Once the recruits undergo the baptism of the knife, they are escorted to the main camp, where they join the rest of us.

In the massive, debris-strewn foyer of the abandoned convention center, I stand in a line with the council members and greet the recruits as they come in, shaking each of their hands, introducing myself. Some of them are flushed with excitement and exchange loud jokes and hearty greetings. Others are very pale and hardly move their lips when they speak, as if petrified with fear. The latter, I imagine, are the wiser ones.

In the main hall, I walk among the people. Veteran soldiers show the new recruits how to use their weapons and orient them to the mission, but even in their busiest moments, my comrades always take the time to smile as I pass. This is the first time I've really noticed their affection for me. I'm naturally shy, and also—well, I hate most people. So it's surprising to find this many people in one place who genuinely seem to like me. Despite the short time I've spent with the Protectorate, I realize, they are fast becoming my friends and family.

I'm surprised to find that some of those who are new to our ranks seem to know me as well. "You're May Fields!" they say. "The one whose father is this CEO, right? You jumped from that helicopter! You're with the Protectorate? Wow." Then they stare at me goofily, their eyes wide with misplaced awe.

I mumble some assent and walk on through the crowd, blushing.

Then from across the room, I see Clair. The bruises on her face are almost completely healed, and even from here her eyes shine. Her body looks lean and powerful beneath the T-shirt and camouflage pants she wears. Ethan is with her, whispering something in her ear. His hand is on her waist. He goes to leave, and she smiles at him and takes his hand as he departs, letting his fingers slip through hers as he walks away. As I watch, a too familiar, gouging pain of longing stabs through me.

Clair watches Ethan leave, and as she does something about the way she crosses her arms is so familiar, so oddly stirring, that I can't help but stare. Still smiling to herself, she turns and passes through a set of double doors.

Fighting through the crowd, I follow.

Beyond the double doors is a set of stairs. Echoes of my footsteps surround me as I go up and up, many flights. Several times I stop and poke my head through a doorway, only to find the hallway beyond empty. Finally, my legs aching with exertion, I reach the top. Here, a large window is broken, leaving the stairwell open to the outside. Staring outward, her back to me, is Clair. She rests the butt of her white machine gun on one cocked hip. In the air in front of her, two little birds follow each other in dizzying, twittering loops then disappear into the morning.

"I wondered when you'd try to talk to me again," she says, not turning.

Since our little altercation after the prison break, I've avoided her whenever possible. I didn't think she'd even noticed.

"I just . . . " I begin, wondering how to explain myself. The truth would be easy enough to say: I realized that she's with Ethan, and though there's no logical reason it should hurt me, it does. But I can't bring myself to utter the words. I shake my head, frustrated.

She laughs.

"The more people change, the more they stay the same," she says.

What the hell does that mean?

I force myself to come up next to her, so we're both looking out over the crumbling city, the smog-smudged sky and the ruined highway— I-75, it was once called—stretching to the horizon. Suddenly, I feel the urge to pour my heart out to her, to lay bare my entire soul, to confess all my failings, my silly wants, my unattainable desires. Even if she laughs at me, even if she hates me. It would be enough just once to say out loud what I'm feeling inside.

To me, I realize, this war is a war to be *heard*.

But she speaks first. "I've been avoiding you, too," she says.

Why? It can't be because she feels the same way I do. . . . I want to ask her, but again, the words won't come. The silence grinds on for too long, but I still can't find the courage to speak. Finally, I clear my throat and say the first thing that comes to mind.

"I just wish everything was different. The whole world. I wish God would just wave his hand and make it all right."

"God? You still believe in the Company lie?" she laughs, her voice suddenly acidic.

It's funny, although all my recent experiences have made me completely disillusioned with Jimmy Shaw and the Company, I still never doubted God for a minute.

"I think maybe there are two Gods," I say finally, "a false one to imprison people and the real one to set them free."

More silence.

Clair stares out at the ruined city. I watch her. She's so beautiful in this moment, standing there, her hazel eyes as dark as storm clouds. Those eyes are a different shape than I remember them. The face is different, the curve of the mouth, the angle of the chin, the slope of the nose. I don't know how such things can change, but they have. I can't keep myself in denial any longer. The revelation I've kept at bay for weeks now, since the first moment I saw her, hits me like a comet falling out of the sky.

"Kali," I say, and she slowly turns to me. "I would know you anywhere," I whisper.

Fury simmers in her eyes. "You know me?" she asks, "Do you? You know what it's like to live in low-credit-level housing? Or in a work camp? Or to survive on the streets? Do you, Blackie?"

I heave a soul-shaking sigh of relief. It's her. She didn't deny it. It's truly her. She's alive. She's here. There are so many questions—where has she been? Why does she look so different? "Kali—" I begin, fighting back tears.

"Clair! My name is Clair!" she glares at me fiercely, then finishes, her voice low: "Kali is dead. And you killed her."

I stand a moment longer, fighting to dam the flood of emotion rising in me, but finally it becomes too much and I turn to bolt down the stairs. But she grabs my arm hard, wheels me around to face her.

"You don't know me, May," she snarls. "You never did."

I open my mouth to speak, but no words come out. I don't have the breath. "No," I finally manage to say, "but I did love you."

When she moves this time, I'm afraid she's going to strike me, but instead she embraces me, wrapping one arm around my waist, putting one hand behind my head and pulling me to her.

Our lips hit one another's so hard I taste blood, but I kiss her back anyway. I put my arms around her, pull her body to mine, so close I can feel her tears on my cheek.

When she finally pulls away, I can hardly breathe. I'm crying, shaking. Her gaze lingers on me a moment longer, then she turns back to the open window.

"I'm standing guard," she says coldly, her eyes searching the distance for the enemy. And just like that, she is lost to me again.

I want to scream, to beg, to ask her a thousand questions, but the words fall back in my throat. This is enough for now. That kiss was enough. I sniff, take a deep breath, and descend the staircase on weak-feeling legs, trying (failing) to resist looking over my shoulder at her as I walk away. I wipe her taste from my lips and place one hand on my pistol, hoping the feeling of the weapon will bring me back into the world of harsh realities and dire consequences at hand.

But despite everything, I can't help hoping that maybe, just maybe, this is the beginning of something. Maybe, after everything, after all my loneliness, all the misery, all the hollow days and torturous, silent nights I'll finally have my happy ending.

But this is no time for love. This is war.

—CHAPTER Ø2Ø—

As I step out of the stairwell, Grace rushes up to me.

"There you are! I was looking all over for you," she huffs, out of breath. "Ethan needs you, now."

For an instant, as she drags me by one arm through the crowd, I'm overcome with an illogical fear that Ethan has somehow already learned that I kissed Clair and he's pissed. Then, pushing aside my personal fears, I begin to worry that some calamity is coming for all of us, that the Company's learned our location and is at this moment training one of its infinitely deadly weapons on our hiding place. This premonition, too, I set aside. As Ethan taught me during my training, the only mindset befitting a warrior is one of expectant, watchful readiness.

Grace leads me across the great hall. From one wall to the other, restless people mill about. Some are chatting, their conversations often erupting into forced, nervous laughter; others sit quietly, staring at their guns, preparing themselves for the trials ahead. Lovers hold hands. Children run through the legs of their parents, giggling and chasing one another. Old men watch it all and smile, knowing that even as terrifying a day as this will pass, like all the others, into distant memory—at least for those who live to remember it. When we reach the other side of the room, Grace leads me through a door and into a hallway with large, mostly broken windows running along one side.

From the other end of the hallway, a man is coming toward us; he isn't Ethan, I know that much right away—this guy is shorter and heavier than Ethan, his hair darker and longer, his gait lolling and clumsy. His figure is silhouetted, his features unclear.

"He says he knows you," says Grace in a horse whisper, nodding at the approaching figure.

Only when he's right before me do I see his face. He's lost weight since the last time I saw him, and the dark circles under his eyes have become purple bags. Still, there's no mistaking him. I'm overjoyed.

"Randal?"

"May Fields!" he says, his tired-sounding voice full of affection. "I d-do declare!"

We hug. He smells as if he hasn't showered in days.

"What are you doing here?" I ask. "How did you know where I was?"

His eyes tick back and forth among the shadows at our feet. He taps one broad hand on his thigh at a rapid pace. He's worse than the last time I saw him. Too much Peak. "It was easy to f-find you," he says with his sheepish grin, then, as if it were sufficient explanation: "I knew where you'd be before you did."

Grace reads the confusion on my face and steps in. "I might as well tell you now: he's always been with us," she says. "He's the one who disabled the electronic protections and allowed us to break into the prison. He's our genius, our guy on the inside."

"R," I say. Suddenly, the pieces are all fitting together. I look back at Randal, in shock.

"I've always been with the P-Protectorate," he says. "From the beginning."

"Holy crap!" I say, punching him in the arm. "I can't believe you! And you never told me!"

He nods, grinning wanly. "I was watching you. I was the one who told Ethan to send Clair and her Reaper team to recruit you," he says. "I d-d-do it all. I'm the eyes and ears of the Order. I create the e-disguises, crack the codes."

"And he's modest, too," Grace says, rolling her eyes.

"Well, I knew that big nerdy head of yours would come in handy for something eventually," I say, putting an arm around him.

The sound of footsteps from down the hall, crunching across broken glass, cuts our conversation short. Ethan approaches and, like Randal, he looks a little more haggard than usual.

"Hello, all," he says. "I see your friend found you."

I'm not sure whether he's speaking to me or to Randal, but I reply: "Yeah. Why didn't you tell me Randal was one of us?"

"His identity was one of our most closely held secrets. It was too important to jeopardize, although he seems to have jeopardized it himself." He glares at Randal.

"Ethan's mad at me for coming," Randal explains.

"And with your cross, too. They could track you right to us, and you'd have the blood of three thousand people on your hands," Ethan says.

"I disguised the signal in the computer," says Randal. "They can't track me."

"You hope," Ethan amends.

"I had to give you this information in person. It was the only way."

"You could have used a pigeon," says Ethan.

"Pigeon?" I say.

"We use homing pigeons for our most important communications," Ethan explains. "Any electronic method could be decoded and human messengers can be followed. It's the only safe way." He turns back to Randal. "I'll assemble the council in an hour and we'll hear your briefing together. Meantime, get some rest. You look like death. Grace will show you to a room."

Ethan turns on his heel and is gone. It's hard to say what the difference in him is, but I've never seen him act quite like this. I resolve to talk to him before the meeting and find out what's really going on.

Randal, Grace, and I look at one another.

"Okay," Grace sighs. "Come on."

On the way to Randal's quarters, he speaks very little. He looks about nervously and blinks too fast. His lips make words, though no sounds come out. I wonder with vague dismay whether it's just an overdose of Peak or some new, more insidious drug coursing through his system.

After a moment's walk, we arrive at Randal's room. Grace tries the knob but the door is stuck, so she slams into it with her shoulder a couple times until in swings in.

She gestures dismissively into the open doorway. "There's a lantern and blankets. I think there's a bottle of water if you want to drink or wash. I suggest you do both. We'll get you when we're ready."

She seems even gruffer than usual, and I'm glad when the door closes behind her, leaving Randal and me alone. He sniffs and wipes his nose, then pats both legs with his open palms. He won't look at me.

"Randal, what's up with you, man? Are you okay?"

"Yeah, yeah, yeah," he says. I don't know if it's just the dim light spilling into the darkened room from the open doorway, but his normal, disarming smile seems disturbingly counterfeit.

"Are—you—sure?" I say, speaking with mocking slowness that makes us both laugh.

"Sh-sh-sure," he says.

I cross to the table, which I can hardly make out in the half-light, and find a book of matches next to a kerosene lantern. I strike us a light.

"You don't mind if I stay with you for a few minutes?" I ask. "You've got a lot of explaining to do, and I . . . I could use somebody to talk to." After finishing my sentence, I'm a little horrified by my words. Never can I remember admitting to another person that I needed help of any kind. Part of me panics, wishing I could snatch the words from the air and stuff them back in my mouth, but of course it's too late.

Randal just raises his eyebrows.

"Well . . . " he says, then laughs silently. Everything he does is so awkward. So unlike the Randal I first met so many years ago.

"What drugs do they have you on now?" I ask. "It's something new, isn't it?"

"It's nothing," he says, biting his fingernail. "Just new stuff. There's always something new. New, new, n-new s-stuff. Yep. It doesn't stop, this stuff. You just f-f-flat out don't sleep. Don't have to, actually. My w-work has gone into new realms. I've s-s-seen things."

"What do you mean?"

"Oh," he says with a wave of his hand. "Just new ways of seeing. New ways to get around the Company's e-security measures. New ways of integrating c-c-cross implants with p-people's brains. Ooh, they were mad when you took your implant out! Nobody thought you would really do it! But you did. . . . "

"How did you know about that?"

"I know everything. The C-C-Company network is nothing but a big b-brain. And it has its own c-cross," he says, giving me an exaggerated wink.

I pretend to understand. Really, what I want to talk about is myself.

"You wouldn't believe everything I've learned here, Randal. I've learned to shoot; I've been shot at, I've seen people killed, I've killed people, I've rescued people, saved lives! And I've met some really amazing friends—the people who are with us in the Protectorate, some of them are just incredible. Even old Grace. And the prison, some of the prisoners we freed, you wouldn't believe what the Company's done to these people. And in the work camp, there's one in the old city called In-something . . . Indianapolis! These people there are real slaves, not just indentured workers like the rest of us were, but *slaves*"

"I know," Randal says with a distant sigh. "I saw."

"What do you mean, you saw?"

"Company c-cameras. Everything everywhere is on camera. Of course, if there's an important Protectorate mission going on, I'll black out the c-cameras in that area when Ethan asks me to, but for something like your trip to the work camp, it's all recorded. You just need to know where to look."

"I see," I say. Something in Randal's demeanor disturbs me, no matter how hard I try to shake the feeling. Still, I feel like a piece of tinder about to catch fire. I've had so much to say—and nobody to say it to—that I can't hold myself back.

"I've been reading, too," I continue. "About the American government. Did you know they used to break Companies up when they got too big? It was called antitrust legislation, the big companies were called monopolies, and it was illegal! Then the Companies took over the government and put a stop to it, the bastards. And . . . Kali, Randal. Kali is alive. But of course you know all that, don't you? You know everything."

Randal nods distractedly. When I look at him more closely, I see that he's about to cry.

"What's wrong?" I ask.

He sighs, sniffs. "I missed you," he says.

"I missed you, man."

He opens his arms and we embrace. I give him a hardy pat on the back, and we pull apart.

The lamplight flickers. In it, I see a cavalcade of emotions cross his face, from yearning, to anger, to worry, to regret, to anger again. He stares into my eyes, his gaze more intense than I ever remember it, and his lips form silent words—threats, maybe, or an accusation.

"What Randal? It something wrong?" I ask him. "Say it."

But he only shakes his head, takes a deep breath, and forces himself to smile.

"Nothing, nothing, nothing," he says. "I'm just t-t-t-t-t-tired."

"Okay. Should I let you get some rest?" I ask.

He nods, and I take a blanket from the corner and help him lay it out on the floor. I fold another one up for him to use as a pillow. I throw a third one over him, letting it fall over his face playfully.

"Get some rest," I say. "You want me to turn out the lamp?"

He shakes his head emphatically.

"Alright." I take a few steps toward the door, then stop. "Hey," I say. "So, I won't tell anyone before the big meeting, but what's so important that you came all the way here? I mean, that was a big risk. And if it was that important, why didn't you tell Ethan right away? Why are you waiting for the council to assemble?"

"My message is for the whole council, not just one person." Randal says. "You'll see. . . ."

I don't know why, but I'm overcome again with a strong sense of concern for him. Now, after all this time, after all I've learned, it's easy for me to see what I was afraid to admit to myself before: Randal and I really are friends. Despite what happened all those years ago with him and Blackwell and Kali, we always have been. We are connected. In some way I still can't completely comprehend, we are the same. And I care about him, deeply.

"Well, whatever it is," I say, "we'll face it together, alright?"

The only answer is his breathing, slower now, and steady.

"Hush little baby, don't say a word . . . " I sing softly, playfully. That's all I can stomach of my singing voice, so I stop. I can't see him in the shadows, but I imagine his eyes closed and his pudgy, pale, sweat-slicked face finally relaxed and cherub-like in sleep.

I smile. It's the most beautiful thing in the world to have friends. Too bad I found it out so late. I walk out the door and pull it shut very slowly behind me, releasing the knob carefully so that even the tiniest *click* won't disturb Randal's slumber.

Then, as I turn to leave, I hear it. The sound is low at first, low and heart-wrenching, then it rises in pitch and volume like a siren's wail. I lean close to the door and listen.

Behind it, Randal is crying.

Something is horribly wrong with Randal. I decide the only one I can share this concern with is Ethan, but McCann tells me he's indisposed. I consider finding Clair at her lookout post, but at the thought of our last encounter my resolve to find her wilts and I turn away at the foot of the stairwell.

So I walk aimlessly for about an hour or so, tangled in restless thoughts.

The battle is coming. The words ring in my brain like a bugle blast and my heart beats as fast and steady as a marching cadence. Though I can hardly admit it to myself, I am in love with war. The feeling of firing a gun, like holding thunder in my hand, is intoxicating. The power to kill compensates for all I've been deprived of in my life. The love, respect, and freedom I've missed out on all amount to nothing compared to the force I wield with the simple, one-millimeter movement of a trigger. I remember the cries of the men I killed in the prison, the way their bodies twisted in agony as they fell, and all I can think is: *good.*

I never wanted to hurt anyone, of course; I could never want that. I want to be happy. I want others to be happy. But in the absence of that happiness, I want revenge. I want the curtain separating "what is" from "what should be," torn down and I want to do the tearing with my own bloodstained hands. Let the war come. I'm ready.

When Grace finally finds me, I'm lost in thought, watching Michel and a group of young boys playing soccer in a corner of the great room.

"May," she says, and I turn. "Stop disappearing, would you? Come on!"

She tells me the council has assembled, awaiting Randal's news.

"Thought you might like to be the one to wake him and bring him in, since you two are such great buddies. . . . " Her tone is laced with an even more lethal dose of sarcasm than usual, but I ignore it and go to get Randal. This time when I approach his closed door, there is no sound on the other side. I enter slowly, not wanting to wake him abruptly, and am startled at the creak of the door's hinges. I'm even more startled to find Randal not sleeping as I had expected, but sitting up, staring at the lamp's wavering flame.

"Hey," I say. "No sleep?"

His jitteriness seems to have ebbed in the hour since I last saw him, and there's even an air of weariness as he shakes his head.

"Randal," I say, "what's going on?"

He looks up, making eye contact with me for the first time since our reunion. His smile seems fragile. "You'll find out soon," he says. He bites his lip, seems to consider something, then says, "So, so, are you and that old grizzly bear Grace an item, or what? I saw you checking out her caboose back there."He laughs a wheezy little laugh.

"Jackass," I say. "I'd hook up with you before her, and that's pretty bad."

He laughs harder.

"Come on," I say. I walk over to him, hold out my hand, and pull him to his feet. His hand feels plump and moist as bread dough in mine. On his feet now, he blinks at me without moving. "Let's go before we piss them off." I put one hand on the lamp to turn it off, but Randal stops me.

"Wait—"The urgency in his manner catches me off guard. "I need to give you something." He holds a hand out to me, with something pinched between his fingers; it's small and flat, the size of a small coin but triangular in shape. I recognize it instantly: it's a data stick for the new IC. We don't use them much—it's far easier to transfer files using the Company network. But for the rare times when greater security is needed, like if we don't want someone to hack in and look at a new ad campaign before it's released, we use data sticks like this one.

"What's on it?" I ask.

"It's my gift to you," he says, chewing on his lip, tapping one foot. "I was going to g-g-give it to Ethan, but he won't want it anymore. Just remember, no matter what happens . . . I always loved you."

"Randal, what's going on?" I'm not surprised by the "I love you" part coming from him—it's the "no matter what happens" that's a little too ominous for my taste.

He stares into my eyes, his smile fading. "I know, May. About *her*."

"Know what? About who?"

"About Rose," he whispers, his lips trembling, "I know about our daughter."

I'm too bewildered to reply. First, he isn't the father. Second, how could he possibly know about Rose?

"You should have t-told me, May," he says, shaking his head. "You should have told me. For a s-spy and a rebel, the worst thing in the world is having something to lose."

Still confused, I open my mouth to ask what the hell he's talking about, but before I can, Grace barges in. "You gonna keep the whole council waiting while you two play grab-ass? Let's go."

I glance at Randal, hoping to catch his eye, to get some clue about what my daughter has to do with the council meeting, but he's not even looking at me. Head bowed, he follows Grace through the doorway. I slip Randal's data stick into my pocket and follow.

All eyes are on us as we enter the meeting room. At the council table, Ethan sits in the middle seat, with McCann on his right and Clair on his left. Grace takes her seat with the rest of the council, while I take the folding metal chair near the door, leaving Randal standing alone under the scrutiny of the assembly.

Ethan sits up very straight. His expression is grave. "You know how much danger you put us all in by coming here, Randal, so I'm sure your news must be urgent. Speak."

My heart beats fast. I'm nervous for Randal, standing up there all alone. I know how terribly shy he is, how lousy he normally is at speaking in front of people. For the first time, as he shifts from one foot to another and wipes his brow, I truly pity the odd genius standing before me. Then, all at once, he pulls his shoulders back, straightens up, and takes a deep breath. His voice is clear and his eyes firmly fixed on the council as he begins:

"For years, we have all been brothers and sisters together. I would have d-died for any of you. I will die for you. But," he looks down and seems to be biting his lip. When he raises his head again, there are tears in his eyes.

"I have betrayed you." The room holds its collective breath. "The Company was going to kill my child. A ch-child I didn't even know I had until a few months ago, and . . . I know I'm weak, I don't need anyone to tell me that. I know I'm selfish, but to me, that one life was worth more than all of yours. Blackwell found out about me altering a security code. When he interrogated me, he threatened my daughter, and I agreed to cooperate—but I told myself I would only tell them a little bit. I thought I could lie to them, maybe even throw them off your trail. But . . ." His voice cracks. Snot and tears drip from his face. "They changed me. My b-b-brain. There was a surgery—and—I told them where you are. I told them everything. I couldn't stop myself. After they let me go, I knew I had to warn you. I couldn't just let you all die. So here I am. And now they'll probably kill her anyway, my Rose. . . ."

Ethan is standing now. Several other council members are on the verge of rising, too, but he stays them with a gesture. "What are you saying, Randal? Be very clear."

Randal meets Ethan's glare. "By sunset, we'll all be dead," he says. "It's over. They're coming."

From outside, the sound of first one air horn, then another, bleeds through even the concrete walls. Alarms. We hear screams. In a blur of motion, Ethan draws his gun. Two deafening cracks cut through the air, and Randal is on the ground, writhing and squealing. The room is in a tumult, some council members dashing for the door, some standing and looking around in confusion, others still sitting, frozen in morbid disbelief.

Ethan turns to me: "Get your *friend* out of here. Send him out the front door, now. He resists, shoot him. The rest of you, spread the word and evacuate the building. Scatter throughout the city. Go underground if you can, and try to stay in tight quarters where the Ravers can't get to you. Go!"

In an instant, the room is empty, save for the now-disordered furniture, me, Ethan, and Randal.

"Ethan," Randal says, writhing in his own blood, "I'm sorry. P-please! I'm so sorry!"

Ethan pauses in the doorway. "No," he says. "I am."

And just like that, he's gone.

I walk over to Randal, standing over him as he moans on the floor. Right away, I can see he's not dying. Ethan's two shots were not meant to be fatal. Randal has only been wounded—in both his hands.

He notices my puzzled look. "*If any a Benedict Arnold becomes, shoot both his hands so he can't hold a gun,*" he murmurs, holding his blood-soaked hands in front of him. "So says the P-Protectorate."

He sits up, trembling violently. "I t-tried to redeem myself by coming here . . . ."

He looks so pitiful sitting there, but I'm so angry at him at the same time, I don't know whether to hug him or kick him. He destroyed us all. Maybe ruined the whole revolution. But he did it for our daughter. My daughter.

"Randal . . ." I say, shaking my head, fighting my anger. "You probably killed three thousand good people today." I haul him to his feet. "Come on."

He rises on unsteady legs and follows me. As we head out of the meeting room and into the main corridor, there's a deafening explosion somewhere. The air seems to crackle and the building shakes all around us. Dust descends like a veil.

Randal gazes up at the blank, white ceiling of the corridor. "It's b-beginning," he whispers.

I give him a little push, herding him ahead of me.

The hall soon opens into the high-ceilinged lobby, the conference center's grand foyer. The room's massive skylights were all blown out by the explosion, and the marble floors under our feet are slick and crackling with broken glass. From above, a few shards still drop like falling stars, hitting the floor around us with what might be lethal force. There's a ferocious screaming sound and, looking up, I see two sleek, black drones streak past, preparing for a second bombing run.

Randal is talking, but whether the nonsense he's prattling on about is directed to me or only to himself, I can't tell.

"All this blood, this drug. I . . . I just wanted to live! All I wanted, and n-never could . . ."

To the exit, now. The doorframe is a sagging parallelogram. The doors are half fallen from their hinges. I push Randal gently through one of the openings.

"Go."

He turns back to me, suddenly very lucid. "We . . . we had a lot of fun, right May?"

Tears rise in my eyes. "Ah, don't get all sappy. This isn't goodbye. It's just . . ."

Randal takes a small step toward me. "I did it f-for Rose," he says. "We c-could have been together, May! Why? Why didn't you tell me?"

I clamp my teeth together, trying to hold back the torrent of conflicting emotions I'm feeling. *Because the world is ruined,* I want to say to him. *Because I don't love you, Randal. I can't. I love someone I can never have. Because Rose isn't even yours. She was conceived in blood and tears. Because Jimmy Shaw was right, we are a fallen people. But not fallen for want of hard work, like he claims. We are fallen because of greed, endless greed. Endless selfishness. And as for redemption . . .*

The blood on his hands shines, thick and slick. He reaches out to me, pleadingly. "D-d-do you think . . . maybe I could just stay?" His eyes are full of tears. He looks so sad, my old friend. This is killing me.

"Randal," I say, "I can't."

"No one w-would know!" he says, taking another step forward. I can see a frenzy building within him, the Peak-fever rising. "P-please, May! They'll kill me out there! They have a thousand ways!"

"I'm sorry—" I begin, but he lunges forward and grabs my arms. His face is inches from mine, now. He's trembling, spitting, desperate.

"I don't want to d-die alone! I want to be here, with you! Just another J-J-Judas—the ones and zeroes—over and over and over again!"

"Stop!" I shout, and shove him.

He falls to the ground and blinks up at me, as if startled out of sleep.

My hand rests on my gun. We stare at one another, both of us fighting to catch our breaths.

Finally, he cracks a smile and I know he's himself again. "May Fields, Protectorate soldier!" he says. I can tell that despite everything, he's proud of me.

An instant later, the smile has already faded. He stumbles to his feet. "I'll go," he says. "I'll go."

He looks at me, and for a moment his eyes are the same as they were in our childhood.

"You get that data stick to an IC," he says.

"I will," I say. "I promise."

"And if you see Rose again . . ."

"I'll tell her that her daddy loves her," I say.

Randal smiles through the prism of my tears. We clasp hands for a moment, then he pulls away and heads out the doorway and down a long, concrete footbridge leading from the convention center entrance to the parking lot below.

Something on my hand is sticky and moist, and I look down to find my fingers reddened with Randal's blood. Down the causeway, he grows smaller with each step. Though I somehow hate to take my eyes off him, my responsibility lies with the others—so grudgingly, I turn away. Back across the foyer now I hurry, dodging bits of falling glass.

Work to do. I have to help with the evacuation before the drones make another pass. . . . Now, again, the rumble of nearby explosions. My stomach is in knots. I redouble my pace.

Suddenly, I stop. The hairs on the back of my neck are standing up. My skin seems to be crawling with electricity; my teeth vibrate and my scalp feels as if it might creep off my skull on tiny insect legs. Something tells me to turn back, and I do.

Through the skewed rectangle of the door, I see Randal's figure, stopped halfway across the bridge. Slowly, he tilts his head to the sky. Without warning, white light sears my eyes. There's a sound like a whip cracking inside my head, and a wave of heat brushes my cheeks, then disappears. My eyes are closed, but the image is still superimposed over my eyelids: Randal standing on the bridge, and the lightning striking him.

When I finally open my eyes, he's still smoking.

He falls to his knees then topples over, charred black as coal from his head to his waist.

I don't have to look up to remind myself that the sky is a clear and cloudless blue; I already know. This is the power the Company has. Just like Randal said. The Black Brands—lightning sats—death from the sky—insurmountable.

Somehow, I knew it all along.

Beyond Randal's smoldering body, a cloud of swarming Ravers rises. Hundreds of thousands of them, coming fast. Ashes of Randal drift in the wind. There's nothing left but to turn and run.

—CHAPTER 021—

The nightmare has come.

I run as hard as I can through the halls of the abandoned convention center, the buzz of the Ravers behind me growing louder every instant. My shirt is already soaked with sweat and clinging to my chest. I know I need every ounce of concentration I can muster to stay alive, but the image hangs over my vision, obscuring everything else: lightning striking Randal.

The whirr is getting closer.

Turning a sharp corner in the hall, I take four long strides and stop short, my boots skidding across the carpet. I turn back, gun up and ready, and see three darts stick into the wall where I just was. An instant later, a Raver shoots around the corner, faster than I had expected, and I open fire.

CRACK-CRACK-CRACK-CRACK!

Three Ravers round the corner, three fall.

I wasn't sure my bullets would bring them down, but they did— at least temporarily. The Ravers might buzz back into flight at any moment, but I don't wait to find out. I'm already tearing off again, sprinting for my life.

Maybe twenty yards ahead, a set of fire doors stands propped open, flush against the walls of the hallway. I can hear the buzzing behind me again and feel the breeze as darts hum past my ears. My life depends on making the right decision now. If I can close the heavy double doors, I might be able to keep the Ravers out—they can't be capable of opening doors, can they? But if I can't get the doors shut fast enough, I'm going to be a dead pincushion in a matter of seconds.

From what I can judge, the Ravers are maybe twenty-five yards back, and closing. This is my only chance. The doors get closer, closer. I'm going to do it.

Now! I spin to a stop, my back slamming against the wall, and fling the near door shut with my left hand while firing two shots with the pistol in my right. My shots miss. The door swings closed.

I watch the darts coming, my death on their tips. Two sink into the door, one passes through my hair and disappears down the hall. The Ravers are fifteen yards away, now ten.

I kick the other door. It's hooked open somehow, doesn't close.

Ravers: five yards away.

I yank the door, yank again. More darts coming.

Screaming, one foot against the wall, pulling the door with all my strength. There's a splintering, snapping sound as the hook holding the door open gives way, and now I'm on my back. Darts pass over my head, the door drifts closed. The Ravers are two yards away, close enough to see the blood-red lenses that serve as their eyes, close enough to see the tiny N-Corp logo on their underbellies.

And the door closes. There's a loud bang as the first Raver slams into the thick metal. The others turn away in time.

I stand. My lungs hurt, my hands are shaking. Sweat drips, burning, into my eyes. I stand and place my hands on the doors, bracing against them in case my mechanical assailants try to push them open. I hear them buzzing around on the other side, see their black shapes crisscrossing through the crack between the doors, but they can't get through. For the moment, I'm safe.

As if to negate my last thought, the floor jitters beneath my feet and the whole building seems to jump in a thunderous explosion. I'm safe—unless the bomber drones bring the roof down on my head.

Running again. Black smoke collects around the ceiling. I hear more bombers pass overhead, and somewhere outside the sound of gunfire erupts and continues, unabating. It sounds like the demolition of the world.

I run down several hallways through ever-thickening layers of smoke, until I pass what must be the only unbroken window in the place. It looks out onto a courtyard, and what I see there stops me dead. Outside, thirty or so members of the Protectorate, some with children, are pinned down, hunkered behind cement benches and flattened in weed-choked drainage ditches. Scores of Ravers rake the sky above them, raining death. About a hundred yards away, across a deserted roadway, several squad trucks are parked. The black-uniformed squadmen sheltered behind them fire ceaselessly at the cornered rebels. From my position behind the glass, it's like seeing an exhibit in a museum of death.

Unable to help, I run on.

I encounter Ethan, Clair, and McCann and the rest of the survivors a few minutes later. They've made their way to a shipping-and-receiving area, and from there are planning to escape the convention center via a loading dock door and pass to an adjacent building, hopefully undetected. We all listen as Ethan lays out the plan.

"McCann, you and a few others will make your way up to the café area and fire on the troops positioned across the road. Hopefully you can put enough heat on them to distract them while we make it across the parking lot to the old shopping mall. The rest of us will be running across open blacktop with very little cover. It's a risk, but in another twenty minutes this place will be ashes. It's our only option. Everybody got it? Okay, who's going with McCann?"

"I will," I say.

Ethan's expression darkens. "Bear in mind," he says, "whoever goes will be drawing a lot of fire, and will have to cross after us, with no cover. You'll be in the open with a lot of Ravers. It's extremely dangerous. Clear?"

I nod.

"Fine. Who else?"

"I'll go," says Grace. She has a long, bloody gash down one side of her face and is limping badly. No doubt, she knows she couldn't cross two hundred open yards if she tried. Better to be of use with us. She smiles at me—it's probably the only time I've ever seen her smile.

A tall Hispanic kid, one of the ex-prisoners, (his name is Chris, I think), raises his hand. He has two massive machine guns strapped over his shoulders and a fiery look in his eyes. Ethan nods at him.

"One more, at least," Ethan says.

Clair glances at me.

"I'll do it," she says.

A look of concern passes over his features, then melts into resolve again. "Are you—?" he begins.

"I'm sure. I'll catch up with you," Clair says.

He looks at her hard, and some unspoken communication passes between them. Finally, he sets his jaw and looks us all over for a moment, no doubt expecting this may be the last time he'll see any of us. "Okay, then," he says, "Godspeed."

McCann musses his son's hair, then winks at me. He might actually be insane, I think to myself—for even in this, the most dire of moments, he still wears a gigantic smile. He surmises my thoughts and puts a strong hand on my shoulder. "If you gotta die, you should be grateful to die right," he explains. "Isn't that right, lady-lover?"

Though a moment before I would have thought it impossible, I smile back at him, and place my hand on his shoulder, too. "That's right," I agree.

Before we all part ways, I see Ethan grab Clair's arm. He pulls her to him. I try not to watch, but out of the corner of my eye, I see him kiss her softly, just beneath her eye. Even amid all this, I still feel a pang of jealousy. But there's no time to dwell on it. In the next instant, McCann is running like a gazelle down the pastel-painted hallway, a war cry on his lips, and we follow.

When we reach our position, I see that Ethan was right: this is a place one goes to die. The café is a wide, jutting oval of a room with all glass walls, designed to look out upon the broad lawn below. To our right is the courtyard where, by now, the cornered rebels I saw earlier have all probably been killed. Ahead, beyond a wide bomb crater and debris-strewn yard lies the road where the squadmen have taken position.

To our far left, sheltered for part of the way behind a wing of the building, we can see the crumbling parking lot across which our comrades must escape. And all round us, on every side, are nothing but windows, floor to ceiling. The only shelter to be had is behind a serving counter that stretches along the back of the room, and that's where McCann leads us. Above the counter is a sign: a big, yellow, arched M. In a brief flicker of curiosity, I wonder what it used to mean—then my mind is back on the battle again.

We take position, check our clips, and look at each other one last time.

"Ethan and the others should be in place by now," McCann says, then nods across the way at our enemy. "Pick one out, get him in your sights, and fire on my signal. Remember to aim for the head; they've all got body armor. On three. One . . ."

"Well," Clair says, leaning over to me, "this is it."

Something tells me this isn't true; we aren't dead yet. But I don't contradict her. Instead, I close my eyes and take a whiff of her scent. Even in the heat of battle, she smells of jasmine. I think of all the things in my life that I've wanted and never had, or had and took for granted, and am almost overcome with tears. I don't want to die now;

I don't want to die ever, and certainly not like this. What I feel most is not fear, though I am afraid, it's regret. I never saw the regions controlled by B&S, or took a nap with Rose, or went to the beach with Clair—Kali. I never did a million things.

"Two . . ." says McCann.

I take aim at a squad member through the window, but can't help glancing over at Clair again. For all I know, it might be the last time. With one luminous hazel eye, she winks at me.

"THREE!"

We all fire at once. Across the road, a couple squadmen fall.

"Don't let up!" says McCann. "Until your last breath, don't stop!"

And we don't.

The kid, Chris, seeing me firing with only my pistol, passes me one of his machine guns. Within seconds, the fury of hell is unleashed on us. Bullets come in torrents, breaking away every bit of glass in the windows then battering down the window frames themselves.

Swarms of Ravers amass outside, hovering just above the line of fire. Every few minutes, dozens of the little planes swoop into the windows. We desperately rake them with gunfire, somehow miraculously dispatching wave after wave of them. All around us, every surface resounds with the clatter of bullets. The empty chairs skitter across the floor as if dancing. Tables overturn. Hanging lights fall, and the counter before us splinters and sags. We keep firing, but the end is inevitable.

Chris takes a bullet in the throat.

McCann is hit in the left arm and falls back. An instant later, he is up again, screaming curses and taunts at the Company, redoubling his efforts.

We successfully force back another wave of Ravers, but by now we have a new enemy: a fire in the building, from the bombing, I guess, is catching up to us. The floor is hot to the touch. Smoke fills the air, and it quickly becomes too thick for us to see our enemies or for our enemies to see us. Still, we keep firing blindly—if we were to stop now, we would free up the squadmen to track down our fleeing friends.

The reeking smoke makes me dizzy. My eyes water, and when I turn away for a second to wipe them, I see Grace. She's sitting with her back against the counter, facing away from the fray, clutching her gun to her chest. Her face is white, her breathing shallow. I step around McCann, dodging the hot casings as they fall from his gun, and stoop next to her.

"Grace?"

She turns her face toward me, but her eyes don't focus on mine. I look for a wound, but see nothing.

"Grace?"

"May?" she says, smiling weakly.

"Yeah. It's me. You okay?"

She can't hear me over the din. "What?"

I lean toward her ear, placing one hand on the floor. The surface is slick beneath my fingers, and I don't have to look down to know the puddle I'm kneeling in is red.

"You're going to be okay!" I yell.

There are tears in her eyes, but she's still smiling, or trying to. She pants, seemingly building herself up to speak.

"You're my favorite," she says. She's trying to yell, but it comes out a whisper.

"What?"

"I bet you always thought there was nobody else in the world who understood you," she says, "but I was just like you once. Just like you."

I try to fight the tears that well up.

"Yeah?" I say. "I always thought you hated my guts."

"No," she huffs. "I liked you. I'm just a mean old bitch."

She tries to laugh, and her face pinches in pain, then gradually grows lax. She's sweating badly, but when I touch her forehead, it's frigid.

"Grace," I say. "Come on, Grace!"

She doesn't respond, but I can still see her breathing shallowly.

I reach out with one weightless-feeling hand and slowly pull the gun away from her chest. At first, she resists, but a second later her strength gives way. Beneath the gun, her stomach is torn open; I can see nothing but her shredded, soaked shirt and pools of thick, dark blood. I place the gun back over her wound. Soon, she'll be dead. Not even Ada could save her.

"May!" says McCann.

He doesn't have to say anything else. I resume combat, though there's no way of telling what I'm firing at through the black, billowing smoke. It's all I can do to stay conscious, breathing in the thick, hot, poisoned air.

Seconds later, the structure all around us begins groaning, creaking, crackling. The final disaster comes with a single ear-splitting *pop*. At first I think it's the sound of a bomb exploding beneath us, then the floor tilts and I'm sliding downward.

Everything is in a tumult—arms, legs, guns, shards of glass, ragged bits of wood, warm blood—mine or another's, I can't tell which. I'm tumbling, sliding. Heat lashes my face and debris hammers my shoulders.

Then I'm on the grass. Coughing, dizzy, and nauseated, I get to my hands and knees, staring through the rolling smoke.

"May!" a voice cuts through the haze. I hear another cracking sound, this one coming from above, and throw myself toward the sound of the voice. Behind me, a deafening crash.

I'm kneeling in chest-high grass. McCann is pulling me to my feet.

Clair stands next to him, eyeing me with concern. "You alright?" she says.

"I don't know," I mumble. My heart is beating fast. I'm so light-headed I don't know if I'm alive or dead.

I look over my shoulder. The near side of the cantilevered room we were in has collapsed. The floor we had been standing on, once the second floor of the building, now forms a ramp down to the ground. And the second crashing I heard must've been the roof caving in, for now its tarred surface extends from the grass at my feet and up through clouds of smoke to the second floor, where the other half of the room still stands. Now, the whole structure is being engulfed in flames. Only God knows how we made it out alive.

Somewhere, there's another explosion—either another part of the building falling or a drone dropping some massive bombs.

"She looks like she's hit," Clair says, studying me with concern.

"I don't see the wound," says McCann. He glances at me and then over his shoulder, eager to be moving out of this exposed spot.

"I think I slid through Grace's blood," I say. "I'm okay."

"Let's go," McCann says. "We get caught in the open like this and we're done." And he leads us away.

We run blindly through the choking haze, across the parking lot, toward the old shopping center. The sun is just a pale place in the drifting soot. Large bits of ash float around us like will-o'-the-wisp, and burning embers glide past, bright and fleeting. I watch Clair from the corner of my eye, thinking how I wish I could hold her hand right now. It's an absurd thought, but I can't help it. I'm buoyed with con-fidence and bravado and an illogical certainty that Clair will be mine.

The smoke masks our retreat beautifully, and for a minute, I almost smile with triumph at the thought that despite all the firepower the Company has thrown at us, we're about to escape.

The next disaster comes without warning.

"Down!" yells McCann, his voice choked with terror. He dives away from us into the smoke and is gone. Clair and I both dive in the opposite direction and land together on the crumbling, weed-cracked concrete.

Above, two Ravers buzz past.

Hardly breaking her momentum, Clair rolls back onto her feet. She holds her hand out to me and with one surprisingly strong pull brings me to my feet. "Come on!"

We might be running through clouds. There are no landmarks to measure our progress, only the thick, vile curtains of smoke and the never-ending, teeth-grating buzz of the Ravers. Their dark forms fade in and out of the oblivion surrounding us, forcing us to dodge and weave, duck and sprint. Tears run down my face from the particles in my eyes. My lungs ache.

Then I suddenly realize: Clair's still holding my hand! It's a dream come true nestled inside a nightmare.

Raver darts whistle past us, terrifyingly close, but I feel invincible. Then without warning, a gust of wind comes by, sweeping away the smoke for a moment, and the sight that it reveals stops my breath: hundreds of Ravers swarm around us. The density of their numbers obscures the sky. The murmuring buzz of their propulsion drowns out even the crackle of gunfire.

Now, ahead and to my right, I see my death coming. A dozen or so Ravers veer toward us and fire a volley of darts all at once. With preternatural clarity, I can see each stinging point as it approaches me, sharp, deadly, inexorable. Clair, on my left, sees them too, and suddenly I am pulled off my feet. My left shoulder shoots with pain, as if jerked out of its socket, as I'm swung to the ground. I hit hard, feeling each piece of broken asphalt cutting into my back, tasting the dirt in my mouth, wincing at the sting as the skin is shredded off my right arm where I tried to catch myself.

Clair threw me down and now she's on top of me, her face an inch from my own.

Then comes a sound, like a brief drumroll on a muted drum, and I feel her body tense up against mine. Her hair flutters as the Ravers pass over.

She stares down at me, her hazel eyes moist and red-rimmed from the smoke.

"No," I say. "No, no, no . . ."

I reach around her, tracing one hand up to her back. My fingers pass from dart to dart. There are probably hundreds of them. In that instant, the world seems to cease its turning. I stop breathing. The gunfire that had rattled in my ears only a moment before fades into nonexistence. The flames, the smoke, the pavement, the bullets, the explosions, the Company, the Protectorate, all of it disappears from my mind, and there is only me and Clair, and the incomprehensible horror of what has just happened, the overwhelming desire to undo it, and the terrible knowledge that it can never be undone.

"Clair, why? Why did you do that?" I can't hold the anger out of my voice.

She blinks slowly, and her eyelids flutter open again. I hear the buzzing swarm above her. Her body is hot, pressed against mine.

She shakes her head slowly. Her words are barely audible. "Not Clair," she says.

I open my mouth and search for the breath, for the courage to say what I have to say next. "Kali?"

Her features soften into a smile. I want to memorize every feature of her face, so beautiful but so unlike the face I remember from the love of my youth, but my tears blur her beauty.

"Kali," I whisper, "why didn't you tell me earlier that it was you? Where have you been? Why do you look so different? Why did you throw me down, goddammit? I was supposed to die for *you*."

She doesn't answer, but she brings her face close to mine. Her smooth, perfect cheek is cold.

"I'm sorry," I tell her. "I'm so sorry about your dad. I should have helped you. We should have run away together. I'm so sorry."

I put my arms around her, careful to avoid the bristling darts in her back.

"I love you," I croak through tears.

Shaking, I hold her to me. It wasn't supposed to be like this. Through the silken strands of her hair, I watch the smoke above billow and shift, capricious and black, but the Ravers are mostly gone, moved on.

It wasn't supposed to be like this. In my arms, Clair twitches once then goes perfectly still.

A sound comes from my throat, something between a moan and a growl. It resonates up from my chest, my crotch, my gut, low and horrible. I grope the ground and find Clair's—no, Kali's—gun, and slip out from beneath her. I brush the hair from her brow and kiss it. As I stand, the sound in my gut erupts into a scream so primal and horrible that it makes the hair on the back of my neck stand up.

I sprint, sightless, fearless and screaming, through the nothing-scape. I fire the gun indiscriminately, just to hear the deadly report. I am utterly hollow, as if an atom bomb had exploded in my heart. All I want is to die, and I run toward my death desperately, hungrily.

In the shifting smoke, I can almost see my Kali again: her face, her body, her hair—and the parts of her precious life that I missed.

I don't know any of this, of course—not for sure. But I can see it. I can feel its truth in the marrow of my bones. And I know this is how it was. . . .

I see my Kali leave her home and wander the streets. Forgetting her father, herself, her life. Forgetting me. I see her hungry, weak, unable to face the reality of her life, her utter incompatibility with the world. I see her taking pills she wishes will kill her, but will not. I see the pills stealing the light from her eyes and the flesh from her bones. I see her lost.

To survive, she must steal, fight, hurt others, and allow herself to be hurt. She becomes a killer, a cold, wandering wraith, stalking the night in search of sustenance. For her crimes, she is placed on the squad's "wanted" list.

Now she cannot enter a Company building, because the cameras of the e-security system are programmed to scan something called the Face Database for any criminal matches. If her face is seen on a Company camera, it will instantly be connected with her identity in the computer system, then an alarm will sound at squad headquarters and within minutes she'll be arrested. She is an unprofitable, reviled and exiled.

She cannot venture indoors where the cameras are, so instead she lives on the streets—and on the streets, she is prey. Huge, black squad trucks stalk her through alleyways. Black-suited squadmen find her huddled beneath overpasses and kick her awake. When these predators catch her, she must give them what they want, whatever they want. When she's lucky, it's just affection. The unlucky times, she wills herself to forget.

Within a few years, something terrible happens: squad cameras are put not only inside Company facilities, but on the streets, too. Now there is no hiding from the Face Database anywhere. Before, if a squad member had caught her on the street, he would just mess with her, maybe hit her, maybe make her perform some humiliating act. Now, if she were to be spotted by a camera and identified in the Face Database, it would become official Company business. The squadmen wouldn't have the option of simply having their fun with her and letting her go; they would have to bring her in. And the Company is not as lenient as its sadistic employees.

The only way to escape the cameras and the database is to alter herself. This is performed at great expense, and the only currency she possesses is her body. The procedures are done by a series of unsavory, sometimes amateur surgeons, often in strange locations, with disturbing instruments and in disgusting conditions. Afterward, she will awaken on the street again, her face wrapped in blood-soaked gauze, a new bottle of pills rattling in her pocket. In a week or so, when she gets up the nerve, she'll stop at a storefront window to look at her reflection. The feeling that washes over her is one of mingled revulsion and relief. She is herself, but she is not herself.

And that's good. Perfect. That's just how she wants it.

The pill "trips" that make her vision spin out of control, the mutilation, humiliation, and beatings, the endless fleeing, fighting, fearing that she endures—these are not the worst parts of her life. The worst comes after. When the squadmen or surgeons are done with her, when the pills wear off—then, she is horribly, inexorably herself again. No matter where she runs, what she does, she cannot escape herself: Kali, the little girl who broke her father's heart. Kali, the sinner. She steals things, hurts people. She changes her name, changes how she speaks, walks, talks, and thinks, but no matter what, she is the same: a selfish little girl, a lesbian, an addict, a whore.

But there is a solution, she knows, an absolution, a comfort, yes. Sooner or later, she will end herself. This thought alone sustains her. At least she will accomplish this. But before she dies on the streets;

perhaps only months, weeks, or days before she is able to bring herself to die, a man finds her. A man named Ethan Greene.

He finds her in the men's bathroom at a plastics factory, sleeping in a pool of her own urine—how she got through the door without a cross is anyone's guess—and he carries her home.

All she knows is that he's a mid-level tie-man in the psychology division of the Company's HR department. He will tell her no more. She likes that about him. He asks her no questions. He has a lot of illegal guns. She likes those things, too. Never does he ask to kiss her or touch her—although later she'll insist on it. He is handsome, and often reads, and sometimes stays out all night with no explanation of where he was. She likes all those things. Slowly, painfully, she begins to trust him.

As years pass, Ethan takes the pieces of her, the scattered fragments, and puts them back together. The surgeries she's had on her face, designed to make her someone else, someone anonymous and lethal and irresistible and immune to suffering—he sees through them. He takes her to a real doctor, who fixes the sloppy work those back-alley surgeons have done on her. With his help, she is remade.

Finally one day, Ethan tells her of his secret—and of the special role she might play in it. Because she has lived for so long outside the Company, she is in a unique position to help his cause. She can be an agent of something called the Protectorate. Her life and death, finally, can stand for something besides shame.

Eagerly, she begins her new incarnation, the last in a seemingly unending series of rebirths. Kali is dead. Now, she is Clair—strong, healthy, and clear-minded (no pills now, no; Ethan would never have it). She is Clair, strong, ruthless, and beautiful.

But even now, having run so far from her old life, from the awful summer when her sinful love drove her father to madness, she cannot quite forget that she was once just Kali, a quiet girl who loved butter-flies and lying in the hammock, eating grilled-cheese sandwiches and kissing a pretty girl named May. May, who eventually betrayed her. She has not forgotten, no. Memory is an incurable and painful disease.

A few years later, when May finally reappears, a woman now—dark, powerful, mysterious, and strong—Clair cannot help but love her again. Nor can she help loving Ethan. There is no escape, she decides: no escape from her feelings, no escape from herself. The years of run-ning were all in vain. There is no shame anymore. No right, no wrong, no heaven or hell. No change, no beginnings or endings.

There is only Kali, right or wrong.

There is only this one, fleeting life.

There is only her love.

She embraces it, lives, fights.

And finally, she dies as she lived—beautiful and wreathed in smoke.

—CHAPTER Ø22—

Still screaming, still shooting, I run blindly through the vacant parking lot.

Then, as if the smoke solidified before my eyes, a wall appears. The shopping center rises before me, a bleak beige mass of crumbling stucco. I look left, and against the wall I see a dark shape moving. I train my gun at it, starving, lusting to kill something, but for some reason I stay my trigger finger. Instead of firing, I rush the thing. I'll beat it to death with my own hands! Crush it! Rip it apart.

Drawing close, though, I can tell even through my tears that the figure isn't a squad member or a Raver. Still I run, eager to see its blood fanned out across the wall, eager to be the bearer of death.

As I approach, words gradually seep into my mind. "May! May, it's me. May! Me, McCann!"

He stands against the wall his hands up, his gun pointed heavenward. "You okay?" he says.

I realize I'm still screaming. My teeth are bared like a rabid dog's. When I close my mouth, all is horribly silent. I'm shaking. My gun is aimed at McCann's head, and I lower it, suddenly embarrassed.

"Where's Clair?" McCann asks, but I can see by his face that he's already guessed the answer.

"Kali," I correct. I don't say anything else, but somehow McCann understands. He motions for me to follow him, and together we creep along the wall, through the smoke.

Shots still ring out, but they're more distant now and we know enough not to shoot back and give away our position. After following the wall for a few hundred feet, we find a set of glass doors—shattered, presumably, by Ethan's entry—and McCann leads me inside.

Here, what dim light there is comes from skylights, which are periodically obscured by the shifting, drifting smoke. It is a world of half-light and shadow. The sounds of destruction outside are stifled. We traverse cracked tile floors covered in a half inch of dust. Every shop window is broken, the glass scattered across the floor. Everywhere, strange paintings and curse words adorn the walls and ceiling, looking as if they were painted by cave people. If I could see anything but Kali's face before me, I might be amazed; never in a Company area have I seen so much as a single white wall defaced. If I were capable of thought, I might delight in the bravery, the will it must've taken for somebody to create these sloppy murals. But as things stand, the sight awakens a strange fear in me. This looks like a world of Chaos, and Chaos, like the deadly order of the Company, is the enemy. *We are not anarchists*, Ethan's words from one of our training sessions come back to me. *Anarchy means letting animal greed go unchecked—that's what the Company does. We stand on the side of order.*

McCann puts two fingers in his mouth and makes a strange, high-pitched whistle. A moment later, another whistle answers. We follow the sound down the long, dark hallway, passing desolate shops, broken skylights, and twisted, abandoned clothing racks. Ahead, the hallway ends and a great, black opening, like the mouth of a whale, gapes at us. Above, a dingy-looking sign can still be read: *Macy's*. I've never seen a store by that name, but I imagine it must've been one of the many independent retail stores swallowed up years ago and rebranded by the N-Style division.

From the shadow of the store's arching entrance, eyes peer out. Perhaps a hundred people wait here. Some crouch, resting, others pace restlessly, with eyes scanning the darkness around them and fingers on the triggers of their guns. Still others sit on the floor, their eyes closed in either despair or prayer. Out of the shadows, Michel appears, running like a terrified cat and finishing in his father's arms.

"I'm safe," McCann says. "It's okay. Daddy is still working. Sit back down there by the others and everything will be fine." He kisses his son on the head, and the boy runs back into the shadows.

From among the figures, Ethan emerges.

First, he sees McCann and me—then, as his eyes search the shadows behind us and find them empty, his expression of relief dissolves.

"Clair?" he asks.

"She saved my life," I say. The words seem miserably inadequate, but I can't find any others.

Ethan nods stiffly and glances at the survivors huddled in the shadows. "I figure twenty minutes, tops, and they'll realize they've cleaned out the convention center and start on the other buildings," he says, his words fast and low. "They probably already have the perimeter surrounded. So how do we get out? Any ideas?"

"It's a tough one," says McCann, thinking.

I try to think, too, but I am incapable of it.

Even now, with almost certain doom waiting around every corner and through every door, even with the agony of Kali's loss, none of this seems real. Though I still see Randal's hair burning when I close my eyes, though Grace's blood is still smeared all over me like war paint, even their losses seem like something out of a fast-fading dream. And my own predicament, even in this moment, is beyond my power to comprehend. Maybe it's my N-Corp schooling, an education so rooted in fiscal practicality and disconnected from visceral reality that even now I'm unable to see myself as a mortal, precious life. Maybe I'm just afraid to think too hard about the situation we're all in—surrounded, hunted, haunted. I just want to be alone, to be in silence, to lie down and waste away and meet Kali again in a brighter world beyond all this strife and misery. I wander a few steps away from the others.

"May," says a little voice.

In the shadows I see Michel, sitting cross-legged against the wall. His face is smudged with soot. He picks at a scab on his knee.

"Hey," I say.

He looks up at me expectantly. As much as I want to turn away, to be alone with my wounds, I am unable to ignore the pain I see on his face.

"What's the matter?" I ask.

"Well . . ." he says. "Ada was taking care of me. You know Ada?"

I nod.

"She always watches me when Father is fighting."

"Where is Ada?" I ask, though I'm almost afraid to hear the answer.

He nods his head toward the convention center. "One of the little black planes was coming, so she threw me into a closet. I skinned my knee, see? I stayed in there a minute, hiding, then when I came out Ada was lying down. She didn't move. She had some, like, darts in her, but I took them out. I couldn't wake her up, so I just left her there. Do you think she was dead?"

"Do you?" I ask.

"Yeah," he says. "For sure."

He doesn't cry. He just looks gloomy and picks at his knee.

"I wish the fighting would stop," he says. "I want to play football again."

I nod. What else can I do?

"May," Ethan calls.

I lean over Michel and rub his little head. "Hang in there." I tell him. "We'll play football again soon," and I turn away from him.

When I rejoin Ethan, his expression is as dark as obsidian. "We need your help," he says. "We can't figure a way out of this. There are no underground tunnels leading out of this building. The sats will be scanning for us, and I'm sure we're surrounded, so we can't sneak out. And if we stay here, the drones will eventually bomb this place and kill us all," he pauses, regarding me darkly. "So?"

"So . . . what?"

"What have you come up with?"

I think for a second. What's left? We're surrounded. The forces arrayed against us are too great. The Company's technology has us wrapped up in a cocoon of death. And without Randal to help us. . . .

"What's left," I say, thinking aloud, "but to rush them?"

From somewhere, the low cough of a bomb comes, vibrating the air around us. Ethan glances at his watch.

"Glorious death," says McCann, smiling with weary irony. "What a warrior she is. I'll see you in Valhalla!"

"Actually," says Ethan, "that's not a terrible idea."

I think to myself, *Of course it's a terrible idea! Even with the best of luck, three-quarters of us will be mowed down before we reach the squad trucks; that's if we aren't caught up in a swarm of Ravers and completely decimated the minute we step out the door.*

But Ethan seems to be thinking the same thing I am: *What other choice do we have?*

"It *is* the last thing they'd expect," McCann agrees grudgingly.

"They're positioned on the other side of the road," Ethan says, thinking through the problem. "There's a lot of open space between us and them, but we should have smoke to cover us for part of the distance."

"What about the Ravers?" asks McCann.

"You gotta go somehow," I joke.

There is another option, I think to myself. *We could surrender.* The thought sends a shiver up my spine as I imagine things magically reverted back to what they once were: sitting in my office, eating frozen dinners alone in my apartment, daydreaming about the next big product, sustained only by one thought: of becoming a Blackie.

No, even if there were a magic pill I could pop that would take me back in time, I would never, never take it. Even the final loss of Kali can't change that. The only way for me is forward.

Ethan nods to himself. "If we can make it to their lines and hijack some of their trucks, some of us might make it out."

McCann looks at Ethan. "You ready to die, brother?"

Ethan nods. "If you're ready to follow me."

Another explosion rattles the building. Again, Ethan glances at his watch. He takes a deep breath and turns to our restless comrades.

"Alright, everyone," he says. "We're charging the squadmen line. Anyone who stays behind will likely be captured or killed. For those of you who come with us, I'm afraid odds look bleak, but there is a chance some of us will make it through. So decide now, are you going or staying?"

There is hesitation, a collective sigh of resignation, of hardening resolve, and one by one, the remaining members of the Protectorate rise to their feet. Despite all the horror, I think to myself that this moment is beautiful. Everyone is standing.

"Good," Ethan says. "We all go together."

Through a dim, musty-carpeted hall we walk, three or four abreast. Our pace is neither quickened with urgency nor slowed by fear. Ethan, McCann, and I are at the head of the column. I glance over my shoulder and see a hundred pairs of eyes looking back at me out of the darkness, as hardened as steel-shuttered windows. Glancing down, I see Michel. The expression on his face is outwardly calm, if a little sad, but beneath its surface lies a deeper feeling, which simply can't be translated into words. McCann slows to walk at his side.

"Hey, small man," he says, "are you sure you want to come with us? It's going to be dangerous."

The kid nods. "Ethan said it's dangerous either way. And I don't want to stay back alone."

He's right, I think. What difference does it make? Either way . . . I can't finish the thought.

"Do you know what this means?" McCann says. "Where we're going?"

"We're going to maybe die," he says, matter of factly. "For freedom."

"Praise God, boy," says McCann, squeezing his son's shoulder. "You make me proud."

There's no resisting it. I speak. "You aren't afraid?"

"A little," Michel says. "But like my father says, if we fight today, maybe somebody else won't have to fight tomorrow."

I suck my teeth, willing the tears to stay out of my eyes.

"You're a brave kid," I say. "Maybe a lot of other kids will get to be happy because of what you do today."

"You think so?" he asks.

I sigh, trying to ponder his question. With all the terrible losses we've suffered in the last few hours, it's hard to hang on to any remnants of hope. The chances that we will survive this battle seem slim. We've lost Clair, Randal, Grace, and countless others already; if the rest of us die in the next few minutes, who will be left to carry on the fight? Who will even remember the Protectorate? What meaning will any of our efforts have when the last of us is gunned down and forgotten? But even in the face of such bleak thoughts, I can't help thinking that there still might be a way. . . .

"I think you're very brave," I tell Michel. And in his smile, I find the hope I was looking for.

Ahead, Ethan has reached an emergency exit. Everyone checks their weapons, says their prayers. I look over the machine gun in my hand, check the clip.

"God bless you, Michel," I say.

"God bless you, too," he says, "and God bless America." Then, by way of explanation, he adds: "Dad taught me to say that."

McCann kisses his son on the forehead; then we turn to the doorway as Ethan prepares to lead us into the mouth of hell.

For the last five minutes, we've stood tensely in the doorway of the shopping center, waiting to make our charge. With each passing second, my nerves grow more frayed—but still, Ethan does not lead us out. He merely stares out the tiny crack at the edge of the door, still as a statue.

Another explosion thunders close by. Dust rains down on us from the ceiling tiles above. Ethan glances at his watch. It's the third time he's looked at it. I'm starting to think he's lost his nerve.

"What's with the watch?" I ask.

"The drones are on an automated loop," he explains, his eyes still trained on his watch face. "The bombing runs are forty-six seconds apart, which means they've locked onto us. We're going to take advantage of it."

Someone, one of the Order members in the back of the column, has attached a tattered American flag to an old piece of steel tubing—probably a curtain rod—and passes it up to us. I go to hand it to Ethan, but he waves me off.

"You hold it," he says, and he calls back to everyone. "Alright, soldiers. During the charge, I want you to fire on my signal, not before.

We need the element of surprise. Listen, this is very important: when we reach the squadmen line, dive and take cover under the squad trucks *immediately*. That's an order."

He puts a hand on my shoulder and surveys his troops. "It might be hard to see the way through the smoke. Follow the flag." Everyone nods. Then, to me, he says, "Hold it high, May, so they can see it."

Now his hand is on the door knob. We all breathe one last breath together, listening to the brittle crackle of gunfire calling us from without.

"Go!"

Ethan throws the door open, and suddenly we're all charging through the smoke.

At first, all is quiet. Then, through the haze comes the crackle of gunshots and the flashbulb blinks of muzzle flares. We run faster. The ground trembles under our feet with the concussion of explosions. The sky melts with the shrieks of streaking drones. My shoulders already ache, but I hold the flag high and it snaps in the wind as I bear it forward.

"Fire!" Ethan shouts, and the air around me sounds as if it will split in two as our guns report as one.

Bullets whistle everywhere, death like swarming locusts. Our calls cut the air, sharp, fierce, piercing. We do not hold back. We run as fast as our legs will go, fire until our clips are empty.

I think, *This is the longest two hundred yards imaginable.*

Then, things get worse. There's a succession of explosions behind us, one, two, three, four, five, six of them, each one closer than the last. The ground beneath us bucks with each detonation. I look over my shoulder and am horrified to see a squadron of low-flying drones racing toward us, their bombs coming closer and closer.

I look forward again and run even faster.

Now, through the grayness, black hulks of the squad trucks grow larger, and in the next instant, we are upon them. Several squadmen lay dead beside their vehicles. I watch two more get shot to pieces as we approach.

"Dive!" Ethan calls as we reach the trucks, and without slowing, I throw myself headfirst under the nearest squad truck.

Instantly, I explode. My eardrums shatter. My eyelids melt. My lungs burn.

Then, all is silence.

Slowly, I open my eyes and peer out from my hiding place. A few yards away, a squad member's body lies sizzling on the pavement. There's another, and another and another. The smell of burning explosives stings my nose. Slowly, with trembling arms, I pull myself out from under the squad truck, and am amazed by what I see. The pavement all around is littered with dead squadmen—hundreds of them. The truck I just dove beneath is a charred, burning shell, but somehow I'm unharmed.

The bombing drones, having locked on to us, must've followed us to their own line and wiped out their own men. Ethan is a genius.

McCann, Michel, and two other rebels emerge from beneath one squad truck. Ethan crawls out from beneath another.

I tilt my head back and scream in triumph. We've taken the squadmen line! We did it! But when I turn back, looking for someone to celebrate with, looking for the one hundred Order members who followed us, I see no one.

Ethan steps toward me as I look around, confused.

"Where are the others?" I ask.

Ethan is silent. I glance at McCann. No one answers me.

"Didn't they follow us?" For a second, I'm flooded with a wave of bitterness, thinking they were too cowardly to come. Then, I glance back at the parking lot just as the wind shifts, lifting the veil of smoke. And there lies the Protectorate.

Their shredded bodies lie in various postures, some facedown and alone, others in jumbled piles of tangled limbs. Some lie in twos, as close to one another as lovers.

"Oh, God," I whisper.

Michel clings to McCann, his little face buried in his father's chest.

The other two survivors, both young men, look around with flickering, frightened glances. The afternoon has grown quiet, a silence that holds greater horror than the preceding din. Ethan climbs down from the seat of one of the few intact squad trucks.

"Ignition is coded. You have to have a cross to use it, and without Randal to tweak the coding, our pocket transmitters are worthless. We'll have to go on foot."

"What about the others?" says one of the young men. "There might still be some alive back there." He glances at the still-rolling wall of black smoke.

Ethan shakes his head. "If anyone's alive, they'll find their way. We have to find ours."

McCann takes the nearly shredded flag from my hands (I discover I'm still stupidly holding it). He pulls it from its pole, and drapes it over my shoulders. "Don't lose it," he says.

"Yeah," I reply, failing at my intended smile.

"Let's move," Ethan says, and we take off on foot.

Five minutes later we're running through a rundown neighborhood. The houses are all abandoned, of course, but somehow the colors of the paint cracking and peeling from the walls are still vivid, beautiful. Dandelions and other flowering weeds poke up from brown grasses in overgrown yards. The flag around my shoulders smells musty and strangely sweet, old and good. Death might come from anywhere, and I guess part of me wants to soak up the last ounces of beauty I can, before it's too late. Even now, after all these years of strangling it, the romantic in me won't quite die.

As we run, I keep glancing at the sky, half expecting a lightning bolt like the one that struck Randal to blast from the heavens and fry us all. Maybe without crosses in our cheeks they can't target us, I tell myself, but I'm terrified anyway.

"When we reach the next block," Ethan says breathlessly, "look for a good building to hole up in. We have to get out of the open."

No sooner have the words left his lips than the jittering, chugging sound of a chopper grows from nothing to a blasting roar. Seconds later, the helicopter appears above one of the buildings behind us. McCann scoops Michel up into his arms and quickens his pace, sprinting a step behind Ethan and me. From behind us I hear the two young rebels firing on the chopper, trying to cover our retreat. After a second, the sound of their gunshots is punctuated with a low, hollow-sounding explosion. Without breaking stride, I glance back.

Behind me, a curtain of green smoke rises, ghostlike, and swoops toward us. I drop my gun, letting it hang from its strap, and run my hardest. Instinctively, I am terrified of the rising gas. A moment later, when I glance over my shoulder again, I can see only one of the guys covering our retreat. He's still running, but unsteadily, weaving first left, then right, then finally going limp and falling like a rag doll, skidding across the pavement face first. Behind him, the other rebel is already sprawled out in the street, twitching violently. And the poison gas is coming closer.

"Don't look back," Ethan wheezes in front of me. "Just run."

I follow Ethan. We sprint hard for one more block before taking cover behind a row of old, burned-out cars.

Only then do we look back and see that the unthinkable has happened.

There, in the middle of the street, stands McCann. With one hand, he holds Michel's little body clasped to his chest. *Oh, God, Michel!* I think. Could he have inhaled some of the poison gas? Did a bullet intended for McCann strike him?

Either way, he's gone, his limbs hanging limply from his father's embrace. And McCann is getting revenge. His white machine gun blazes, unleashing an unrelenting hail of lead at the helicopter. Even from here, the sound of McCann's scream is piercing. Slowly, the chopper turns its massive machine gun toward him.

"Stay here!" Ethan growls to me, and he's gone, dashing across the pavement, firing on the chopper. McCann's and Ethan's bullets clatter off the helicopter's armored body, with no effect.

"McCann!" Ethan screams. "Retreat!"

But I know already, McCann isn't going anywhere.

From my position behind the car, I watch as the chopper's side door slides open. I watch as a squad member takes position at that door. I see the muzzle flare from his gun, and I see Ethan fall mid stride.

Now, it's my turn to dash down the street, screaming, "Ethan!"

But he is already back on his feet, rushing toward McCann, toward the chopper.

The helicopter finishes rotating and faces them now. The African warrior stands, his son clasped to his chest, his feet planted wide, tears streaming down his cheeks, his gun rattling away at its target.

The helicopter's huge machine gun opens fire. Instantly, McCann falls.

Ethan screams in fury and skids to a halt. He sets his feet and shoulders his gun, firing mercilessly. I come up next to him, firing too.

It must be my imagination, but I think I can hear the laughter of the squadmen inside even over the roar of the chopper. But our relentless barrage is too much for the helicopter's armor, and we manage to damage the back rotor. The squad chopper spins around once, buzzing like an injured fly, then slams into a large office building. Dust belches toward us as the wall crumbles and the roof of the place caves in.

I want to go to McCann and little Michel, but Ethan is already dragging me onward. I want to weep, but there are no tears left in me.

There's an explosion where the helicopter crashed, and bits of shattered rotor skitter across the road toward us. Dodging, ducking, leaping over flying debris, we run two more blocks before finally coming to a gray, stone office building with a marquis on the front that says: *Fox Theatre*. Ethan leads me inside.

—CHAPTER Ø23—

The drones pass over again, rattling the front doors of the theater.

I'm staring out the dirt-streaked glass while Ethan sits with his back to the door of an old ticket booth, gazing in at the darkened theater. The lobby of the place is like an art deco palace, arrayed with columns, ornate plaster work and beautiful (though dusty) marble floors—but we aren't here for the décor.

"How long was that?" I ask.

Ethan glances at his watch. "Sixty-five seconds," he says. "They're homing in again. The satellites must've picked up on our body heat."

With each blink, the day's horrific events flash through my mind: Grace stewing in her own blood, Randal fried by lightning, McCann and poor Michel cut down by the chopper's gun—and of course, Kali. But I fight to push these images from my thoughts. In a day, the Company has reduced the glorious rebellion to two solitary people. And if we're not smart, there will be no one left.

I glance at Ethan and notice for the first time that he sits with one hand pressed to his side. In the dim light, I can see no blood, but his teeth are on edge.

"You okay?" I ask. "It looked like you were hit going after McCann."

"Fine," he says. He grunts as he takes an IC from his pocket.

"What are you doing?" I ask.

"Checking on the other Protectorate groups."

Staring at the screen, his expression grows even darker.

"How are they doing?" I ask.

He snorts. "No worse than us."

Above, the drones roar past again. This time when the bombs fall, dust rains down on us.

Suddenly, I realize something.

"Ethan," I say, "let me see that IC. Randal gave me a data stick—"

Ethan's eyes widen. "The Protectorate Education Initiative. He must have finished it." I hold my hand out for his IC, but he shakes his head. "It won't work on this thing—it has to be tied into the Company network, and this one isn't. Besides, Randal betrayed us. That damn data stick probably doesn't even work."

One more flicker of hope, lost. I shove the data stick back into my pocket, and Ethan and I fall silent again. As the minutes drag on, I find myself thinking of Randal. I remember his cryptic and feverish talk of digital coding, of reducing all things to their common denominator. Were his words empty, just the product of his brilliant but drug-addled mind, or was there meaning behind them? Was he talking about the human propensity for creating abstract systems: language, mathematics, digital coding? Or was he referring to the codes inherent in nature, like those in DNA? Was his message one of bleak empiricism, a reminder that in the end, we're all just a combination of molecular elements, stuck together in semi-unique combinations? Or—my mind returns to the writings I've read from the first Revolutionary War—did he mean that in the end, when reduced to our common denominator, we're all actually the same. Equal. Could Randal have meant that after final analysis, when all the codes are broken and the variables reduced, we are all truly alike? Truly one? Could he, in his troubled, gifted mind, have found the proof of a real God after all?

I think again of the tiny card in my pocket. Despite Ethan's skepticism, maybe Randal did leave us a final scrap of hope....

We hear the drones coming around again. This time, they're even louder than before.

Reflexively, I look up. "Uh-oh," I say.

That's when the ceiling caves in.

❖   ❖   ❖

When the dust settles, all that remains above us is a sky of the purest blue.

"Ethan!"

I am buried in the rubble, immobilized, staring heavenward.

The sound of the explosion still rings in my ears. Tiny bits of shattered masonry and drywall dribble down my arms, tickling like the march of ants across my skin.

Trapped.

"May."

The sun, warm on my face, is eclipsed. The silhouetted figure above me stoops, grunts as it heaves away pieces of rubble. The pressure on my body lessens.

"How bad are you hurt?"

When he stoops to pick up another brick, I see Ethan's face above me, black with dust, streaked with sweat and blood.

"I don't know. Everything is tingling."

Above, I can see that most of the building is still intact—it was just the lobby roof and the marquis that tumbled down onto our heads. Still, it's a miracle that we're alive. If we're still here when the next drone pass happens, we won't be. . . .

"May Fields," Ethan says, casually tossing a brick. "Your name has always cracked me up. Sounds like a scent for laundry detergent."

"Bite me," I say. "You want to hurry up?"

After a minute, Ethan has cleared most of the debris off me and offers me a hand. I wince as he pulls me up and the last bits of rubble fall away from my body.

"I feel like I've been sleeping in a waffle iron," I mutter, but neither of us has the energy to laugh. As if to punctuate my sentence, the sound of sirens rises, first to our left, then to our right. I hear a heli-copter coming up from behind us, though it's not yet visible over the buildings.

I struggle to my feet. Automatically, my hand goes to my holster but finds it empty. I've lost my gun.

Clumsily, I climb down from the heap of rubble, ready to run. But when I look over for Ethan, he's no longer at my side. I find him sit-ting on the top of the rubble heap, lighting a cigar.

"What are you doing?" I ask.

He looks at me. "Smoking."

Smoking, a violation of Company policy. He's a rebel to the end.

Ethan reaches over and gingerly pulls the flag that had been draped over my shoulders from the rubble. He presses it against the wound on his side, wincing. Instantly, it is soaked through with blood.

I climb back up toward him.

"Let me see."

He waves me off. "I'm fine," he says. "Go on. Run. Who knows, maybe Randal's program will work after all, right?"

All around, the sirens grow louder. I glance over my shoulder, des-perate to keep moving.

"Go," he repeats.

"I'm not leaving you," I say.

He smiles. "Well you don't want to go where I'm going, believe me."

He takes another drag off his cigar and clenches the flag tighter to his side.

"You can't give up!" I say. "This isn't about you, or me, or McCann or Clair! This is about the Protectorate! Since seventeen eighty-three—"

Ethan laughs bitterly.

"What?"

He smiles at me, shakes his head. "Of all the strong, brave, jaded people I know, you have the biggest heart of them all, you know that?" He pauses. "George Washington didn't start the Protectorate, May. Randal and I did."

The silence that passes between us is filled by the chuckling approach of a still-unseen chopper. I suddenly feel ill.

"What are you talking about?" I ask.

Ethan sighs. "I was with the N-Corp psych evaluation division. We decided which criminals were unprofitables and which were redeemable," he says, looking off into the distance, remembering. "Every day, people would tell me these stories of all the horrible things the Company did to them. After a while, I had to do something about it. Randal was my friend. He felt the same way. We wanted to find a way to rally people to the cause. I guess the story of the Protectorate just sounded better than the truth."

A moment passes while I try to process this new realization.

"So . . . you lied to us? There was no Protectorate?"

"Not until we started it."

I'm shaking, furious. I open my mouth, but it takes a second for me to make words come out. "So you lied to us," I say again.

To my surprise, a glimmer of hurt passes through Ethan's face, and he inhales on his cigar, long and slow. An instant later, his expression becomes unreadable again. Sirens are all around us now. Any minute now, they'll be upon us.

"If you're telling me this to make me leave," I say, "it won't work."

Ethan seems hardly to hear me. He winces in pain. "All those lives," he murmurs to himself. "Who's even going to remember them?"

He looks up at me suddenly, a hint of a smile crossing his lips. "At least we tried," he says. "We did something, May. That's a lot more than most people can say."

Even if I knew what to say, I would have no chance to respond.

Shadows pass overhead and a swarm of Ravers wheels and dips toward us. The screech of sirens becomes deafening as, from around the corners of buildings on both sides of us, squad trucks appear, rumbling and skidding to at halt.

Neither Ethan nor I run as the doors of the black trucks open and the squadmen pour out. The Ravers swoop down and encircle us, hovering. Despair clamps my heart and nausea twists my stomach.

Ethan gives a mighty sigh as he rises to his feet. "Here we go," he says wearily.

With one hand, he nonchalantly slides his gun to his back and raises his hands—the American flag hanging from one, his cigar in the other.

From among the ranks of squadmen, Blackwell appears. "Don't hit the woman," he calls out. "They want her alive. Take the other one out on my order."

This, of course, infuriates me. I step in front of Ethan.

"No!" I shout at Blackwell. "You want him, you shoot me first! Go ahead, Blackwell! Do it!"

A hundred gun barrels gape at us.

"Do it!"

From behind, I feel Ethan's hand on my shoulder. Gently, he turns me around to face him. His face is pale. Blood drenches his shirt. He smiles at me wanly.

"Step aside, Blackie," he says.

I open my mouth to protest, but he shakes his head. "That's an order."

This time, I obey and move away from him.

"Standby for the kill order," Blackwell says, then puts one finger to his ear, listening intently for the order from his unseen commander.

Ethan steps slowly forward, his expression a cipher. He takes one last drag from his cigar, then flicks it away. With the other hand, he raises the bloodstained flag high over his head. It stirs in the breeze.

Ethan's voice booms over the silent squadmen: "In the words of Patrick Henry," he says, "Give me liberty, or give me—"

With incredible speed, he draws his gun and fires one shot. Below, Blackwell stumbles and falls.

Instantly, then squadmen open fire.

Ethan falls backward, his body already limp, and slides down a few feet before coming to rest in a pocket of debris. The flag, still clutched in his fist, settles down over his head and face.

Not a bird calls. No one speaks. No one moves. My mouth is open, but I haven't the breath to scream.

Ethan is dead.

All now is indistinct, the world blurred with my rage. I jump forward, snatch a hovering Raver from the air and fling it down on the bricks, stomp on it once, then sprint toward the squad trucks.

From the corner of my eye, I see Blackwell rising, waving off a squad member who tries to help him. "I'm fine," Blackwell mutters. "Hold your fire!"

I am pure fury. I slam into the nearest squad member, sending him sprawling to the concrete. My hands are already gripping his heavy, black gun, yanking it, trying to tear it free with desperate force, but its strap holds. I squeeze the trigger, but the weapon won't recognize my palm print and refuses to fire, so instead I slam the butt into the squad member's startled face.

Then, breath departs my lungs as I'm tackled to the pavement.

Several huge squadmen are on top of me now, crushing me with their weight. I struggle to get free, to push myself up to my knees and fight, but strong hands grab my wrists and twist my hands behind my back. I scream, bite, spit like an animal, but it's no use. They lift me, drag me, throw me in the backseat of a squad truck and slam the door in my face.

No matter how hard I kick the window, it will not budge.

The Protectorate never existed.

Kali, Ethan, McCann, Randal, Michel, Ada, all dead.

Even I, all that I have been and all that I ever hoped to be, have passed away.

It's all over.

—CHAPTER 024—

This is where the revolution ends.

Here, in this holding cell that smells like rancid ass—or maybe that's just the stink of my own sweat. Of course I haven't showered. I haven't even eaten in three days, but it doesn't matter. The hunger pangs haven't come today. Today, I feel nothing at all. I don't lift my arm, don't flex a single muscle. The only part of me that's still alive is my eyes, and they roam about the room, from the dirty steel crapper to the blaring imager on the far wall, outside my cell. Maddeningly, it's too distant for me to smash it, so I have to listen every few hours when they announce details about my soon-to-be televised execution.

A ring of anarchists was broken up and several unprofitables killed when the security squad raided an anarchist camp yesterday in the old city of Detroit, according to an HR department spokesman. While there was no official word on what crimes were perpetrated by this particular group of anarchists, an unnamed squad source says they may be connected to the August 16 attack on N-Corp headquarters that killed seven people. Well, we'll all certainly breathe a lot easier with those criminals off the streets. Hallelujah!

In financial news, the release of the new IC has earned the Company record sales, adding an exclamation point this historic week marked by the N-Corp/B&S merger. A statement released by N-Corp CFO Bernice Yao today confirms that the Company is now once again on track to report a profit for the coming year. . . .

Somehow, through the genius of digital image manipulation and simple lies, everything, from the headquarters attacks to high interest rates, has been blamed on me and my anarchist friends. And why not? At this point, what does it matter anyway?

I've made my peace with things. Sort of.

356

I do not hate Randal. He was simply weak. I do not hate Kali/Clair for not telling me who she was. She did what she had to do to survive. And I don't hate Ethan, either, though the hurt of his lie and the suddenness of his death still make my gut feel sour—or maybe that's just the feeling of my stomach eating itself as I starve to death.

Footsteps approach and I look up. It's the Reverend Jimmy Shaw, with Blackwell in tow.

"Time for your debriefing," says Blackwell cheerfully. It's the first time I've ever seen him cheerful. One arm is in a sling, but otherwise he appears to be in perfect health. The bastard. He sets his suitcase down on the concrete floor and takes out a device that looks something like a black traffic cone.

"Your performance as a spy was quite disheartening, May," says Shaw, shaking his head. He leans heavily, almost wearily on his cane. "There's nothing left but to make an example of you, I'm afraid."

A litany of colorful retorts fill my mind, but I discard them all. It's too late for wisecracks. It's too late for anything.

Blackwell points the traffic cone at me and nods to Shaw.

"Now," Shaw says, "what can you tell us about your good friends the anarchists?"

"For starters, they weren't anarchists," I say, "and they're all dead."

When I speak, I can hardly feel my lips. Maybe it's the dehydration. It's a strange sensation.

"Do I really have to explain to you that we'll be torturing you if you aren't forthcoming?" Shaw says. "That should be obvious, my dear."

Blackwell makes a movement and the device in his hand clicks on.

Suddenly, my head feels like it's a hive filled with a million furious wasps. My vision blurs. My skull might collapse at any second; the pain is tremendous. Have to get it out, out of my skin, out of my mind, I'm dying—then it stops.

There's a sound, a terrible gurgling, which I discover is me, puking and screaming at once. My face is pressed against the concrete wall behind my cot. My fingertips throb, bleeding. Apparently, I was trying to claw my way out of the cinderblock cell. Slowly, my skull regains its previous dimension and my brain ceases to feel crushed.

Blackwell is nodding, "See? Works pretty well, right?"

Shaw waves a hand dismissively, looking at me. "It's a beam weapon of some sort. What did you say, Blackwell? Long wavelength microwaves? Anyway, it has enough battery power to last for four hours, so we can keep it on you for as long as you want, May—but I have a meeting at noon, so I'd rather keep it brief. What can you tell us?"

I glare at Shaw.

"You know it all," I say, wiping vomit and sweat from my face with the bottom of my T-shirt. "We lived in the tunnels and basements in the industrial arc. Randal used his inside knowledge of Company security systems to keep us safe and informed. And . . . what else? I'll tell you anything. It doesn't matter. They're all dead, everyone's dead. It's over."

"What about the leader?" says Shaw.

"Ethan? He worked for N-Psych then started the Protectorate. He was just a regular guy," I say.

Shaw nods, "What else?"

"Nothing. He never told me anything else. You can cook me with that thing until I'm black."

Blackwell raises the weapon again, but Shaw waves him off. "It's okay. I believe her. The leader of that group was too smart to trust the likes of her." Shaw turns back to me. "And what about the group, the organization?"

"The Protectorate," I say.

"How strong are they now?"

I'm about to answer, *I told you they're all dead,* but I hesitate. Suddenly, a thought dawns on me: maybe Ethan wasn't really lying after all. Maybe founding fathers *did* envision a fourth branch of government, one designed to fight for democracy against any element of government, or foreign military, or greed-blinded corporation that might come to threaten it.

There has always been a Protectorate. It's the people.

Shaw repeats: "How strong is this Protectorate now?"

A smile curls on my lips. "Strong."

"Well, that's funny, Miss Fields. You just said they're all dead."

Blackwell brandishes the cone of death, but Shaw stays him again.

"They're strong anyway," I say. "Stronger than before, if anyone will remember them."

"I assure you, they won't." Shaw smiles. "But that was an interesting bit of rhetoric. Really, May, did you think you'd change the world? There are forces much larger than you, or anyone, at work here. Money is power, and power consolidates. The biggest fish gobbles up the rest. A child could understand that. It's not evil; it's evolution, nature. It's inevitable, that's what you people don't understand! Money is the only power there is, it always has been, and the lure of it is unstoppable. Even if you killed us now, May, there'd still be a million more just like us fighting to take our place."

"And when you kill me, Jimmy, there'll be a million more like me, I promise you that."

"Well," Shaw says brusquely, "I think we'll take our chances and kill you anyway."

He nods to Blackwell, who puts the wave-gun away. "God have mercy on your soul, May," Shaw says, and turns to leave.

I'm shaking with rage, but still smiling. Marshaling my strength, I fight to my feet and surge to the door of my cell, holding the cell bars with both hands, and call after them: "I have a debriefing for you, Shaw," I shout.

He turns back to me, looking mildly amused.

"When you get to the gates of heaven and find out God exists after all, when the real Christ stands to judge you for all the killing and lying and stealing you did in his name, what will you say for yourself then?"

Shaw raps his cane on the floor, his face an unreadable, grinning mask, wilted and pink. "Then, May, at least I'll have the comfort of knowing I died rich, fat, and smiling," he says. "God bless."

The hallway door hisses open as they depart.

"God bless *you*," I yell. "You'll need it!"

But the hall is empty, and so is the threat.

So here, finally, is the end. I'll die with puke on my shirt, exhausted, with no food, no water, no blanket, no hope. So I take the one comfort I can and lay down to sleep.

Tomorrow, they'll execute me. Even my dreams are miserable.

Awake again. I sit up instantly.

There's a rush of air on my face as the heavy, Plexiglas door on the far end of the room whooshes open. When I stop blinking, I see a man standing before me, leaning against the bars.

He looks like my father, except older, more tired.

"Well, well. My little Napoleon," he says.

"Dad?" My tongue feels dry and swollen. I glance over and realize that while I slept, the guards must've tossed a bottle of water in to me. It sits in one corner of the cell, tempting me, but I feel too weak to walk over and pick it up.

"You don't look good, sweetie," he says. "They feeding you?"

I shake my head. "I guess they want me to look appropriately gaunt when they fry me," I say.

Dad sighs. "Why did you do it, May?"

Our eyes meet.

"You know why. And if you don't, I can't make you understand."

He nods. He looks a bit sick, I suddenly realize. Unhealthy.

"First, May, I promise you I didn't know what they had planned for the merger. I asked around once you left, and after I found out you tore out your cross and went to the other side, that's when I started really digging. The more I learned, the more I realized you were right. I found out that they did kill a lot of people in Africa Division, and I swore I'd get to the bottom of it. I hopped the first plane I could find and went there myself, started interviewing members of the security squad who'd carried out the murders. They all said they were just doing their job—following orders. So I went to their supervisor; she said that the head of the division told her to do whatever was necessary to create a hospitable environment for Company growth. So I went to the head of the division, Elton Weiss. He got all defensive and told me that his salary was entirely based on the profits of Africa Division, so he'd simply told his underlings to do whatever was necessary to generate a profit, as long as it wasn't prohibited by the Department of Expansion Policy Handbook. So I talked to the VP of Expansion Denise Willard and asked her who on earth authorized her to write a policy that allowed such horrors to take place. You know what she said? Her eyes got wide, and she says, 'You did, sir. You told me to make Africa Division profitable or I'd be out on my ass. You said you didn't give a damn how I did it. You said, *Denise, there are four things that are important in this world: first-quarter profits, second-quarter profits, third-quarter profits, and fourth-quarter profits. Now get the hell out of my office and make me proud.'"*

Dad shakes his head bitterly. "I remember saying it, too. . . . All of them thought they were just doing their job, fulfilling their duty, making the Company profitable. And no one took a damned bit of responsibility. *It wasn't me, it was the Company,* they said. Africa Division wasn't the only place things like that happened, either," he said. "No, it happened all over the world. Then this horrible business with the merger. . . . You were right about it all. I was sick when I learned about all of it. Furious. I spoke about it in a board meeting, too. Pissed a lot of people off. You'd have been proud," he smiles wanly.

"It won't make a difference, though. I used to have power, but not anymore. Nobody does. The Company is too big now for any one person, or maybe even any group of people, to change its course. That's what I've learned. It's just . . . too big."

"I noticed that," I say. Only my lips move. I feel for a second as if I might black out, but fight back into consciousness.

"I could have told you it's impossible to change things by force, May. Blackwell has a hundred weapons systems he hasn't even played with yet."

"Well . . . " I begin, but don't know what to say. I almost nod off. When I open my eyes again, they're drawn to the cross on my father's cheek. Beneath his haggard, gray skin, it looks less like a tattoo or an implant and more like a lesion, like a cancer eating him from the inside out.

"A lot of things changed for me after you left," he continues. "I realized things. I got rid of the drugs—although it was hard, let me tell you. They were marvelous drugs, and now, without them, I feel like a steaming pile of horse manure. I got rid of the whore, too. And that was hard, because she was a marvelous whore," he pauses, as if collecting his thoughts. "I've been offered a severance package, since I've had so many differences of opinion with the board lately. I got an island in the Caribbean. Just a small one, but it has a house, servants. I'm taking it, flying out tomorrow. This is the last thing I'm doing before I leave, and they didn't even want me to come and see you. They warned me not to, actually. By coming here, I might lose the package altogether. I don't know, I didn't check the fine print. . . .

"Oh, God," he says, realizing something. He takes an N-Nourishe bar out of his pocket and tosses it to me. "I completely forgot I had that with me, and here you are, starving."

The bar hits my chest and falls into my lap. It takes me a minute, but I peel the wrapper open with leaden fingers and manage to nibble off a small bite. At first, the food elicits only nausea, but as I eat more, a small measure of strength returns to me. At last, I'm able to stand up on shaky legs, cross the room, pick up the water bottle, and take a careful sip.

My father watches all this silently. When I glance over, he's holding a cell bar with each hand, staring at the empty space between them.

"May," he says finally, "I'm sorry."

"I know," I say.

Dad nods. He glances over his shoulder. "They're watching us now, I'm sure. Blackwell, Yao, and that damned Jimmy Shaw. They never trusted me completely; now they don't trust me at all. They're listening to us right now, reading my thoughts, I guarantee it."

I notice something.

"Is that the new IC?" I ask, pointing at a small, metallic green device strapped to his arm like an old-fashioned wristwatch.

"Oh," he says, sounding distracted. "It's marvelous. Worth every dollar. . . . " he trails off, staring at nothing again, seemingly fighting some massive struggle in his mind. "They use tiny cards instead of the old memory sticks. Little triangles, but they hold unbelievable amounts of data. Marvelous. . . ." he trails off again.

I drop the health bar wrapper on the floor and go to my bunk. I slip my hand under my pillow. There, between two fingers, I grasp the tiny data stick Randal gave me. When I was captured, I carried it under my tongue through the cavity search, through the questioning, through it all, carefully concealing its location from my captors and the many cameras they certainly had trained on me for the last few days.

Dad clears his throat. "Those bastards on the board always hated me. Hated the way I cursed, the way I walked. Hated me for the way you were. They never trusted me. For good reason, I guess it turns out."

He looks at me, filled suddenly with emotion, eyes brimming with tears, but his mouth twists into a grin. This behavior is so unlike him, I'm too startled to speak.

"Cell door, open," he says.

And it does.

I stand there, astonished.

"One of the perks of being CEO," Dad reminds me. "My voice is encoded as a master command for all Company doors. Come on, before they see what we're doing and override my command," he holds out a hand to me. I take it, and he pulls me through the open door, to freedom.

"There goes my severance package," he says. "Run, go. I won't be able to keep up!"

"But, Dad," I say, "with the sats and everything, neither of us will get away. They'll catch us in five minutes."

"We'll live until then," he says. "Now go!"

"Wait," I say. "Give me your IC."

"What? Why?"

"No time!"

"But it's brand new."

"Dad!"

He pulls it off his wrist and hands it to me.

"I love you, May."

"Love you, too," I say.

"All compound doors, open," he says. "Emergency override blocked, code three-four-seven-nine-six-one."

The Plexiglas door ahead of me opens, and I run.

"I'm proud of you," Dad calls after me.

As far as I remember, that's the only time he's said it. Despite everything, I smile.

The data stick! Running fast on wobbly legs, I jam the triangular card into a slot in the side of the IC. It beeps at me. A moment later, I hear Randal's voice.

"Hello, Ethan—or Clair or McCann or May, whoever's alive to use this card. As I'm sure you know, this is the last help I'll be able to give you. . . . "

As I turn a corner, sliding haphazardly on the smooth floor, I see a squad member standing at the far end of the hall. He sees me and yells, "Hey!"

I spin and sprint the other direction and around a corner.

Randal's voice continues: "This is a transmittable p-program, designed to reformat all five billion ICs on the Company network. Once the new program is uploaded, all normal IC functionality will cease. It will be replaced with a manifesto of the Protectorate, a summary of American and Company history, proof of Company transgressions, and finally, an address by you, giving the people the instructions for action. All you have to do is record that last portion and say the words 'transmission final,' and our message will be passed to every Company employee in the world."

Gunshots from behind me. I hear a bullet glance off the wall near my shoulder, but my legs are feeling stronger now. Imager screens on every wall blink on. My picture is there.

The automated voice in the ceiling drones: *"Code red, escape: prisoner May Fields. Code red."*

The clamor grows as, throughout the facility, more guards are alerted. I can feel their pursuit rising behind me like a wave.

"It's up to you, now," Randal says. "I love you guys. God b-bless the Protectorate, and God bless America."

A female squad guard appears around a corner and squawks as I bowl her over. Her gun skitters across the floor, and I snatch it up and keep running, hardly breaking stride. A security checkpoint lies just ahead, and behind it, a huge bank of windows, extending many stories high. Squadmen stand next to a row of body-scan machines, talking to a handful of perturbed-looking people trying to get past the security checkpoint. By the time they notice my approach, I'm already on top of them. I scream a vicious war cry and level the gun, but because of the palm coding, it doesn't fire. Still, the squadmen are startled and duck, buying me just enough time to sprint past them. Behind me, I hear calls of "That's Fields! Stop her!"

Ahead: a huge window.

Bullets buzz over my head and strike the glass in front of me with several dull *cracks*. Where each one hits the glass, a shatter pattern appears like a giant snowflake.

This is my only way out, my only chance. They're close behind me, now. I charge the window, lower my head—

"Please commence recording audio message at the tone—" says the IC in my hand.

Through the window. Shatter.

Falling within the musical clink of broken glass, among a thousand twinkling shards. A story below, I hit a grassy slope, roll, and am back on my feet again, running.

Cuts on every part of my body protest at each step, but the pain only spurs me on. Above, behind me: murmurs of consternation. No squad member dares to jump after me.

I look down at the IC in my hand as it beeps. Mouth gaping like a fish, I capture enough breath to speak.

"I am . . . May Fields. . . . Like you, I was a grateful slave. . . . Now, I know the truth. You are about to learn about all the evils of the Company, and the virtue of the Protectorate. . . ."

I pause, glancing over my shoulder then dashing across a busy street, narrowly missing several cars. Ahead, a few blocks away, N-Corp Headquarters looms. With nowhere else to go, I fight my way toward it, hoping to disappear into the morning rush.

"Our intention is not to create chaos, or a new order," I continue. "It's to reinstate the democracy that was stolen from us. It was supposed to be a government for and by the people, not a Company *owning* them."

Sirens coming. Cars honk at me as I stumble across a street. Feeling weak now, like my legs might give out at any second. My mind reels. What to say?

"If guns can't change things, then use words. And if words won't work, then use action, and leave your job, boycott the Company church, burn your N-Apartment to ashes."

Squad trucks ahead and the shriek of sirens behind. I turn off the street.

Under the shadow of the headquarters building, I shove my way through a throng of tie-men and women, drawing a thousand strange looks. I fight through the crowd, into the square outside the N-Corp Headquarters entrance, up to the steps of the building.

"If some of us will die for freedom, the least you can do is stand up and demand it. . . . And if everyone stands up and yells together . . . "

Like a bee sting in my back, the first bullet.

". . . We cannot fail."

Next, a pain in my arm, like a pinch, nothing more, but when I look down, I see my own torn flesh.

"Transmission final."

I turn to face my attackers, raise my useless gun to them. Maybe twenty squadmen are there—young men, mostly. Their scared faces are probably paler than mine, but still they fire.

I see the mist of blood on the steps at my feet. My blood.

What I feel is not so much pain as the uncomfortable feeling that something inside my torso is wrong. Organs shifting, being rearranged.

And here it is, that instant where your whole life is revealed to you, played out before your eyes, just like they say it will be. All the beauty and heartache, loneliness and triumph compressed into a single, flickering, achingly vivid instant.

When it's over, I am here, under the shadow of the headquarters, with the squadmen still firing bullets into my body.

I hear a low, grinding moan escape my mouth.

Somehow, I am still standing. No, now I fall. Something comes out of my mouth, but whether it's spit, puke, or blood, who knows? Funny, it's as if I'm sitting outside myself, watching it happen.

And strange thoughts wash over me: I think of my poor body, and what will become of it, where it will be buried, whether it matters at all. I think of the blood seeping out from me, vibrant crimson, thick against my cheek, warming the pavement beneath me.

I think of the concrete, cold under my skin, and the mirrored glass of the buildings above, reflections of reflections, of the parade of empty zeros and ones and the machines making shoes and guns and wedding dresses. The Company.

I think of God, and hope he isn't really a close friend of Jimmy Shaw's, or I'm screwed. My eyes roll upward and I see the vapor trail of a jet, painted a vivid pink by the dawn, trailing to the end of a flawless blue sky. A path of magical light, ending.

Then, I think of the people. The real Protectorate. They had filled the square, heading in to work. Now they cringe away from me. They hide their eyes. Some run. Only a few stand and watch.

Pain comes in a huge, dizzying convulsion, then ebbs away.

The people. I imagine them watching me die, hearing my last words on their brand-new, state-of-the art ICs, and, one by one, standing up from their desks.

I imagine them, one by one, walking out of their offices and into the sunlight, refusing to work again until they are free.

I imagine them, holding hands, billions and billions of them, and in that one act of simple defiance accomplishing what all this spilled blood never could.

And somewhere in her N-Academy cell, I imagine my Rose listening to my message on her IC and beginning to dream of a different life.

I imagine a better world, and in imagining it, there is hope.

This is how the revolution begins.

—EPILOGUE—

Dearest Protectorate,

When I first wrote *Blood Zero Sky* back in 2005, I couldn't get it published. The people I showed it to felt that it was rife with hyperbole, a depiction of a future so exaggerated that it wasn't believable. In the following years, however, the world has marched steadily in the direction that the book foretold. Corporations consolidated. Government agencies privatized. A multibillion-dollar bailout blurred the lines between the federal government and our nation's "too-big-to-fail" corporate giants. Consumer debt soared, and the middle class in America became increasingly marginalized. Now the world of *Blood Zero Sky*, far from being hyperbole, actually seems a bit too close for comfort—and indeed, the first rumblings of a peaceful revolution have already begun. As a result, I feel compelled to issue a word of caution.

The preceding novel tells the tale of a world in which the only path to freedom for the characters is armed revolution. Though this world seems eerily similar to our own, it is not our own. Let me be clear: this novel is not a call to arms. It is a call to awareness. Violence is not the answer to our problems, and, personally, I reject it on every level.

Only truth can defeat lies, only generosity can defeat greed, and only love, patience, and long-suffering can defeat violence.

Let us come together peacefully to restore what our forefathers envisioned: a vigorously competitive capitalist system regulated by a democratic government that is truly controlled by the people.

If you wish to combat the injustices of the world (and I hope you do), then first educate yourself, then educate others, then demand change with a spirit of brotherly love and cooperation. That way, the power of the Protectorate can reign in peace for another generation.

Yours in Gratitude,
J. Gabriel Gates

—ABOUT THE AUTHOR—

 J. Gabriel Gates is the nationally acclaimed coauthor of *Dark Territory* and *Ghost Crown*, Books 1 and 2 in The Tracks series, and the author of the horror novel *The Sleepwalkers*. A native of Marshall, Michigan, Gates discovered his passion for writing and performing at a young age. He received his bachelor's degree in theater from Florida State University and relocated to Los Angeles, where he acted in numerous television commercials and penned several screenplays.

When Gates is not writing, Gates can usually be found reading, working out, hanging out with his friends, or watching college football. He is an advocate for social justice and has participated in the Occupy Detroit and Occupy Lansing. He currently lives in Michigan with his dog and faithful writing companion, Tommy. Visit him online at www.jgabrielgates.com.

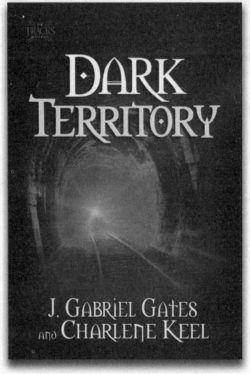

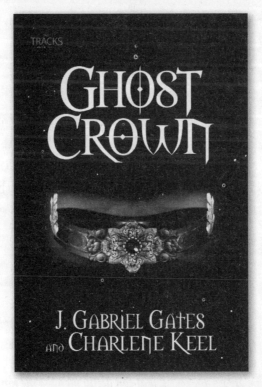

ISBN 9780757315886 • $12.95

J. GABRIEL GATES

Sixty-six murdered souls will bring about the end of the world. Discover a truth that could only be uttered by the lips of the dead.

What people are saying about The Sleepwalkers . . .

Scan this code on your smart-phone or visit jgabrielgates.com